Praise for Sharon Bolton

"Bolton's narrative is taut and twisty and dark, and her pacing unrelenting." —*StarTribune* on *Lost*

"A number of superlatives could be used to describe Bolton's new work, but a simple 'wow!' will do . . . The story's atmosphere is dark and spooky, the main characters are strong yet vulnerable, and the plot is refreshingly unpredictable. This stunning psychological thriller is well worth your time." —*RT Book Reviews* (4½ Stars, Top Pick) on *Dead Scared*

"Outstanding . . . Bolton never eases up the tension; her tightly coiled plot and heroine on the edge work perfectly in tandem." —*Publishers Weekly* (starred review, Pick of the Week) on *Dead Scared*

"*Now You See Me* is really special: multilayered and sophisticated, but tough too." —Lee Child

"Excellent . . . *Now You See Me* is a cerebral thriller that avoids clichés. Each twist and turn is unpredictable, as are the fully drawn characters' actions." —Oline H. Cogdill, *South Florida Sun-Sentinel*

Also by Sharon Bolton

Dead Scared
Now You See Me
Blood Harvest
Awakening
Sacrifice

LOST

Sharon Bolton

Minotaur Books ✠ New York

LOST. Copyright © 2013 by Sharon Bolton. All rights reserved. Printed in the United States of America. For information, address St. Martin's Press, 175 Fifth Avenue, New York, N.Y. 10010.

www.minotaurbooks.com

The Library of Congress has cataloged the hardcover edition as follows:

Bolton, S. J.
    Lost / S.J. Bolton.—1st U.S. ed.
        p. cm.
    ISBN 978-1-250-02856-3 (hardcover)
    ISBN 978-1-250-02855-6 (e-book)
    1. Murder—Investigation—Fiction. 2. London (England)—Fiction. I. Title.
    PR6102.O49L67 2013
    823'.92—dc23

                                                            2013010680

ISBN 978-1-250-04223-1 (trade paperback)

Minotaur books may be purchased for educational, business, or promotional use. For information on bulk purchases, please contact Macmillan Corporate and Premium Sales Department at 1-800-221-7945, extension 5442, or write specialmarkets@macmillan.com.

First published in Great Britain under the title *Like This, For Ever* by Bantam Press, an imprint of Transworld Publishers

First Minotaur Books Paperback Edition: March 2014

P1

For Hal, who peeps out at me through every child in this book; and for his mates, who gamely played along.

"Do you not know that tonight, when the clock strikes midnight, all the evil things in the world will have full sway?"

Dracula, Bram Stoker.

Prologue

'*T*HEY SAY IT'S LIKE SLICING THROUGH WARM BUTTER, WHEN you cut into young flesh.'

For a second, the counsellor was still. 'And is it?' she asked.

'No, that's complete rubbish.'

'So, what is it like?'

'Well, granted, the first part's easy. The parting of the skin, that first rush of blood. The knife practically does it for you, as long as it's sharp enough. But after that first cut you have to work pretty hard.'

'I imagine so.'

'The body's fighting you, for one thing. From the moment you cut, it's trying to heal itself. The blood starts to clot, the artery or vein or whatever it is you've opened is trying to close and the skin is producing that icky, yellowy stuff that eventually becomes a scab. It's really not easy to go beyond that first cut.'

'It seems to be largely about the first cut for you, would that be fair to say?'

The patient nodded in agreement. 'Definitely. By the time the knife touches skin, the noise in my head is close to unbearable — I feel like my skull's about to blow apart. But then there's that first drop of blood, and the next, and then it's just streaming out.'

The patient was leaning forward eagerly now, as though the act of confession, once begun, was unstoppable.

'I'll tell you what it's like — it's like that first heavy snowfall in winter,

7

when suddenly everything's beautiful and the world falls silent. Well, blood does exactly the same thing as snow. Suddenly, the pain means nothing, all that noise in my head has gone away. Somehow, with that first cut, I've gone to another place entirely. A place where, finally, there's peace.'

Gently, almost apologetically, the counsellor closed her notebook. 'We're going to have to stop now,' she said. 'But thank you, Lacey. I think, at last, we're getting somewhere.'

PART ONE

1

Thursday 14 February

THE SADNESS WAS INSIDE HIM ALWAYS. A DULL PRESSURE against the front of his chest, a bitter taste in his mouth, a hovering sigh, just beyond his next breath. Most of the time he could pretend it wasn't there, he'd grown so used to it over the years, but the second he felt his focus shift from the immediate on to the important there it was again, like the creature lurking beneath the bed. Deep, unchanging sadness.

Barney waited for Big Ben to strike the fourth note of eight o'clock before pushing the letter into the postbox. The sadness faded a little, he'd done everything right. This time could work.

Important task over with, he felt himself relax and start to notice things again. Someone had tied a poster to the nearest lamppost. The photograph of the missing boys, ten-year-old twins Jason and Joshua Barlow, took up most of the A4 sheet of card. Both had dark-blond hair and blue eyes. One twin was smiling in the picture, his new adult teeth uncomfortably large in his mouth; the other was the serious one of the pair. Both were described as 1.40m tall and slim for their age. They looked exactly like thousands of other boys living in South London. Just like the two, possibly three, who had gone missing before them.

Someone was watching. Barney always knew when that was

happening. He'd get a feeling – nothing physical, never the prickle between the shoulder blades or the cold burn of ice on the back of his neck, just an overwhelming sense of someone else's presence. Someone whose attention was fixed on him. He'd feel it, look up, and there would be his dad, with that odd, thoughtful smile on his face, as though he were looking at something wonderful and intriguing, not just his ten-year-old son. Or his teacher, Mrs Green, with the raised eyebrows that said he'd been off on one of his day-dreams again.

Barney turned and through the window of the newsagent's saw Mr Kapur tapping his watch. Barney kicked off and in a steady glide reached the shop door.

'Late to be out, Barney,' said Mr Kapur, as he'd taken to doing over the last few weeks. Barney opened the upright cool cabinet and reached for a Coke.

'Fifty pence minus ten per cent staff discount,' said Mr Kapur, as he always did. 'Forty-five pence, please, Barney.'

Barney handed over his money and tucked the can in his pocket. 'You going straight home now?' asked Mr Kapur, his last words drowned by the bell as Barney pulled open the door.

Barney smiled at the elderly man. 'See you in the morning, Mr Kapur,' he said, as he pulled the zip of his coat a little higher.

There was a fierce wind coming off the river as Barney picked up speed on his roller blades and travelled east along pavements still gleaming with rain. The wind brought the smell of diesel and damp with it and Barney had a sense, as he always did, of the river reaching out to him. He imagined it escaping its confining banks, finding underground passageways, drains, sewers, and seeping its way up into the city. He could never be near the river without thinking of black water flowing beneath the street, an invasion so subtle, so cautious, that no one except him would notice until it was too late. He'd confided his fear once to his dad, who'd laughed. 'I think you're overlooking some basic laws of physics, Barney,' he'd said. 'Water doesn't flow uphill.'

Barney hadn't mentioned it again, but he knew perfectly well that sometimes water did flow uphill. He'd seen pictures of London sub-merged by floodwater, read accounts of how high spring tides had coincided with strong downstream flows and the river's cage had been unable to contain it. Given a chance of freedom, the water had leaped from its banks and roared its way through London like an angry mob.

It could happen. There had been snow in the Chiltern Hills. It would be melting, the thaw water making its way down through the smaller tributaries, reaching the Thames, which would be getting fuller and faster as it neared the capital city. Barney picked up speed, wondering how fast he'd have to skate to outrun floodwater.

When Barney reached the community centre the building looked deserted. No lights, so even the caretaker had gone, which meant it had to be after nine o'clock. With a familiar feeling of dread, he looked at his watch. He'd said goodnight to Mr Kapur just after eight o'clock. The newsagent's was a ten-minute skate away. It had happened again. Time, inexplicably, had been lost.

A voice from beyond the wall, the sound of wheels on iron. The others were waiting for him in the yard, but suddenly Barney wanted nothing so much as to go straight home. Sooner or later – sooner if he was smart, and he was, wasn't he? Everyone agreed that Barney was clever, a bit weird sometimes, but bright – he would have to tell someone about these missing hours of his.

A low laugh. He thought he heard his own name. Barney pushed the worry to the back of his mind and carried on round the corner. The community centre had once been a small Victorian factory. Surrounding it were various outbuildings and a tarmac yard, all encased within a high brick wall topped with iron railings. Inside the main building were a library, a crèche for pre-school children, an after-school club and a youth club. Barney and his friends hung out at the youth club several nights a week, but it was after the centre closed that the place became their own.

In the alleyway at the back, Barney reached for the loose railing and got ready to pull himself up.

In this city, someone is always watching.

What was that doing in his head right now? Why, now, should he remember the talk they'd had at school from the local community police officer? She'd been talking about how every Londoner could

13

expect to be caught on CCTV several hundred times a day. But Barney knew for a fact there were no cameras in the alley and the surrounding streets, or overlooking the centre. It was one of the reasons his gang hung out here.

He ran his eyes along the row of houses opposite, looking for the light in the window, the undrawn curtains, the gleam of eyes that would confirm what he knew – that someone was watching. Nothing.

Except they were, and with that certain knowledge came a knocking in his chest as if his heart had suddenly moved up a gear. OK, here he was, in the city where five boys his age had disappeared in as many weeks, on his own in the exact part of London where they had all lived, and someone he couldn't see was watching him.

Barney scrambled through the gap in the railings, skates still on his feet, knowing it was a stupid thing to do, but adrenaline and determination just about kept him the right way up. He rolled forward. Right, which side of the wall were the eyes? Street side or factory side? Cut off from him by nine feet of solid Victorian brick-work and iron railing, or trapped inside with him? The contents of his stomach turned to something like cold lead as he realized he might just have made the biggest mistake of what was going to be a very short life.

He could no longer hear the others. For now it was just an eleven-year-old boy, a very high wall, and an unseen pair of eyes.

Directly ahead, between Barney and the main yard, was the Indian village: five small wigwams in which the younger kids played during the day. Even on a normal night, Barney couldn't look at them without imagining someone – maybe a toddler left behind by an absent-minded parent – peeping out at him from the blackness. He never liked being near the Indian village at night, even without . . . he checked each dark interior in turn before moving on. Nothing.

Nothing that he could see.

Just beyond the wigwams was one of the murals that had been painted on the inside of the perimeter walls. Scarlet-clad pirates, their sights on distant treasure, clung to the rails of a galleon on a troubled sea. In the daytime, the murals were faded, the paint peeling in places. During the hours of darkness, the tangerine glow of the streetlights brought them to life. The green forests around the gates had depth and a sense of secrets lurking behind giant trees, the starry night sky beyond the skateboard ramp seemed endless. Without the sun's harsh scrutiny, even the pirates seemed to be watching him.

At last, from the corner of the factory building, he could peer round into the quadrangle that was the main part of the yard. The relief almost hurt. At the top of the skateboard ramp sat four still figures. His best mate, Harvey, then Sam and Hatty, two kids in Harvey's class, and finally Lloyd, who was a couple of years older. Against the streetlamp light they seemed entirely clad in black. Barney caught a gleam of eyes as one of them looked round. He could also see the tiny red glow of a couple of cigarettes. At the sight of his gang, doing what they always did, looking completely relaxed, Barney started to calm down too. For once, his instincts had cried wolf.

A sudden noise, loud and shrill, blared directly above his head. Then someone jumped down, grabbing him around the throat.

2

THE CHILDREN WERE BEAUTIFUL. THEY LAY CURLED ON their sides, spooned together. The fingers of the boy in front looked as though they were about to twitch and stretch, as sunlight and his internal body clock told him it was time to wake. Even in the flat light of the tent, he didn't look dead. Neither did his brother, snuggled up behind him, one arm slung carelessly across his sibling's chest.

'Boss!'

Dana started. Her gloved hand was reaching out towards the closest boy's forehead, where a damp lock of hair had fallen forward. She'd been about to brush it out of his eyes, the way a mother would. She still wanted to – to smooth it back over his head, pull covers up over their shoulders and keep the night air from their skin, bend and brush her lips over the soft cheeks.

Stupid. She didn't have children, had never known maternal feelings in her life. That they should kick in now, that a couple of dead, ten-year-old boys should be the ones to awaken them.

'Boss,' repeated the other living occupant of the tent, a heavy-set man with thinning red hair and an indistinct chin-line. 'Tide's coming in fast. We need to get them out of here.'

Detective Inspector Dana Tulloch, of Lewisham's Major Investigation Team, let Detective Sergeant Neil Anderson help her to her feet. They moved out of the police tent and into the smell of salt, rotting vegetation and petrol fumes that was the night air by the tidal Thames. The waiting crowd on Tower Bridge wriggled in anticipation. Light flashed as someone took their photograph.

As she and Anderson moved away, others took their place, moving quickly. In a little over thirty minutes, the spot would be under several feet of water. The two detectives walked up the beach towards the embankment wall.

'Right under Tower Bridge,' said Dana, looking up at the massive steel structure. 'One of the most iconic landmarks in London, not to mention one of the busiest spots. What is he thinking of?'

'He's a cheeky bastard,' agreed Anderson.

Dana sighed. 'Who was first on the scene?' she asked.

'Pete,' Anderson replied, looking around. 'He was here a minute ago.'

Dana watched as more SOCOs made their way gingerly down Horselydown Old Stairs, the slimy concrete steps that offered the only access point to this stretch of the riverbank.

'He's killing them faster, Neil,' she said. 'We've never found them this quickly before.'

'I know, Boss. Here's Pete.'

Detective Constable Pete Stenning, thirty-one years old, tall and good looking with dark curly hair, was jogging lightly down the steps to join them.

'What can you tell us, Pete?' she asked, when he was close enough.

'They were spotted at 20.15 by the local florist,' said Stenning. 'I was with him just now. He's had a busy day, what with it being Valentine's Day, and he's got a big wedding on tomorrow so he and a couple of assistants were working late. He needed a fag and smoking is frowned upon in the street so he tends to wander down the lane and up Horselydown Steps. Finds it soothing to watch the river, he says, and there's shelter if it's pissing it down. His words, not mine.'

'And he spotted them?'

'There was just enough light from the Brewhouse behind and the bridge in front, he says, although he wasn't entirely sure what he was looking at till he went down to the beach. And before you ask, he saw nothing else. The two women in the shop confirm his story.'

'Any thoughts on how they were brought here?' asked Anderson.

'Could have come by water,' said Stenning, 'but personally, I doubt it. This is a bloody treacherous place to bring a boat in at anything other than very high water.' He gestured over towards the river's edge. 'There's the remains of a Victorian embankment just under the water there,' he went on. 'If your boat hits that at any speed, chances are you're going down.'

'Road, then?' said Dana.

'More likely,' said Stenning. 'One thing you should see,' he went on. 'Just a bit further under the bridge.'

Dana and Anderson followed Stenning into the shadows beneath Tower Bridge, trying to ignore the craning necks and intense stares just a few feet above them. Then all attention switched from the police officers to the small black bags being carried out of the police tent. The boys were being taken away. A few outraged cries broke out, as though the police on the beach were responsible for what had happened to the children.

Beneath the bridge, uniformed officers with torches were still combing the short stretch of the bank that remained accessible. A small area had been cordoned off with police tape. Stenning shone his torch on to it.

'Footprints?' asked Anderson.

'Large wellington-type boot,' said Stenning. 'Looks to be the same tread as the ones we found at Bermondsey. Thing is, there would be no need for him to come here. Look.'

He was pointing back towards the stairs.

'He carried them down the steps, then a few yards along the beach to where we found them. He'd want to get it over with as quickly as possible. And yet he walks all the way over here, a detour of – what – eight metres, to leave a footprint.'

'On the only stretch of sand I can see on this beach,' said Dana.

'My thoughts exactly, Ma'am,' said Stenning. 'On the rocks and gravel, he wouldn't have left any prints. So he comes over to a patch of sand that, conveniently, happens to be beneath the bridge and sheltered from the rain. He wanted us to find it.'

'Cheeky bastard,' said Anderson.

18

'Who's that, Sarge? Him or me?'

'Both. You OK to accompany the bodies?'

Stenning agreed that he was and then set off to follow the mortuary van as it took the boys' bodies away.

'I'll get on with the door-to-door, if it's alright with you,' said Anderson.

Dana nodded. Anderson invariably got twitchy if forced to keep still for more than a few minutes during an investigation.

'Somebody will have seen something,' he went on. 'Even if they don't know it yet.' He turned to go, then half turned back again. 'What's up, Boss?' he asked her.

She ought to tell him nothing, that she was fine. The team needed her to be fine.

'This one scares me, Neil.'

She saw his head draw back, his eyes narrow. 'You're the DI who caught the Ripper,' he said. 'My money's on him being scared of you.'

Anderson loved to say what he thought was the right thing. Even when the right thing was an obvious cliché.

'Mark and Lacey caught the Ripper,' she said. 'I just got the credit. And I was never as scared by the Ripper as I am by this one. Four boys dead in two months. Another one still missing. And he's speeding up. He's taking them faster and he's killing them faster. How long have we got before the next one?'

3

A S LONG FINGERS CLOSED AROUND HIS NECK, BARNEY dropped his Coke can, the wheels of his skates slid and he almost fell. Two strong hands kept him upright.

'Steady, Barney Boy. Don't piss your pants.'

Aw, shit-shit-shit! Every nerve-ending singing, sweat breaking out all over his body, Barney wondered if being proved right was any consolation for being made to look an absolute tit. What the hell was Jorge playing at?

'Prat,' he managed.

Jorge, his best mate's older brother and the gang's undisputed leader, had been hiding on the roof of the bikeshed. To cover up the fact that his face would be bright red and that he'd snorted snot out of his nose, Barney bent to pick up the now-dented Coke can. 'How long have you been up there?' he asked, when he'd wiped his nose on his sleeve and straightened up.

'Couple of minutes.' Jorge didn't even bother trying not to grin. 'Spotted you at the corner.'

OK, deep breaths. It was dark, maybe no one would see the sweat on his forehead. He hadn't wet himself, thank God. 'You been rehearsing?' he asked, in an attempt to sound normal.

Jorge nodded. 'Mum texted me to say I had to collect Harvey on the way home. Come on.'

Leaping on his skateboard and kicking off, Jorge set off towards the others, leaving in his wake a sense of pent-up energy that was unusual, even for him. Harvey had been complaining lately that Jorge came back from rehearsals completely hyper. That it took him several hours just to calm down. If he pulled tricks on a regular basis like the one he'd just played, Barney could understand Harvey being pissed off.

The rest of the gang watched as first Jorge and then Barney made their way up the ramp towards them.

'Your hair's green,' said Hatty, looking at Jorge.

Jorge tossed his head and ruffled his short, usually silver-blond spikes. 'Hairdressing wanted to try it out,' he said, as though it were perfectly normal for 'hairdressing' to take an interest in a fourteen-year-old boy's hair. 'Green hair to match the green costume. They're going to stick leaves in it as well. The other two are well pissed off because they both have dark hair and it just doesn't look as good on them.'

Jorge wanted to be an actor. A couple of months previously, he'd successfully auditioned for a West End show. To his annoyance, though, because he was only fourteen, he had to share the part with two other boys. Boys who, if Jorge were to be believed, didn't have a fraction of his talent.

'Did I miss anything?' Barney asked, conscious he should have arrived an hour ago.

'Nah,' Harvey told him. 'Lloyd won the darts tournament, but then Sam threw one at Tom Roger's arse and we were kindly invited to leave.'

'Can't leave you lot alone for five minutes,' said Jorge.

'Did you get banned?' asked Barney.

'They said they didn't want to see us for the rest of the week,' said Lloyd, a large-eyed, dark-haired boy who was in the same class as Jorge. 'Then they said we had to go straight home and not hang around outside.'

'Like this?' said Barney.

'Yes,' agreed Lloyd, his brown eyes wide and serious. 'Hanging around like this would be very wrong.'

Hatty got up without a word and set off down the ramp. With the possible exception of Barney, she was the best blader of the group. She raced up the other side and stopped herself at the crash barrier. Lloyd, Sam and the two brothers were looking at a bent wheel on Harvey's skateboard. Only Barney saw Hatty's head lift like a dog's that had just caught a scent. She was looking at something in the middle distance. After a few seconds of staring, she turned and sped back to the boys.

'Guess who's back,' she said in a low voice.

The others all turned, some looking at Hatty, others trying to see what she'd seen.

'Where?'

'You're dreaming again, Hats.'

Barney looked past the factory outbuildings that were used for storage now, beyond the wall and railings that surrounded the property, into the streets of South London. Terraced houses on the other side of the road, beyond them the huge abandoned house with its ornate brickwork and blank, black windows. He stopped blinking, stopped looking for anything in particular and waited, letting the focus of his vision shift, until he didn't see the outline of buildings, the line of the pavement, the skyline. As he knew they would, the pictures in front of him began to break down, to lose their structure and reduce themselves to their simplest form. He waited for the patterns to emerge. And then the discrepancy was obvious. There she was, her face pale against the brick wall, her dark coat smoother, reflecting more light, than her surroundings. He wondered how long she'd been there this time, and whether the being-watched feeling he'd had earlier had been entirely down to Jorge. He blinked and what he could see became normal again.

'She's behind the red car,' he said. 'You can just see her head and shoulders.'

'Weirdo!'

'What she want, anyway?'

'Bleedin' perve, spying on kids. I think we should call the filth.'

'She *is* the filth,' said Barney. 'She's a detective.'

Silence, then, 'Are you sure?' asked Jorge.

Barney nodded. 'She lives next door to us,' he said. 'Her name's Lacey, I think.'

'So what's she doing? Keeping an eye on you?'

22

'We hardly know her,' said Barney, knowing he'd be in big trouble if Lacey told his dad where he went at night.

Jorge stood and stretched his neck, staring directly at the detective. She carried on watching. Jorge's upper lip began to curl.

'Shit!' said Hatty, in a shrill voice.

'What?' The others turned from the detective to the girl in their midst.

'Lost my earring,' said Hatty, pushing back her hair to reveal her tiny ears. One had a small gold stud in the shape of a leaf. The other was empty.

'Keep still,' said Barney, reaching out. He didn't think he'd ever felt anything as soft as Hatty's hair, except perhaps the fur on the longhaired rabbits at the pet shop. Touching it sent a sharp sensation right down into the pit of his stomach, making him want to squirm on the spot. Got it! The tiny piece of gold was between his fingers and he dropped it into Hatty's outstretched hand. Not the earring, just an integral part of it.

'That's just the butterfly,' said Hatty. 'Shit, it could be anywhere.'

'Jump up and down,' instructed Jorge. 'It's probably caught on something.'

As Hatty jiggled, making the steel beneath them twang and groan, Barney stood up and rolled down the ramp. Keeping his eyes down, he made his way up and down it several times. No sign of the lost earring.

'I have to go,' said Sam. 'I still haven't done that friggin' field-trip write-up.'

Hatty announced that she was leaving too.

'Me and Harvey will walk you,' said Jorge, as the brothers rolled down the ramp to join Barney. 'There's a perv around, remember?'

'A perv that kills boys,' replied Hatty, whose face was still twisted with disappointment at the loss of the earring. 'What you trying to say?'

'And just what part of "bring your brother straight home" did you not understand?'

The gang practically jumped in unison. They'd been so fixated on the detective watching them from beyond the gates that they'd completely failed to notice the other woman, who'd appeared in the yard without any of them, even Barney, seeing her.

'How did you get in?' said Harvey, turning to check the gates.

'Jorge weighs more than I do,' the small, silver-haired woman replied, 'and is an inch taller. If he can squeeze through a gap in the railings, so can I.' She looked round the yard, at the high walls, the dark building, the gates. 'Why do I get the feeling you lot aren't supposed to be in here?'

'You said you were working,' said Jorge.

Jorge and Harvey's mother was a freelance photographer. Sometimes she stayed out all night, on call at the offices of a news agency, and Harvey and Jorge were left in the care of their elderly grandmother. Their dad, who'd been a war correspondent for the BBC, had died before Harvey was born.

'The job's over,' replied his mother. 'And so is this little party. Goodnight, everyone. Straight home now.'

The brothers and Hatty said their goodbyes before making their way across the yard behind Jorge and Harvey's mum.

'You coming?' Lloyd asked Barney.

Barney nodded. 'My dad'll be on my case if I'm much later,' he said. 'I'm just going to have a quick look for Hatty's earring. See you.'

Alone, Barney made one last circle of the yard, steering clear of the Indian village. The rain of earlier had made for a narrow drain that ran around the edge of the yard. Barney moved slowly, following the flow of the rainwater, until the pipe disappeared underground and an iron grille held back debris. Then he stopped blinking and let his eyes lose their focus. The patterns always took longer at night, but after a moment or two they came. And there it was. Clinging to the underside of a Mars wrapper. He bent, picked the wrapper from the drain and rescued Hatty's earring.

Beaming, Barney looked round, having for a moment completely forgotten that the others had gone. He'd never been alone in the community centre before. He hadn't realized quite how high the walls were, or how dark the shadows beneath them became when there was no one around to distract him. He was looking directly at the painted face of a long-haired girl on the opposite wall. She sat on a rock, in the middle of the ocean. She was smiling

24

at him, not in a pleasant way, and her strange green eyes seemed to say that she knew a secret, and she was only biding her time before she told.

A sudden rustle behind him made him jump. The wind, which normally couldn't make it past the walls, was blowing a crisp packet around. Time to go. He left the yard and skated round to the main street. Maybe he'd get chance to give the earring back to Hatty when they were alone. He'd reach out and gently push it into the hole on her left ear.

'Barney!'

He jumped again as though he'd been shot. He hadn't noticed the policewoman approaching, had forgotten about her completely.

'Hi,' she said, when she'd reached him. 'You on your way home?'

He nodded.

'We should go together,' she said. 'It's pretty dark.'

'OK,' he agreed. He could move at a walking pace if he wanted to, although in fairness, she didn't hang around. She was taller than he, and thin, with long hair scraped back into a ponytail. She never seemed to care what she looked like. On the other hand, she always seemed to look OK.

'Are you on duty?' he asked after they'd walked halfway down the street.

'No,' she said. 'I'm not working at the moment. I'm on sick leave.'

He sneaked a sideways glance. She didn't look sick. For one thing, she went out running every morning, he heard her leave as he got ready to go to the newsagent's and often they'd both get back to the house at the same time. Sometimes he'd see her riding off on her bike, a gym bag slung over one shoulder. And in the evenings, she often left the house on foot, coming back hours later.

They'd reached the corner and Barney had a second's gratitude that he wasn't on his own. This was the only bit of the journey home that bothered him, having to pass the old house. Even with the security fencing, even with all the ground-floor doors and windows boarded up, he couldn't help the feeling that someone could be in there, waiting to jump out.

'This house gives me the creeps,' he said.

'You should see it on the inside,' she replied. 'Kids and homeless people used to break in before all the windows were properly boarded up. We used to get called out to it quite a lot.'

They reached the corner and left the old house behind.

'Barney, it's not really any of my business, I know,' she said. 'But I'm not sure it's very safe for you and your mates to be out after dark at the moment.'

'We stay together,' replied Barney. 'We look out for each other. And Jorge and Lloyd are nearly fifteen.'

He waited for Lacey to point out that he'd been alone when she'd met him and got ready to respond that he was fast. That no one could catch him on foot once he got some speed up.

'Five boys of your age have gone missing recently,' she went on. 'None of them lived very far from here.'

'What happens to them?' he asked her. 'The TV never says how they died. Do you think the Barlow twins are dead as well?'

'I hope not,' she said, in a voice that told him she was pretty certain they were.

4

ALONE ON THE RAPIDLY DWINDLING BEACH, DANA WALKED to the water's edge. Just over a year ago, when she'd moved to London from her native Scotland, she'd fallen in love with the river at night. She loved the way it curled its way between the buildings like a sleek black snake, mirroring only what was beautiful about the city – its lights, its architecture, its colour. Now, the spot around Tower Bridge would always remind her of two small, pale bodies, two boys who should have run squealing along this beach, not been carried from it in body bags. She took her phone from her pocket.

'Hey,' said a deep male voice with a South London accent.

'Hi. Where are you?'

A pause. 'Just in my car. Parked, not driving. What's up?'

'It was them. The Barlow twins. As we knew it would be, I suppose.'

A whispered curse. 'You OK?'

'I'm on my way to tell the parents. Mark, their mother . . .'

Another pause. 'Want me to come?'

Dana smiled to herself, shook her head. 'No,' she said. 'I'll be fine. What are you up to anyway?'

A sigh came down the line. 'Dana, there are some things it's better you don't know.'

'Enough said, I suppose.'

Silence.

'What's up?'

'I shouldn't say this,' said Dana. 'I wouldn't to anyone else. I haven't the faintest shred of—'

'Dana, just say it.'

'I think it's a woman.'

Silence for a heartbeat, then, 'Oh?'

'No sexual abuse, Mark. No physical abuse of any kind, except the wound that kills them. Their bodies are perfect and we find them curled up like they're asleep. Just looking at them – oh, I can't explain it, but they inspire such love. I know it sounds stupid but I think the killer loves them, in her own way. I don't think she wants to hurt them, I think she can't help herself. I think maybe she lost her own son at that age, and something is making her re-enact it with proxies.'

'Anything to back this up, other than what your gut is telling you?'

'Nothing.'

'Then the chances are you're having the normal reaction of any woman your age confronted with dead kids, and you're projecting what you feel on to the killer.'

'Yes, but . . .'

'Not done yet. On the other hand, as theories go, it's not completely off the wall. You can soon run a check on boys of that age who've died in London in recent years. If any died of extensive blood loss, if any of the mothers have had unusual difficulties coping. It's a lead.'

'Yeah, I can get that started tonight. Look, I've got to go. Thanks, Mark.'

Dana disconnected the line and heard a lapping sound at her feet. In the minute or so that she'd been talking, the water had crept closer. She took a step back and stumbled, then turned round and found herself walking faster than was sensible. The lights had been taken away, most of the people had gone from the beach and from the bridge, and she really needed to watch her step. Miss your footing on one of these beaches at night, hit your head as the tide crept its way in, and it could be the end of you.

Only when she'd reached the first step that wasn't encrusted with riverweed did Dana feel her heartbeat begin to slow down. She turned back, one last time. By this time, it was impossible to tell where the beach ended and the water began. She could still hear it though, the soft, whispering sound it made as it crept towards her.

5

'WILL YOU BE WORKING ON THE MURDERS WHEN YOU go back?' Barney asked Lacey, as they turned into the road where they both lived. Lacey looked down at the boy, only a few years away from turning into a man, and yet whose face was so fresh, whose skin so clear and whose thought processes so blindingly obvious. He was thinking that his stock with his gang of mates would soar if he had an inside track on a murder investigation. Especially one involving kids. People were invariably most interested in murders when they were potential victims themselves.

She was almost sorry to disappoint him. 'No, I don't work on murders,' she said. 'My job isn't anything like that exciting.'

She could see him watching, waiting for her to tell him what her job was, hoping it would be something like Drugs, Vice or the Flying Squad. But how could she explain to a boy she barely knew that she didn't think she would ever work as a police officer again?

'You and your mates are good,' she said. 'I've watched you a couple of times now. If the light catches you the right way, especially against the mural with stars on it, you look like you're flying.'

'My mates are scared of you,' he said.

The words seemed to take them both by surprise. Barney's lips were clenched tight and he had an *oh shit* look in his eyes.

'Are you?' she asked him.

30

'No,' he said after a second. 'But then, I knew you before.'

Before. This child, whom she'd spoken to less than a dozen times, could remember what she'd been like before. Jesus, even *she* couldn't remember that any more.

Barney had stopped moving. 'He's here again.' His voice had lowered, giving a hint of the man's that was to come in a few years, and something about its tone put her on full alert. She stopped, too.

'Who's here?' she asked. Two middle-aged women were walking away from them further up the street. There was one at Barney's front door.

'The man that watches you.'

Lacey wondered at the complexity of the human heart that could feel fear, misery and joy, all at the same time. All with the same root cause. 'What man?' she asked, although she knew perfectly well.

'The one who sits in his car outside your house,' the boy replied. 'Who knocks on your door a lot.'

'Where is he?' she asked him. 'Don't point or look, just tell me.'

The kid was bright, he did exactly that. 'He's in a green car on the left-hand side of the road about six – no, seven – cars away from us.'

So strong, the temptation to look for the car, to make sure he was right. 'How on earth did you spot that?'

Barney shrugged, looked uncomfortable. 'I just see things,' he said.

'What do you mean, you just see things? I wouldn't even have known there was a green car that far down the street, but you not only see the car, you see a man sitting inside it, in the dark.'

He sighed. 'The colours of the cars are reflected in the water on the road,' he said. 'There's a silver one, a black one, red, two more silver, white van, then his green one.'

He couldn't see the line of parked cars any more. She was blocking his view. If he was right, it was extraordinary. Incredible powers of observation and recall.

'The street lights are shining through the cars,' he went on. 'The light comes straight through most of them, but in the green one there's something that gets in its way. A dark, solid shape, which can only be a largish head and shoulders. A man, sitting inside a green car. It's obvious.'

'I think we need to get you working for the Met,' said Lacey.

His face softened. 'I've always been good at finding things,' he said. 'When I was a kid, I used to find four-leaf clovers in the grass. My mum collected them in a box for me. I've still got them. If you lose anything – you know, jewellery and stuff – just give me a ring. I'll probably find it.'

'I have very little jewellery,' said Lacey. 'But I could use a four-leaf clover, next time you find one.'

'I don't really see them any more,' he said, taking her seriously. 'I grew out of that. I see other things now. Lost things.'

They crossed the road and stopped at Barney's front door. Neither of them had looked back at the green car but Barney's eyes couldn't settle. 'Are you worried about him?' he asked her.

She shook her head. 'No, we sort of work together. Actually, he's more of a friend.'

A look altogether too mature for an eleven-year-old appeared on his face. A friend? Who hung around outside her flat, banging on the door because she wouldn't answer his telephone calls?

'He's worried about me,' she went on. 'I've been ill, you see. I just don't want to talk to anyone right now.'

The too-grown-up look disappeared, to be replaced by one that was all kid. 'Except me,' he said, smiling at her.

It was surprisingly easy to smile back. 'Yeah, except you.'

Lacey was about to wish Barney goodnight when she thought to glance up at the house. All the windows were in darkness. There wasn't even a light in the hallway.

'Is your dad home?' she asked him. It was after half nine. Kids of his age, mature or not, shouldn't be on their own that late. If some-one reported it to her at the station, she'd be duty bound to check it out.

'Probably,' said Barney. 'He may have nipped out. Or he could be in his study. It's at the back of the house, so you wouldn't see a light.'

He couldn't make eye contact any more. He was lying. He knew perfectly well his father wasn't in the house.

'Do you want me to come and sit with you till he gets back?' she asked, knowing it would keep the occupant of the green car at bay a little longer. Maybe he'd even give up and go home.

Barney shook his head. 'I'll be fine,' he said. 'He's probably in. I'm just going to go to bed.'

'Do you have a phone?'

He pulled it from his pocket and held it out. 'Have you cut yourself?' she asked him, holding back from taking it.

A look of panic, as sharp and unexpected as a slap, crossed his face. He looked down quickly, as though noticing for the first time that his fingers were smeared with something that looked a lot like blood.

'Yuck!' He wiped his hand backwards and forwards on his jacket, a look of extreme distaste on his face. Then he shuddered. 'No,' he said. 'Just something I must have touched.'

Lacey smiled, took the phone and tapped both her mobile and land-line numbers into his contacts list. 'Just in case you need me,' she told him. He nodded, unlocked his front door and turned to say goodnight.

'Wash your hands before you eat anything,' she called. He was looking over her shoulder, at the line of parked cars in the road.

'I expect he'll be knocking soon,' he said, before disappearing inside.

6

THE HOUSE WAS A MESS AS USUAL. BARNEY LOOKED ROUND at the supper remains all over the granite worktop, the skewed window blind, his dad's sweater abandoned on a stool, two drawers not quite shut, one cupboard door wide open. Somehow, the rule that said grown-ups were supposed to tidy up after their kids had skipped the Roberts' house.

He turned on the hot tap and ran it over his hands. He hadn't cut himself, he was pretty certain he hadn't, but that icky stuff on his hands had looked, for a second, like blood. He soaped and rinsed them several times before getting to work on the kitchen. Tidiness had been important to his mum; it was one of the few things he could remember about her.

At the kitchen sink, Barney raised the blind to straighten it. Light in the garden next door told him that Lacey was in her conservatory at the back of her small flat.

Lacey could help him find his mum.

The dishes done, Barney let the water drain away. He couldn't understand why he hadn't thought of it before. The police tracked down missing people all the time. But if he told anyone what he was doing, he'd jinx it and it would fail. Somehow he knew that. He couldn't tell anyone. And what if she told his dad?

When everything had been put away and all the surfaces were clean again, Barney went up two flights of stairs to the top floor. On the way, he switched off the divert that sent all incoming calls to his mobile. He wasn't supposed to go out when his dad wasn't home.

On the second floor of their house were Barney's bedroom, bathroom and his den. On one wall of his den was a giant poster of the solar system, on the other a large artist's impression of a black hole. He wasn't particularly interested in astronomy, the two posters had just been the biggest he could find on Amazon. He pulled out the eight map pins that held them to the wall and rolled them up. Underneath were his investigations. The first was about the boys who'd been killed. Their photographs, taken from news sites, ran along the top. Beneath them, he'd fastened a map of the river with tiny coloured stickers marking the spots where the bodies had been found. Barney didn't think there was much chance of his dad finding his investigation, he hardly ever came into his den, but he had a plan just in case. He would say it was for a school project about the work of the Metropolitan Police.

He ran his finger along the course of the river, starting way downstream in Deptford where the first body had been found. The killer was working his way up-river, getting closer. Barney's finger hovered near Tower Bridge.

On the wall opposite was another large map, this time of all the London boroughs. Right now, he was doing Haringey. The envelopes he'd posted earlier each contained a classified ad to go into the *Haringey Independent* and the *Haringey Advertiser*. BARNEY RUBBLE was the bold heading at the top, because that had been his mum's name for him when he was little. Barney Rubble, after the Flintstones character. That was the attention-grabber. The message below he changed often, because he still hadn't decided which would work the best. Sometimes it just said: MISSING YOU. Other times it was chatty, quite informal: WOULD LOVE TO CATCH UP SOME TIME. Once, he'd even tried: DIES A LITTLE EVERY DAY WITHOUT YOU, but he'd regretted that the moment he'd posted it. It just wasn't the sort of thing you said in a newspaper, even if it was anonymous. Even if it was true.

The ads always ended with an email address, the one he'd set up in secret, which only he knew about. The one he checked every morning of his life because this could be the day his mum finally got in touch.

Next month he'd move on to Islington. By the time he was thirteen he'd have done the whole of greater London and it would be time to move on to the Home Counties.

It didn't matter really, if his dad found this map. He would never guess what it was all about. It was just important, somehow, to keep it to himself.

Replacing both astronomy posters, Barney crossed the room to his desktop computer. In his in-box were a couple of emails from friends at school, one from his PE teacher, Mr Green, about a fixture that weekend, and a long list of notifications telling him people had replied to a comment stream he'd contributed to on Facebook. Strictly, Barney wasn't old enough to be on Facebook, but most of his class had their own pages. They just lied about their year of birth. He looked at the time; he had a few minutes before he was supposed to go to bed.

On Facebook he went straight to the Missing Boys page that had been set up a few weeks earlier, when Ryan Jackson had become the second South London boy to vanish. 5,673 people were now following the site and, as always, there were a huge number of posts, ranging from the sensible to the downright weird.

One guy thought the boys were being used for unorthodox medical experiments in a secret research facility somewhere along the riverbank.

Some comments appeared to be from genuine friends of the boys, others from strangers offering best wishes for their safety. Not all the comments were good-natured, and there were the usual people expressing outrage that a social media site should encourage this sort of 'wallowing' in others' misery.

Finally, Barney neared the bottom of the clist. God, some people were weird. And this guy, Peter Sweep, was probably the weirdest of the lot. No profile picture, for one thing, just a photograph of some blood-red roses. No personal information either, although that wasn't so unusual for kids on Facebook. He had nearly five hundred friends, but they all seemed to be others who'd 'liked' the Missing Boys page. It looked like a page set up purely to comment on the murders. Barney sat looking at Peter's latest post, the last in the thread.

Very exciting – two dead already. Now maybe two more!

The thread updated itself and Barney read with interest. It was Peter Sweep again.

Update on the Barlow Twins case. Lewisham police have recovered two bodies from the banks of the Thames this evening. Announcement expected shortly. RIP Jason and Joshua, now to be known as the Heavenly Twins.

Peter Sweep was one of the most regular contributors to the Missing Boys site. His posts always started out factual, almost official sounding, and in the early days, more than one person had speculated that Peter was connected to the police investigation in some way. Certainly everything he posted turned out to be right. But then he always added a sick little message at the end, which made it seem highly unlikely he was a police officer.

In the few seconds since Peter had posted, a flood of comments had followed. Barney spotted Lloyd joining in with the conversation and, a few seconds later, Harvey. As usual, people were eager for more information, including how Peter had come by his scoop. As usual, he didn't respond.

A thought struck Barney from nowhere. If he went missing, if his face was on television every night, in newspapers, on posters and flysheets that were handed out at train and bus stations, would his mum see them? Would that be enough to bring her back? He could spend years steadily making his way through all the regional papers, spending every penny he had, and not get close. But if he went missing, in one fell swoop he'd get national coverage. That would have to work, wouldn't it? She'd have to come back then.

Barney stood up, suddenly tired of the Facebook site and its contributors faking sympathy for emotions they'd never feel. How many of them had any idea what it felt like to love one person more than anything in the whole world, and have no idea where she was?

He was getting it again, the feeling that made him want to break something, throw something fragile against the wall, or hurl a chair at the window. Pour ink over the carpet. Deep breaths. In for four, out for four. Where was the box? Barney's breathing was getting away from him, he couldn't control it. In for four, out for four. He left his den and went into his bedroom. The simple, square rosewood box was in the exact centre of his bedside table. Inside it were small, wizened, green pieces of foliage sitting on tissue paper. Seven of them in total, his four-leaf-clover collection.

He'd been just two when he'd found his first one. He and his mum had been in the park, with a group of other mums and toddlers. He couldn't remember the occasion himself, but he remembered his mum telling him about it later. 'I was talking to one of the other mums and you squeaked for my attention like you always did. Then you held your hand out to me and said, 'Mummy four. Not free. Four.' And there it was in your chubby little hand, the first four-leaf clover I'd ever seen in my life.'

Over the next couple of years, he'd become obsessed with the idea of finding four-leaf clovers. He looked at the ground and saw the patterns among the grass and the clover. The ones with four leaves jumped out at him. 'How do you do it?' his mother would ask. At almost four, the age he'd been when his mother had left, he'd found his last one. He couldn't remember whether she'd seen it or not.

Barney's breathing had settled. He closed the box and put it back down beside the bed. Tears filled his eyes. He could find four-leaf clovers. He could find any number of things that were lost. Why couldn't he find his mum?

7

THE DOOR OF THE TERRACED HOUSE WAS OPENED BY THE
Family Liaison Officer. She took one look at Dana's face
and stepped back quickly so that the two of them could get
inside, away from the reporters who'd been positioned outside the
Barlow family home for the past two days. Inside the house,
Dana could hear voices on a television programme and music
upstairs.

'Where are they?' she asked.

'Lounge,' replied the FLO. She knew. They always did.

Dana let the FLO lead the way along the hall and through a door
on the right. The room was long and narrow, running almost the
full length of the house. The family was sitting on easy chairs,
pretending to watch television. The mother, father and one of the
mother's sisters, who seemed to have worked out a rota between
them, and the twins' fourteen-year-old brother, Jonathon. Their
sixteen-year-old sister was in her room, if the music drifting down
the stairs was anything to judge by.

Seeing Dana, Mr Barlow rose and turned off the television set.
He stood by its side, waiting. His wife seemed to have frozen in
place on the sofa.

'I have news,' said Dana, her eyes flicking from the mother to the
father. 'Would you like me to speak to you alone?' Her eyes
wandered to their son. He caught her meaning instantly and moved

across the sofa to sit next to his mum. He took hold of her hand, looking frightened and much younger than fourteen.

'Go on,' said the dad. He knew, too. They all did. 'Get on with it.'

'I'm very sorry, but we found the bodies of two young boys this evening. We believe they're Jason and Joshua. I'm so very sorry.'

'Two?' he said. 'Both of them?'

Dana wondered whether, if she listened to the mother's howl for long enough, it might actually drill a hole in her head.

8

THE KNOCKING HAD STOPPED. HE'D FOLLOWED THE USUAL pattern. Three sharp knocks, loud enough to be heard in the garden but not so loud as to sound aggressive or threatening. Repeated twice. Nine times his knuckles made contact with the wood of her front door. She never heard him climb back up the steps.

In the old days, he'd have been able to break into her flat using a credit card. The state-of-the-art security he'd had installed himself had put paid to that. Funny, really. It had been intended to protect her from a killer; now it was protecting her from him.

At least two minutes since the last knock. He'd gone. Feeling herself breathe easily again, Lacey walked the length of her long, narrow garden. The walls around it were high, but whoever had planned the space had chosen carefully and its plants all thrived in the shade. In summer, the sweet scents of jasmine, honeysuckle and old-fashioned roses cloaked the acrid smells of the city. In winter, the frost and occasional snow made fairytale ice-sculptures.

There was light coming from the top floor of the house next door. She could see the top of Barney's head, just above his computer. Strange, sweet kid. He was on his own in the house after all, there wasn't a single other room lit up. It was getting on for ten o'clock. It wasn't right. He was sensible enough but he'd be scared, with everything that was going on, with the newspapers and the television news full of stories of boys his age going missing from their homes.

A scuffling noise on the other side of the wall. For a second, adrenaline pumped, then Lacey recognized the head and shoulders of the man who appeared over the top. He pushed himself up and swung his legs over the top of the wall before dropping down on her side.

'Hi,' he said.

'What are you doing?'

Detective Inspector Mark Joesbury, of the special crimes directorate that handled covert operations, rotated one shoulder, as though he'd tweaked a muscle. He'd cut his hair short again, close to his scalp, making him look tougher, less attractive. 'You don't answer my calls, you ignore my emails, you don't even open your door,' he said. 'What am I supposed to do?'

'Get the hint.'

A sharp blink and the tiniest jerk back of his head. The lines of his face hardened. 'I thought you should know that the Cambridge gang have all been officially charged and a date set for their first hearing. Next month. The twenty-eighth.'

Cambridge. Just hearing the name of the city made her feel sick. 'Good,' she said. 'But you could have sent a constable to tell me that.'

He turned to look at the conservatory door. 'Can we go inside?' he asked.

'I was about to go to bed,' she said. 'So it wouldn't really be appropriate, would it?'

Joesbury gave an exaggerated sigh. 'Perish the thought. They're all expected to plead not guilty.'

'I wouldn't expect anything else.'

The twenty-eighth of March. She'd known it was only a matter of time. The British legal system was slow but relentless. They probably wouldn't need her at the first hearing. The evidence-gathering would take months. She had time. Time to deal with the panic, rising like molten load inside her every time she thought about the events of January.

'There'll be a trial,' said Joesbury. 'You'll have to appear.'

'I know.'

'Can you cope?'

No, she really didn't think she could. 'Of course,' she said.

He sighed, took a step closer. 'Dana tells me you've been signed off sick for another month. She says that other than official communication that you can't avoid, no one's heard anything from you since you got back to London. You won't see anybody. You won't even talk on the phone and you're showing no interest in going back to work.'

Where was he going with this?

'Lacey, this isn't you.'

'No disrespect, DI Joesbury, but you know nothing about me.'

Another heavy sigh, as though her natural desire for space and privacy was somehow childish and indulgent.

'I know how much the job means to you,' he said. 'What did you tell me last year? Your career is all you have? If you're going to throw that away as well, what's left?'

He knew far too much about her. That had always been the trouble with Mark Joesbury. What he didn't know instinctively, he ferreted out somehow.

'I heard a whisper the Sapphire Units are recruiting again,' he said.

The Sapphire Units were a relatively recent initiative in the Metropolitan Police, set up to handle crimes involving sexual violence. She'd joined the police service to work on crime against women and joining the units had always been her long-term goal. Of course, that was before Cambridge.

'I can't,' she said.

He'd been edging closer, almost without her noticing. If he reached out now, he'd touch her. She couldn't let that happen. She took a step back.

'I meant it,' he said.

It was probably just the light but his eyes didn't look turquoise any more. They were the colour of storm clouds and the scar on his right temple looked fresh and vivid.

'Every word I said on that tower – I meant it,' he went on. 'Jesus,

Lacey, can we only be honest with each other when one of us is about to die?'

Lacey wasn't sure whether the sound she made next started out as a laugh or a sob. What came out of her mouth was a sort of strangled howl. A second later she was pressed tight against his chest, wailing like a child with cut knees. This! This was why she couldn't be near Mark Joesbury.

'I know, I know,' he whispered in her ear, playing the parental role to perfection. 'No one should have to go through what you did.'

This had to stop right now. Much more of this and she'd tell him everything. She forced her breathing back under control, gave herself a minute until the sobs subsided, then pulled back. She ran both hands over her face to wipe the tears away before looking up.

'What?' he said. 'Still pretending you don't remember the tower?'

Look him in the eye. 'I'm fine, Sir, really. I just need some more time. Thank you for your concern.'

Joesbury's tender moments never lasted long and this one vanished as quickly as it had appeared. 'I just hope you're clear about what you do and don't remember before the trial,' he said. 'The last thing we need is a prosecution witness who's fuzzy about the details.'

Maybe all he really cared about was that she'd be able to hold it together as a witness. Well, life would be a lot less complicated if that turned out to be the case.

'I won't let you down,' she told him.

'I know you won't. I suppose I should let you get some sleep.'

'Thank you.'

'Come out with me tomorrow night.'

'What?'

'Dinner. Nothing heavy – actually there's someone I'd like you to meet. Would seven be too early?'

She shook her head. 'It's not a good—' She didn't get to finish. An electronic beeping came from his jacket pocket. He took a couple of seconds to read the text message. It was the chance she needed. She moved away, as though to give him privacy, edging closer to the conservatory door. She could see his reflection in the glass. He was tapping out a reply with his thumbs and wasn't it ridiculous, to feel cross and jealous that someone had taken his attention away from her, when she really didn't want it in the first place?

'That was Dana,' he said, making eye contact with her in the glass.

Dana. Who else?

'They found the missing kids earlier this evening.'

Instinct made Lacey turn and look him full in the face, seeking information. Police instinct, which she no longer wanted to be part of her make-up.

'I suppose they're . . .'

He nodded. 'Bodies were found by Tower Bridge a couple of hours ago. Dana's on her way to the mortuary with the father.'

There was nothing to be said. It was the part of the job that was unbearable. Somehow they forced themselves to bear it, because that was what they signed up for. Except she couldn't any more.

'It's all going to get ugly,' he went on, as if she didn't know that already. 'Four dead kids, one still missing, no closer to finding out who's doing it.'

'Are you involved?'

No, don't ask questions. It's not your business any more and information, of any kind, will eat away at those barriers.

Joesbury shook his head. 'No, I'm just Dana's punchbag, someone for her to yell at when it all gets too much. Do you need one of those too?'

Oh, did she ever. But if she started yelling, how would she ever stop?

'The MIT will have to get bigger now,' Joesbury went on. 'Dana could really use your help.'

'I can't.'

'She can have you transferred – just in an admin role if that's all you feel up to. When the case is over, you'll be a strong position to apply for promotion.'

She'd run out of words. All she could do was shake her head.

Joesbury looked at his watch. 'I've got to go,' he said. 'Tomorrow?'

Another shake, eyes on the ground this time.

'OK, you win. You going to make me jump over the wall again or can I go through the gate?'

Without replying, Lacey took the set of keys from the conservatory door and unlocked the gate that led to the alleyway outside. She crouched to release the lower bolt, as Joesbury pulled back the upper one. In the months since she'd last opened this gate, a winter jasmine had wrapped itself around the hinges. They had to pull together to open it. Tiny yellow flowers fell to the ground.

'See you around, Flint,' he said as he left the garden.

Deep inside Lacey, something shrivelled up tight, like paper in a flame, then lay still.

9

'THE BODIES OF JASON AND JOSHUA BARLOW WERE formally identified by their father an hour ago,' announced Dana to the team in the incident room, including her immediate boss, Detective Superintendent David Weaver. 'OK, for the benefit of those new to the investigation, these are the facts.'

Behind her, the photographed faces of five young boys stared down at those who were expected to come up with some answers.

'In the last eight weeks, five boys aged either ten or eleven years old vanished from in and around their homes,' she said. 'No one saw them leave, no one saw anyone take them. There were no obvious signs of forced abduction. The first of those boys to vanish, Tyler King, was last seen on the twentieth of December. He is still missing and may be nothing to do with this investigation. Four bodies have now been recovered.'

Weaver was slightly built for a police officer, with thick dark hair, thin lips and a hooked nose. His resemblance to a bird of prey, Dana always thought, was due in no small part to his habit of sitting perfectly still, allowing only his eyes to move around the room.

'Ryan Jackson vanished on the third of January, was held somewhere for seven days and then found on a muddy bank at Deptford Creek,' she went on. 'Noah Moore was taken on thirty-first of January, found at Bermondsey five days later. In both cases, death had occurred within a few hours of the body being dumped. On first sight, this appears to be the case with the Barlow twins.'

Eyes flickered to the photographs of the two identical dead boys, lying on an oil-slicked, stone-strewn river beach. Weaver's gaze remained fixed on Dana.

'Neither Ryan nor Noah were sexually abused or tortured in any obvious way,' said Dana. 'Early indications are that the Barlow boys weren't either. Cause of death in each case was extensive blood loss following the severing of the carotid artery.'

'Do we think the killer is someone they know?' asked Weaver.

'Seems likely, Guv,' answered Anderson, after a nod from Dana. 'Kids of ten and older, especially in London, are usually quite savvy. They wouldn't go off with a stranger without putting up a bit of a fight.'

Not a strange bloke, maybe, thought Dana. *An unknown woman, on the other hand . . .*

'When Noah disappeared, we started looking for connections between him and Ryan,' Anderson told the team. 'Obviously, two days ago, we brought the Barlow twins into the circle. Trouble is, there's nothing obvious.'

'Although the four boys – five including Tyler – lived within roughly the same area,' Dana said, 'and are of the same age and ethnicity, unfortunately the similarities seem to end there. They went to four different schools and we can find no evidence that either they or their families knew each other.'

'Families all had different backgrounds,' explained Anderson. 'Ryan Jackson lived with his mum, who's a single parent, and two younger siblings. Noah Moore was an only child of affluent, professional parents. Jason and Joshua's father has been out of work for six months, their mother works part-time in a supermarket.'

'Two of them were Cub Scouts but with different packs,' said Dana. 'All four – five including Tyler – played football, but you name me a ten-year-old boy who doesn't.'

'There'll be a link somewhere,' said Weaver.

'I agree, Guv, but we've talked to everyone who knew those boys, including all their mates. Every detail has gone into the system and nothing's come up other than the football connection, which we spotted ourselves.'

As she spoke, Dana looked over at the HOLMES operator for confirmation. The Home Office Large and Major Enquiry System was a sophisticated intelligence system into which details of all major crimes across the UK were routinely fed. It could spot similarities, connections, links to other crimes in minutes. The operator, a drab middle-aged woman, shook her head. HOLMES, so far, hadn't helped.

'What about the coaches?' asked Weaver. 'Have you checked them out?'

Anderson nodded. 'Nothing,' he said. 'And boys' football coaches are usually dads themselves. I can't see this being a family man somehow.'

The detective superintendent stood and walked closer to the board. The five boys grinned down at him. Ryan had a missing front tooth from a playground injury.

'What's he doing with them?' he asked. 'We know what he's not doing, and we can all be grateful for that, but what does he want them for?'

No one replied. They'd asked themselves the same question too many times. They'd got rather tired of endless answers that didn't fit.

'It's not about rage, is it?' he went on, looking from one boy to the next. 'It's all too cold, too careful. OK, tell me about the scenes. They're not being killed where they're found, are they?'

'Pete,' invited Dana.

Stenning cleared his throat. 'No, Sir,' he said. 'They're not. There's been no trace of blood at any of the sites where we found the bodies. They're bleeding out somewhere else and that's significant in itself, because each victim suffered extensive blood loss. It would be messy.'

'Not to put too fine a point on it,' said Weaver, fingering his shirt collar. He wore expensive shirts, Thomas Pink and Brioni, always perfectly laundered. 'We've got prints, is that right?' he went on.

'Yes, sir. Size ten wellington boot, the sort that sells several hundred pairs a week. But there are distinctive marks in the prints, other than just the tread of the boot, so we know it's the same pair at each of the three sites and if we find the boots themselves, we can match them.'

Weaver nodded. It was something.

'Pete, can you talk to the people who are analysing the prints,' said Dana. 'See if they appear normal?'

Several pairs of puzzled eyes looked at her.

'Normal how?' asked Stenning.

'I'm not sure. Can you ask, for example, whether they can get any idea of the weight of the person leaving the prints? A big, heavy bloke would make deeper prints than a fairly light one, don't you think? So are these prints consistent with the size of man you'd expect to have size-ten feet?'

Stenning still looked puzzled but he nodded. 'I'll ask,' he said.

'Neil's been in charge of processing the immediate areas,' Dana told Weaver. 'What can you tell us, Neil?'

'At first he seemed to be choosing his sites carefully,' said Anderson. 'Deptford Creek where we found Ryan, and Bermondsey where Noah was left, are both some distance from residential properties. They're also generally quiet as far as traffic is concerned. He seemed to be keeping to a minimum the chances of someone spotting him, although the site at Bermondsey is directly across the river from Wapping police station. Tower Bridge, though, is a whole different ball game. It's as though he's growing in confidence all the time.'

'Cameras?' asked Weaver.

'Not at the sites themselves, Sir. Although quite a number of the roads accessing the sites do have cameras. We've got footage from seventeen different roads taken in the time window when our killer must have driven along several of them to offload Jason and Joshua. Fourteen for the Noah Moore investigation. Similar number for Ryan Jackson.'

Weaver's eyebrows had risen an inch. 'How many hours are we talking about in total?'

'A hundred and seventeen,' said Dana.

Weaver sighed. 'I don't even want to think about how many cars would have been caught on camera in South London in a hundred and seventeen hours.'

'Four hundred and twenty-one thousand and two hundred,' said Dana. 'We assumed one per second to be on the safe side. It's going to take a while.'

Weaver nodded. The footage from the cameras could be sent away to a company that specialized in Automatic Number Plate Recognition. It wasn't foolproof, because so much depended upon lighting conditions, speed of vehicles, angle of number plate, even the font used, but most of the systems offered a reasonably good rate of recognition. If the same vehicle were spotted en route to both Tower Bridge and Bermondsey on the nights in question, it would be one they'd be very interested in.

'Start with the most likely routes,' he said. 'We could get lucky. In the meantime, I want to bring a profiler in. I know you don't—'

'Good idea,' said Dana.

For once, Weaver let what he was feeling show on his face.

'There's something very odd about this one,' said Dana. 'It'll be good to have a fresh perspective.'

'Ma'am.'

Dana turned. One of the detectives on her team, a blonde woman in her early thirties called Gayle Mizon, was at her computer. 'You might want to know that Peter Sweep posted on Facebook at 21.37 hours this evening,' she said. 'Announcing quite correctly that Jason and Joshua's bodies had been found.'

Several members of the team moved closer to Mizon and peered over her shoulder at the screen. More than one helped themselves to an open jar of sweets on the desk. Mizon seemed to eat continually.

'What's this?' asked Weaver, glancing over.

'We've been monitoring social network sites, Sir,' replied Mizon. 'A hundred and sixty of them, to be precise. A couple of dozen mention the murders on a reasonably regular basis, mainly the London-based ones and the parents' chat sites. They all seem pretty innocuous, but we are interested in a Facebook site called the Missing Boys.'

She paused to get her breath and Weaver nodded to show he was following.

'Quite a few of the contributors seem to have known the boys personally,' Mizon said. 'Which is the main reason we've been taking an interest, in case one of them let something slip that they wouldn't necessarily say to us. Nothing so far, but this chap called Peter Sweep keeps popping up. He knows about developments in the case before anything's been officially released.'

'I assume we've tried to trace him,' said Weaver.

'Facebook have been quite helpful,' replied Mizon. 'They let us have the email addresses of the site's main contributors. Then it was a question of getting in touch with the internet service providers to get the IP addresses and the Mac addresses. Most of them are coming from normal family computers in homes, occasionally schools. A lot of them are using their real names and they all check out. Peter, though, doesn't. He uses computers in public buildings or a mobile phone. No profile, just a completely random picture of roses, and no personal information of any kind, which is just odd for young people on Facebook. They normally like to tell the world everything. And, to me, he just doesn't sound like the other kids.'

'Not a kid?' asked Weaver.

Mizon shrugged.

'So far, he's not used the same building twice,' said Dana. 'If we could pin him down even to a few, we could put cameras in and catch him that way. All we know at the moment is that he probably lives in the same area of South London that most of the murdered boys did.'

'Any number of people will know what we're up to before official announcements are made,' Weaver said. 'On the other hand, his try-ing to conceal his identity is interesting in itself. It's worth keeping an eye on.'

The door to the incident room opened and a woman in civilian clothes made eye contact with the superintendent. She tapped her watch and gestured towards the corridor.

'Five minutes,' Weaver told her. She left the room.

'Press conference at eight,' Weaver said to Dana. 'Will that give you enough time?'

As Dana nodded, Weaver walked back to the incident board. He took his time, looking from one young face to the next. 'We had to wait a week to find Ryan,' he said. 'Noah was missing for five days, and now Jason and Joshua turn up after only two.'

'We know, Guv,' said Dana. 'Whoever he is, whatever he's doing, he's killing them faster.'

10

Friday 15 February

BARNEY WOKE IN DARKNESS AND KNEW SOMETHING WAS different. He often woke at exactly four o'clock in the morning and then lay for what felt like ages staring up at the ceiling. Usually, though, his head wasn't anything like this fuzzy. He turned and looked at the clock. Well, that explained it – only just gone midnight. He'd not been asleep much more than an hour and a half.

He sat up, wondering what had woken him. London was never quiet. There was always noise coming up from the street: traffic, sirens, older kids screeching, the occasional drunk. In the back gardens and alleyways, rubbish bins would clatter when cats or foxes got amongst them. He was used to all that, though. Normally, nothing woke him until four o'clock.

He got out of bed, crossed to the window and lifted the blind. If there'd been something in the garden the security lights would be on. They weren't.

Years ago, Barney's dad had hired a landscape designer to make the best of the long, narrow, shady plot behind their house. The young man came fresh out of college with grand ideas of Zen gardens and Japanese influences that had worked surprisingly well. From the back door of the house a mosaic path led in gently curving lines down to the very end of the space. The undulating beds on either side were filled with tall, architectural plants that kept their shape and foliage throughout the winter. Quirky sculptures lay amidst the shrubs like random surprises on a treasure hunt, whilst wind chimes and water features kept silence at bay. There were few flowers, even in spring, and no scent, but thanks to the presence of several small ponds, dragonflies, frogs, even newts could be seen and heard throughout the summer months.

Right at the very end of the garden, only just visible behind the bordering plants, was a tall mirror. It reflected the garden, the mosaic path being the predominant feature. From the house, it gave the impression that the winding, colourful path went on for ever.

As Barney looked out, the moon appeared, only fleetingly, but long enough to cast a soft, silver light across the garden. The mirror glowed and in its very centre a small, pale face looked back at Barney.

Barney stared back, more curious than alarmed, knowing that the pale face was his own reflection. And yet it seemed to have taken on a life of its own out there. As though there were two Barneys: the one he knew inside-out, the constant, the familiar; and then the other one, the one who was him and not him, the boy in the mirror who was both smaller and thinner than he, spectral pale and with a smile on his face that Barney was sure he never saw in the bathroom mirror. He almost expected to see the phantom Barney wave, turn and walk away.

The moon vanished and so did the other boy. Barney let the blind fall back into place then crossed to his bathroom and used the loo. He reached for the flush, then stopped. There was something about the flush of the cistern that always sounded so unnaturally loud at night. He found it a bit unnerving, if he was honest, and if it wasn't for the fact that he hated to get up and see the mess the next day, he'd never flush the loo at night. Usually the forces of tidiness won, but tonight felt different.

For one thing, there was that pressing cold weight in his stomach that told him he was alone in the house.

He realized then, for the first time, that he had no idea what time his dad returned home on his evenings out. The pattern they'd established was always the same. Dad went out at 7.30, immediately after dinner, and phoned on the half-hour, every hour, until 9.30pm when he checked that Barney was in bed and the light was about to go out. He always asked if both doors were locked and Barney always had to get up and check, even though he knew they were. When Barney woke again, at 4am, his dad was always back.

'Dad!' he called from the bathroom doorway. No reply.

Barney stepped out on to the landing. On the first floor of the house, the doors to his dad's bedroom and study and to the two spare bedrooms were all shut. Barney had closed them himself on his way to bed as he always did when he was alone, because it was impossible to go to bed with open doors in the house. So there was really no way of knowing whether his dad was home or not.

Except he knew. Apart from him, this was an empty house.

'Dad!'

No, don't say that again. Too freaky to keep calling out for a parent who wasn't there.

Downstairs, in the kitchen, something fell to the tiled floor. Dad was home, after all.

Except he wasn't. He couldn't be. The first floor and the ground floor were in darkness. Barney reached behind and pulled the draw-string that switched off the bathroom light.

It had to be his dad. Barney had locked both doors before he'd gone to bed. Both had deadlocks, and the back door that led to the garden had bolts top and bottom. The windows were locked – he had a ritual, he checked them every night, running his hand along the aluminium, making sure the lock was in place. And then he always got up to check after his dad's last phone call. No one could have broken in.

Except someone was downstairs, he could hear footsteps. The gentle, stealthy footsteps of someone who didn't want to be heard.

His dad would have switched lights on. His dad didn't sneak around. Barney had a sudden flashback of the boy in the garden, the thin, pale boy, who was him and not him, slinking round the back of the house, looking for a way in, groping, feeling, pulling. Finding one.

OK, he had to stay calm. His dad's study was the only room with a lock, he just had to get down the first flight of stairs without being heard and lock himself in. He'd phone Lacey. She could be here in seconds.

On tiptoe, Barney took the first step and then the second. There was definitely someone in the kitchen, he could hear a distinctive and familiar sound. That made him pause. Why would a burglar, let alone a phantom, open the door of the washing machine?

He reached the first-floor landing and stopped outside the study door. Lock himself in, or carry on down? Could he phone Lacey and say someone had broken in and was doing their washing? And what if the police did turn up, and found him alone in the house? They wouldn't like it. They might take him away and put him in a care home like the two brothers who'd recently joined his school. They weren't quite right, those two. They were way behind the rest of the class and had all sorts of what adults called behaviour issues. The rest of the kids had got the message loud and clear. Care homes were not the sort of places you wanted to be.

Barney left the door of the study behind and carried on down, knowing from years of practice how to walk at the left edge so that the stairs never creaked. From the hall at the bottom he could see that the kitchen door was open, and he knew it hadn't been when he went up to bed.

A hand touched his shoulder and Barney screamed like the kid he hadn't known he still was.

'Barney, for heaven's sake, it's me.'

His dad, as startled as Barney, had stepped back and raised both hands in the air in a surrender gesture. His dad, looking different somehow. Flushed and excited and nervous. His hair was untidy, there was colour in his cheeks, his clothes looked dishevelled. There was alcohol on his breath, too, not the bitter smell of beer but the sweeter one of red wine. The bottom couple of inches of the left leg of his jeans were wet. He caught Barney's eye and looked away immediately.

'Why didn't you put any lights on?' asked Barney, whose entire body was still trembling with fright.

'I didn't want to wake you up.'

His dad's right hand was tucked behind his back, as though he were holding something he didn't want Barney to see. Then he shoved his hand into his jacket pocket. Whatever he'd been holding was now tucked inside. He raised his other hand and looked at his watch.

'It's gone midnight,' he said. 'Come on, back to bed.'

For some reason, his dad seemed to have trouble looking at him.

'You're wet,' Barney said.

His dad looked down, saw the wet trouser leg. 'Stepped in a puddle,' he said.

'Where've you been?' Barney asked.

'Working.' His dad's eyes drifted up to Barney's face, then back down to the tiled floor. 'You know I have to work sometimes.'

Till midnight? How many people worked till midnight? Barney wanted to say it, didn't quite dare. 'They found those two boys,' he said instead. 'They found them tonight. Did you know?'

Something that looked a bit like pain and a bit like anger crossed his dad's face. 'I didn't,' he said. 'I haven't seen the news. Were you worried?'

'No,' said Barney. 'Not till just now. I thought you were a burglar.'

'Burglars can't get in, we talked about that. Come on, up you go.'

Barney did what he was told. On the first landing, he looked back. His dad was standing at the foot of the stairs, in the still-dark hallway. His eyes were shining in the light from the street lamp outside and there was something about them that looked very different.

Back in bed, Barney realized he wasn't getting back to sleep any time soon. He heard his dad draw the chain on the front door and climb the stairs. He listened to the sounds of the bathroom and then two doors being closed. Sometimes, his dad remembered Barney's dislike of open doors at night.

As silence fell over the house once more, Barney got up. He could have another wee, he supposed, although he didn't need one. Maybe get a drink of water. Then he would need a wee.

As he crossed the landing, he saw a light shining from his dad's study. He'd have to be very quiet. He took extra care opening the door of his den and closing it behind him. The desk-lamp made no sound and he turned down the volume on his computer before switching it on.

He went to the news site first. The discovery of Jason's and

Joshua's bodies was official now. There was even a photograph of the crime scene taken from Tower Bridge. You could see the police tent, the crime-scene tape, detectives looking as though they didn't know what to do next. Barney wondered if Jorge and Harvey's mum had taken it – it was typical of the sort of factual but, at the same time, slightly depressing and really rather hopeless pictures she always seemed to take.

He read that the twins' dad had identified his sons' bodies earlier that evening and there would be a press conference at Lewisham police station the next day.

Further down, the webpage carried pictures of all four boys, Ryan, Noah, Joshua and Jason, with details of their disappearances, including the dates they'd vanished and the dates they'd been found. Seven days, five days, two days, respectively, the boys had been missing. He was killing them faster. Barney sat back to think about that, and then immediately saw something else. He blinked, double-checked. Blimey, had nobody spotted that? It all happened on Tuesdays and Thursdays.

Barney made sure, cross-checking the dates on the webpage with his electronic calendar, but he hadn't been wrong. Ryan had disappeared from the garden of his house at 6pm on a Thursday evening. His body had been found a week later on Thursday. Noah had been taken on a Thursday and found five days later on Tuesday. Jason and Joshua had disappeared just two days ago, a Tuesday evening, and had been found this evening – Thursday. The news pages didn't mention days of the week, just dates, so Barney knew there was a good chance most people wouldn't have realized. But the police would have, surely? What about the other one, the one they weren't sure was involved? Barney found his files on Tyler King. Vanished on a Thursday.

Barney flicked away from the news page and on to Facebook. As most kids would have gone to bed, the comment stream had slowed down in the last couple of hours. Barney hovered the cursor over his status box and started typing.

Has anyone else spotted that this is all happening on Tuesday and Thursday evenings? Check it out! Do the police know they should be looking for someone who doesn't have an alibi on Tuesdays and Thursdays?

He pressed Update without thinking about whether or not it was a good idea. Then realized it almost certainly wasn't. Of course people would have spotted it. It had probably been picked up ages ago. He'd just made himself look a proper jerk. The piss-taking he'd get tomorrow.

Within seconds someone replied. It was that rather odd Peter Sweep character. Bracing himself, Barney started to read. After one sentence, he felt like someone had placed large, cold hands on his shoulders.

I was wondering when someone would spot that. Oh, the cleverness of you. Are you busy next Tuesday?

Barney sat for a second, looking at the comment, waiting for someone to respond. No one did. He checked back up the thread. The last comment before his own had been left at 11.30pm. Still nothing else. It was as though he and Peter were alone on Facebook. Barney logged out and closed his computer down. He'd go back to bed and tell himself very firmly that there was nothing to get uptight about. Peter was just a twat trying to freak him out. Peter had no way of knowing where he lived. He could only get to him on Facebook.

Barney closed the doors, switched off the lights and climbed into bed. As he lay in the darkness, he realized that Facebook felt quite close enough.

11

'*I*T'S THE BLOOD THAT I REMEMBER. OUT OF EVERYTHING THAT *happened that day, it's the blood that won't go away. There was this splash – spatter, I think you'd call it – on the windows and I remember I couldn't take my eyes off it. Bright red. Like rose petals. Or rubies. Or balloons. Little red droplets. The colour they made in the sun was just incredible.'*

'*Blood is a beautiful colour,*' *agreed the psychiatrist.*

'*And the way it moves in water. Have you seen that? It doesn't mix, like a water-based paint, it hangs, suspended, twisting and turning like one of those lava lamps, forming its own shapes. Sometimes I think I'll never get it out of my head. The blood.*'

12

THE COLD, SOGGY LIGHT OF A WINTER DAWN SEEMED TO BE snaking its way up the Thames and settling over the city when Barney got back from the newsagent's the next day. Strictly, he was too young to have a job, and there was no way his dad would have allowed him to have a paper round, but Mr Kapur had never been able to find a child he trusted to sort and organize the papers in the morning until Barney came along. Barney had the neatest, most logical mind he'd ever come across, he said at least weekly.

There had been nothing from Mum in his secret mail account this morning. It was getting harder, somehow, to look at that empty in-box every day. Still, he'd only just sent off the latest ads. He had to give them time.

As Barney walked along the hall towards the kitchen, he heard the sounds of *Daybreak* on the kitchen TV and something else that was wrong.

The washing machine was on. They never did washing on Friday. Saturday was washing day. They did four loads every Saturday. A whites wash, a coloureds wash, bed linen and then towels. The washing was Barney's job, because he quite liked the sorting into organized piles, and the idea of putting dirty stuff in and getting clean, sweet-smelling, damp clothes out. His dad did the ironing.

'What's going on?' he said, as he walked into the kitchen, his eyes going straight to the washing machine. Yep, there it was, something pale and stripy sloshing about.

'Breakfast's ready,' said his dad, who was sitting at the central island, a cereal spoon in his right hand. Barney didn't move. His dad had used too much soap. There was too much froth in the machine.

'I spilt a mug of tea in bed this morning,' said his dad. 'I didn't want it staining. That's OK, isn't it? For once?'

''Course,' said Barney, making himself look away from the washing machine. So did that mean they'd only do three loads the next day? Odd numbers had a way of making him feel twitchy inside.

'Barney!' His dad was reaching out across the island towards him, putting his own large hands over Barney's small ones. 'You're doing it again.'

Barney shrugged and concentrated on making his hands relax. He couldn't remember it, but he knew they'd been tracing patterns on the granite surface, his fingers moving in repetitive squared shapes, over and over, even when his hands started to hurt, either until someone stopped him or he was distracted by something else.

'Raisins,' said his dad.

The raisins were by his right hand. The bran flakes had already been poured into the bowl. Barney counted four raisins into his bowl as the 8am news came on, his dad adjusted the volume and a tall man in a suit told the world what most of it already knew – that the bodies of Jason and Joshua Barlow had been found the previous evening and that the police believed they'd been killed by the same person who'd previously abducted and murdered Ryan Jackson and Noah Moore. He reminded them that a fifth boy, Tyler King, was still missing.

The tall man, a senior police officer of some kind, was sitting behind a table with three other people. As the next four raisins landed on the bran flakes, the cameras moved along the table to the parents. The bones of the father's skull seemed to be pressing themselves out through his skin as he asked the viewers to help find their sons' killer. The mother didn't manage to articulate a single word. She was crying too much.

At least Jason and Joshua had had a mother.

As the last four of his sixteen raisins went into his cereal bowl, a dark-skinned, dark-haired woman appeared on the screen. The name card on the desk in front of her said that she was Detective Inspector Dana Tulloch.

'Someone knows who this killer is,' she was saying. 'This killer doesn't appear from nowhere and then vanish again. He lives among us. If you have any information that you think could be helpful, however small, however unimportant it may seem, please get in touch.'

The news moved on to the next story and Barney's dad turned the volume down again.

'Toast?' he said, getting up.

'Please,' said Barney. 'Can I have maple syrup and honey?'

'No, because that would be disgusting.'

'I mean honey on one half and maple syrup on the other.'

With a heavy sigh and a resigned shake of the head, his dad reached up into the cupboard. 'Barney, I'm not sure I want you going out in the mornings at the moment.'

Instant panic. Barney looked from the TV over towards his dad. 'Why not?'

His dad turned to face him. 'It's too dark,' he said. 'Maybe when it gets lighter, in the summer.'

'If I give my job up now, I won't get it back again just because the working conditions become better,' said Barney.

His dad almost smiled and then caught the look on Barney's face.

'I just don't feel comfortable about you being out on your own right now.'

But he felt perfectly comfortable leaving him on his own two nights every week. OK, that was hardly fair. Barney was the one who refused ever to have babysitters in the house, who'd kicked up a massive fuss on the few occasions, now years ago, when his dad had arranged one. Babysitters just never understood how things needed to be done. Babysitters moved things. Babysitters came into his room when he was working and asked nosy questions. Babysitters . . . yeah, his dad had finally got the message, and for years Barney's dad just hadn't gone out at all. Only in the last few months had he started to trust Barney on his own.

'Don't glare at me, Barney.'

'I'm not,' Barney said, although he knew he had been. Then the toast popped up and his dad began the process of buttering and spreading. While his dad's attention was elsewhere, Barney reached for the remote control, turned down the volume and switched the channel.

'You wouldn't answer the door, would you?' his dad said, as he handed him the toast. 'If anyone knocked when I'm not here. You'd phone me.'

'Course,' said Barney through a mouthful. On the TV, three men in swimming trunks, yellow beanie hats and goggles were getting into three bath-tubs. One had been filled with chicken curry, the second with soy sauce and the third, blackcurrant juice. It was an experiment to find Britain's stainiest food.

'Are you sure you don't want me to organize someone to keep you company? We can find someone you like. Maybe an older boy? Jorge, perhaps?'

The men on the TV screen were sponging themselves down. Just gross!

'Barney!'

'What?'

'Can we think again about a babysitter?' said his dad in a voice that made it clear it wasn't for the first time. 'For Tuesdays and Thursdays, when I have to work late.'

13

'MIKE, PLEASE.'

The pathologist, Dr Michael Kaytes, turned round in surprise. He'd been about to switch on the iplayer in the corner of the mortuary examination room. Whilst cutting open bodies and removing internal organs, Kaytes liked to listen to Beethoven. Dana was convinced he did it for effect. Usually it didn't bother her. Usually.

'I'm sorry,' said Dana, knowing she looked anything but apologetic, and not caring. 'I'm just not sure I can cope with the music. Not this time.'

Kaytes nodded slowly. 'As you wish.' He walked back to the two gurneys in the centre of the room where Jason and Joshua Barlow's bodies lay under blue plastic. Dana knew Stenning and Anderson were exchanging uncomfortable glances behind her back. Well, it was just tough. These were ten-year-old boys they were dealing with and if anyone could be blasé about that, she wasn't sure she wanted them on her team.

Jesus, she had to calm down.

She watched, teeth clenched, as Kaytes and his young technician, Troy, peeled back the sheets. Kaytes was a tall man, barrel chested and with a thatch of thick grey hair. His eyes were bright blue. Beside him, thin, small, colourless Troy looked like an under-nourished teenager.

The gurneys had been labelled, to make it obvious which twin was which. Those little faces would have been so cute, so cheeky in life.

'We got straight on to it,' said Kaytes. 'I thought you'd want the facts as soon as possible.'

'Thank you,' said Dana. 'Is it the same killer?'

Kaytes nodded. 'Almost certainly,' he said. 'Same cause of death: extensive bleeding following the severance of the carotid artery. Neither boy was sexually abused, no evidence of prolonged physical brutality of any sort.'

'Are you sure?' asked Anderson.

Kaytes nodded. 'Hair missing around the wrists and ankles, consistent with strong packaging tape being wrapped around them,' he went on. 'Some bruises that would indicate struggling, the most recent of these along the left side of Joshua's body.'

Kaytes positioned himself on the far side of the gurney from the three police officers and reached over the body. He towered over the small, thin child. 'Can you see?' he said. 'One on the left thigh, a couple of smaller ones on the calf. Then this one on the shoulder. None of them much more than a day or so old. If I were hazarding a guess at what happened to him, I'd say some time yesterday, he fell on to his left side.'

Dana nodded. Yesterday, Joshua had been a prisoner for almost two days. He'd have been scared, but the will to live, to escape if possible, would have been strong.

'Like our previous two victims,' continued Kaytes, 'these both have a scattering of wooden splinters on the back of their shoulders and upper arms, consistent with their being held immobile on some sort of wooden bench or trestle table.'

These children had been strapped down for two days. They'd squirmed and wriggled to get free, and at some point Joshua had probably tipped the table over and landed heavily on his left side.

'Their last meal was crisps and some sort of chocolate candy bar,' said Kaytes. 'They ate about two hours before they died. Again similar to the stomach contents of the previous two victims. Whoever's holding them, he's not big on healthy eating.'

A woman would make them eat properly, wouldn't she? Dana felt her conviction wavering. On the other hand, would you worry about vitamins if you knew you were going to cut the kid's throat days down the line?

'Same murder weapon?' asked Anderson.

'Like the previous two victims, these two chaps were killed by a straight-edged, sharp blade, seven to ten inches long. Difficult to say, beyond that. But I am glad you brought that up. Because in one respect, Jason at least does differ from the previous two. Come and look.'

He stepped closer, extended a gloved hand and laid it on Jason's forehead. As he tilted the boy's head back, Troy shone a lamp directly at the wound on the throat.

'We're going to get this photographed and blown up to make it clearer, but for now, can you see?' Kaytes ran his gloved index finger close to the edge of the wound. A millimetre or so beneath the cut was a thin, pink line.

'Is that another cut?' asked Dana.

Kaytes nodded. 'That's exactly what it is,' he said. 'And whilst it's very indistinct, we're pretty certain there's a third cut here as well.'

'Hesitation wounds?' asked Dana.

Kaytes shook his head. 'No. The previous two were made earlier – sorry to sound a bit *Blue Peter*. They had chance to start healing.'

Dana straightened up, looked at Anderson and then Stenning.

'What the hell's he doing? Practising?' said Anderson.

'To be absolutely honest with you, we saw something on Ryan's corpse that made us wonder,' said Kaytes. 'It just wasn't clear enough to draw any conclusions from. But what seems to be happening is that your perpetrator starts making cuts on his victims' throats some time before he kills them. They'll be much smaller cuts, of course, or else they'd bleed out. He cuts them, and lets them heal.'

'And then he cuts them again,' said Dana.

Silence for a moment, as each person in the room seemed to be mulling over what that could possibly mean.

'Anything else, Mike?' asked Dana after a while. She watched the pathologist glance at his assistant then nod his head fractionally.

'I'll let Troy tell you,' he said.

The younger man's vowels were straight out of Southend. 'I noticed some bruising I thought was interesting,' he said. 'I spotted it on Joshua, but there's some marks on Jason too, although fainter. Come a bit closer.'

Troy put his fingers gently beneath Joshua's chin. Fractionally, he tipped the child's head back and his boss increased the amount of light shining on the boy's face.

'Faint bruising, can you see?' said Troy. 'On the neck, under the jawbone, both sides of the head.'

Anderson and Stenning were nodding thoughtfully.

'Same thing on Jason?' asked Stenning.

'There is, but fainter.'

'Were they made when the boys were killed?' asked Dana. 'They look like restraint marks to me.'

'They look exactly like restraint marks, but they're older than the wounds. I'd say these marks were made on the day the boys were taken, not the day they died,' said Troy. 'It's also my view, and Dr Kaytes doesn't disagree, that these marks are on the exact site of the carotid baroreceptor.'

'Troy studies martial arts,' said Kaytes. 'I'd have written them off as restraint marks; he thinks they could be more significant.'

'Nothing on the others?' Dana asked, speaking directly to Troy now. 'The earlier victims?'

'Not in this exact spot, but to be honest, these are very faint bruises. I'd expect them to disappear after a day or two,' Troy told her.

'So Ryan and Noah could have had them, but there was chance for them to fade?' said Anderson.

'Exactly,' said Troy.

'Could explain a lot,' said Anderson. At his side, Stenning was nodding in agreement.

14

'COULD YOU TELL *ME* WHAT THEY DID TO YOU?' ASKED THE counsellor.

'I assumed you'd read the files,' replied Lacey. 'That you'd already know.'

'I've read all the files on the Cambridge operation. But this isn't about what I know or don't know, it's about whether you're strong enough to talk about it yet.'

The small room in Guy's Hospital was windowless and Lacey could never quite remember whether she'd pressed the lift to go up to one of over thirty floors, or down into the basement. She could be underground, she could be fifteen storeys up. Once in the room, there was no way of knowing.

And the corridor outside was always so silent; as though no one but she ever walked it, no one but she ever came to this small, square, dimly lit room, in which sharp edges probably existed but faded to ambiguous shadings in the gloom. There was a couch, two semi-comfortable chairs and a desk. A reading lamp was the only source of light. Lacey sometimes wondered if the woman she came to see twice a week was nocturnal, unable to face sunlight, even bright artificial light. Perhaps she was doomed to lead a subterranean existence, dependent upon the needy and the disturbed for her interaction with the outside world.

Lacey watched the second-hand glide round the face of the wall clock. Two pounds a minute, this woman's time was worth. Every thirty seconds, ching, another pound gone. It was worse than being in a black cab stuck in traffic. Thank God she wasn't paying the bill herself.

And once again, she was expected to talk about the time, not much more than a month ago, when she'd come up against a new kind of evil. A depravity in which victims were stalked relentlessly, tortured with their own worst fears, before being thrown headlong into a downward spiral that ended only in self-destruction. She'd come so close to being one of those victims and now this woman, who knew nothing about real evil, was interpreting her reluctance to share details as weakness.

'I'll have to say it all in court,' Lacey said at last. 'I'll have to spell out every last detail in front of a hundred strangers. I think that will probably do me.'

She could never bring herself to lie on the couch. Having to talk about herself made her feel vulnerable enough; doing it prone would be a step too far. So she sat, in the chair directly facing the counsellor. Sometimes she and the counsellor held eye contact for long seconds without speaking.

'Well, that won't be easy,' the counsellor said, after the better part of a minute. 'It might help to go through it with me first.'

'I had to make statements from my hospital bed,' said Lacey. 'Then, when I got out, I had to go through it all again, just in case there was any question of statements made in hospital somehow being inadmissible. I've done it twice already, I think third time should pay for all, don't you?'

The woman glanced down at her notes, as though to check which of her prepared questions she'd reached. 'Are you ashamed of what happened?' she asked.

The counsellor's eyes were grey, like her hair and her clothes. She was a grey lady, but her skin was too pink to belong to a ghost. 'I'm not sure I understand,' said Lacey, although she understood perfectly.

'Do you feel embarrassed? Weak? As though your colleagues are judging you?'

'*Are* they judging me? Is that in the file too?'

It was a game they played, twice each week. The counsellor asked questions and Lacey dealt with them, just occasionally, when she judged the moment was right, giving a little bit more away. She'd played the game before, years earlier, trying to convince police counsellors she was fit to be a police officer. Strange that it should be so much harder, convincing them that she wasn't.

'You were sent in to investigate, you became one of the victims. Some people might consider they'd failed.'

The woman was trying to get a rise out of her. Did she really imagine it would be that easy?

'I'm still alive. Most of the other girls aren't. I'd say that makes me a survivor, wouldn't you?'

The counsellor pulled one of her rare smiles out of the ration-book. She wasn't unfriendly, Lacey had decided at one of their earlier sessions, just one of those people who didn't smile easily.

'Yes,' she agreed. 'I would. And you caught the people responsible. From what I understand, they're all going to prison for a very long time. Not that you can always prejudge these things, of course.'

Time to give a little. Lacey gave a deep sigh, dropped her eyes to the carpet. 'I never think about it,' she said in a low voice. 'About what they did to me that last night. If I catch myself on the verge, I have to push it right away, because if I let all those thoughts in, I think my head might explode.'

The other woman was leaning forward in her seat, the way she always did when she felt she was getting somewhere. 'Go on, Lacey,' she said.

'I have to keep active,' Lacey went on. 'I wake up and go running, two hours every morning. In the afternoons I go to the local pool or out for a bike ride. I have a gym at home and I use it most days. In the evenings I walk, sometimes for miles, and when I get in, even though I'm exhausted, I stay up till about two in the morning watching romantic comedies and sit-coms. Nothing dark, because if I think about anything even remotely unsavoury then I can feel it, everything that happened, hammering on the door. I'm living in a La-La land of my own making, wearing out my body and flooding my brain with fluffy pink crap.'

'Because you can't allow yourself to think about anything real?'

Lacey dropped her head forward into her hands. Between her fingers she saw the counsellor's hand stretch out and leave a box of tissues within reach on the carpet. Lacey pressed one to her face. A second later, she crumpled it to hide the fact that it was bone dry.

When she looked up, the counsellor's face had softened. Christ, it was almost too easy. Come in edgy, difficult, have a bit of a sparring match and then let something get to you. Break down and give a bit of information. It never failed because, luckily, counsellors employed by the Met just weren't bright enough to spot what you were up to.

'Tell me more about Mark Joesbury,' she asked Lacey.

On the other hand, maybe this one was brighter than she looked.

'He was my senior officer on the Cambridge case,' said Lacey, knowing she wasn't going to get away with that. 'And I worked with him last autumn, on the Ripper murders. Do you remember?'

'Who doesn't?' replied the counsellor. 'And you became close?'

Not by choice, they hadn't. And yet there was no denying Mark Joesbury had got a lot closer to Lacey Flint than she'd allowed anyone in a long time. He was the one who, albeit for just a second, had seen through the mask . . .

'DI Joesbury was suspicious of me from the start. When we met I was soaked in another woman's blood.'

The mask that was Lacey Flint, the mask that her true self hid behind, the mask that could never be allowed to slip again.

'For a while he thought I was the killer,' Lacey went on. 'I'm not sure he's ever really learned to trust me. Even when he sent me to Cambridge, it was against his better judgement.'

'I read the transcript of what happened on the tower.'

That bloody tower! 'I remember very little about the tower,' said Lacey. 'They'd pumped me full of LSD, I was away with the fairies.'

'He told you he loved you.'

Lacey forced a smile. 'He was on quite a lot of medication too, from what I understand.'

'You think he didn't mean it?'

Every word I said on that tower – I meant it.

'I think he would have said anything in the circumstances.'

'Well, either he meant it, or he knew it would mean something to you. Either way, it seems significant to me.'

Much brighter than she looked. Not stupid at all.

'Are you worried about getting involved with another police officer?'

'I just don't want to get involved with anyone right now.'

'When were you last involved with someone?'

'It's been a while,' said Lacey, thinking that never probably qualified as 'a while'.

'Months? Years?'

Jesus, was it not enough that they'd pulled the insides right out of her body? Did they have to hang them up for all to see and let them scorch in the sun for good measure?

'I'm leaving the police.'

The announcement seemed to hang in the air between them.

'This is a little sudden.'

'Not really, I've been thinking about it for a while. I'll wait till after the Cambridge trial, of course.'

'Have you told anyone?'

Lacey shook her head. How could she have done? She'd only made the decision ten seconds ago. 'I just can't do it any more,' she said.

'Can't do what, exactly?'

'I can't look into people's eyes and see the dark.'

15

'BARNEY?'
The usual midday smells of congealing gravy and chemical sweeteners were seeping through the air-conditioning system when Mrs Green called Barney back. He stepped to one side and let the other children walk round him. 'Push the door to,' she told him, when the last curious face had disappeared.

Mrs Green was Barney's form teacher. She'd joined the school just under a year ago when she and her husband had moved south to London. Mr Green worked at the school too. He was the games teacher and Barney's favourite teacher ever. Not that Mrs Green was bad. She never lost her temper, but somehow always managed to keep control of the class. And she was tidy. The books on the shelves were always neat, arranged in alphabetical order, and she always cleaned the whiteboard completely after each lesson. As she walked towards him, she pushed chairs back under desks, neatening the rows.

'You look tired,' she said, when she'd reached him. 'I thought you were going to drop off during science. Is everything OK?'

Barney nodded. 'Everything's fine,' he said, because that's what you always said, even if it wasn't. He hadn't checked Facebook that morning, but he'd felt it, hanging over him, since he'd got up. Sooner or later he'd have to log back on and see what was waiting for him. Whether Peter Sweep had left him another message.

Mrs Green was giving him an *Oh, really?* look. 'So those shadows under your eyes are just purple paint to make me feel sorry for you and give you less homework?'

'Well, less homework would be good,' he said, keeping a perfectly straight face. 'Because actually, my dad woke me up last night with the washing machine.'

At that his teacher blinked hard in surprise, then half frowned, half smiled. It was a nice sort of look. Friendly but puzzled. Mrs Green had pale-red hair that she'd worn long until a couple of months ago and then cut in a more complicated style that flicked around her shoulders and chin. Barney decided Mrs Green looked quite nice for an older woman; when his mum came back, he hoped she would look a lot like that.

Jesus, he had no idea what his mum looked like!

'Barney, what's the matter? Look, sit down for a second.'

Mrs Green had pushed him gently into a chair and was at the back of the classroom, running the tap. Her heels clicked on the floor as she came back and she left a trail of splashes behind her. She'd overfilled the glass.

Concentrate on something. Don't cry in front of a teacher.

'What time did you go to bed last night, Barney?' she asked him, in a low voice that told him she knew she was being nosy.

'Half nine,' he lied.

Mum would have light-brown hair, wouldn't she, like him? His dad's hair was grey, but he'd seen photographs in which it had been darker. And his dad was tall. So was he. Did that mean Mum was too? Jesus, tall with light-brown hair, was that all he had?

'Barney, Barney, you're going to hurt your hands.'

He was doing it again, that thing with his fingers, tracing a square pattern on the desk. He watched his hands jabbing and darting as though they belonged to someone else and then Mrs Green did something very odd. She reached out and stroked her own hands over his. Very lightly, first the left then the right, then the right and then the left again. Just like his dad did when he was trying to soothe him. Funnily, it worked better when Mrs Green did it. Must be her softer hands.

Barney felt himself calming down. It was OK, there'd be a photo of his mum somewhere at home, he just had to find it; finding things was what he did, and what did it matter what she looked like? It didn't matter what mothers looked like, you just loved them anyway.

'Feeling better?'

Barney nodded. He was.

'Early night tonight?'

He nodded again.

'Off you go, sweetheart.'

Mrs Green stood and pushed her chair back. As Barney walked past her she reached out a hand and stroked the top of his head. Teacher's weren't supposed to touch children. He could get her into trouble if he told on her. And he'd never heard her call another child 'sweetheart'. He wouldn't though, he decided, as he ran along the corridor to the playground. He quite liked the way Mrs Green's soft hands had stroked over him.

'Barney, over here!' Harvey was by the playground equipment store with Sam. Harvey had been Barney's best mate for as long as he could remember, but because Harvey was an August-born baby, whereas Barney's birthday was in October, he'd always been in the year above Barney at school. The previous September, Harvey had started secondary school, but as the two schools shared the same site the two boys still saw each other most days. Harvey, loyal and independent-minded, refused to see a problem in being friends with someone still at primary school.

Children from the secondary school weren't supposed to come into the primary school playground, and both boys were keeping an eye out for prowling teachers. Harvey turned to Sam, as Barney got close. 'Go on,' he said, 'tell him.'

'These kids on Twitter were talking about how they were hanging out at Lewisham College the other night, near where Ryan Jackson's body was found, and they saw his ghost,' said Sam.

Barney screwed up his face the way his dad did a second before he'd say, 'Barney, does my head look like it zips up the back?'

'Straight up,' insisted Sam. 'He was as pale as anything and he had this long white thing on and he was clutching his throat and moaning.'

Barney shook his head. He liked a ghost story as much as the next guy, but come on!

'We're going up there tomorrow night,' said Sam. 'When it gets dark. See if he comes back.'

'Knowing your luck, whoever bumped him off will come back,' said Barney, and was suddenly conscious of Peter, crouching like a troll in the back of his mind. 'And will your mum and dad really let you go down to Deptford Creek at night? I don't think so somehow.'

'Well, duh! We don't tell 'em that. I'll say I'm going to Lloyd's and he'll say he's coming to mine. Jorge and Harvey are up for it.'

The expression on Harvey's face said that, actually, that might be pushing it a bit.

'It'll work,' said Sam, 'because Lloyd can't play football tomorrow morning, so none of our mums and dads will be able to talk to his about it.'

'We'll still need to keep them apart on Sunday morning,' muttered Harvey.

'You need to watch the tides there,' said Barney. 'The Creek fills up quickly. People have drowned in it who haven't known what they've been doing.'

'How do you know?' asked Sam.

'We've got a boat there,' said Barney.

'No shit?'

Barney nodded. 'It was my granddad's,' he said. 'He lived on it. Dad keeps saying he's going to sell it, but he hasn't yet. We go sometimes to check it's OK.'

'Is it locked up?'

Barney nodded. 'And so's the yard that you have to go through to get to the boats. I might be able to find the key though,' he said.

'Cool.'

'Ryan's body wasn't found near the boat, though,' said Barney. 'So wouldn't it be a bit pointless looking for ghosts there?'

'Still be cool, though. I could bring some lager,' said Sam.

'So is your dad going to let you go to Deptford Creek at night?' asked Harvey.

Barney thought about it. He'd always liked Granddad's boat, always secretly wondered what it would be like to sleep on it. 'I could tell him I'm going to Lloyd's house,' he said.

16

'I CAN'T QUITE BELIEVE THESE WORDS ARE COMING OUT OF my mouth, but I'm actually looking forward to hearing what this profiler has to say,' said Anderson as they drove back towards Lewisham.

'Steady on, Sarge,' muttered Stenning from the back seat. 'You'll be saying next that women on the force is a good thing.'

'The timing's important,' said Anderson, ignoring Stenning. 'Jason and Joshua and Noah had been dead for two to six hours when we found them, meaning they were killed earlier in the evening. Ryan was killed around twenty-four hours before we found him, again making the time of death some time in the evening. All three disappeared in the early-evening period too.'

'He has a job,' said Stenning. 'Blue-collar job, most likely, if he's finishing work by around five.'

'He has a job and he doesn't live alone,' said Anderson. 'He's not going to stand out from the crowd.'

'What do you think, Ma'am?' Stenning said.

'I think it's a woman,' she said, a second before she could have bitten her own tongue out. Lord, it was one thing to indulge in wild speculations in front of Mark, another entirely with people who depended on her judgement being spot on.

Silence in the car for a second.

'Blimey,' said Anderson. 'Why? Because of what happened . . .'

'No,' said Dana, twisting round in her seat so she could look at both of them. 'Look, I shouldn't have said anything. Please don't repeat it to anyone until we've had the profiler's report. I don't want to influence her thinking in any way.'

'No, course not,' agreed Anderson. 'Blimey, it would make a lot of sense, though, wouldn't it? Kids would be far more likely to go off with a strange female.'

They pulled into the station car park. 'You know,' he went on, 'I am going to be a bit disappointed if all this profiler lass tells us is we're looking for a blue-collar worker who doesn't live alone.'

'You're looking for someone who has a regular nine-to-five job,' said the profiler, who was a thin, dark-haired woman in her early forties called Susan Richmond. 'Possibly a blue collar worker because he seems to finish quite early in the day. He doesn't live alone.'

Anderson took a deep breath and breathed out heavily. Stenning was biting his lower lip. From across the room came the sound of Mizon trying not to crunch crisps too loudly.

'But then I'm sure you've worked that out for yourselves,' said Richmond. 'You also know that he's organized and careful. He plans everything he does very thoroughly.'

'We know he's clever,' said Mizon, through a mouthful of cheese-and-onion flavoured.

'Careful's not the same as clever. Serial offenders are rarely unusually intelligent,' said the profiler. 'Hannibal Lector is a bit of a one-off. More commonly they're of average to slightly-below-average intelligence.'

'Sadly, so are most coppers,' muttered Anderson.

Richmond got to her feet. 'I'm not going to give you a report,' she said. 'We do that together.'

Around the room several eyebrows raised.

'So do we break into syndicates and role-play?' asked Anderson. Dana caught his eye and glared. He had the grace to look sheepish.

'I'll keep that in reserve,' said Richmond, walking to the white-board at the front of the room. 'For now, we're going to start with the building blocks.' She picked up the pen and started writing.

'Access to the victims,' she said, as she wrote. 'All four disappeared from in or around their homes. The first boy, Tyler, was last seen at the school gate, waiting for one of his mates who'd been kept behind. Ryan was spotted turning the corner into his street after school, but never actually made it home. The third boy, Noah, was watching television with his childminder and got up to answer the door. Jason and Joshua were in the front garden of their home. No one saw anything and that tells me two things. First, that the killer can make himself very inconspicuous, and second, that he's patient. The chances are he had to lie in wait more than once, waiting for the opportunity to get at the boys.'

'You're assuming Tyler King is part of the investigation,' said Anderson. 'We haven't as yet.'

'There's a very good chance,' said Richmond. 'He matches the victim profile completely and the circumstances of his disappearance are the same. I suspect his body was dumped like the others but not found. It'll have been washed out to sea.'

'Actually that doesn't happen,' said Anderson. 'If someone goes in the river, sooner or later, we pull them out.'

'Then sooner or later I think you'll pull Tyler out too,' said Richmond. 'Does anything else strike anyone about the abductions?'

'He's not threatening,' said Mizon. 'All four – five – went with him without a struggle. If they'd cried out, someone would have heard them. No one did.'

'So he's either someone they know or someone they would instinctively trust,' said Richmond. 'Yet you've found no common denominator other than that they were all football players, albeit for different clubs.'

'Someone in uniform,' suggested Tom Barrett, one of the DCs on Dana's team. Barrett was young, black and handsome, and seemingly incapable of taking life sriously. 'Someone posing as one of us.'

'Kids of that age still instinctively trust the police,' said Richmond. 'And most people in uniform. So, we've got inconspicuous, unthreatening, possibly known to the victims, and patient – maybe someone in uniform or a figure of authority.'

'Actually, we do have some new information on how he might be abducting the boys in the first place,' said Dana. 'The pathologist found evidence of carotid baroreceptor compression on both the latest victims.'

Of all the people in the room, only the profiler looked mystified.

'You've heard of pressure points?' Dana asked her. 'Points of the body where relatively modest amounts of pressure can cause disproportionate levels of pain.'

Richmond nodded slowly.

'Police officers are trained to use pressure points to restrain and subdue difficult and violent suspects,' Dana continued. 'They're of limited use, frankly, because people's natural reaction when faced with pain is to fight against it rather than submit. The trick is to take them by surprise, then get them in some sort of limb lock, then get the cuffs on quick.' She got up and crossed to where Richmond was sitting. 'I'll give you an example,' she said. 'Let's imagine you're a protestor, sitting on the ground, refusing to budge, and I want to move you.'

She moved to behind Richmond's chair and placed three fingers beneath Richmond's jawbone on either side of her chin. 'OK with that?' she asked.

'OK so far,' replied Richmond. 'Whoa!'

With barely any effort, Dana had pulled upwards, lifting Richmond just a centimetre or two off her seat. She let her go.

'Wow,' said Richmond, rubbing her jaw.

'Another second or so and you'd probably have pulled free,' said Dana, 'because you and I are very similar in terms of weight and strength. If Pete did it to you, on the other hand, you'd probably have to do exactly what he wanted you to.'

'So with a size advantage as well, pressure points can be a very effective way of subduing someone?' Richmond asked, still looking uncomfortable. 'So was that used on the Barlow brothers?'

'No,' said Dana. 'The bruises on the boys were lower on the neck, round about here.' On her own neck, she indicated two points on either side of her throat. 'Baroreceptors are a sort of gauge that control blood pressure in the body. One on either side of the neck. Apply pressure to both of them and they send a signal to the brain that the body's blood pressure is dangerously high. So the brain responds by lowering it. What happens when your blood pressure falls?'

'You feel dizzy, faint,' said Richmond. 'Eventually you pass out. Well, that would certainly explain how he got them away quietly. They were in a faint.'

'It's not that easy though, is it, Boss?' said Anderson. 'It's not like the Vulcan Death Grip, one squeeze and you're down. It takes a minute or two, from what I can remember. And it's far from reliable.'

'Neil's right,' Dana told Richmond. 'It's also exceptionally risky, which is why the police don't use it. But if an adult is using it to subdue a child, I'd say the child could be incapacitated in less than a minute.'

'Who would know about this?' asked Richmond.

'Anyone trained in combat of any sort,' said Anderson. 'Police, armed forces. Even people who study martial arts. Frankly, though, I've seen kids doing it. My son and his mates went through a phase of torturing each other with pressure points.'

'OK, well that is helpful,' said Richmond, giving her neck one last rub. 'Thank you. I'd like to look now at what he does with the bodies. And the first thing that strikes me is that he wants them to be found quickly. Leaving Tyler to one side for a moment, he leaves them in places where they'll be seen within hours. He's making no attempt to hide them, he wants everyone to know what he's up to. He's enjoying the attention. But he's still careful. He knows the river will cover his tracks after a few hours. He picks places where there's no CCTV and where he has a good chance of getting in, offloading the body and disappearing again. Quiet, but not too quiet, and always at low tide.'

'He knows the river very well,' said Mizon.

'Yes, he does,' agreed the profiler. 'OK, now we get to the interesting stuff. All five victims are Caucasian males, aged ten or eleven. When boys of this age are killed, it's usually either gang related, involving a close family member or sexual. This appears to be none of those. Something on your mind, Sergeant?'

Anderson had been making faces at Dana, gesticulating that now was the time to bring up her killer-as-a-woman theory. She looked at the floor.

'Apparently not,' he said.

'Is the means of death important?' asked Stenning.

'The means of death is probably the key to it,' said Richmond. 'Our guy doesn't want to mark the bodies, I think we're all agreed on that. He wants to keep his boys nice and neat and clean. So why isn't he smothering them with a pillow? It would be quick and easy, far less messy. Why isn't he strangling them? He has a thing about pre-teenage boys and he has a thing about blood. That's what we need to work on.'

17

BARNEY WAS LATE LEAVING SCHOOL BECAUSE THE THIRD Friday in the month was the day he stayed behind to clean the animals' cages and make sure they had enough food and water for the weekend. It was just after four when he made his way to the main school door. Mrs Dalley saw him look through the sliding window of the office. She was on the phone and pressed the mouthpiece against her shoulder.

'Be with you in a sec, Barney,' she called.

Barney nodded and went to wait by the door. A boy from Year Five was already there, looking out across the yard.

'Right, Huck,' said Barney.

'Right, Barney,' replied the younger boy.

Huck Joesbury played in the Under Eleven football team, even though he was only nine. He was supposed to be a genius on the rugby pitch too, although as rugby wasn't played at the school, this was something that remained a rumour.

'Is your mum late?' asked Barney.

'My dad's picking me up,' said Huck. He was smaller than Barney, with dark-brown hair that stuck upright and bright-blue eyes. There was something about his small face that always made Barney think of elves. Not that he ever mentioned it. You couldn't really tell a kid, even a younger one, that he looked like an elf.

'The dad with the most boring job in the world who never leaves his computer?' said Barney, remembering a previous conversation he'd had with Huck. Barney had argued that being a university lecturer in old books was far more boring than working with computers.

The smaller boy nodded. 'He phoned to say he'd be late. Computer trouble.' Then his little face lit up. 'Here he is.'

A tall, broad-shouldered man in jeans and a black leather jacket and with a big grin on his face was approaching the school door. When he reached it, he bent and pressed his face against the window. His nose and mouth squashed up and spread out against the glass.

'Dad!' moaned the child, glancing round at Barney.

'You should see my dad if you think that's embarrassing,' said Barney as Mrs Dalley appeared behind the boys and reached over them to unlock the door.

'Afternoon, Mr Joesbury,' she said to Huck's dad, who apologized for being late. 'Good afternoon, Huck. Good afternoon, Barney, I hope you're going straight home now.'

Barney agreed that he was and followed Huck and his dad across the yard.

'So we'll spend an hour at the public library, then drop by the salad bar on the way home,' Huck's dad was saying. His right arm was slung around his son's shoulders, his left was carrying Huck's school bag, overnight bag and guitar case.

'Rec, then movie, then Trev's,' replied Huck.

Barney dropped back. Obvious affection between parents and children always made him feel uncomfortable. At the gate, Huck's dad turned round.

'Is someone meeting you, mate?' he asked Barney, before glancing up and down the street.

Barney shook his head. 'I'm going to a friend's house,' he said. 'It's only five minutes away.' He stopped and let his skates drop to the ground.

'Barney's the best blader in the school,' said Huck. 'He's faster than everyone.'

'All the same, it'll be dark soon,' said Mr Joesbury. 'Can we drop you off, Barney?'

Barney smiled and said he was fine, thank you, it really was just around the corner. Even then, Huck's dad seemed reluctant to let him go. Barney pulled his skates on, hoisted his bag on to his shoulders and set off. Just before he turned the corner he looked back. Huck and his dad were getting into a green Audi convertible. Barney recognized the registration number immediately. Huck Joesbury's dad was the bloke who knocked on Lacey's door late at night, and who sat in the car for ages waiting for her to come home.

Barney watched as Huck and his dad drove away, Huck waving at Barney as the car disappeared. Most boring job in the world? Lacey had told him she and the man in the green Audi worked together and that would make him a police officer. Somebody was lying. Barney didn't like lies. There was something untidy about them.

'Barney, great. Catch this. Oh, nice catch.'

In the doorway of the Soar family kitchen, Barney looked down at the plastic sword he'd just caught. Jorge, striding towards him, was holding a matching weapon. There was a thin film of moisture on his fair skin and his cheeks were bright pink. The green dye had been washed from his hair. 'I just need to practise a couple of moves,' he said, taking a defensive, swordsman's pose directly in front of Barney. 'Harvey was helping me but he's not much good at fencing.'

On a stool at the counter sat Harvey, holding a freezer bag of ice to his forehead. Like his brother, he was pink in the face. He was also a little red around the eyes and his bottom lip looked swollen, the way it did when he was cross or upset. The boys' mother, Abbie, was stirring a casserole dish on the worktop.

'Your brother was doing fine till you stabbed him in the eye,' she said. 'Can you put the swords down now, please?'

Jorge barely acknowledged her. 'Five minutes. I just need to get this move right. OK, Barney, I come at you like this, you lift your sword up to meet mine and then we hold them together while we—'

'Jorge, there is no room in here.'

Barney had a choice: defend himself against the sword sweeping

88

down towards him or be slashed across the face. With an apologetic look at Abbie, he blocked Jorge's move. Jorge danced back, feinted left, then struck at him hard from the right.

'There's as much room in here as on the stage – oh, nice. How did you know I was going to do that?'

'Saw it in your eyes,' said Barney.

Jorge froze, the sword hovering just in front of Barney's chest. 'Straight up?' he asked, his blue eyes looking searchingly into Barney's. Over Jorge's shoulder, Barney could see both Abbie and Harvey watching them.

Barney shrugged. 'Probably just a lucky guess,' he said.

Abbie left the counter. With an effort, she wrenched Jorge's sword off him. 'Before someone gets hurt,' she said, holding her hand for Barney's sword but continuing to talk to her oldest son. 'Now I'm going to check on Nan. Tea in ten minutes.'

The boys waited until the door was closed. Then, without looking, Jorge gave a massive leap backwards and landed on the kitchen counter. 'So what's the plan tomorrow night then, Barney?' he asked.

Since when had it been his plan?

'It's not my plan,' he said. 'I'm not even sure I can get the key to the boat.'

Jorge shrugged. 'So we break a window. Send Hatty in to open it up. She's tiny.'

'We can't do that,' said Harvey. Barney gave him a grateful smile. If they broke a window, he'd have to pay for the replacement, sneaking the money into his dad's wallet somehow. Anything else just wouldn't be fair.

'Harvey says you've been studying the murders since the first boy went missing,' said Jorge. 'That you've got all sorts of theories about who the killer is and how he gets them.'

'A few,' Barney admitted.

'So what we should do, is visit all the murder sites,' said Jorge. 'See what they have in common, work out why he's choosing them.'

The kitchen door opened and the boy's grandmother appeared. She was easily the tallest of the family, a giant of a woman with bobbed white hair and big blue eyes. Her make-up always looked like she'd put it on in a dark room with a very shaky hand. As a young woman she'd been a dancer, Barney had seen photographs of her in costumes that seemed nothing but feathers and sparkles. She nodded at Barney and patted Jorge on the head, but her eyes didn't quite meet those of any of the boys. She made for the sink and rinsed out the glass she'd been carrying. In her wake, she left the same stale, sweet smell that always seemed to follow her around.

'We don't know where the murder sites are,' said Barney, keeping his voice low, although he knew the old lady didn't hear too well. 'Just where the bodies are being left.'

Jorge smiled. 'True. Still, be fun to look though.'

18

RIGHT, PHOTOGRAPHS OF MUM, WHERE WOULD THEY BE? Barney was in his dad's study, knowing he had an hour at most. The room was lined with bookshelves. His dad taught eighteenth- and nineteenth-century literature at King's College and sometimes Barney thought every book printed in two hundred years was right here in this very room. Still, finding things was what he was good at. The first set of bookshelves housed textbooks. Books about books.

He moved on around the room, wondering how his dad ever managed to find anything. Before Barney could spend one day in here he'd have to organize the shelves so that they were in alphabetic order at least. And probably by date of publication. In a locked case under the window were first editions.

Not a single photograph album in the room. If they weren't here, they could only be in the attic. On the back of the door hung the jacket his dad had been wearing the previous evening. Barney remembered how odd his dad had seemed, how he'd been holding something in his hand that he obviously didn't want Barney to see. Something that he'd tucked into his jacket pocket.

From downstairs came the sound of a key being turned in the front door. Barney reached out, pulled the small, soft ball of something woollen from his father's pocket and looked at it. A child's glove. Black, with bumps on the palm side to help the wearer grip a tennis racket or something. Not his. For one thing, it was too small. It was like a little kid's glove. He shoved it back into the jacket pocket.

'You home, Barney?' called his dad from the hallway, as he always did.

'Yeah,' called back Barney as he slipped out on to the landing and up the next flight of stairs. First mission aborted. On to the next.

In his den, he took down the solar-system poster and swivelled his chair round to face the missing boys' wall. When he'd first started following the investigation, he'd used both official news and social media sites to find out where the bodies of the abducted boys were being dumped.

Barney sat and looked at the map, letting his focus slip and waiting for the patterns to emerge. After a couple of minutes he knew it wasn't going to work. Three sites just didn't give enough data for any sort of pattern to stand out. All the location of the sites told him was that the boys had probably been taken by someone who knew that part of the river.

On the other hand, it might be possible to learn something from the roads. The killer must have brought the boys by car, and there were only a certain number of roads he could have travelled along. So if he plotted where the boys had disappeared from, then marked the most likely route to the dump sites, if those lines crossed anywhere, wouldn't that indicate where he might live?

Movement outside caught his attention. Lacey was leaving the shed at the bottom of her garden. As usual she was in gym clothes. Her face was red and the hair around it damp. Would he tell her that he knew the name of her stalker? That he was one of the dads at his school? Whatever she might say, it wasn't normal behaviour, was it? To hang around outside someone's house at night?

Then Barney forgot about Huck's dad when his own appeared carrying the laundry basket. As Barney watched, he took a sheet and hung it up. Then another. Sheets from his bed, he'd explained that morning, which needing washing early because he'd spilled tea on them. Except, to Barney's certain knowledge, there were no striped sheets anywhere in the house. His dad had washed sheets that didn't belong to them.

*

'Just had a text from Lloyd's mum,' his dad said when Barney walked through the kitchen door. Luckily, because Barney hadn't had much practice lying to his dad, his back was turned. He was at the worktop by the sink, preparing vegetables in the food slicer.

'What's she want?' said Barney, trying to sound uninterested.

His dad lifted a saucepan down and scraped the vegetables into it. 'Inviting you to a sleepover tomorrow night. Want to go?'

As the delicious smell of frying garlic came sneaking up towards Barney's nostrils, he told himself to be careful, not to sound too eager.

'Suppose so.'

'Why they call them sleepovers is beyond me. Overnight rampages might be more to the point.'

'So can I go?'

His dad paused in the act of stirring and looked at him. 'What's the homework situation?'

'French vocabulary test on Monday, two sheets of long division and a book review. I can do it all after football tomorrow.'

'If I say yes, what are the chances of you getting any sleep?'

Barney's eyes started to sting. That would be the ginger his dad was using, possibly chilli. He loved Friday-night dinner. 'I can sleep on Sunday,' he suggested.

'Well, that's going to be a fun weekend for me. On my own on Saturday night and you in bed all Sunday.'

'I won't go if you don't want me to,' offered Barney, surprised to find that he meant it.

His dad smiled. 'I'm kidding, course you can go. I'll give Lloyd's mum a call now.'

Not good! Lloyd would have borrowed his mum's phone to text his mates. If parents started phoning her, the game would be up. Barney picked up the morning's newspaper and turned it round as though he were reading the heading. 'She keeps her phone on silent when she's in the house,' he said, without looking up. 'I'd text her.'

His dad glanced round. 'You'd better do it,' he said. 'Tell her I'll drop you off at five.'

Oh, this wasn't going well.

Barney picked his dad's phone up off the counter. 'They're only ten minutes away,' he said. 'You don't need to take me. I'll tell her I'll arrive about five.'

'No, you won't,' said his dad. 'I'll drive you and I'll pick you up.'

'Dad!'

The two of them made eye contact. 'Deal-breaker, Barney.'

When his dad said that, there was no point arguing. OK, all wasn't lost. Lloyd could tell his mum, who thought they were having a sleepover at Sam's, that Barney would be picking him up on the way. His dad would drop him off, watch him disappear inside Lloyd's house, then five minutes later the two of them would set off, supposedly for Sam's. He quickly tapped out the message to Lloyd's mum's phone, which was temporarily in Lloyd's possession, and sent it. Then he deleted it. Finally, he tapped out the one his dad would see if he checked Sent Messages. Sneaking around and covering tracks was hard work.

'Dad, do we still have Granddad's boat?'

His dad spun on the spot, wooden spoon still in hand. 'What on earth made you ask about that?' he asked.

Barney shrugged. 'Some kids were talking about boats today. I just remembered. We haven't been for a while, have we?'

His dad turned back to the hob. 'No,' he said. 'Well, it's not much fun in winter, is it?'

'We should go and check, though,' said Barney. 'Just to make sure it's all right and not leaking again or anything.'

'I'm sure it's fine.'

'How do you know?'

His dad spoke slowly, as though explaining something difficult. 'One or other of the neighbours would have let me know if there'd been any trouble.'

'Do you keep the key safe?'

'Yes, thank you. It's on my keyring with my car and house keys.'

No, this was not going well at all. And since when had his dad got so blinking organized?

'By the way,' said his dad, over his shoulder again, 'the kitchen knives are getting blunt again. Want to sharpen them for me?'

19

LACEY SPENT A LONG TIME IN THE SHOWER. ONLY WHEN the water was starting to cool did she step out. Seven o'clock on a Friday evening. Less than a year ago, Fridays were the nights she went out, when she dressed carefully, drove across London and spent the evening around the Camden Stables Market. She'd liked to think of it as her hunting ground. A place where no one knew her, where so many people gathered you never saw the same faces from one week to the next. She'd take her time, spot her target, make sure he was alone before moving in. She'd had her stock-lines, some funny, some a bit weird; getting the initial conversation going was always the hard part. After that, no problem. Only rarely did she have to cut her losses and move on.

A few months ago, her life had consisted of hard work during the day, and casual, uncomplicated sex on Friday evenings. Now, she couldn't work and the very thought of sex was revolting. She hadn't had much in her life, and now she'd lost what little there'd been. How on earth was she going to get through the next—

No, don't think about the future. Just concentrate on getting through another Friday evening.

She pulled on her robe and walked through into the living space with its small, galley kitchen. For the first time, it struck her that her flat was too plain, too white, too cold. The minimum of furniture, nothing decorative, nothing that was really hers. Nothing in the fridge either – a perfectly normal state of affairs these days. Somehow supermarkets were just too much of an effort.

The Wandsworth Road was busy, people in cars driving home from work, buses offloading, early-evening drinkers making their way to and from the pubs and bars. The Chinese restaurant was quiet, though, she could see through the glass. It was the sort of place that didn't normally fill till later. The door made a chinging sound and Trevor, the middle-aged Chinese owner with the northern accent, appeared a second later.

'All right, Lacey?' Over the last few months she'd become something of a regular.

'How you doing, Trev?'

'Not so bad. Usual?'

'Please.'

The restaurant was almost empty. A table of students. A couple of men eating alone. In the furthest booth, half hidden by the intricately carved screen, sat a man with his back to Lacey, a man she knew immediately, with broad shoulders and short dark hair. Joesbury.

He wasn't alone. Directly opposite him sat a child. A boy, around nine or ten years old, with short, dark hair that grew vertically up from his forehead and a heart-shaped face. It was the eyes that gave him away, though. Large and oval shaped, and even from a distance she could see they were the exact shade of turquoise blue as his father's. This was Huck. Joesbury had invited her out to dinner this evening. He'd wanted her to meet his son.

Lacey peddled hard, heading for the river, away from the traffic, hardly aware of how she'd made the decision not to go home, only knowing that four walls around her right now might make her scream.

Trevor would have heard the door chimes as she'd left. All the same, she'd go back later and pay, when she could be sure the two Joesburys had gone. She'd make up some excuse about feeling ill or an urgent phone call. She couldn't fall out with Trevor. What would she eat?

She rode beneath the underpass, garish with graffiti, where kids were gliding around on skateboards and roller blades, weaving in and out of each other like a strange street-ballet.

Huck? Such a funny name for a child. Why would he call his son Huck? The hair and the eyes had been Joesbury's but the face was nothing like his dad's. The boy's face had been pretty with small features and very fair skin. His mother's face. Joesbury had fallen in love, married and had a child with a woman whom Lacey had never even thought about before. A woman who would be slim with dark hair and a delicate, heart-shaped face.

Even in the dark, even in the cold, the embankment was busy with pedestrians. Everywhere around her the life of the city was going on. People were crossing the Millennium Bridge, travelling up and down the river on passenger ferries, crossing the water on trains; on the north bank the traffic flow seemed endless. Everywhere around her people moved with a sense of purpose. They knew where they were going and why. No one else looked lost.

The wind seemed to be coming directly from the east tonight, hurling its way up the river, almost throwing her off balance. Lacey tucked her head down and pressed on. Her muscles were trembling, the way they always did when she'd exercised too much, or not eaten enough. Or both.

And she had that feeling again, that sense of a scream building inside. Of something churning and pressing, trying to get out. When it came over her, all she could do was run, or swim, or cycle, or pound the punchbag in her shed until she was too exhausted to think about what it was she couldn't possibly let come to the surface.

Cycling too fast, but unable to slow down, Lacey passed through an avenue of small trees, their bare branches strung with blue and white fairy lights. Huck had been wearing a blue football shirt with white stripes on the shoulders. What did that make him? A Chelsea supporter? She knew so little about London football clubs. What on earth would she have talked to a nine-year-old boy about?

She was leaving the busiest part of the river behind. Once past Tower Bridge, the lights and colour started to fade quickly. Pleasure craft rarely came this far downstream. The tide was high but going out. When she cycled past boats moored in the water she could see it pulling against them, trying to tug them out to sea. Not so very long ago she'd found herself in the Thames. Twice. The first time hadn't been intentional, she'd been pulled in, had narrowly escaped drowning. A couple of weeks after that she'd jumped in to try to rescue a young illegal immigrant. The first time had been terrifying, but the will to live, to keep fighting, had taken her by surprise. The second time, though, it had been oddly soothing, as though the river had tried to scare her again and failed. Now there was something about its black, swirling depths that looked almost inviting.

The police notice caught her eye and she stopped before she had time to think about whether it was a good idea. The yellow, laminated card referred to an incident several weeks ago and asked for eyewitnesses to contact a central London telephone number. This had to be where one of the boys' bodies had been found.

She closed her eyes and could picture her old colleagues, who'd almost become her friends, making their way around the crime scene, working as fast as they could before the tide came in and stole it from them. She could see their faces, white and drawn as the small corpse was taken away. She could feel their anger, their growing sense of helplessness.

The river below the embankment wall was dappled black and silver like the battered shield of a medieval knight, and it seemed to be the only thing she could see clearly. If she looked up for a second, everything lost its focus. Colours became blurred, like lights she'd looked at too long. Edges disappeared, as though her eyes were full of tears.

'You all right, love?'

'Dozy cow, she's going to fall in.'

A hand on her shoulder. Two curious, half-afraid faces staring at her. She'd left her bike behind and was standing on the steps that led down to the river. Below her black water swirled and eddied. The two men stepped back, letting her move away from the top step. Both were looking searchingly into her eyes.

'You want to be careful, love,' said the man who'd touched her, the less judgemental of the two, the one who didn't yet have her down as a drug-addled loon. 'Fall in here and you're a goner.'

Lacey smiled and knew she'd lost him too. 'Well, you know what they say,' she said. 'Third time lucky.'

20

'*I SEE THEM IN MY DREAMS, YOU KNOW. THE DEAD BOYS.*'
'*All of them?*'
'*Yes, every one.*'
'*What are they doing when you dream about them?*'
'*They watch me. Sometimes I dream I'm walking through the room, the one they all died in, and they're all in there, not buried or taken away or anything but still there, watching me.*'
'*Do they ever talk to you?*'
The patient lurched forward, startling her. '*How can they talk? Their throats are gaping open. Some of their heads are practically hanging off. Do you have any idea what a kid looks like when his throat has been sliced open? Well, do you?*'
'*I think you need to take it easy. No, stay in your chair. Take a second or two, just get your breath back.*' *The psychiatrist's eyes strayed to the panic button.* '*Just concentrate on your breathing. OK, well done. Would you like to carry on? OK, good. So they just watch you. And what do you do?*'
'*I look at the patterns.*'
'*The patterns?*'
'*On the walls, the patterns on the walls and ceiling and floors made by the blood. It's a bit like – I'll tell you what it's like – it's like when you go to a school and all the kids' pictures have been put on the walls for you to look at and you wander round, pretending to be interested and muttering*

nice things like, "Oh that's a good one, I like the way he used the colour blue in this one." Well, that's what I do. I walk round the room and I look at the patterns each boy made when the blood came out of him and I smile and say, "Yes that's good, well done." Like it's artwork and they're in a show and they're proud. And the weird thing is, it is interesting, the patterns that blood makes. They're like snowflakes, blood spatters, every one is different. Amazing thing, blood. Did I mention that? Sometimes I think I'll never get tired of looking at blood.'

21

Saturday 16 February

FOR ONCE, WHEN THE PHONE RANG, DANA DIDN'T WAKE UP instantly. She'd been up late the night before, combing the internet for cases of female serial killers, or killers who'd fixated on pre-adolescent boys. By the time she realized someone was calling her, she knew it had been ringing for a while. Her landline. Mark. She picked up and saw the clock at the same time. Nearly ten. Christ, she was supposed to be at Heathrow in an hour.

'Hi, you watching TV?'

'No, why?'

'Turn it on.'

Mark waited while she ran downstairs, found the TV remote and took it off standby. 'ITV1,' Mark told her. Somewhere in his flat, she could hear Huck singing.

The channel flicked on to the usual mid-morning news and current affairs programme. The two presenters, one male, one female, were sitting on the blue sofa along with a well-dressed man in his late forties with swept-back red hair and an unusually pale face.

'For those who have just joined us,' the male presenter was saying, 'our guest in the studio this morning is clinical psychologist Dr Bartholomew Hunt. We're talking about the serial killer who has taken four young lives in just six weeks and who, in spite of huge resources pumped into their operations, the Metropolitan Police seem to be no closer to finding.'

The red-haired man was nodding in the way people only ever did when they knew they were being observed.

'Now, if I've got this right, Dr Hunt,' the presenter went on, 'these young victims all died from extensive blood loss.'

'Massive blood loss following the severing of the carotid artery,' replied Hunt. 'The bodies were, quite literally, drained of blood.'

'Jesus,' whispered Dana. 'The parents could be watching this.'

'More importantly than that,' the red-haired man went on, 'wound patterns on at least one of the victims – it wouldn't be proper to say which one – indicate that the carotid artery was cut several times before death, each time allowing some blood to be lost before clotting began.'

'Oh my God.' Dana dropped to the sofa, landing on its edge.

'You've got a mole, sweetheart,' said Mark.

On the screen, Hunt and the presenter were still talking. 'And this is the point at which some viewers may struggle to deal with the implications of what you're telling us,' said the presenter, 'but you believe this blood loss is particularly significant.'

'The Metropolitan Police are working under the erroneous assumption that the severing of the carotid arteries is simply the means of death,' said Hunt. 'It isn't. It's the motive for abducting the boys in the first place.'

The presenter blinked. 'He takes them because he wants their blood?'

'Absolutely. What we're dealing with here is a case of Renfield's Syndrome, an unnatural obsession with blood, particularly with the drinking of blood. People with this condition crave the taste of blood in their mouths. It's also known as Clinical Vampirism.'

Dana's mobile was ringing. She leaned over to see who was calling and realized she wasn't going to make it to the airport. Helen, her long-term partner who worked in Scotland, would have to make her own way across the city. 'Weaver's on the other line,' she told Mark.

'You know where I am.' The line went dead.

'I'm just watching it now, Sir,' Dana told her boss, a second later. She was on her feet again, pacing across the rug, her eyes never leaving the TV.

'Vampires? What the hell's going on, Dana?'

'Give me a minute, Sir.'

'This condition is a lot more common than people realize,' Hunt was saying. 'Try Googling "obsession with blood" and you'll be awash with evidence of people who crave the smell and taste of blood.'

'We did do that, actually, when we knew you were coming in,' said the presenter. 'And it's certainly true. But these people are invariably talking about self-harming. They cut themselves, and the sight of the blood, often the taste of it, too, seems to bring them some sort of odd relief.'

'Oh, these are very sick people, make no mistake about it,' replied Hunt, as Dana could hear Weaver's breathing down the phone line. 'But cutting and tasting their own blood is just the start. Quite often they move on.'

'To cutting others?' asked the female presenter, who had the raised eyebrows and pursed lips of someone exhibiting physical revulsion. 'Just to be clear, are you saying the police should be looking for a vampire?'

Hunt shook his head, gave a rueful little smile. 'I'm not talking about someone who sleeps in a coffin and turns into a bat at will,' he said. 'What we're dealing with here is an unusual but all too real clinical condition. There are many documented cases of serial killers who have committed acts of vampirism on their victims. Richard Trenton Chase, a American serial killer in the 1970s, was one of the more notorious cases.'

'Jesus, Dana, where the hell has this come from?' demanded Weaver, unable to keep quiet any longer.

'Chase was a very dangerous man,' Hunt was saying. 'As a teenager, he killed rabbits and ate them raw, sometimes putting their entrails into the blender to make a drink. He caught birds to kill and eat, other small animals too. Then, as these people often do, he moved on to drinking human blood. He killed and cannibalized six people before he was caught.'

'Have you shared your theories with the police?' asked the female presenter.

'Bloody good question,' muttered Weaver down the line.

'From the studio I'm travelling to Lewisham police station to offer my services to the Major Investigation Team,' said Hunt, checking the buttons on his jacket as though ready to get up there and then. 'Let's hope that together we can catch this maniac before another boy is taken and murdered.'

'I'm sure they'll be pleased to have you on board,' said the presenter. 'They certainly seem to have been at a loss so far.'

22

DANA LOOKED ROUND THE ROOM. WHAT SHE WAS ABOUT to say shouldn't be easy. Trouble was, she was so bloody angry, it wasn't going to be any effort at all.

'When I find out who released the information about the repeated cut marks on Jason Barlow's throat, I will wipe the floor with him,' she said. 'If I find out it's a serving officer, I will have him on traffic till he claims his long-service medal. If he works for an associated organization, which we are supposed to be able to trust, I will make it my personal mission to end his career. And, ladies, the fact that I'm using the male gender for convenience does not let any of you off the hook. Now, does anyone in this room have a problem with what I've just said?'

There were twelve people present, including herself, Detective Superintendent Weaver and the criminal profiler, Susan Richmond. One of them was the middle-aged civilian woman employed to input data on to HOLMES. The rest were detectives, people she'd trusted.

'No, Ma'am,' said Anderson quickly. A couple of the others were shaking their heads. Richmond looked nervous but she met Dana's eye continually.

'I understand where you're coming from, Dana, but it's not necessarily someone on the Force,' said Weaver. 'Could be someone at the mortuary, one of the SOCOs at the scene.'

'I'll be talking to Kaytes,' said Dana. 'But I think we can rule out SOCOs. The repeated cuts just weren't visible at the scene. They wouldn't have known.'

Weaver nodded, looking troubled. He knew as well as she did that a mole would seriously undermine the work of the investigation. 'Right,' he said. 'What about this vampire business?'

All eyes turned to the profiler.

'Renfield's Syndrome *is* a recognized psychiatric condition,' said Richmond. 'But it's very rare. On the TV this morning, Dr Hunt gave quite the opposite impression, but I'd be willing to bet a lot of practicing psychiatrists have never heard of it. I've spent the last hour trawling the internet, printing off every published article I can find and there isn't much.'

She opened the blue file on the desk in front of her and took out several sheets of paper, website pages that she'd printed off. Several members of the assembled MIT glanced over; no one moved to pick one up.

'What is it again?' asked Anderson, who was picking at a loose piece of skin just below his right ear. 'What that Hunt geezer called it?'

'Renfield's Syndrome.'

'And it means an obsession with drinking blood?'

Richmond nodded. Around the room, people were shooting uncomfortable glances at each other. Dana could feel Weaver stiffening at her side. 'Human blood?' he asked.

'Ultimately, yes, but not exclusively,' said Richmond. 'People who have this condition experience a craving for blood that gets out of control. It's believed that it stems from the idea that blood has life-giving powers. It makes you stronger, more potent, live longer, that's the general idea.'

'I knew I shouldn't have had black pudding for breakfast,' said Anderson.

'The term was coined by a psychiatrist called Richard Noll,' said Richmond. 'He named it after a character in this book.' From her bag, she took a paperback with a black cover and handed it to the nearest person, Stenning.

'Bram Stoker's *Dracula*?' he said.

'Stoker's Renfield is a character in an asylum,' said Richmond. 'He's insane and he's obsessed with consuming other creatures. He eats every insect he can get his hands on and spends his days trying to capture birds. He begs his doctor to get him a kitten so he can eat that, too.'

Weaver's nostrils twitched. Without turning his head, he reached out towards Stenning for the paperback.

'According to Noll,' said Richmond, 'the condition begins with a key event in childhood in which an injury involving blood, or the swallowing of blood, is seen as exciting. The child will then experience a growing interest in blood. He'll be fascinated by road-kill, he might enjoy licking his own wounds and scratches.'

'We all do that,' said Weaver, looking up from reading the cover blurb.

'Yes, but for most people it's an instinctive reaction, we're trying to soothe the wound and keep it clean. These people are enjoying the taste, and the sensation of blood in their mouths. As they get older, they're likely to start inflicting wounds on themselves, so that they can swallow blood. This stage is known as auto-vampirism. They start with self-induced cuts and scrapes and eventually learn how to open major blood vessels.'

She paused, giving the team time to take it all in.

'The next documented stage is called zoophagia,' she went on. 'That means eating living creatures and drinking their blood. When the child reaches puberty, he or she starts to associate the swallowing of blood with sexual arousal. After that, the next stage is clinical vampirism in its true form, acquiring and drinking the blood of living human beings. Sometimes the blood is stolen, from hospitals and laboratories, quite often it's consensual. It's often linked with consensual sex. But in the more extreme manifestations, the sexual activity and the vampirism may not be consensual.'

'Why didn't you say anything about this before?' Weaver, as Dana had expected, was running low on patience. She'd learned some time ago that his calm exterior wasn't necessarily a reflection of what was going on inside. He was surprisingly short-tempered for such a still man.

'Please bear with me,' said Richmond. 'On the one hand, I can see where Hunt is coming from with this. When children are taken by strangers and found dead, the natural assumption is that they've been the victim of a paedophile.'

'But no evidence of sexual abuse on any of the boys,' said Dana.

'Exactly,' agreed Richmond. 'So we look at what else he might want from them, and there is no doubt that he is taking their blood.'

Across the room the phone rang. Anderson answered it.

'God, the bloody media will have a field day when we admit we're looking for a vampire,' said Weaver.

'Boss,' Anderson called to Dana. 'Dr Hunt is downstairs, with a posse of reporters, demanding to speak to the officer in charge of the investigation.'

Weaver met Dana's eyes. 'What do you want to do?' he asked her quietly.

'Have someone put him in an interview room,' said Dana. 'Alone. The reporters stay outside until we call a press conference.'

Anderson looked troubled. 'OK. Then what?'

'Then nothing. When we're done here, Pete can go down and talk to him.'

Anderson put the phone back to his mouth, then thought better of it. 'Boss, perhaps I should go . . .' he began.

'I will not dignify that pillock by sending a senior member of my team to talk to him,' snapped Dana, before turning to Stenning. 'When you go down, Pete – and please don't hurry – I want to know where he's been getting his information from and I want to know where he was the evenings all four boys a) disappeared and b) were found. That's six occasions I want accounted for, and don't just take his word for it. I want alibis.'

'Dana . . .' Now Weaver was looking troubled.

'Sir, if this so-called professional had had to face three sets of parents and tell them their ten-year-olds weren't going to grow up, ever, he might have had some qualms about adding to their pain on national bloody television.'

If an attention-seeking pin were in the room, this would have been a good time for it to drop.

'Right,' said Weaver. 'Anything else you can tell us, Susan?'

'Well, as I was saying, although I can see where Hunt's coming from, on the other hand, too many things just don't add up for me,' said Richmond.

'Like what?'

'People with Renfield's Syndrome are overwhelmingly male,' said Richmond. 'But there are no documented cases at all of men with the condition attacking children. They attack other adults, women most commonly, but other men too.'

Overwhelmingly male? Dana could sense Anderson and Stenning looking her way, wondering if she was going to air her killer-is-a-woman theory.

'What about this Richard Chase bloke?' asked Stenning, who'd been reading one of the case notes. 'He killed a kid.'

'Richard Chase was a very disturbed young man,' said Richmond, 'but his problems were almost certainly due to drug abuse and failed medication. He was quite possibly schizophrenic. He killed six people, but with only one of them did he commit cannibalism and drink blood. I'm not saying the condition doesn't exist, just that because of its sensational nature, it's assumed an importance way beyond what it deserves.'

A woman with the condition would need to select victims she could overpower more easily, thought Dana. Could she ask if there was any history of women having Renfield's Syndrome?

'Anything else?' asked Weaver.

'Yes, the sheer amount of blood we're talking about. People with this condition crave the taste of blood in their mouths. They don't drink it like milk because they can't. The body would reject it. You'd most likely vomit it up. If you managed to keep it down, you'd be looking at serious organ damage. Each of these boys lost around three litres of blood. No one could drink that amount of blood and live.'

'No one human,' quipped one of the younger detectives as Weaver stood up to leave the room. 'Word outside, Dana, please,' he said.

In the corridor he turned to face her. 'Everything OK?' he asked her.

'Apart from four dead children, a hysterical media reaction and a mole on the team? Yes, Sir, everything's fine.'

He raised his eyebrows. 'I've not seen you this uptight before,' he said. 'If you want to stay on this case, you're going to have to calm down.'

23

'COME ON, BOYS, WATCH YOUR POSITIONS! SAM, WHO are you marking?'

Barney took a quick glance around. You did not want Mr Green yelling at you on the pitch unless it was something like 'Well-played' or 'Nice work'. The ball went across the pitch towards the opposition's number 8, who had a clear shot. Barney raced across, got to the ball first and cleared it.

'Lovely, Barney,' called a female voice. Barney turned to see his form teacher, Mrs Green, on the touchline, not too far away from his dad.

'Well played, Barney,' called Mr Green. 'Now come on, keep the pressure on!'

Heading into the wind, Barney's team followed the ball up the pitch. Huck Joesbury got possession and Barney dropped back, watching the patterns form again. When he was really in the zone, he could predict, sometimes two or three passes ahead, where the ball was going to go. This morning, though, he was having trouble focusing. The wind was a problem, for one thing. The pitch was surrounded by high lime trees and when the wind blew hard, the swaying and dancing patterns the branches made above his head were distracting.

Huck had lost the ball, it sailed away from him in a fountain of mud droplets and then went hurtling back down the pitch. Nobody was playing well today.

To make matters worse, Barney couldn't stop thinking about the trip to Deptford Creek that night. The creek was dangerous, especially for kids who didn't understand about tides and who couldn't stop themselves messing about. But he couldn't pull out now. The others would be relying on him to find the murder sites, maybe even clues the police had overlooked, and he hadn't even found the key to his granddad's boat yet. His dad, normally rubbish at hiding things, had surprised him for once.

'Barney, what planet are you on?'

And that was his second telling-off. He'd get dropped from the team if he wasn't careful. The wind though! It found its way under shirts, up the legs of shorts, right through his ears and into his head. Broken twigs were scurrying across the pitch like small rodents, catching around studs, crackling underfoot.

One of the opposition's better players, a small blond boy, was racing towards the goal. Sam, the right-back, ran to tackle him and got nutmegged. It was all up to Barney now. Over the blond boy's shoulder Barney could see Huck's dad, clutching a coffee mug from Costa. Barney wondered what he'd say if he found out that he, Barney, lived right next door to the woman whose flat he sat outside so often.

'Barney, that's yours! Oh boys, come on!'

Blondie had dodged to the right. A second later the ball was in the bottom left corner of the net.

'Where was my defence?' called the keeper, glaring at Barney as the whistle for half-time blew. They were one-nil down.

'Why do you think Mrs Green comes to watch every week,' said Sam, as he and Barney jogged back to join Mr Green and the other boys. 'It's not as though she has a kid on the team.'

'We can pull it back, lads,' said Mr Green, as Sam and Barney joined the others. 'We had most of the possession. Have a drink, then we'll have a chat.'

'Well done, Barney,' said Mrs Green, who was standing next to his dad now. 'Will you hand the biscuits round?'

'Other team first,' reminded his dad, as Barney opened the tin. Double chocolate chip. His favourite. An adult hand reached over his shoulder and helped itself. Barney recognized Mr Green's aftershave.

'He's doing well,' he said to Barney's dad, as the other hand patted Barney on the shoulder. 'When he concentrates, his positioning is superb. We just need to work on his ball skills.'

His face glowing, Barney set off with the biscuit tin, just as Harvey came jogging over. He'd arrived late, hurrying up with his mum and brother just minutes before kick-off, and they'd had no chance to talk before the match.

'Any of you see GMTV this morning?' Harvey asked. Barney and Sam shook their heads.

'This bloke was on, right? And he was saying whoever killed those boys, Joshua and Jason, drank their blood. It was a vampire.'

Sam looked startled, then laughed nervously. 'There's no such thing as vampires,' he said.

The half-finished biscuit in Barney's hand fell to the ground. He'd known, immediately, that the adults were different that morning. They'd leaned closer together when they spoke, lowered their voices, given odd, furtive glances around to make sure they weren't being overheard. There'd been something discussed that morning that they hadn't wanted the kids to know about. Saliva was building in his mouth.

'Straight up, he was a proper doctor and everything,' said Harvey. 'He said it was a condition, I can't remember what he called it, but Jorge seemed to know what he was talking about.'

'Renfield,' said Jorge, who'd approached the boys without them seeing him and who obviously had a match himself later because he, too, was wearing football kit. 'People who have Renfield's Syndrome are obsessed with blood. Angelina Jolie has it. Any biscuits going spare?'

Barney handed the tin to Jorge.

'She does not!' Sam was keen on Angelina.

'She does, it was on Facebook this morning. People have known about it for years. When she was married to her last husband – not Brad Pitt, someone else – she used to carry his blood around her neck in a little bottle.'

'And do what, take sips when she got a bit thirsty?'

Barney took a deep breath. If they didn't stop talking about blood soon, he'd have to leave.

'No, dorko. I don't think she drank it. But it's still well weird. Would you want to carry someone's blood around your neck?'

'What's it called again?' asked Sam.

'Renfield's Syndrome. It's got something to do with a book about Dracula,' said Jorge.

Barney swallowed hard. 'My dad has a copy,' he said. 'It's by a man called Bram Stoker. He caught me reading it once – I was just flicking through looking for the scary bits and he told me off. Said it was a work of great literature, not a manga comic.'

The others were all watching him, wanting more.

'Well, it's supposed to be the first vampire story,' Barney said. 'All the other stuff – you know, *Twilight*, *First Blood*, *Buffy*, those old films you see sometimes – they all started with Bram Stoker's *Dracula*.'

'So why's it not called Dracula Syndrome?' asked Sam.

'Well, that would just sound stupid,' said Jorge.

'And it's straight up? These kids had their blood drained out of them so someone could drink it?'

As Jorge shrugged, Barney turned away. The adults were all gathered in small groups, talking quietly; even his dad and Mrs Green seemed deep in conversation. Only Jorge and Harvey's mum stood alone, wrapped in her cream padded jacket, her short blonde hair spiked upwards, ignoring the other adults. She was watching the children, her sons in particular. Barney caught her eye and looked down.

'There's something they didn't want to tell us,' he said. 'They're more worried now than they were before. I'm not sure they're going to let us go out tonight.'

'We can't cancel now,' said Sam. 'We'll never be able to set it up again. I've lost count of what parent thinks who's where.'

'And doing what,' added Harvey.

'With who,' said Jorge. All three of them laughed. Barney didn't quite manage to join in.

'There's us four, Lloyd and Hatty. Six of us. Can six sleep on your boat, Barney?' Harvey asked.

'We've got to get on it first,' said Barney. 'Boat windows are small.

I'm not sure even Hatty will get through. I think we need a back-up plan.'

'The back-up plan is that we all come back to our house,' said Jorge. 'Mum's working all night and Nan is always comatose by nine o'clock. We could have the entire football team sleeping over and she wouldn't know.'

'What if your mum comes home early?'

'Barney Boy,' said Jorge, giving him a pat on the shoulder, 'sometimes you just got to wing it.'

24

'NO LESS THAN FIVE OF THE ONLINE NATIONALS ARE running the vampire story, as well as several of the big regionals; we've had over a dozen requests for interview from the media on this subject specifically and Bram Stoker's *Dracula* is currently climbing up the Amazon chart,' said Anderson as he and Dana approached the incident room. 'My younger, hipper colleagues inform me that the social networking sites are talking about nothing else. Suddenly it's cool to be undead.'

'OK,' said Dana, raising her voice to get the attention of the room and walking to the front. 'I want to knock this vampire business on the head once and for all. Then at least we can say we considered it fully. I've asked Gayle to do some research on known cases of so-called vampirism. What have you got for us, Gayle?'

Gayle Mizon stood, brushed biscuit crumbs off her skirt and came to join Dana at the front. 'Right, two cases this decade of note,' she began. 'Both in 2002. First, a young Scottish man, Allan Menzies, who became obsessed by vampires after seeing a film called *Queen of the Damned.*'

'That the one based on an Anne Rice book?' asked Tom Barrett. As heads turned to him, he shrugged. 'I had a girlfriend loved that sort of stuff,' he said.

'Yes, *Queen of the Damned* is a vampire story by the American author Anne Rice,' said Mizon. 'Anyway, Menzies killed his friend and buried him in woods near his home. At his trial, he claimed to be a real vampire and to have drunk the dead man's blood.'

'Trying for an insanity plea?' asked Stenning.

Mizon nodded. 'The jury thought so. He was given a life sentence and committed suicide in prison. The same year, a German couple, Manuela and Daniel Ruda, stabbed a man sixty-six times and drank his blood. They claimed to have been indoctrinated into a vampire cult while they were staying in England and had met several willing donors over the internet.'

'You can get anything on eBay,' muttered Barrett.

'Thank you, Tom,' said Dana.

Mizon glanced at her notes. 'A few years earlier, in 1998, Joshua Rudiger in San Francisco claimed to be a two-thousand-year-old vampire,' she said. 'He ran around slashing the necks of homeless people. One woman died. He was diagnosed as psychotic, schizophrenic and bipolar.'

Richmond made a gesture with her hands to indicate extreme frustration. 'Not a vampire,' she said. 'Just a very sick man with exotic fantasies. As was Menzies, if you ask me.'

She put a pen down noisily on the desk and addressed the group. 'What we have to understand is that vampires are seen as immensely glamorous,' she said. 'If you go back to Bram Stoker's book, the female vampires in Dracula's castle are as intent on seducing Jonathon Harker as they are on killing him. At the moment, thanks to Stephanie Myers and all the rest of them, the popularity of vampires is at an all-time high. They're beautiful, sexual, incredibly powerful and immortal. It's not surprising that seriously disturbed people latch on to them.'

'Comments noted, Susan,' said Dana. 'Carry on, Gayle.'

'In the 1940s, another Englishman, John Haigh, was arrested for the possible murder of a missing woman,' said Mizon. 'He confessed to killing six people and drinking their blood. 'But nobody believed him. For one thing, no bodies. It was generally believed he was making it up to convince people he was insane and avoid the death penalty.'

'Has anyone else noticed most of these bozos are British?' asked Barrett.

'Go on, Gayle,' said Dana.

Mizon had been glancing nervously at Susan Richmond. 'Well, to cut a long story short, I found just seven cases in over a century,' she said. 'In some, there is indication that blood was a sexual stimulus, but in only a couple is there real evidence tht blood was drunk. Others seem to have been nothing more than violent crimes involving perpetrators fantasizing about vampires, and with all due respect, Ma'am, I might fantasize about being in a successful girl band. It doesn't make me Cheryl Cole.'

Dana gave the banter a minute to run its course. 'Any thoughts, Susan?' she asked, turning to the profiler.

'In the last twenty-four hours, I've read nothing to convince me that Renfield's Syndrome is something to take seriously,' said Richmond. 'I think people want to believe in it, because it's scary and sensational, and I think they've combed through the history of violent crime trying to find cases that fit. The fact that there are so few, and that most of those are pretty unconvincing, suggests to me they failed.'

'OK, but some people are turned on by blood,' said Anderson. 'You have to admit that?'

'Any number of offenders have been sexually stimulated by violence,' replied the profiler. 'Blood is usually an integral part of that. But here we have four cases of murder with no evidence of sexual abuse or violence. This is not about sex, it's not about violence, and I'm not even sure it's about blood.'

'Well, let us know when you decide what it *is* about,' said Anderson.

'Neil—'

'Actually, there is something else I want to ask, Mrs Richmond,' said Anderson.

The profiler looked at him, wary. 'Of course,' she said.

'We've all been talking about the killer as though he's a bloke. Tell me I'm away with the fairies, but is it possible it's a woman?'

Dana saw Stenning give a sharp glance her way. Anderson kept his eyes firmly on the profiler. She looked back at him steadily.

'No evidence of sexual abuse or violence,' said Anderson. 'When men kill kids, they don't do it gently – not in my experience, anyway.'

Richmond was looking troubled. 'Female serial killers are rare,' she said.

'But not unheard of,' said Anderson. 'Myra Hindley, Rose West and Beverley Allitt, all of whom killed children.'

'Two of them didn't act alone,' said Richmond. 'Both West and Hindley were luring victims for their partners. And sex was a motive.'

'Not with Allitt, though,' said Dana, thinking that if Anderson could go out on a limb for her, the least she could do was give him a bit of support. 'Allitt's motives were altogether more complex. With her it was all about the power, being needed, being important.'

'There are plenty of precedents for women killing their own children,' said Mizon. 'Though that's often a result of post-natal depression.'

'What about a woman who's lost her own child?' said Dana. 'I can soon produce a list of nine-, ten- and eleven-year-old boys who died in London in recent years.' Very soon, actually – it had been sitting on her desk since noon the previous day. 'Neil, do you want to take a look at it when it's ready? See if anything stands out?'

Anderson nodded, not quite meeting her eye.

'OK, thanks everyone. Neil, can I have a word please?'

Anderson stood up, and followed Dana out of the room. She walked several yards down the corridor then stopped and turned. He stopped, too.

'Ma'am, it's an idea and I thought it needed airing,' he said. 'If it turns out it's a duff one, I'll be the one to look daft and that's never bothered me in the past.'

He was right, of course, she should have said something herself. She was just frightened of what it might have revealed about her.

She forced herself to smile. 'And if it turns out to be spot on, you'll share the glory?'

'Nope. I'll graciously accept my promotion to DI and then I won't have to call you Ma'am any more.'

'You don't have to call me Ma'am now.'

'We all need something to aspire to, Ma'am.'

25

'DAD, CAN I GO INTO THE ATTIC?'
His dad looked up from the ironing. 'What for?'
Barney had planned for this. 'Sam's younger brother is into Lego,' he said. 'I don't play with mine any more, so I thought I'd let him have it.'

His dad looked surprised but pleased. He was always nagging Barney that they had too many toys and that he really should give some of them away, especially stuff he hadn't played with in years.

'You'll be careful near the hatch.'

Barney agreed that he would and left the kitchen. On the way out, he had to move the laundry basket because it was half blocking the doorway. Three loads of washing had already been done, the fourth was in the machine. The first load had dried while they'd been at football, and Barney had folded and piled everything up according to colour and pattern. Plain, darker colours at the bottom, brighter colours next, and stripes and whites at the top. His dad had long since given up asking what would happen if he ironed the dark stuff first, he just got on with the ironing in the order Barney gave it to him.

As Barney climbed the stairs, he realized the striped sheets his dad had washed the day before hadn't been in the ironing pile.

He found the Lego quickly, and put it next to the hatch so that when his dad came looking for him he'd be able to claim he'd just that minute found it. Then he started looking for photographs. Barney knew he was going back seven years, at least. That meant starting towards the back.

The attic was in the roof space of the house, low ceilinged, with exposed beams criss-crossing the space. Barney made his way round cardboard boxes and plastic crates, past an old bookcase full of paperbacks no one could ever possibly read again, they were so completely covered in dust and cobwebs and insect husks. By the time he reached the far wall, there were cobwebs in his hair and dust in his throat and his eyes were stinging. This was the place, though. The boxes were cardboard and looked damp in places. He pulled open the first and took a ball of old newspaper off the top, flattening it out until he could read the date: 20 December, six years earlier. The box was full of old china, nestling safely down in newspaper. The next one he opened contained old textbooks of his father's. Next box – toddler clothes. Barney's heart started to beat faster. Dads didn't save baby clothes. That was definitely the sort of thing mums did. His mum had packed this box. Next box – baby books. She'd saved his books and his clothes. Some time when she'd lived in this house, his ultra-tidy mum had hoarded away things she'd never use again, because she couldn't bear to throw them away.

Four boxes later, he found the albums. He lifted the first, a faded crimson colour, out of the box and sat with it on his lap. This was it. It was like exam results, or waiting to hear if you'd been picked for the cross-country team. Just a second away from information that would change everything.

The first page had nothing on it but three Polaroid-style pictures on thin, shiny paper. Each was in black and white and showed a hazy mass of nothing. Black space, grey shadows and something that might just, if you screwed up your eyes, resemble a human face. They were of him, photographs of an unborn Barney, in his mother's stomach.

'Not quite what I had in mind,' he muttered, turning the page.
Oh God!

It was as if someone had hit him hard in the chest. How could a picture cause so much physical pain? He couldn't even see her face properly. She was in profile. The picture was mainly of him as a tiny baby. But she was so beautiful. That was obvious, even in what little he could see of her. Her hair was short and a shiny dark brown, the colour of conkers. It curled around her chin, showing off her long neck. Her hands and her wrists looked large for a woman's and she was holding him close to her face, smiling down at him. He was looking back up at her, as though her eyes were the most fascinating thing he'd seen in his short life. They looked like they might be the only two people in the whole world.

'Barney, you all right up there?'

For a second, Barney didn't trust himself to speak. He gulped, tried to sniff without making a sound and ran his hands over his eyes. He had no idea how long he'd been in the attic. He'd turned the pages of the album, watching tiny baby Barney turn into bigger baby Barney and eventually toddler Barney. Most of the pictures had been just of him, but his mum had been in several and his dad in one or two. Her hair had got longer, sometimes she'd worn it pulled back in a ponytail. He thought she looked less happy, even less pretty, in the later photographs, but she always seemed to be smiling at Barney. She always seemed to love him.

'Barney!' Steps on the ladder. His dad was coming up.

'Coming!' Barney managed, shoving the album back into the box and turning to face the hatch. His dad's face appeared.

'What's up?' he asked.

'Nothing,' Barney replied, hoping his dad couldn't see past him to where the boxes were disarranged. 'Just the dust up here. It's been making my eyes water.'

'I see you found it,' said his dad, who was looking at the Lego. 'Shall I carry it down?'

His dad climbed back down the ladder and Barney followed. Next time, he'd take a couple of the pictures of his mum out of the album. He'd learn them, until his mum's face was as familiar to him as his own, and then he'd go out looking for her. He'd go to supermarkets and busy shopping centres on Saturday afternoons. He'd let his focus drift and concentrate on finding his mum's face. He could do it, he knew he could. In any crowd, he could find that face.

123

26

'FOUR PROPOSALS OF MARRIAGE, SIX DEATH THREATS, TWO job offers and five churches claiming eternal salvation will be mine once I embrace Jesus and join their flock.'

Lacey nudged her chair further under the table, closer to the slim young woman on its opposite side. All around her in the visitors' suite people were making the same effort to give their conversations an outside chance of privacy. Trouble was, given the noise levels in the room, at times they invariably had to shout to make themselves heard. 'And is that this week?' she asked.

The woman smiling at her across the table looked nothing like the photograph that had appeared, not quite a week earlier, in a Sunday supplement about female serial killers. The photograph had been taken several weeks after her arrest, when the strain of incarceration and the slow grinding of the legal system were taking their toll. This woman – face free of make-up, hair grown longer and its natural toffee brown – didn't look much older than twenty. She was slim and strong and had great posture. Her skin glowed and her eyes shone. She looked as if she'd never had a sleepless night or a bad dream in her life.

She gave a half shrug, as though conceding a small defeat. 'Since you were last here.' Then she grinned. 'I'm still in the lead though.'

Impossible for Lacey not to smile back. The woman serving a life sentence for murder was brimming over with life. You could almost look into her eyes and see her heart beating. And her conversation was so quick, so full of energy, ideas just poured out of her. This woman, more than anyone, made Lacey acutely conscious of how sluggish her own thinking had become, how dulled her reactions to what was going on around her. This place, more than anywhere, made her feel as though she were viewing life through a thick screen of opaque glass.

'I'm very happy for you,' said Lacey. 'And at what stage is the winner determined?'

Hazel-blue eyes blinked. 'It's more of an ongoing challenge. We just update the board in the dayroom as and when. One of the warders rubbed it off the other week and there was nearly a riot.'

'Volatile places, prisons.'

The woman tucked a strand of hair behind one ear. 'You're telling me,' she said. 'Then we had the allegations of cheating, so now we have to supply proof. One of the older women is in charge of the board. Only she can update it, and she wants to see the letters or the emails before she'll change the scoring.'

'Strict.'

'Rachel Copping. You've probably heard of her. She put weed-killer into her husband's tea when she found out he'd emptied their bank account. Took him three days to die and she kept him locked in the bedroom the whole time.'

'I'm glad you're making friends.'

A conspiratorial grin. Then a second of silence as both women momentarily ran out of conversation. Lacey's eyes drifted up to the wall clock and saw that twenty minutes had gone by already.

Time behaved differently in here, she'd noticed. Or rather it misbehaved. It skidded, dragged its heels, sprinted forward and doubled back, catching itself on loose nails and grinding to sudden and unpredictable halts. It was as though the laws governing real time didn't quite make it through prison security.

'Are they treating you well?' she asked, when the silence was nudging towards awkward and even a stupid question seemed better than nothing. As if anyone were treated well in prison. But this woman was probably one of the most notorious killers of modern times. She'd be bound to attract attention.

'Not bad. I wonder if they're a bit afraid of me, even the staff.' As she spoke, she glanced at the middle-aged man in uniform standing just five yards away against the wall. He caught her eye and looked down. 'If any of them get a bit lippy,' she went on, 'I just sort of stop and stare. And I can see them thinking about what I did and they just back down. Nobody really gives me any trouble.'

For a second, the warmth in her eyes flickered out and her pupils took on a darker cast. For a second, it was possible to see the woman who had killed, pre-meditatively and brutally; who, despite what she might pretend to the prison authorities, psychiatrists and social workers, felt not a shred of remorse. It was good though, good that she was tough, good that she was feared. It would keep her safe.

'Good,' said Lacey.

A second more of silence. Lacey leaned back and took a deep breath, unconsciously pushing back her shoulders to give her lungs more room to move. She still hadn't got used to how thin the air felt here, as though the place was part of some underhand experiment to find out if prisoners and their visitors might be a bit more manageable if the oxygen content of the room were reduced. Come to think of it, didn't they do that on airplanes?

The prisoner was watching her thoughtfully. 'Are you still getting headaches?' she asked.

Lacey nodded. 'Sometimes,' she admitted, although headaches were something she was suffering from increasingly. Especially on visiting days. The thin air in the visiting suite, the noise and smell of people around her, then the exhaustion that several hours on public transport brought. And yet, she realised with a surge of warmth, it was all a small price to pay for the sheer joy of having this woman back in her life again.

'You know what? Having an education is the most enormous advantage in prison,' said the prisoner.

'It's generally considered an advantage out of it as well. But you left school at fifteen.'

'Yeah, but I didn't waste my time when I was there. I can read. I can string a sentence together. Loads of the women in here ask me to write letters home for them. Or read the ones they get. One girl even asked me to teach her to read. I said I'd have a go, but you wouldn't believe how bad the library is. I've written to the minister.'

'The minister?'

'Secretary of State for Education. I mean, you've got all these women locked up – talk about a captive audience, makes sense to give them something useful to do. And people learn through books, don't they? You taught me that.'

'And you want the minister to . . .'

'Provide some decent books, of course. Even if they're only secondhand. I've only been here a couple of months and I've read everything in the library already. Ten years down the line I'll be able to recite them. Imagine it, Lacey, ten years reading the same thirty-seven books. What? What's the matter?'

Lacey had reached across the table, taken hold of the other woman's hands. 'I'm so sorry,' she said. 'I'm so sorry you're in here. It's all my—'

The prisoner was looking round, alarmed. If they made a scene, Lacey might be asked to leave early. Then she leaned forward. 'No, listen to me,' she said. 'I've been in prison since I was fifteen years old. A worse prison than this, by a long shot. Here, it's warm and clean. There's food and company. I can plan for the future. By the way, are you involved in the vampire murders?'

Even here, there was no respite from the evil that was following her around. Even here? What was she thinking? Here was where the evil of humanity was concentrated. Even if it never felt that way.

'They're calling them that already?' said Lacey.

The prisoner nodded. 'Since that bloke on GMTV this morning. The twenty-four-hour news channels have been full of it. The girls here have been talking about it all day. Funny how uptight they get about kids being murdered. So is the Lewisham team dealing with it?'

'They are. But I was never part of that team. I was just drafted in to help out with – well, you know, last autumn.'

'But you told me you'd been asked to join them.'

Lacey nodded. A couple of months ago, Dana Tulloch had told her she had a place on the Lewisham Major Investigation Team if she wanted it. She'd been seriously considering the idea. Then she'd been sent to Cambridge.

127

'I'm not sure it's for me, after all,' she said, thinking that most people would assume she was talking about a specific posting. On the other hand, the woman across the table wasn't most people.

'What? Lewisham in specific or the Met in general?'

Lacey's eyes fell to the tabletop.

'What else will you do?'

Lacey looked up. 'I'll think of something. Private security, maybe.'

'This isn't you.'

'We all have our tipping points.'

'I could help.'

'What with? Career advice?'

'If you want, but I meant the case.'

'Well, first up, I'm not part of the investigating team, and I know nothing more than what I've heard on the news. Second, how can you possibly help with the abduction and murder of four young boys?'

The woman shook her head. 'Oh, typical police two-dimensional thinking. Do you have any idea of the criminal knowledge in this room alone?'

Lacey looked round. As usual, most of the visitors were men and children. Some older women, who looked like they might be prisoners' mothers. The prisoners themselves all sat facing the same direction, the north wall, all dressed alike in royal-blue overalls. Women of varying ages, the oldest in her sixties, the youngest barely out of her teens. None appeared to be anything out of the ordinary. They were the sort of women you'd see on a bus, in the supermarket, waiting for their children outside school. Perfectly ordinary-looking women, who'd been convicted of some of the most serious crimes in British history.

'I can get a focus group together,' the ordinary woman across the table was saying. 'Brainstorm a few ideas. Try and come up with the motivation. We could build you a profile of the killer. I'm sure we'd do a pretty good job. There are some very twisted people in here, you know.'

'You don't say.'

'Seriously, we've been talking about little else all morning. What do you think about this clinical vampirism business?'

'I haven't really given it much thought,' said Lacey,

'Oh, come off it. I know you, you'll be poring over every single detail you can get your hands on. The consensus here is we're not sure. A lot of the women in here cut themselves, you know. My roommate does it. I asked her about it once. She said it's like tension builds up inside you and it gets to the point when you just can't keep it in any longer. Like a really nasty festering sore that you know you have to burst. You know it's going to hurt like hell when you do, but afterwards it'll feel so much better.'

It was actually a pretty good analogy. Like the inside of your body was festering.

'Still with me?'

'Of course,' said Lacey, blinking herself back.

'So we get the idea of blood-letting to release tension, but nobody had ever heard of doing it to someone else. And as for drinking blood, that's just gross.'

The bell rang to signal the end of visiting time. The two women had established a pattern. They never lingered, that just made it harder. They stood up, kissed, held each other for a second, and then Lacey walked away without looking back. This time, though, the brief second didn't feel nearly long enough. Lacey held on to the young woman's slim, strong body, felt her soft cheek against her own.

'You're really OK, aren't you?' she said. 'It's not just a brave face you're putting on.'

Fingers stroked the underside of her chin. 'I'm fine,' she said. 'You're the one we need to worry about.'

Lacey pulled away and made for the door. Noise levels in the room always picked up at this point. Chairs were scraped along the floor, people invariably raised their voices to say goodbye.

'You have to go back to work, Lacey,' called the voice across the room. 'You can't do anything else!'

27

'OH, MY LIFE, WHEN DID YOU GET SO BIG AND UGLY?' Turquoise eyes blinked at her. 'That's no way to talk to my dad.'

At the door of Dana's small office on the first floor of Lewisham Nick, the older of the two Joesburys gave a muffled laugh, the younger kept a dead-pan face.

Dana felt her first smile in days pushing at the corners of her mouth. 'If hugs are on the agenda, I'm willing,' she said, getting to her feet.

'If I must,' grumbled Huck, who was already halfway across the room. They smelled of the outdoors, these two men, of dry mud and damp sports clothes, of petrol fumes and, God, how had she never realized how strong and warm and solid young boys' bodies were? Huck's hair smelled of apples, his skin was the softest thing she'd ever touched.

'OK, you're being weird now.'

She looked up, over Huck's head, to see Mark with that crease between his brows that meant he was worried about her. She let Huck go, stepped back and tilted his chin up. 'You're right,' she said, 'you're much better looking than your dad.'

'He got his mother's looks and my brains,' said Joesbury. 'I never tire of telling him how lucky he is.'

'But my natural athleticism is all my own,' said Huck, pulling back the sleeve of his rugby shirt. The bicep muscle looked as if someone had pushed a ping-pong ball under his skin.

'Nearly ready?' Mark asked Dana.

'Yep,' she said. 'I've got my phone if they need me. Do you want to take a look downstairs first?'

'Back in a sec,' he told Huck. 'You two decide where you want to eat.'

'Are you going to the incident room?' asked his son.

'No, I'm going to ask the desk sergeant who he fancies in the 4.15 at Haydock.'

'Can I come?'

The two squared up to each other. 'Since when have you been interested in horse racing?' asked the bigger of the two.

'I mean to the incident room.'

Mark pulled the door open. 'Of course,' he said. 'Your mother said to be sure I showed you lots of photographs of dismembered corpses.'

'Mark!'

Quick as a rat, Huck had one foot in the corridor. 'Cool, can I?'

'No,' said Dana firmly.

'No,' repeated Mark, 'because I am not going to the incident room and the desk sergeant doesn't approve of children gambling.'

Huck waited for the sound of his father's footsteps to fade. He looked at Dana, then back at the door, then at Dana again. She waited.

'While my dad's in the incident room, can I ask you something?' he said eventually, his bright-blue eyes wide and staring.

Dana sat down again. 'Of course.'

Huck leaned against the back of the chair facing her. 'Actually, three things. First, is it true that you're looking for a vampire?'

'No. And where on earth did you hear that rubbish?'

Huck started swinging the chair round in the usual manner of boys who can't keep still for a second. 'On the radio on the way over,' he said. 'The bloke said that in view of latest developments – I think that's what he said – the investigation team would be bringing in Van Helsing to act as an advisor. My dad called him a Ducking Bat and switched the radio off.'

'A Ducking Bat?'

Huck grinned. 'No, he didn't say that, just something that sounds a lot like it. He's not supposed to swear in front of me, but I don't tell on him because I know more swear words than anyone else in my class.'

'You must be very proud.'

Huck's eyes narrowed. 'I know who Van Helsing is, though.'

'Do you?'

'He's the black guy in *Young Dracula*. The one with the stupid hat who's always trying to catch the vampires but never manages it. I don't know why you'd want him on your team, he's a twit with a different vowel sound.'

'A what?'

'Twit with a different vowel sound. You know, twit, twot, tw—'

Dana held up her hand. 'Yeah, I get it. Well, there are no such things as vampires. I'm looking for an evil, but otherwise very ordinary man or woman, and I will not be hiring anyone called Van Helsing. Now, what was your second question?'

Huck spun the chair right round and sat in it, then looked down at the desk, and arranged the pencils into a square shape. His mouth twisted into a lopsided pout.

'Auntie Dana,' he began, without looking up.

He hardly ever called her that.

'Yes, Huckleberry?'

He looked up, down, up again. 'Are you still gay?' he asked her.

Oh God, the last thing she'd expected. He'd been teased at school. This child, probably the closest she'd ever come to having one of her own, was embarrassed by her.

'Yes, Huck,' she said, watching his little face fall. Kids could never really hide what they were feeling. 'Why, has someone said—'

'No, I thought you probably would be. It's just . . .'

She really didn't want to be having this conversation right now. Except when these conversations arrived, there was no avoiding them. 'Just what?'

His eyes were on his feet, his trainers kicking the leg of her desk, his hands tucked in his pockets. Then he looked up again.

'I really think my dad needs a girlfriend,' he said.

'Oh? Why?'

'Even Mum's starting to say he does. He's just in such a bad mood all the time. Always grumpy.'

The little face in front of her looked so sad.

'Is he grumpy with you?' she asked.

Huck shook his head. 'No,' he said. 'With little things. You know, when the traffic lights change at the last minute, or he spills some coffee on the worktop. Or if he forgets something. If you're happy, you don't get cross with little things, do you?'

'No, I guess you don't.'

Footsteps outside. The two of them exchanged a glance that was half guilt, half intrigue. 'We'll talk about this some more,' said Dana. 'In the meantime, what's the third thing you want to ask me?'

'Are you going to make us eat vegetarian muck again?' said Huck as the door opened and his dad reappeared.

'Matey, will you get me some water?' he asked Huck, holding the door open. 'Water fountain at the end of the corridor.'

'OK,' said Huck, getting up and sauntering out.

'What?' said Mark, when his son had gone.

'Nothing. Anything strike you downstairs?'

'Just the blood, for the moment. Lot of it to get rid of. It's going to make a hell of a mess in a house. So, either he lives alone, in which case it doesn't matter how much mess he makes . . .'

'We're pretty certain he doesn't though,' interrupted Dana. 'Circumstances allow him a certain amount of freedom in the late afternoons, early evenings. Then he's expected to be home.'

'So he has somewhere else to work. An outbuilding, a lock-up, even a garden shed. Which tend not to be connected to the sewer system.'

'I'm not following.'

Mark lowered himself into the chair Huck had just left, only he sat on it with the chair-back facing his chest. 'If the blood is being poured down a domestic sink, it'll go straight into the foul-water drain and join the municipal sewerage system. In this city, with hundreds of thousands of litres of sewerage being processed every day, it'll soon get lost.'

'Right.'

'On the other hand, if it's not getting into the sewerage system, it most likely is going into a storm drain.'

'When did you become an expert on sewerage?'

'Not sewerage, water pollution. You forget Adam and I spent most of our weekends when we were kids driving up and down the river with Granddad.'

She nodded. Mark's maternal grandfather had worked for the marine policing unit. His uncle still did.

'One of the things we'd get involved with was river-pollution incidents,' Mark continued. 'Strictly, it's not the responsibility of the Marine Unit, but typically it's their patrol boats that spot problems. And one thing I did learn was that if an unauthorized substance enters the river via a storm drain, it leaves some trace behind. I've watched these blokes from the Environment Agency find traces of oil, or chemicals, or raw sewerage at the points where the storm drains meet the river, then track it back up through the drains, right to the point of origin.'

'So, if they spot blood, then they can—'

'Track it back to where it was spilt in the first place.'

Dana pushed her chair back from her desk. 'I had no idea,' she said.

'It's a long-shot, sweetheart. A typical pollution incident is a lot bigger than a few litres of blood, but it's worth a go. Talk to the Marine Unit, they'll put you in touch with the Environment Agency, you can pin-point the storm drains along the stretch of the South Bank between Tower Bridge and Deptford and then you can send a team out. Take a couple of days at most.'

'I'll get on to it tomorrow,' said Dana, glancing at her watch. 'Huck's been a long time.'

'Speak of the Devil,' said Mark, as the small boy pushed open the door. 'Where've you been?'

'Having a word with David,' said Huck. 'On the next floor up.'

Mark raised one eyebrow at Dana.

'David Weaver, the Detective Superintendent,' explained Dana. 'How was he?'

'Good,' said Huck. 'Worried about the vampire. He didn't

mention it, but he had a copy of that book on his desk, the one that's just gone into the top fifty on Amazon.'

'So now even the Super is reading Bram Stoker,' said Dana.

'Did you give him my water?' said Mark.

Huck gave his dad a withering look. 'You didn't want water,' he said. 'You wanted me out of the way so you could tell Dana what you thought of in the incident room.'

'You see,' Mark said to Dana. 'Kid got my brains.'

28

LACEY'S TRAIN GOT INTO KING'S CROSS JUST BEFORE EIGHT o'clock. As she left the station she saw the late edition of the *Evening Standard* and stopped to take a copy. The masthead had caught her attention. VAMPIRE AT LARGE IN LONDON.

The world had gone nuts.

It was a thirty-minute Underground trip home. The front page of the paper showed artist's sketches of the four young boys who had died and the one still missing. Each looked paler and thinner than the photographs Lacey remembered seeing. Dwarfing all of them in size was a colour photograph of the psychologist who'd been in the news all day: Bartholomew Hunt, an attention-grabbing pillock, if ever she'd seen one.

Hunt was miffed at not being taken seriously and was happily accusing the Metropolitan Police of being narrow-minded and bigoted in their thinking. A spokesman for the MIT had told the paper that they were taking all new information seriously and were currently pursuing a number of lines of inquiry.

Lacey folded the paper on her lap. The team hadn't a clue. Pursuing a number of lines of inquiry was as good as saying they had no idea where to turn next. She pulled out her iPhone and pressed the Twitter app. During the day, some wag had christened the murderer the Twilight Killer and #TwilightKiller had been attracting new posts at the rate of several a second. As was the

Missing Boys Facebook page. Lacey had also followed comment streams on MySpace and Mumsnet. Several wanted to know of any shops that hadn't sold out of garlic. There were rumours of holy water and crucifixes being stolen from churches and Bram Stoker's *Dracula* was predicted to hit the bestseller chart for the first time since its publication. It seemed safe to say hysteria was building.

At Stockwell, Lacey climbed up to street level realizing that old habits died hard. She'd wanted to know nothing about this investigation and here it was, churning around in her head as if she'd been right in amongst it from the start. Even the country's incarcerated wanted in on the action. A focus group of some of the world's most notorious female criminals, working directly for the Met and using her as their main channel of communication? It was almost funny.

Except, was it actually such a bad idea? Who better to get inside the head of a cold and calculating killer than several more of them with time on their hands?

Yep, the world had gone nuts.

29

BARNEY LOOKED ALONG THE EMBANKMENT, AND THEN down to the map. They were some distance from the nearest street lamp and he had to use his torch. 'This is it,' he said. 'This is where they found Noah.'

The six children lined up along the wall and peered over to look at the beach below. Long way down. Lloyd took a step back. 'He went down these steps?' he said. 'Can't have been easy with a body over his shoulder.'

Close to where the children were standing, a dozen concrete steps led from the embankment to the beach. All but the top two were covered in green algae. Threads of river-weed had knotted around bumps in the concrete and the metal handrail looked anything but secure.

'He could have just tipped him over the wall,' added Jorge. 'No point making unnecessary work.'

Barney was looking at the opposite bank. 'The thing about this site is that it's almost directly across the river from the headquarters of the Marine Unit,' he said.

'What's the Marine Unit?' asked Harvey. He and the other boys were pressing closer, all trying to see the map at once.

'The river police,' said Barney, nodding to the large brown-brick, Victorian building on the north bank with its industrial-length pier. 'Part of the Metropolitan Police but in charge of the river. People at the time said it was really cheeky of the killer, to dump the body here, right under their noses.'

'That's where they're based, is it?' said Jorge, who was also looking at the building. 'I didn't know.'

'Are you alright up there, Hatty?' asked Barney. Hatty and Sam had climbed up on to the embankment wall. It was only about five feet high on this side, but a good fifteen-foot drop on the other.

'Hatty'll be fine,' said Jorge. 'Sam will probably tumble to his death though.'

'Heard that,' muttered Sam.

'The police didn't find him though, did they?' asked Lloyd.

'No, a couple on their way home from work,' said Barney. 'The point is, there was a lot of talk about whether the killer was taunting the police, you know, saying. "Look at me, look what I've left on your doorstep."'

'Maybe he just didn't know,' said Jorge, whose eyes were still fixed on the north bank.

'One thing everyone is agreed on is that this bloke knows the river,' said Barney. 'If you know the river, you know where the Marine Unit are based.'

'So where was the body?' asked Sam.

Barney shone his torch down on to the beach. 'Hard to know for definite,' he said. 'There were sketches in some of the newspapers but they'd be based on guesswork. I think we have to work it out for ourselves.'

'Go on then, Sherlock,' said Jorge.

'Well, he probably carried him down these steps,' said Barney, 'and we know he leaves them where the tide will cover them after a couple of hours. If we go down, we can probably figure it out.'

'What's the tide doing now?' asked Lloyd, looking nervously at the black water.

'It's coming back in. In another couple of hours you won't be able to get down there. It'll be muddy even now. I did tell you lot to wear wellies.'

Of the whole group, only he and Lloyd were wearing wellington boots.

'Watch it,' Barney said, realizing he was expected to lead the way down to the beach. 'These steps will be slippy.'

Shining the torch on the crumbling concrete steps, Barney made his way down to the beach. The first few yards of it were dry. The tide didn't usually reach all the way back to the wall. After a few paces, though, the stones became damp, interspersed with patches of mud. Four yards away from the river's edge, Barney stopped.

'Somewhere round here,' said Barney, looking down. 'I can't see any reason for him to have walked left or right. I imagine he wanted to get rid of it and get away from here as soon as possible.'

Jorge had walked another pace further on. 'Here, I reckon,' he said.

'How come?' asked Harvey.

'Had a good view of the river in both directions,' said Jorge. 'He could see if any traffic was coming. But that pier would provide a pretty good screen for what he was up to.'

'Here then,' said Barney, stepping closer to Jorge. One by one the other children joined them. They stood in a circle, looking at each other.

'We should switch these torches off,' said Jorge, doing exactly that with his own. 'People up on the embankment might see us. And there's still people on the pier. We should work in the dark. Like he did.'

The three remaining torch beams disappeared and the children were left in darkness on the riverbank. Barney felt a twang of nerves. This close to the water's edge, the sound of the river was surprisingly loud. It seemed to groan, somehow, as though with the effort of continual motion. Or as though there was something beneath it, pushing to be free.

'This is freaky,' giggled Hatty. In the dim light, Barney thought he saw Sam sneak his arm around Hatty's waist. She stepped to one side, away from him.

'Quiet,' said Jorge. 'Let's just listen.'

A second of silence from the children, then another muffled giggle. Jesus, was Barney the only one who could hear the noise the river was making? It sounded like it was alive. With a start, Hatty turned to look out across the water. Had she too heard the low-pitched moaning, like half-dead creatures waking up? Then the spell was broken when Harvey pulled a plastic water bottle from his rucksack and started to walk round the others in a big circle. The children watched, increasingly mystified, as Harvey held the bottle out at arm's length and let the water inside trickle down on to the stones. He drew a circle around them and stepped into it.

'What you doing?' asked Jorge.

'Holy water,' said Harvey. 'I've just drawn a protective circle around us.'

The noise from the children bounced across the beach.

'Daft pillock!' 'Prat!' 'Dickhead!' Only Barney stayed quiet. They weren't going to start talking about vampires and drinking blood again, were they?

'Where the hell did you get holy water?' demanded Jorge.

'St Nicholas's,' said Harvey, looking defensive. 'They have a bowl of it at the back by the door, I just waited till no one was looking. Everyone knows vampires hate holy water.'

'So we're perfectly safe from vampires as long as we stay in this circle all night,' said Jorge. 'Course we might drown, but at least our jugulars will be intact. OK, own up, who brought garlic?'

Sam and Lloyd laughed nervously.

'Stakes?' said Jorge.

With a grin on her face, Hatty reached inside the neck of her fleece and pulled out a small, silver crucifix.

'OK, guys, quieten down,' said Lloyd. 'We came here for a reason, not to piss about.'

'So what do we do, look for clues?'

'There won't be any clues left,' said Barney. 'I think we just have to get a feel for the place. Any special reason for choosing here? Did he definitely come by road or is it too soon to rule out the river?

'He's bringing them by road,' said Lloyd. 'At Tower Bridge, he could get a car right to the steps, then it would be just a couple of minutes to carry them up, through the alleyway and down again to the river. All he had to do here was park in the road, carry him a few yards down the steps and he was on the beach.'

'Convenience then,' said Jorge. 'Does your map show all the steps with road access, Barney? We can try and predict where he might leave the next one.'

141

'Glad you think there's going to be a next one.'

'Serial killers don't stop unless they're caught or die,' said Jorge. 'Course there'll be a next one.'

'It's raining,' said Hatty, stepping away from the circle, a step closer to the river. Barney followed, resisting the temptation to pull her back. 'I keep forgetting,' he said. 'I found your earring.' He opened his hand. The tiny gold leaf sat in the centre of his palm.

'Cool,' said Hatty. 'Where was it?'

'In the drain that runs round the edge of the community-centre yard,' said Barney.

'Yuck!' She tucked it into her pocket.

'I cleaned it. It was covered in something grotty, but I cleaned it with my dad's white spirit.'

'Thanks.' She gave him that cute, shy smile of hers, the one that made her cheeks plump up like she had gobstoppers inside them. Although she was older than Barney, she was smaller. Sometimes, when you looked down at her, you couldn't see her eyes, just long black lashes.

'How deep is it?' she asked, turning back to the river.

It made him feel good that there was stuff he knew that she didn't. 'Right now, about five metres in the middle,' he said. 'Gets deeper when the tide's in, obviously.'

Five metres of cloudy, dark water. Barney had a sudden vision of himself stepping out and sinking down, through the silt and the oil, feeling the pull of friendly hands, only to realize it was weed clinging and that it wasn't friendly at all, that it was taking him further, down to the wrecked boats, the mud and rock at the bottom. To spend the last seconds of his life in an underwater city, peopled by corpses that had never managed to float free.

'What?' said Hatty, who'd seen him shiver. 'Someone walk over your grave?'

'Something like that,' he admitted. 'We should go, we can't get into the Creek if the tide's high.'

The others were reluctant to leave the riverbank. Sam and Harvey were trying to skim stones, Jorge seemed strangely fascinated by the river in the fading light and Lloyd had discovered shells among the rocks. A bit like a Collie dog with badly behaved sheep, Barney chivvied them along. He was careful not to overdo it, he never forgot he was the youngest. Even so, more than once he was told to chill out.

But it was difficult to chill when the sense of the river behind him was so strong, when the temptation to look back over his shoulder, like a nervous girl walking alone down a dark street, was close to irresistible. And when pictures were forming in his head of waves like tiny creatures, snapping at his ankles, getting ready to bring him down.

He was an idiot. It was just a river, black and mighty and relentless, but still nothing more than an urban watercourse.

'Guys, it's raining, come on,' complained Hatty and finally they started to leave the beach. Barney was the last to climb the steps. As he put his foot on the first, he had a feeling that the river called out to him. That it told him it would always be here, and it would be waiting.

Riverside lanterns, round and pale like puffball mushrooms, were glowing softly when Dana arrived at the restaurant. Mark and Huck had gone on ahead; Helen, punctual to a fault, would have arrived fifteen minutes ago. They'd all be waiting for her.

The river, just yards away, was racing past, and had taken on the fuller, more urgent sound it made when the tide was heading in. By the time they left the restaurant, the water would be pushing against the embankment wall.

The restaurant was busy. She could almost feel the heat seeping out from the giant glass windows and doors. Most of them had steamed up already. Needing one last moment before she forced herself to be happy and upbeat – for Huck's sake, at least, there was no fooling the other two – Dana walked to the railings and leaned out over the water.

To her left, on the beach where the two Barlow boys had been found, all was in darkness. Only the reflection of lights from Tower Bridge told her where the water ended and the rocks began. Someone walking around down there, wearing dark clothes and moving without light, would not be spotted.

On the other hand, the figure stepping out from the bridge's shadow, wearing a light-coloured padded jacket, could be seen very clearly. He or she, it really wasn't possible to tell, reached the concrete steps and began climbing. Slim, not too tall.

Dana ran, away from the river, heading for Shad Thames, knowing the chances of cutting off the figure in the padded jacket were slim. The streets around Butler's Wharf were busy, even in February, and she had to dodge her way around more than one group idling along, looking for somewhere to eat.

Ahead, about thirty yards away, was the light-coloured jacket.

'Hey!'

Several people turned, including the one she was fixated on. Definitely a woman, a little older than she, thin face, hair hidden beneath a dark woollen hat. The face turned away, a group came out of a building and got between them. Dana picked up her pace as much as she could but she was wearing heels and the street was cobbled. She reached the corner and turned.

No sign of the woman.

By the time they reached Deptford Creek, Barney had a sense that several of the group were starting to think this wasn't such a good idea after all. It had rained persistently since they'd left Bermondsey and all the children had wet hair and damp clothes. On Creekside they chained their bikes to a railing and Barney led them to the tall iron gate.

'Nobody should be here at this time, but we'll be on private property so we still have to be careful,' he said. 'Jorge, can you give us all a leg over?'

One by one, the children stepped on Jorge's clasped hands and scrambled over the railings. 'What is this place?' asked Jorge, when he'd joined them.

'Creekside Educational Trust,' said Barney. 'They're a sort of charity that look after the Creek. Be quiet – people live close by.'

The children made their way down the side of the Trust building, past rubbish that had been pulled from the Creek over the years, including several rusting shopping trolleys, and down a path that led through a roughly tended garden. Slowly, the twin towers of the old railway-lift loomed above them.

'What's that?' asked Hatty, eyeing the massive iron structure nervously. In the darkness it looked far bigger than it ever did in daylight, like a mechanical monster leering over them.

'The railway-lift,' said Barney. 'It's not used any more. In the old days, it would lift train carriages from one track and put them down on the other. This way.' He led them across the grass until they could see down to the Creek itself.

'Down there?' asked Sam, staring down at the narrow, steeply sloping beach that led to the black slick of water. All around them, granite-black buildings loomed.

'Down here,' confirmed Barney. As he led the way, he had a sense of the others hanging back. Not that he really blamed them. The Creek was freaky, especially at low tide, especially at night. As they neared the water he stopped.

'It's like the friggin' Grand Canyon,' said Lloyd. None of the others spoke. They were all staring round at the massive river walls that soared seven metres high in places. Their construction was completely random, adding to the bizarre effect. Originally, they'd been built from vertical timbers, but many of those had rotted away, to be replaced by steel piles, or concrete sheets. There were even patches of brickwork. Dark, dank vegetation sprang from wherever it could, as though, despite man's best efforts to colonize this stretch of water, nature was determined to claim it back.

Above the walls, three- and four-storey warehouses and dockyard buildings stretched up even higher. The impression was of a dark and narrow tunnel between massive black cliffs.

'It looks like this because the tide's low,' said Barney. 'When it's high the water will reach right up to where we're standing. It can be seven metres deep. That's why the walls have to be so high. When the tide's completely out, there's nothing but mud here. We can go a bit further, but be careful if you're not in wellies.'

The children crept forward, mainly keeping to the stones and gravel that lined the sides of the beach, only Barney and Lloyd sensibly enough shod to walk through the mud. 'Yuck,' complained Hatty, as the mud seeped up over her trainers and into her socks.

'This is well freaky,' said Sam, when they had gone as close to the narrow stream as they could. To their left, through the arch of the railway bridge, they could see the last stretch of the Creek before it joined the Thames. The huge iron lift looked alien and predatory in the poor light.

'We need to stay together now,' said Barney, spotting the others starting to drift off and feeling increasingly nervous. He'd never been in the Creek without a supervising adult before, and it had always been impressed upon him how dangerous it could be.

The tall buildings around them kept out just about all light from the surrounding streets and the river-bed was black as pitch. Any of them could fall, get stuck. The tide was on its way back but tide was never the biggest danger in the Creek. Rain was. Heavy rainfall higher up the River Ravensbourne could wash down here at lightning speed, and once you were walking the high-walled channel, there weren't many escape routes. It would be stupid to go any further.

'So where was Ryan found?' asked Lloyd.

Barney looked beneath the arch of the bridge, and then down at his feet.

'Just about here,' he said.

'Aw, Christ,' said Sam, shuffling backwards in the mud, further up the bank.

'The thing about the Creek,' said Barney, 'is that there's practically no public access to it. Where we're standing is one of the few points where people can actually get into it without climbing down a ladder. This is the only beach on the Creek.'

'This isn't a beach, it's a mud bath,' said Sam.

'So he must be bringing them by road,' said Lloyd. 'If he'd come up the Creek by boat, he could have left Ryan anywhere, couldn't he? By road, it had to be here.'

'Can you even get a boat up here?' asked Harvey, looking at water that didn't seem more than a foot or so deep.

'When the tide's in, yeah,' said Barney. 'All the boats where we're going next sailed up the Creek. In a couple of hours, this spot will be under four metres of water. It's deeper further in.'

There was a second's silence, while all the children imagined the deep, narrow tunnel they were standing in filled to the brim with seawater.

'I'm ready to go now,' said Sam, who was looking nervously up-river.

'It comes that way,' said Barney, pointing under the bridge.

'All the same.'

'Thing is, though, even though Ryan was found here, he may not have been dumped here,' said Barney. 'Some newspaper reports said that the body was soaked in salt water, which it wouldn't have been if it had been dumped at low tide. If it was soaked in salt water, that means it was dumped higher up and got washed down.'

'But dumping bodies at low tide is what he does,' said Harvey.

'It's what he does now,' said Barney. 'But what if, the first time, he just wanted to get rid of the body, but then when it was found and there was a huge fuss, he found he quite liked the attention?'

'You've given this guy a lot of thought, haven't you, young Barney?' said Jorge.

'This water is getting higher,' said Sam. 'Please can we go now?'

'Right, we have to go over this gate and through the yard on the other side,' said Barney. 'Then we have to climb down a ladder to get to the boats.'

Just before Creekside met the main road, the properties on the river side of the street became working yards and lock-up areas. High walls, higher gates, barbed wire and forbidding signs told them that security was taken very seriously.

'How do the owners get to the boats?' asked Sam.

'They have keys to the gate,' said Barney. 'I couldn't find ours. I tried.'

'What if there's dogs?' said Hatty nervously.

'There weren't last time I was here,' said Barney. 'Just vans – ice-cream vans, builders' vans, fish-and-chip vans. Nothing worth having guard dogs for. But if there are, they'll go for Sam first.'

'Hey!'

'Once we're over the gate, no one can talk,' said Barney. 'People live on most of these boats, and they're not keen on people just wandering through the yard to gawp at them, so we have to be quiet.'

Repeating the process that had got them over the fence at the

Educational Trust building, the boys and Hatty clambered over into the yard.

'Oh, well skanky,' said Hatty, looking round. The quarter-acre-sized yard was little more than a car park for vehicles that owners didn't feel comfortable leaving on the street overnight. Small Portakabins around the outside of the yard suggested that work of some kind went on here, but the general run-down feel of the place indicated it probably wasn't work you wanted to inquire too deeply into the nature of. Rubbish and discarded tools littering the ground made plain that no one ever gave a thought to clearing up.

'I never said it was the Riviera,' replied Barney.

'I can't see any boats,' said Sam.

'That's because they're still low in the water. Come on.'

The children followed Barney through the yard to the moorings. Like everything else in the yard, the two-foot-wide strip of concrete that edged the Creek bank was strewn with rubbish, discarded tools and scrap metal, and Barney remembered another reason why his dad was often reluctant to bring him. *It's too friggin' dangerous for a kid.*

Barney dropped to his knees, the others followed his example and they looked out across the eleven houseboats currently moored in this stretch of the Creek. Music was drifting from one of the boats. If they were lucky, it would mask the sound of them creeping across.

'This isn't part of the main channel of the Creek,' said Barney. 'This is an offshoot they call the Theatre Arm. Dad told me why once, but I wasn't listening. Across the water is Lewisham College and there's sometimes a nightwatchman, so we have to be extra careful.'

'Which is your granddad's boat?' asked Hatty.

Barney pointed to the left. Three large houseboats, at one time fishing boats or dredgers, were moored to the bank. Tied up to them were four smaller boats and, in the third line along, five boats that were smaller still. To get to his granddad's boat in the third row, the children would have to creep across the ones in between.

'It's the yellow one with two masts,' Barney said. 'We should go in two groups, tread quietly and not talk. I'll go first. Who wants to come with me?'

Sam was looking nervously across the line of boats. Dim light shone from several of them. 'Why can't we all go together?' he said.

'Because you lot can't keep from talking. All of us together will sound like a herd of elephants, someone will hear us and that'll be the end of it,' said Barney.

'He's right,' said Jorge. 'I'll come last. Barney, you go with Sam and Harvey, Lloyd and Hatty will follow. If anyone comes, I'll crow like a cockerel and you can all hide.'

A second, whilst what Jorge had just said sank in.

'Crow like a cockerel?' said Lloyd. 'Won't that be a bit obvious? I don't see any chickens round here.'

'Hoot like an owl then,' said Jorge. 'Whatever.'

Barney, Harvey and Sam climbed down the ladder on to the first houseboat. The rain was falling faster and the air was punctuated by thousands of plopping noises. As they made their way around the deck, which could hardly be seen beneath the pots and planters, the sound of a Saturday-evening quiz show drifted out towards them.

'They have TV?' whispered Sam, as he followed Barney over the guardrail and on to the next boat.

Barney had been looking carefully at the cabin windows of the middle boat. The curtains weren't closed and no light shone from below. He nodded at Sam. 'A lot of them have their own generators,' he said. 'No mains power though.'

'What about gas?' asked Sam.

What was this? A lesson in domestic utilities?

'Calor,' he said, hoping that would be the end of it. 'Comes in bottles.'

'What's with all the plants?'

Barney raised his eyes to the night sky. 'They don't have any gardens.'

A couple of seconds' silence while Sam thought about that one. Then, 'Neither do we, but we don't cover our veranda with plants.'

'Sssh!'

'What?'

Barney put his finger to his lips. He dropped into a squat and peered into the water. It was about five or six feet deep, he judged, and getting deeper every second. It was also moving very fast, not smoothly the way it would in the main river, but sloshing backwards and forwards, swirling and slopping. It was noisy, and yet there'd been something that wasn't quite . . .

'What?' Sam was looking left and right, and making rude gestures to the group still waiting up on the wall. For crying out loud!

'Listen,' Barney mouthed.

A few seconds of silence, then, 'Can't hear anything,' said Sam.

Barney got to his feet. It had probably been nothing.

'What?' asked Harvey as they set off again, treading carefully around the front deck of the middle boat. 'What did you hear?'

'I thought there was something in the water. Probably just a bird feeding.'

The light grew fainter and the streets of Deptford began to feel a long way away. Barney tried to ignore the uncomfortable feeling in his stomach. The splashing sound he'd heard had been too loud to be a bird, even supposing they were still feeding in the dark.

When they reached the side deck, they could look down on to the yellow yacht in front of them, which seemed smaller and at the same time neater than Barney remembered. He turned back to signal to the others. He had to hope that Lloyd and Hatty would be quieter than he, Harvey and Sam had been. The next two children climbed down the ladder and began making their way towards them.

'What a pair of dorks,' muttered Sam.

Lloyd and Hatty were scuttling along the deck of the first boat at a slow run, bent double, glancing to left and right like commandos. At least they were moving quietly, though, and they weren't stopping to talk. Lightly, they jumped on to the middle boat and ran round to join Barney and the others.

'This place is freaking me out,' said Hatty in a low whisper when they were close enough. 'Why's it have to be so dark?'

'It's private land, so the Council don't put in street lights,' said Barney. 'And we're a long way from the road. Just watch what you're doing. If you fall in here we might not be able to get you out again.'

Sam responded to that sensible piece of advice by leaning out over the guardrail and looking down.

'Now what?' said Harvey, as Jorge arrived.

'Now we climb aboard and break a window,' said Jorge. 'I'll do it, then I'll help Hatty climb through. Only the two of us should go on board because if we make a noise, it'll be easier for us to hide. You lot stay here till we're in.'

'This boat's empty,' said Barney, indicating the one they were standing on. 'Let's get down into the cockpit. And I'm coming with you. We may not have to break a window. I'll try the hatches.'

As Harvey, Sam and Lloyd stepped into the cockpit of the larger boat, Hatty took hold of the boat rail and swung herself up. The yellow boat didn't register the extra weight. Jorge followed and the boat rocked gently. Then Barney was on board, following Hatty across the cabin roof, towards one of the main hatches. She dropped on to all fours on one side of it, he did the same on the other.

In spite of his misgivings, Barney had to admire the way she could move so lightly, making no sound at all. Following her lead, he slid his fingers under the edge of the hatch and pulled gently. The hatch moved two inches and they heard music from below. Hatty peered inside and froze. Barney looked, too. And didn't believe what he was seeing. A sharp nudge on his shoulder brought his attention back to Hatty. She was frowning at him, signalling urgently with her eyes. She wanted him to help her lower the hatch.

But, I mean, what . . . ?

Sharp gesticulation on Hatty's part and Barney pulled himself together. Between them, they lowered the hatch, just as gently as they'd lifted it. Signalling to Jorge to follow, Hatty stepped off the roof, over the rail and back on to the middle boat. Barney followed slowly.

'What?' hissed Harvey.

'There was someone on board,' replied Hatty.

Everyone looked at Barney, who could do nothing but shake his head.

'What did you see?' asked Jorge.

'A bloke,' said Hatty. 'Just the back of him. Couldn't see his face, not even his head. Just a blue and yellow sweatshirt.'

A blue and yellow sweatshirt that Barney knew well.

'Did he see you?' Jorge asked.

'No, I don't think he even heard us, there was music playing. And he was leaning into some sort of cupboard.'

'You sure that's your boat?' asked Lloyd.

Barney nodded. Of course he was sure, he'd discussed it with his dad just that afternoon.

'What if it's . . . you know . . . him,' said Sam.

'Who?' said Lloyd.

'The vampire,' hissed Sam, hardly audible.

The vampire was the killer. Sam thought the man on the boat was the killer.

'In a blue and yellow sweatshirt?' said Jorge.

'What was that?' asked Hatty, looking round.

'I heard it too,' said Lloyd.

'Someone threw a stone in the water,' said Jorge, looking round the group. 'Come on, own up.'

'We heard something before,' said Sam, who seemed to have forgotten he'd been talking too much to hear anything. 'Me and Barney and Harvey. Like a bird or an animal in the water.'

'Shush!'

Splash, splash.

The children fell silent. No one seemed to know what to do next. Then Harvey stepped a little closer to the boat's edge. Leaning forward, he raised the torch and shone it down. A second later, he gave a strangled scream, the torch fell to the deck and he was running away from the others, round the front of the boat, slipping on the damp deck.

'Harvey!' yelled Jorge, giving chase.

Making far too much noise, but hardly knowing what else to do, the others followed, on to the big houseboat and then over to the ladder. Jorge and Harvey were already up and out of sight. Hatty put her foot on the bottom rung of the ladder.

'He's pissing about,' said Sam, who didn't look sure.

'You lot! What the hell do you think you're doing?' On the next boat along, a man on deck was shining a torch towards them. 'Get back here, now!'

The children scrambled up the ladder, Barney the last to leave the boat. Halfway up, he turned back. Two men were visible now, shining torches around, checking to make sure their boats hadn't been damaged, angry, but not enough to give chase along wet decks in the dark.

Then there was movement on Barney's boat and in the light from the cabin he could see the man in the companionway, watching the commotion but staying out of sight of just about everyone but him. The man in the familiar blue and yellow sweatshirt who'd scared Hatty away. It hadn't been a mistake, a cruel trick of the light. The man on the boat was his father.

'Barney, come on!'

The others had run in the wrong direction, not back to the large yard gates, but towards the very tip of the Creek's backwater. They were huddled in the shelter of the massive steel pilings that supported the A2009. Jorge, unusually protective, had his arm round his younger brother. They were very close to the water and the tide was coming in fast now.

Had anyone else seen his dad?

Barney reached the group and turned back to the boats. The men who'd come up to investigate had gone back below. The yellow yacht was in darkness once more.

'What happened, Harvey?' asked Lloyd.

'There was someone in the water.'

The children pressed closer together, turning instinctively to face the black river.

'I think we should go home now,' said Jorge.

'What sort of someone?' asked Sam.

Harvey shook his head. 'Too dark,' he said. 'I just saw, like, an arm coming out of the water.' He raised his right arm in a swimming motion. 'You know, like when you're doing the crawl. And then I saw eyes looking at me. Big eyes like a fish, only a massive fish.'

'I'm out of here,' said Sam, not moving.

'Harvey, it was probably just an animal,' said Lloyd. 'An otter or something.'

'A bloody otter,' said Jorge. 'Since when did you get otters in the middle of London?'

Barney had never seen Jorge scared before. He was trying hard to hide it, but couldn't quite keep his eyes from staring, his mouth from clenching up tight. The hand still round his younger brother's shoulders was trembling.

'I'm just saying,' said Lloyd.

They couldn't have recognized, even noticed, his dad. One of them would have said something. 'It could have been someone swimming,' said Barney. 'People do, in summer. My dad won't let me, he says it's too dirty, but some people do.'

Just talking about his dad felt wrong, as though the others might make the connection between the words coming out of his mouth and the man on the boat.

'It's nearly ten o'clock at night,' said Lloyd. 'Who'd be swimming at ten o'clock? In February?'

'In the rain,' added Hatty. 'I'd really like to get away from the river.'

Barney only had to look at everyone's faces to know they all agreed with Hatty.

'I'm going to ring my dad,' said Sam.

'If you ring your dad, we'll all get murdered,' said Jorge. 'Come on. Lloyd was probably right, it probably was just an otter. Or a badger. Or a walrus.'

'Or a hippo,' said Hatty, who was starting to smile again.

The group made their way back to the yard, heading for the gates.

'A hippo called Hatty.' Jorge gave Hatty a tiny nudge on the shoulder.

'What you sayin'?' She pushed him back, a bit harder.

'Or a crocodile,' said Lloyd.

'Or a mermaid,' said Hatty.

Splash, splash.

'Oh God, no,' whimpered Sam, as the children stopped in their tracks. Jorge raised his torch and directed it on to the river. Oily blackness, the slow flow of water coming in from the Thames, gentle ripples, as though something had disturbed the surface not seconds earlier. Then, just out of reach of the torch beam, movement that they all saw.

'There!'

'Jorge, there!'

Four torch beams fixed on one point. Nothing in the black water. Stillness. Tension that Barney thought would make one of them scream any second. Then all five screamed as the creature hurled itself out of the water at them. A child, like them, but nothing like them. This child was dead. This child was covered in a waxy, sticky substance that looked as though it had leaked out of him. His body had been half eaten by river creatures. His eye sockets stared black and empty and his tongue-less mouth gaped open as if he was screaming too. He rose out of the river, lurched towards them and then collapsed face-down on the bank.

Barney didn't think he would ever stop running.

30

With his long sharp nails he opened a vein in his breast. When the blood begin to spurt out, he took my hands in one of his, holding them tight and with the other seized my neck and pressed my mouth to the wound so that I must either suffocate or swallow . . . some of the . . . Oh my god . . . my god. What have I done?"

LACEY CLOSED HER KINDLE. JESUS, SHE'D FORGOTTEN WHAT a creepy book *Dracula* was. A phantom that gained power from the blood of its prey, that grew stronger with every fresh victim it claimed. It was a truly horrible thought. And now people were being led to believe there was a real one running around South London. It was no wonder they were getting twitchy.

She got up off the sofa and stretched. There was noise in the street outside, people gathered just above her window. Lacey walked across and pulled the curtains apart an inch. Kids – one of whom looked like Barney – and something was up. They were edgy, nervous; waiting for Barney to open the front door, they kept glancing down the street. She was half tempted to go out, make sure they were OK, then they filed into the house and the door slammed shut.

Over at her desk, her laptop was still open and Lacey soon found the Missing Boys page. Honestly, the drivel people were prepared to post was endless. And she wasn't the only one to have rediscovered

Dracula that weekend. The page had any number of posts linking passages in the book with some aspect of the murders. Most of the connections seemed pretty spurious.

A number of the posts were from self-proclaimed vampires, all of them with glamorous names. Others, rejecting outlandish and sensationalist labels, talked about the very real condition of being obsessed by the sight of their own blood.

I can't explain my need for blood. I think about it all the time, craving the smell, the sight, the taste of it. It's like a secret I share with myself. And my sharp knife, I suppose. LOL.

It's like a scream building up inside me. When it gets to the point where I have to let go, I cut. Just those first few droplets of blood oozing up through my skin are enough to make me feel better. Sometimes I don't even have to taste it, although I always do.

It's getting harder and harder to hide what I do from my mum. She's getting suspicious about me sneaking rubbish (blood-stained tissues I daren't let her see) out of the house. And she's always trying to sneak a look at my arms. I'm ahead of her there, though. I cut my legs now.

Some of my scars have got infected. They hurt and they look awful, but I can't see a doctor because he'll know what I've been doing.

Nutters! Stupid, self-obsessed fruitcakes. Lacey logged off and closed the laptop. Nearly eleven o'clock. God, was she ever going to start sleeping again? It didn't seem to matter how much she wore out her body, her mind wouldn't shut down. Was it even her mind anyway? This burning feeling in her chest didn't have anything to do with intellect.

Like a scream building up inside me.

Lacey pushed up the sleeve of her sweater. The scar, running vertically the length of her wrist, was nearly four inches long. It had been itching a lot lately; sometimes in the mornings it looked pink and sore and she suspected she'd been scratching it in the night.

Without realizing, she'd walked into the kitchen. The breadknife was on the worktop. She'd used it earlier to cut bread for toast. It was probably the sharpest knife she had. She picked it up, realizing, possibly for the first time, how comfortable knives felt, how well they seemed to fit in the hand. There were smears on the blade, and crumbs left over from the bread. She should wash it, really. If you were going to cut yourself, it should be with a clean knife. She reached out to turn on the tap and hold the knife in the water, while the saner, smaller part of her yelled, *Lacey, what the hell do you think you're doing?*

The sound of the text message made her jump, as though she'd been caught in the act of something shameful. She dropped the knife in the sink and found her phone. She didn't recognize the number. And yet she could count on the fingers of one hand how many people had her private number.

The words of the text didn't register for a second, but then – good God, was this some kind of sick joke?

Body of Tyler King found at Deptford Creek, Theatre Arm Marina. Enter through lock-up yard. Come now.

31

'SHE'S GOING,' SAID BARNEY, FROM HIS POSITION BY THE window. 'Careful now,' he warned as the other children pressed closer. 'If she looks up she'll see us.'

In the dark sitting-room of Barney's house, six children watched Lacey pull the collar of her jacket up and set off down the street. Her car was parked about forty feet away on the opposite side of the road. As she beeped open the door, she looked up and down the street and, for a second, seemed to stare directly at them.

'Nobody move,' Jorge whispered. 'She won't see us if we stay still.'

If Lacey had seen them, she gave no sign. She got into her car, reversed a few inches then drove away. The children left the window and went back to the circle on the carpet they'd instinctively formed ten minutes earlier.

After seeing the thing that had leaped out of the river at them, they'd fled the yard, jumping on their bikes and speeding off, dangerously reckless on the main road, only stopping when they got to Barney's. They'd piled inside and Barney, with support from Jorge, had persuaded the others not to dial 999. Jorge had made hot chocolate, Barney had found a packet of KitKats, and the gang had huddled low and close, and talked about what they were going to do.

Jorge was looking round now. 'Everyone OK?' he asked.

None of them looked OK. Sam and Hatty had both been crying.

Sam looked like he still was, although he was making some effort to hide it.

'I'm OK,' said Barney. He wasn't, but he knew from experience that sometimes, if you pretended for long enough that you felt a certain way, sooner or later you did.

'I'm OK,' said Harvey, who looked close to tears but was holding it together.

'Me too,' agreed Lloyd. 'But what the hell was that thing?'

'Not what,' said Jorge. 'Who. I think it must have been Tyler King. You know, the first boy to go missing. I think we found him.'

'Jorge, it jumped out of the bloody water,' said Sam, unable to keep his voice from trembling. 'It wasn't dead.'

'It *was* dead,' said Hatty. 'It didn't have any eyes.'

'And I saw it swimming,' said Harvey. 'I did, Jorge. It was swimming and then it jumped out of the water. What if it followed us?'

Hatty shuffled along the carpet, a little closer to Barney.

'It didn't.' Jorge put his hands on his brother's shoulders. 'You need to get a grip. We all do. I know it was a massive shock but it was a dead body, not some sort of zombie. You didn't see it swimming and it didn't hurl itself out of the water.'

'What happened, then?'

'A wave,' said Jorge. 'It's a river, isn't it?'

'Yes, and it's tidal,' said Barney. 'The tide's on its way back in.'

'There you are then. A freak wave picked it up and dropped it on the bank.'

'So who did I see swimming?' insisted Harvey.

'I still think we should call the police,' said Sam. 'We should have called them before we left Deptford.'

Barney sighed. Sam wasn't going to let it go. But Barney could not let his dad know he'd been down at the boat this evening. 'Lacey *is* the police,' said Barney. 'She'll check it out herself, then she'll call the others. If we own up to being there, we're all in big trouble. Everyone thinks we're at Lloyd's house, remember?'

'They might think we killed him,' said Harvey.

'They won't think that,' said Lloyd. 'He'd obviously been dead a long time.'

'What if they find out we sent the text?'

'You can't trace text messages from a pay-as-you-go phone,' said Jorge. 'I'll just throw the SIM card away and that's that.'

'Why've you got one of those, anyway?' asked Harvey.

The brothers looked at each other. 'It's not mine, it's one of Mum's old ones,' said Jorge. 'I borrowed it. Mine's out of battery. She won't notice. You know what she's like.'

'It'll be on the news tomorrow,' said Lloyd. 'Everyone will be talking about it and no one will know we found him.'

'They can't know,' said Barney. 'We'll never be trusted again. We'll be grounded for months, if not years.'

Jorge, Hatty and Lloyd were nodding. Harvey would do what his brother told him. It was Sam he was worried about.

'Is your dad out all night?' asked Jorge.

'No,' said Barney, who had no idea at all. 'He'll be back before midnight.'

'It's not far off that now,' said Jorge. 'We should all go.'

'Go where?' asked Harvey.

'Ours,' said Jorge. 'Mum won't be back till morning and Gran will be away with the fairies by now. We just have to make sure we're all up before Mum gets back. Barney, you coming?'

Barney shook his head. 'I'll just go to bed,' he said. 'Dad never checks on me.'

Barney watched his mates cycle to the end of the street and turn the corner, before closing the door. Back in the sitting room, huddled close to the fire, he took out his own phone. No messages from his dad. Quickly he tapped out a text.

Bit hectic here. Not sure when we'll get to sleep. You OK on your own?

Then he sat, waiting, bothered by the dirty mugs and discarded chocolate wrappers but not having the heart to do anything about them.

Beep. His dad had replied.

House is quiet without you. About to go to bed. Have fun.

161

32

'NO! NO! GET OFF ME! I WON'T.'

Dana sat up, struggling to understand why there was a frightened child in her house. Helen, always a good sleeper, didn't stir. Of course. Huck and Mark were in the next room – Huck always liked to stay over when Helen was down. She heard Mark spring out of bed and cross the room.

'It's OK,' she heard him say. 'Just a nightmare. I'm here.'

'He's at the window. Dad, he's trying to get in.'

Dana got out of bed and left the room. She knocked gently on the door of the guest room and pushed it open.

Mark, wearing nothing but checked pyjama bottoms, was sitting on Huck's bed. He'd pulled his son's small body on to his lap and his arms were tight around him. 'There's no one at the window,' he was saying. 'You had a bad dream, that's all.'

'Mark?' asked Dana from the doorway. 'Is Huck OK?'

'He's fine. Bad dream. Want to tell me about it, buddy?'

Huck pressed his face against his father's bare shoulder and shook his head.

'Wouldn't be vampires by any chance, would it?'

The small head clamped against his father didn't move. Mark looked up and caught Dana's eye. Then Huck's head was up, alert again. 'There is something at the window! It's a bat!'

'Huck, it'll be a pigeon.' Dana crossed to the window and pulled back the curtain. 'They nest on all the house-roofs round here. They're a darned nuisance but we can't seem to get rid of them. Look, there are three of them on the window ledge across the back. Want to see?'

Huck shook his head, but he wasn't clinging quite so tightly.

'There are no bats in London,' said Mark.

Dana opened her mouth to correct him and thought better of it. After all, it was February, the bats that regularly flew around the trees in the gardens were all hibernating. She watched Huck raise his head and look at his dad. 'They can get under doors,' he said.

'What? Vampires?'

Huck nodded. 'They turn into mist and sneak under doors. Some boys at school were talking and it's on this Facebook page as well. They come into your room at night and drink your blood and after a few days you die because you've got no blood left, just like those boys Auntie Dana found, and if you've drunk the vampire's blood, you become one of them and then you have to kill everyone in your family.'

'I have never heard such bollocks in all my life,' said Mark.

'Actually, as a summary of the vampire legends, it's pretty accurate,' said Dana. 'But Huck, they're stories. They're no more true than Harry Potter.'

'And by the way, Huck, since when have you been going on Facebook? You're not old enough.'

Huck's scared look became half defiant. 'I use Mum's page,' he admitted.

'I'll be having a word with your mother.'

'So, who is killing these boys then?' Huck asked, deftly moving the conversation on.

'A man,' said his father. 'Very bad, but otherwise very ordinary. And your godmother will catch him.'

Downstairs, Dana put the kettle on and immediately wondered why she'd bothered. She didn't want tea or coffee. In the cupboard by the fridge she found the single Highland malt that Helen had brought down.

She'd been waiting ten minutes when Mark appeared. He'd

pulled a sweatshirt on and she was glad. Normally, male nudity held no more interest for her than a well-executed painting, but just lately, it seemed, she never felt entirely comfortable close to Mark.

'Is he asleep?' she asked.

He nodded. 'You've got to get this guy soon, Dana,' he said. 'Kids are terrified. They think there's a monster out there and he's after little boys.'

'Trouble is, they're right.'

'This frigging Facebook business is a menace. Can you not get this site they're all obsessing with closed down?'

Dana pulled a face. 'Possibly. But we've been monitoring it quite closely. A lot of the contributors knew the victims.'

'You think the killer could be using it?'

'Quite likely he is.'

'Can we have a look?'

Dana led the way to her study and switched on her desktop computer. The page was saved under Favourites.

But just then the moon, sailing through the black clouds, appeared behind the jagged crest of a beetling, pine-clad rock and by its light I saw around us a ring of wolves, with white teeth and lolling red tongues, with long sinewy limbs and shaggy hair. They were a hundred times more terrible in the grim silence which held them than even when they howled.

Yeah, I love that quote. One of my favourites. Wolves or vampires – which does it for you?

Wolves every time. The ripping apart of flesh. Something well savage about a wolf.

'Christ,' said Mark, after flicking through the latest postings. 'I'm going to have to talk to Carrie. I don't want Huck reading this crap, let alone getting involved.'

'There's a chap called Peter we're particularly interested in,' said Dana. 'He's quite often ahead of the game when it comes to talking about the case. He announced we'd found the Barlow twins a couple of hours before we made it public.'

Mark was flicking down the postings. 'This one?' he asked, the cursor hovering over a quote from the book that Peter Sweep had posted.

There are such beings as vampires, some of us have evidence that they exist. Even had we not the proof of our own unhappy experience, the teachings and the records of the past give proof enough for sane peoples.

Dana leaned closer. It was funny, how different to women men smelled close up.

'Yeah, that's him. He's been quoting from the Bram Stoker book ad nauseum since Bart Hunt put the idea into his head. He's clever, though. Sweep, I mean, not Hunt. Uses public computers, never the same place twice. He's hiding something.'

'What's with the red roses?' asked Mark, indicating Peter's profile picture. 'If they're supposed to be symbolic, you'd think a dagger dripping blood would be more to the point.'

'Do roses seem a little on the feminine side to you?' said Dana.

'How is your killer-wears-a-dress theory shaping up?'

'I did what you suggested and pulled up a list of boys aged eight to twelve who died in Greater London in the last five years. Not a long list, thankfully. Some road traffic accidents, a few natural causes. Nothing struck me. Neil's going through it too, but I'm not hopeful.'

He nodded. 'Worth a try.'

Dana thought for a second. Made her mind up. 'I saw a woman on that beach tonight,' she said. 'You know, the one under Tower Bridge where the twins were found?'

'In the dark?'

'That's what I thought. The tide was coming in fast, so there couldn't have been more than a yard or so of shore left. She ran when I called to her.'

'Would you recognize her again?'

'Almost certainly. I've seen her before.'

Mark waited. She gave her temple a little slap, as though trying to shake a memory loose. 'It won't come,' she said. 'I can't think how I know her. Just that, when she turned round, I knew I wasn't looking at that face for the first time.'

'Worth looking through WADS?'

WADS stood for Witness Album Display System, an online database of mugshots. If the woman she'd seen on the beach had been charged or arrested anywhere in the UK in recent years, her photograph would be stored on the system.

Dana nodded her agreement. 'Huck's worried about you,' she said.

His brow creased. 'Did he tell you?'

She nodded. 'He thinks you need a girlfriend.'

'He's probably right, but you're spoken for.'

Suddenly horribly self-conscious, Dana stepped back. He'd said that a dozen times before. There'd been a time when he'd simply refused to accept that she was gay. Why was it bothering her now, knowing he didn't mean it any more? She risked looking up again. There were lines around his eyes that she hadn't noticed before. And his skin was coarser than it had been fifteen years ago when they'd met. He'd aged, of course, and so had she, it just wasn't a process you really associated with people you were close to.

'It's not easy, is it?' she said. 'Wanting something you can't have.'

His eyes narrowed. 'What is it you want?'

He was her best friend, one of the few people in the world she completely trusted. If she couldn't tell him, whom could she tell?

'I think I want a baby,' she replied, knowing in that instant that she had never properly thought about it before, and also that it was completely and undeniably true.

He leaned back in his chair, increasing the distance between them, and pursed his lips into a long, slow whistle. 'I have a huge amount of time for Helen,' he said. 'But I think she's going to struggle with that one.'

Dana couldn't help the smile, couldn't stop the tears.

'Come here,' he said, holding out his arms. She stepped forward, had felt the brush of his hands on her upper arms when her phone started to ring. She turned to look at it, as though to check it really was a phone and it really was ringing. Well past midnight. A phone call at this hour couldn't be good. She walked over, checked the display screen and turned back to Mark in surprise.

'It's Lacey,' she said.

33

LACEY WAS AT THE LOCK-UP YARD GETTING INCREASINGLY cold. Standing ten yards from the corpse, she could just about make out the waxy pale flesh of a body that had spent weeks in fast-moving water. It was badly damaged, most of the skin and hair gone. Identifying it would be almost impossible without dental records or DNA testing.

By attaching police tape to moored boats and to vans in the yard, Lacey had managed to cordon off the scene. Now she just had to wait.

A flicker of blue lights in the road outside told her that uniform had arrived. After a few seconds a police officer appeared over the gate. He dropped down into the yard and was quickly followed by another. Coat collars tucked up around their ears and hats pulled down, they made their way through the debris towards her.

With the human instinct to sense the presence of law enforcement, someone else was watching the two constables through a hatch on one of the boats.

'Detective Constable Lacey Flint, Southwark.' She held up her warrant card. The taller of the two officers shone a torch on it. When he seemed satisfied, she directed her own torch towards the corpse.

'I got a text about forty minutes ago,' she said. 'It claimed this is the body of Tyler King – you know, the kid who went missing just before Christmas. I came down first myself in case it was a wind-up. Once I'd seen the body, I secured the scene and called the MIT, who are dealing with the case. Somebody should be trying to trace the owner of the yard, get those gates opened.'

'We'll just have a look,' said one of the men, stepping past her. His mate looked as though he was about to follow.

'By all means check you're happy with how I've secured the site.' Lacey raised her voice to stop them in their tracks. 'But there could be prints and other trace evidence. You don't want to risk disturbing the scene.'

'What's going on?'

Two people had appeared now on the deck of the nearest boat.

'We're from the police,' Lacey called back. 'Do either of you have a key to the gate?' She turned to the two officers. 'Actually, can one of you get back to the gate and make sure no one leaves the site? People might start trying to slip away once they realize what's going on.'

Neither looked happy at being given orders by a young female, but an unspoken message passed between them and one of them set off back towards the gate, accompanied by a bloke from the boat.

'So you think it's him,' said the other, in a low voice. 'The one whose body wasn't found?'

'The decomposition's pretty bad,' said Lacey, 'but it certainly looks about the right size.'

'Not good for the parents,' said the constable. 'I suppose there's always hope, until the body's found.'

A few minutes later, the gate to the yard opened and more uniformed officers made their way towards them. Lacey could see equipment being unloaded from a large white van. SOCOs had arrived. Then a man in his fifties whom she thought she recognized as one of the police doctors.

'This your guv'nor?' asked the uniform, indicating the slender, dark-haired woman who was making her way towards them. A taller, broader figure was following her like a shadow.

'That's her,' agreed Lacey, looking at the man whose eyes had already found hers over Dana Tulloch's shoulder.

169

Tulloch didn't waste time with social niceties. 'Let me see the text,' she told Lacey. Lacey held out her phone.

'I'll be keeping this,' said Tulloch, a second after she'd read the message.

'Didn't expect anything less,' said Lacey, catching Joesbury's eye again. She thought she saw a softening, a second before he looked up and past her towards where the doctor was crouching over the corpse. His eyes narrowed and then he looked back down at her again.

'You OK?' he asked. She nodded.

'Why you, Lacey?' Tulloch was closer than felt comfortable, looking her full in the face.

Bloody good question. 'I don't follow, Ma'am.'

'Why did you get the text? I can't believe you have no idea who sent it.'

In fairness, she hadn't said that. She'd said she didn't recognize the number.

'I tried calling the number back,' said Lacey. 'No answer. I didn't stop to think, I just came here to make sure it wasn't some sort of joke. I called you the minute I knew it wasn't, and uniform a second later.'

'I'm not having this again. I'm not having some twisted sicko using you as his channel into a major investigation.'

Joesbury gave a heavy sigh. 'Dana, how likely is that, and what the hell could she do about it anyway?'

Tulloch turned on him. 'So you're comfortable with the fact that, yet again, we have a killer fixating on Lacey? That seems perfectly normal to you?'

'We don't know the killer sent the text. We just know it was someone who knew the body was here. Far more likely it was someone who didn't want to get involved in the investigation.'

Well, this was a bit of role reversal going on. The last time Lacey had worked with these two, it had been Joesbury on her case all the time, and Tulloch her defending champion.

'Lots of people have my number,' Lacey lied. 'And it's not difficult to find mobile phone numbers.'

Tulloch glared, but Lacey was saved from whatever response she might have made by the doctor arriving back.

170

'I can confirm he's dead, if that's any help,' he said.

'Oh, for God's sake, when are you lot going to realize how tired that joke is? I doubt it was even funny the first time.'

'Dana,' Joesbury warned.

'This is a child we're talking about.'

No one spoke.

'Is it?' Tulloch asked the doctor. 'Is it a child?'

He nodded. 'On first sight, it appears to be a pre-adolescent child, of a similar age to Tyler King, and could well have been in the water for the eight weeks he's been missing. We're not looking for any other missing children, are we?'

'Not to my knowledge,' said Dana. 'Can you tell how he died?'

'No evidence of a throat wound at first glance, but . . .'

Joesbury took Lacey's arm and gently pulled her away. 'Give her a few minutes,' he murmured. 'She's been off on one since you rang.'

Lacey couldn't resist looking at her watch. Just gone one. Joesbury and Tulloch had been together when she'd made her phone call. Stupid, that that should have the power to hurt.

'Sorry I missed you last night,' he said. 'Trevor told me you popped in. And then out again very quickly.'

Was there any point trying to pretend she hadn't seen him? Probably not. He'd know she was lying and then she'd look stupid as well as furtive.

'Was that your son?' she asked.

'No, just some random nine-year-old I invited out for dinner.'

Lacey stopped walking. 'In the circumstances, that's not remotely funny,' she said.

Joesbury stopped, too, and turned to face her. 'Yes, that was my son. His name is Huck. And I apologize for sounding crass, but Dana isn't the only one who finds you difficult to deal with at times.'

'Why?'

'Why do I find you difficult? Christ, Flint, where would I start?'

'Why is your son called Huck? I don't think I've ever heard that before.'

'It's short for Huckleberry. His mother is a big fan of American classic literature and Mark Twain in particular. I spent most of the pregnancy arguing for Tom. You know, Tom Sawyer?'

'Easily the more engaging of the two characters, in my view, but I quite like the name Huck.'

'It's a bloody ball and chain for the poor kid. Half the kids at school mispronounce it and call him Hook, the other half call him – well, I'm sure you can imagine.'

She could, and if Huck was anything like his dad, she could also imagine he wouldn't have much trouble dealing with playground shit.

Tulloch had approached again. 'Lacey, did you pull the body out of the river?'

Lacey told herself to chill. She was entitled to be pissed off about that. Just not to let it show too much.

'No, Detective Inspector,' she said. 'Had the body been in the water and had I thought there was a danger of its being lost, I'd have made efforts to secure it in some way. And I would have told you the minute you got here. The body was lying face-down on the bank when I arrived and I merely secured the scene, not touching it in any way.'

'So who the hell did pull it out?'

Lacey had never seen Tulloch like this before. It was unnerving. She was used to the DI being on her side. 'I imagine the same person who texted me, but that's mere supposition on my part, Ma'am.'

'Regardless of who pulled it out, it almost certainly went in here,' said Joesbury. 'The chances of a body thrown in the Thames getting washed up here are slim. The flow of the river just doesn't allow it.'

'So now we've got two bodies dumped along the Creek, followed by three along the Thames,' said Tulloch.

'Maybe there's no connection with the other murders. Maybe Tyler wobbled on his bike and fell in,' suggested the doctor.

'Want me to talk to Uncle Fred?' offered Joesbury. 'If he's not on duty, I'll phone him at home tomorrow. I'm pretty certain I'm right about river flows, but it'd be good to have his view.'

'Yeah, that can't hurt,' replied Tulloch. 'Right, can you drive Lacey's car to the station? I want to talk to her.'

'He's not insured to drive my car,' Lacey pointed out.

'Flint, SO 10 will indemnify him for any bloody car he gets behind the wheel of. He can drive it back now or you can collect it in the morning, which will it be?

Lacey handed her keys to Joesbury. He let his left eye close in a humourless wink and walked away.

34

'IS THIS THE FIRST TIME SOMEONE'S TRIED TO INVOLVE YOU IN this investigation?' Dana stared at Lacey, pale and stony-faced, across the interview-room desk.

'Detective Inspector Joesbury has encouraged me to come back to work so that I can join your team, but, other than that, yes.'

Was that intended to wind her up, that little dig about Mark, Dana wondered. And how come it was working? A couple of months ago, it would have amused her. 'How much do you know about the case?' she asked.

'Only what I've heard on the news or read in the papers. To be honest, I've been avoiding it. I'm finding violent crime a little difficult to deal with right now.'

'Another coffee, Lacey?' said Anderson.

As Lacey shook her head, Dana wondered if she'd made a mistake bringing Neil in on the interview. For one thing, men always had a thing about Lacey Flint. For another, he was just too damn reasonable at times.

'One thing I should tell you is that I went to Durham prison today.' Lacey glanced at the clock behind Dana's head. 'Yesterday,' she corrected.

'Again?' said Anderson, before he could stop himself.

Lacey showed no sign of having heard him. 'People in prison hear things. It's not impossible that text had its origins there.'

Dana thought about it. 'Not impossible,' she agreed. 'Just highly unlikely. Prison inmates do not have access to mobile phones, for one thing.'

'Where there's a will,' said Anderson. 'I can have someone follow it up in the morning.'

'I hear you go out a lot at night, Lacey,' said Dana. 'Where do you go?'

'I walk,' said Lacey, with that cold glint in her eyes that Dana had always, secretly, been rather afraid of.

'Where? Where do you walk?'

'Along the embankment, usually. I'm fond of the river.'

'The South Bank?'

'Both. I usually do a circular walk.'

'Not really the time of year for walking along the river.'

'I dress for it.'

'Do you walk alone?'

'Always.'

'Where were you last Thursday evening between 7.30pm and 9 o'clock?'

Hazel-blue eyes narrowed. 'Are you serious?'

Impossible to back down now. 'Perfectly.'

'Last Thursday evening I was out walking.'

'By the river?'

'Yes, for a while, I cut back through Vauxhall.'

'Anyone see you?'

Lacey let a slow, cold smile spread over her face. Her lips didn't part, her teeth remained hidden. 'Actually, yes,' she said. 'Some kids at my local community centre. One of them lives next door to me.'

'We may need to talk to him.'

'He'll be thrilled. He's following the case very closely.'

'Did you know Tyler King?'

'No.'

'Ryan Jackson? Noah Moore? Jason and Joshua Barlow?'

As each name was put to her, Lacey shook her head, slowly and deliberately. Jesus, Dana thought. Now she could see exactly what had been getting Mark so wound up last year, when he'd repeatedly insisted Flint had known more than she was letting on. There was something about this woman that was cold.

On the other hand, she really had to take it easy or Weaver would be on her case again.

'Lacey.' Dana made herself lean forward against the desk, closer to the other woman. 'What you went through in Cambridge earlier this year would have been difficult for anyone to deal with.'

Flint placed one hand on top of the other and tilted her chin upwards. Dana had to admit that for a girl who'd dragged herself up from nothing, she had incredible poise.

'And coming as quickly as it did on top of the Ripper case – well, I can't imagine what's going on inside your head right now.'

I'll bet you can't, said the look in those eyes.

'We can help, you know. We're on your side.'

Two perfectly shaped eyebrows lifted.

Dana waited, gave her time. Flint didn't look away. Dana felt her own eyes start to smart.

'Interview terminated at zero one fifty hours,' she said. 'Thank you for your cooperation, DC Flint. We'll be in touch.'

Flint got to her feet and took her jacket from the back of the chair. For a second, her face softened as she looked at Anderson. 'Good night, Sarge,' she said, before turning and leaving the room. Even after the door had closed and her footsteps had faded, her presence seemed to hover in the room like the faintest trace of a perfume.

'Boss, you're not serious? Lacey?'

Dana let out a breath. She had no idea why she'd just given Flint such a hard time.

'I know you think we're looking for a woman, and I'm happy to run with it, it makes some sense, but for the love of—'

'You know her background, Neil. Abuse, foster-homes, drug addiction. She has a close and ongoing relationship with one of the most vicious killers I've ever come across. You heard her, she was there again today. The heroine detective, best mates with the serial killer she helped to put away. It's a sick joke.'

'Well, I grant you her visits to Durham aren't the wisest—'

'And that's before what she went through in Cambridge. I told

Mark she wasn't ready for an operation like that, but who listens to me?'

'She's one of us.'

'That woman is damaged goods. And she will never be part of a team.'

Silence that spoke volumes.

'I want a warrant to search her flat,' said Dana.

'No.'

Dana turned and looked at Anderson for the first time since Lacey had left the room. 'Excuse me?'

'You've no grounds. You'll never get one, and if by some fluke of luck you do, we'll lose her for ever. I won't be part of that – no disrespect, Boss.'

'You'll do what you're bloody well told.'

Silence again. Suddenly, it was all too much. Dana slumped forward, dropped her head into her hands. For a second or two she felt the heavy load of Anderson's judgemental stare. Then fingers dropped lightly on her shoulder.

'Five dead kids, Boss. It's getting to all of us.'

That was for sure. So why was she the only one sinking?

'It's important, the fact that the body showed up in Deptford Creek,' Richmond told the assembled team. 'If this was our killer's first victim – and, pending the post-mortem report, let's assume so – he hadn't yet established a pattern. The careful arrangement on exactly the right spot of the riverbank, the showing off, hadn't kicked in. He was still finding his way.'

'He could just have got the tides wrong,' suggested Barrett.

'Even if it was just carelessness, it's still significant. He hasn't made the same mistake since. He's upped his game, established a pattern that he's comfortable with.'

'Mark Joesbury was with me at the scene tonight,' said Dana. 'He said it isn't possible for a body entering the Thames to get swept up that stretch of the Creek. Mark knows the rivers well. His grandfather worked for the Marine Unit, his uncle still does.'

Richmond nodded. 'You should definitely check that out. The first victim will always point you to the killer's location. Tyler didn't live anywhere near Deptford Creek, so if he was dumped there, he was probably killed very near by. That's where you need to concentrate your search.

It made sense. On the other hand, Tower Bridge was some distance from Deptford Creek. Was the killer travelling further to dump the bodies? Or was he killing them somewhere new?

'The other significant part of the night's events is that someone pulled Tyler's body out of the river. He didn't jump. Someone could have spotted him, pulled him out and called your colleague, DC Flint, anonymously, but that seems unlikely. Even someone not wanting to get involved could have phoned the police from a call box. I'd say it's more likely that the killer knew Tyler's body was trapped somehow in the Creek, decided the time had come for him to be found and that Lacey should be the conduit.'

Dana waited for someone else on the team to question the co-incidence of Lacey Flint once again being pulled into a serious murder investigation.

'Any thoughts on why Lacey should be the one singled out?' she asked, when it was clear no one else was going to.

'She was involved in a very high-profile case a few months ago,' said Richmond. 'She's also a beautiful young woman. She's going to attract attention.'

'Both true,' said Anderson. 'But Lacey has always gone out of her way to avoid publicity. She didn't do a single interview after the Ripper case. Personally, I'd put money on her prison contacts being responsible for the text.'

The door to the incident room opened and Stenning came in. When she and Anderson had returned to the station, Dana had left him in charge of talking to the residents of the string of houseboats.

'How did you get on, Pete?' she asked him.

'There are twelve residential boats along that arm of the Creek,' said Stenning, perching on the back of a desk and stifling a yawn. 'All owner-occupied. Five of the owners were at home all evening, one couple arrived back shortly after midnight, two families are away for the weekend and one boat hasn't been lived in since its previous owner died.' Stenning stopped to check his notebook. 'New owner is his son-in-law, a Stewart Roberts,' he went on. 'But he isn't seen from one month to the next. I've got names for the other three owners, but no sign of them tonight. There are also about half a dozen vans in the yard and a couple of Portakabins. The site's secured for now, we can do a proper search in daylight.'

'Anyone you speak to see anything?'

Stenning shook his head. 'One chap heard movement in the yard and saw some dark shapes, but he admits himself his eyesight is pretty bad. He yelled and they scarpered. He had a feeling it was kids.'

'What time?'

'Ten-thirty. Over two hours before we got there.'

'Kids would explain all the smallish footprints we found on a couple of the boats,' said Dana. 'I can see kids spotting something in the water and pulling it out before they realized what it was. What I find harder to understand is why they didn't let someone know immediately.'

The door opened again and the desk sergeant peered in.

'Sorry, Ma'am, but Tyler King's parents are downstairs. And a handful of journalists. They've heard we found a body tonight.'

'How the hell?' Dana began.

'Ma'am, it's on Facebook,' said Mizon, who'd been at her computer for the last hour. 'Peter Sweep posted three minutes ago. Shit, there's a photograph.'

'What?' Dana was on her feet. She reached Mizon's terminal first, the rest crowded round her as they read Peter Sweep's latest post.

Badly decomposed body of Tyler King pulled out of Deptford Creek at 10.30 this evening. Slightly damp. Who said he would never be found? Never is an awfully long time and murder will out. Even mine.

A second later the relief sent a tremble through her. 'That's not our corpse,' she said. 'That's not even Deptford Creek. This sick bastard found a picture on the internet and posted it for effect. I tell you one thing, when we find this Peter Sweep, whether he's involved or not, I'm going to throw the book at him.'

'Ma'am!' She'd forgotten the desk sergeant. Forgotten Tyler

King's parents waiting downstairs, wondering if their long ordeal of not knowing was finally at an end, hoping and dreading, in equal measures.

'I'm coming,' she said.

35

Sunday 17 February

'MUMMY'S GOING AWAY FOR A LITTLE WHILE, BARNEY, JUST until she gets better.'

Barney realized he was sitting bolt upright on the sitting-room sofa. Wrong, wrong, wrong. Were the others still here? No, the house was dark and silent, he was alone. He had a vague recollection of them leaving, and then nothing. Had he fallen asleep? Impossible, surely, with all this mess. It had happened again.

He jumped up, saw the mugs stained with the remains of hot chocolate, the KitKat wrappers, the cushions scattered about the floor. All wrong. Not sure what to do first, he bent for the chocolate wrappers and stopped.

Until she gets better.

Had he just made that up? Or was that the second half of the memory, which for some reason had remained hidden until now? His dad's voice telling him that Mummy was going away for a while was one of his earliest memories. How come, until now, he'd only remembered half?

He'd think better when the room was tidy, he always did. He dropped the chocolate wrappers and gathered up the cushions. Two red, two gold, on each of the three sofas, arranged neatly in pairs, that was how it was done. He stood up and, for less than a second, caught another glimpse in the large wall mirror of the boy who wasn't him. The boy who was smaller, and thinner, and who smiled an odd, knowing smile. He stared and the reflection became Barney again. Sad, worried, tired, and far too pale, but definitely him.

Had his mum been ill? Was she, even now, in hospital somewhere? If so, she wouldn't have seen any of his ads. Why was he only remembering this now?

A key was being turned in the lock. Barney remembered, in a split second, that his dad thought he was on a sleepover. No time to hide. He'd have to say he'd felt ill and come home. Jorge and one of the others had walked with him. How to explain being in the sitting room in the middle of the night was another matter.

His dad had closed and locked the door and walked the length of the hall to the kitchen. Barney heard the sound of keys being dropped on to the table, of a tap being run. Then lights switched off. His dad was going upstairs. Movement in the room above, the toilet being flushed, the electric toothbrush, the bed creaking. Then nothing.

Why had his dad been at the boat? Why had he suddenly got so careful about the keys? And why had he lied, why had he claimed to be home when he plainly wasn't?

Barney carried the mugs and the chocolate wrappers into the kitchen. He wouldn't be able to wash them until morning but at least he'd know the living room was tidy. He put the wrappers in the bin and left the mugs on top of the washing machine.

The striped sheets he'd seen in the washing machine, they belonged on the boat. Suddenly Barney was sure of it.

Barney left the kitchen. He climbed the steps slowly and carefully, knowing exactly where to stand to avoid making a sound. On the first-floor landing he paused. The door to his dad's study was open. His coat hung on the back of the door.

Why did his dad have a child's glove in his pocket?

36

EVERYTHING INSIDE HER WAS WRONG. INTERNAL ORGANS swelling, skin tightening, bones pressing closer together. Lacey's body just didn't seem to fit any more. Working parts she never normally gave a second's thought to, systems she took totally for granted, were jarring and clashing like badly made clockwork.

Concentrate. She had to get down the steps without falling. God knows how she'd managed to drive home without killing someone. Maybe she hadn't. Lacey realized she had no recollection of leaving Lewisham police station, of finding her car where Joesbury had left it, of driving across town to her flat. Maybe the screech of brakes on wet tarmac, the glance of terror, the thud of metal against flesh had just slipped her memory. She'd had black-outs once before, years ago, when long hours just slipped from her consciousness. Maybe they were happening again. Maybe there was someone bleeding on the roadside somewhere and it was all her fault.

The ache in her chest was spreading outwards, making her stomach cramp. She was at her front door, with no idea how long it had taken her to get down the steps. She had to go in, and yet the cold air and the rain on her face felt like the only things keeping her together. Noise above. Footsteps. She'd be seen.

Inside her flat, Lacey found herself searching her pockets for her phone, before remembering that Tulloch still had it. And who would she call anyway? Tulloch genuinely seemed to think she might have killed that boy, killed all of them. Hey, maybe she should confess – it wasn't as though she had any plans for the rest of her life. Would prison really be any worse than what she was going through right now? They'd probably send her to Durham. At least then she'd have someone to talk to.

Lacey realized she was laughing. Too loudly. She had to stop, she'd wake the people upstairs.

But it was impossible to stop, even with both hands clamped to her mouth, and now the laugh was turning into a scream. She felt it, behind her hands, a steady, building pressure, like cheap fizzy wine pushing at a cork; she had to let it go, no one could keep this much pain inside them and not howl out loud.

The kitchen drawer slid open, smooth and silent. The knives looked very clean. Lacey's fingers touched the one that was sharpest and she ran the edge of the blade along the length of the scar on her wrist.

The easiest thing in the world. She watched white skin fall apart like fresh snow before a plough. The pain was like an electric current, starting in her wrist and speeding out to every part of her. It was like energy. The blood appeared in tiny, perfect droplets that stretched and met, forming a single scarlet line.

She raised her hand, let the blood flow snake-like down her arm, bent her head and stretched out her tongue. Warm, salty, metallic.

The scream had gone from Lacey's head. In its place was a soft, ivory light.

37

'SOME OF THE BOYS DIDN'T DIE RIGHT AWAY, DID YOU KNOW that?'

The psychiatrist opened her mouth to speak.

'You'd think if your throat was cut, right the way across from one ear to the other, you'd think you'd die pretty much straight away, wouldn't you?' continued the patient.

'Even with very severe injuries, it can take a while for the body to shut down,' said the psychiatrist.

'There was this one kid I remember, his whole body was shivering. I suppose he was scared. He was, like, shaking with fear. I suppose I would have been.'

'More likely his body was going into shock. Loss of blood and lack of oxygen getting to the main organs will send someone into shock. Seizures are quite a common symptom.'

'He was looking at me while he was dying. Never took his eyes off me, all the time he was shaking and pissing himself. I'll never forget that, the way he looked at me.'

PART TWO

38

Sunday 17 February

'SOMEONE KNOWS THIS KILLER,' SAID THE DARK-SKINNED detective. 'He has friends, he goes home at night, he talks to his family. Someone knows who he is.'

By eight-thirty in the morning, Barney had already been up for two hours and it had felt safe to turn the TV on. The news on all channels was covering the discovery last night of the dead body of a young boy. It hadn't officially been confirmed as that of Tyler King, the first of the Twilight Killer's five victims, but no one really had any doubt.

'We believe he lives or works in south London,' the detective, Dana Tulloch, continued. 'We believe he doesn't live alone and that he has some good reason for being out of the house on Tuesday and Thursday evenings. That's when the boys disappear and their bodies are found.'

Tuesdays and Thursdays – what he'd spotted days ago. Barney heard noise on the floor above him. His dad was moving around.

'He doesn't look like a monster. He persuaded five sensible, street-wise boys to leave their homes and go with him. He'll be convincing, plausible. He'll look normal.'

Footsteps coming down the stairs.

Almond-shaped eyes, oddly pale against the detective's skin and hair, seemed to be looking directly at Barney. 'It isn't easy to betray someone you know and trust, maybe someone you love, but if you are protecting this killer, you are doing him no favours because he will carry on killing until he's stopped. If you know something, anything at all, please help us to stop him.'

The picture on the screen switched to a shot of Deptford Creek. Barney could see the yard, the line of boats, the ring of police tape around where the body had lain. The reporter was talking to another detective, a young man with dark, curly hair. Behind Barney, the kitchen door opened.

'Whoever found the body last night contacted the police anonymously,' the detective was saying. 'Whilst we appreciate their efforts to let us know immediately, we do need to ask them some further questions. If you were anywhere near this yard last night, please contact Lewisham police station as soon as you can.'

'Morning, Barney.'

His dad looked tired, a bit more crumpled around the edges of his face than normal. 'I see they found him.' He was looking over Barney's head at the TV screen, at footage taken the night before of a large black bag being carried out of the yard. 'Poor kid.'

'Isn't that where Granddad's boat is?' said Barney, watching his father's face carefully.

His dad screwed up his eyes, stepped closer to the screen. 'Looks like it,' he said after a moment. 'Was he found at Theatre Arm Marina?'

'That's what they said,' said Barney. 'Must have been just by Granddad's boat.'

His dad scratched the back of his neck. 'Well, it's a big area. All the same, we should pop down there soon, make sure it's alright. Maybe when all the fuss has died down.'

Apparently losing interest in the TV, his dad opened the dishwasher to find it empty. Barney had already washed all the cocoa mugs by hand and put them away. The KitKat wrappers were in the outside bin and the sitting room looked as if no one had been near it.

'Why are you back so early?'

Barney shrugged. 'We all woke up early,' he said. 'I didn't really want to hang around.'

'Bit messy, was it?' teased his dad. 'Dirty socks on the carpet?'

'Something like that,' admitted Barney, wondering if he found lying so easy because his dad did. Maybe it was a genetic thing.

'Make sure you marry a tidy woman, son, or neither of you will have any peace.'

Like you did, Barney wanted to say. His mum had been tidy. *Is that a genetic thing, too? Did I get my tidiness from Mum and my ability to lie from you?* He couldn't say it out loud. Mentioning Mum was a taboo he couldn't possibly break. Even now.

'Are we going to watch the rugby this morning?' his dad asked him.

The others from last night would be at the rugby. He could check none of them were having jitters. Reassure them they'd got away with it. The body had been found and no one suspected they'd been involved. It was all fine.

Barney ran upstairs. He just had time to check Facebook before he went. He found his jacket, hat, scarf and gloves while he waited for the system to boot up. He logged on to Facebook and went to the Missing Boys page.

Christ, everyone on the planet had been on the site this morning, he'd never have time to read through it all. Barney started scrolling down. The usual messages of sympathy, expressions of outrage, taunts from the sickos. Barney kept going, looking for the earliest time the news about Tyler's body could have been broadcast.

Shortly after midnight, the boy calling himself Peter Sweep had posted.

Badly decomposed body of Tyler King pulled out of Deptford Creek at 10.30 this evening. Slightly damp. Who said he would never be found? Never is an awfully long time, and murder will out. Even mine.

Peter had finally admitted that he was the killer.

39

'NO, SORRY. I THINK HER FACE WAS THINNER. THE SORT of face that would be pretty, if it had a bit more flesh on it.'

'Like this?'

Dana leaned back on her chair. Her eyes were getting sore from spending too long staring at one image on a computer screen. The image of a Caucasian woman, in her late thirties to early forties. 'Yeah, that's better. But shorter. A smaller face.'

The image on the screen compressed.

'Bigger eyes. There was something a bit elfin about her. Yeah, that's getting closer.'

'How's the mouth?'

The mouth was unsmiling, medium in size, full lips with a good natural colour.

'You know what? I think that's as close as we're going to get,' she said. 'Can you run a check? See if there's anything on the system.'

'No worries. You expecting her to have a police record?'

Dana thought about it for a second. 'I won't be at all surprised,' she said. 'I've definitely seen her before.'

40

WHEN BARNEY AND HIS DAD ARRIVED AT THE RUGBY club, the Chiswick Crusaders were leading ten points to five against the Lambeth Lions. The wind was rough, stirring up hair and scarves and tempers. Barney took in the field, and knew it was a game without the usual rhythm and grace, a game of irritable break-outs, subdued tension and an undercurrent of violence.

He spotted Sam and Lloyd standing with their dads, some way apart as they'd agreed, and Jorge, Harvey and Hatty, who seemed to have come without adults. Also Huck Joesbury, next to a tall woman with long blonde hair. On the other side of the pitch Mr and Mrs Green stood together. Mrs Green spotted them and gave Barney a wave.

As Barney and his dad approached the touchline, Chiswick were in possession and on the attack. A slick back-row move saw Chiswick's number 8 slip the ball to one of the two flankers, who threw a long pass to the other. The second flanker, Barney realized, was Huck's dad. Joesbury senior accelerated forward from the touchline, sidestepped a tackle, reached the try line and dived over. The Chiswick supporters cheered and Huck jumped in the air, both fists raised above his head.

Jorge, Hatty and Harvey were making their way towards Barney. Both Sam and Lloyd slipped away from the adults too.

'Won't be a sec,' Barney announced, stepping away from his dad. Together the boys and Hatty walked down the touchline until they knew they couldn't be overheard.

'Anybody have any trouble?' asked Jorge. One by one the children shook their heads.

'Our mum nearly rang yours, Lloyd, to thank her this morning,' said Harvey, 'but Jorge told her the whole family would be at church.'

'What's church?' said Lloyd.

'I still think we should say something,' said Sam. 'They're bound to find out we were at the Creek.'

'They won't,' said Barney. 'No one saw us, and even if they did, they just saw a bunch of kids. There are thousands of kids in London. And we left it over an hour before sending that text.'

'Barney's right,' said Jorge. 'There's no reason for anyone to connect a bunch of kids in the yard with the body.'

'Is it definitely Tyler?' asked Hatty.

'They haven't said for certain yet,' said Barney. 'They need to do the post-mortem first, but everyone's assuming it is.'

'I still think we should say something,' said Sam. 'What do you call it? Withholding evidence?'

'We're not withholding anything,' said Jorge. 'We saw the body and we reported it. What else could we tell them?'

'We could tell them it leaped out of the water. That Harvey saw somebody swimming,' said Sam.

'Oh, like they're going to believe that,' said Barney. 'If we start talking about people swimming in the river at night, and dead bodies moving around by themselves, they're going to assume we're lying and we know more than we do.'

'He's right,' said Jorge. 'They can arrest kids our age, you know, keep us all locked up for days. I don't like it much either, but I think Barney's right. We say nothing.'

'What about that bloke on Barney's boat? He could have been the murderer.'

'Don't be stupid,' snapped Barney. 'Tyler was killed weeks ago.'

'He could have been keeping the body on the boat, and gone there on Saturday to dump him.'

Why had Barney never realized before how stupid Sam could be?

'That body had been in the river for weeks,' said Jorge. 'The bloke on the boat was probably just some tramp who fancied a dry bed for the night. Next time you go down there, Barney, suggest to your dad that you might need to change the locks again.'

'I will,' said Barney.

Shouts from the spectators nearby distracted them for a second. Three of the players had gone for the ball at the same time and fallen into a ruck, with each player trying to kick the ball away.

'He's gouging, dirty bastard!'

'Come on, ref! Sin bin!'

One player scrambled up, then the other two. Huck's dad had possession.

'Guys, did anyone check Facebook this morning?' said Harvey. 'Dead freaky. That Peter Sweep bloke was on at midnight, while the police were probably still there, saying Tyler had been found. How would he know that if he isn't the killer?'

'Knowing the body had been found doesn't make him the killer,' said Barney. 'There's no reason why the killer would have been any-where near the Creek last night.'

'Peter Sweep must have been there, though.'

'Probably just got contacts in the police, or the morgue,' said Jorge.

'Morning, lads.'

'Since when am I a lad, Sir?'

'I beg your pardon, Hatty. Good morning to you, too.'

Mr Green, the games teacher, wearing the blue and white hooped stripe of Lambeth Lions, had approached without their noticing. They really had to be more careful. He could have heard anything.

'You not playing, Sir?' asked Harvey.

'I'm going on at half-time.' Mr Green looked from one pale face to the next. 'You lot look a bit bleary eyed. Bit of a late night, was it?'

'Study sleepover, Sir,' said Jorge. 'We were up quite late discussing *War and Peace.*'

Mr Green raised his right foot behind him, grasped it and pulled upwards, stretching the muscles in his right thigh. 'Yeah, and I'd call your bluff on that one if I'd ever read it myself,' he replied, with a wobble and a grin. 'Will I see you older ones at football on Tuesday night?'

'Not me, Sir, because I'm a girl,' said Hatty.

'Girls play football,' said Sam.

'Only butch ones,' Hatty told him.

'You alright, Barney?' Mr Green was looking at him oddly. He realized the conversation had been going on without him. He'd been staring at the ground like a dork.

Barney made himself look back steadily. '*War and Peace*, Sir,' he said. 'It's a very thought-provoking book.'

'See you then.' Mr Green nodded at the group and jogged off along the touchline.

'Shit, she's here!' Harvey dodged behind his elder brother, as if trying not to be seen.

Panic hit the group.

'Who is?'

'Where?'

'Don't look, idiot! The policewoman. The one we sent the text to.'

Barney fixed his gaze on the match and then let his eyes wander to the left. Harvey was right. Lacey Flint was walking towards them along the path from the car park. Her hair, which she normally kept tied back, was flying around her head. She looked like a mermaid. Or a siren.

'Crap, she is too,' said Lloyd. 'She's coming towards us.'

'For God's sake, calm down,' said Jorge. 'And don't look at her. She doesn't know a thing.'

'She must do.'

'She can't prove it,' said Barney, before raising his voice. 'Chiswick are having a go at goal.'

'I'm getting out of here.'

'Don't move,' said Jorge. 'If we leave, it will look suspicious. She's probably not in the slightest bit interested in us.'

'So why's she here?'

'She knows Huck Joesbury's dad,' said Barney. 'She's probably come to watch him play.'

'Which is Huck's dad?'

196

'Number 7, open side flanker. Now will you watch the frigging game?'

The kids on the touchline were watching her approach. Lacey studied each in turn. The smaller boy was edgy and nervous. The girl was bold-faced and defiant, just liked she'd been at that age, but scared underneath it. The young were so bad at hiding their feelings. All except Barney, who, she had to admit, was a pretty cool customer. He'd turned back to watch the match again, she'd almost be convinced if it weren't for the angle of his head. He was watching her. Then the taller of the boys followed his lead, turning his back on Lacey, slinging an arm round Barney's shoulders, saying something a little louder than necessary. Then he laughed. Barney laughed too, as though the two of them had just shared something hilarious.

As Lacey drew close, the girl looked her up and down, sizing up everything she was wearing, and then turned her back, as though she wasn't worth any more interest. Little minx. The younger boys couldn't take their eyes off her. They were like small mammals when a snake gets ready to strike.

Lacey was tempted to make them sweat for a while, but she really needed to talk to Barney this morning, away from his father, and if she wasn't careful, this lot would scarper.

'Lacey!'

She jumped, and turned to see the tall, blonde woman with brown puppy-dog eyes and the skinny, dark-haired child. Detective Chief Superintendent Helen Rowley of the Tayside Police, Dana Tulloch's long-term partner. And not necessarily someone she could count on as a friend any more.

If Helen was aware of the spat of the night before, though, she seemed determined to ignore it. She came up close, put a hand on Lacey's shoulder and kissed her on both cheeks. 'And have you met this little fella?' she asked, looking down at the boy whose head just reached her elbow.

Inexplicably, Lacey felt the same pang of nerves she always experienced when the bigger Joesbury male was close. 'Hello, Huck,' she said. 'I'm Lacey.'

Turquoise eyes met Lacey's for a second. He looked away, shyly. Then he seemed to think of something and looked back up again. It was quite astonishing, their eyes were exactly the same.

'Lacey Flint?' he said.

She nodded, intrigued.

'You're number one in Favourites on my dad's phone,' he informed her.

'I'm honoured,' said Lacey, as Helen suppressed a giggle behind Huck's back.

'So am I,' said a voice behind her. 'Did you see me pole-axe that guy?'

The few visible parts of Joesbury Senior that weren't covered in mud were bathed in sweat.

'I saw you flaying around like an upturned turtle, trying to get back on your feet,' replied Lacey. 'Very impressive.'

'Is Lacey your girlfriend?' Huck asked his dad.

'Only in my dreams,' Joesbury replied, without looking at his son.

'Huck, I think we need bacon butties,' said Helen. 'Why don't you and I go and join the queue?'

Helen and an obviously reluctant Huck moved away towards the clubhouse. The child glanced back several times as they went. Then they were lost in the rush of people. Conscious of his eyes upon her, Lacey turned to see Joesbury watching her.

'You look different,' he told her. 'What's happened?'

'Different good or different bad?'

'Good, I think, although it's hard to know for certain with you.'

'I slept,' said Lacey. 'Which I don't normally – not well, anyway. There's something about being accused of multiple murder that seems to relax me.'

Slept? It was almost an understatement. She'd wound a thin, clean tea-towel around the cut on her wrist and fallen into bed. The next thing she knew it had been nine-thirty in the morning. She hadn't slept like that in years.

'Dana's having a hard time of it right now,' said Joesbury. 'There's stuff you don't know about. She took it out on you, which she shouldn't have done, but we're none of us perfect.'

Except you, she thought. *You look close to perfect to me right now.*

And that adorable child of yours. Two perfect men, who could be mine, if only . . .

'And you do seem to have a knack of attracting trouble.'

Possibly the two saddest words in the English language: *if only.*

'Is she at the post-mortem?' asked Lacey.

Joesbury nodded. 'Just to warn you, she'll be wanting to talk to you again. She can't believe you have no idea who sent that text.'

'She's right. I know exactly who sent it.'

Joesbury looked like she'd slapped him.

'Don't you start as well. I can't prove anything,' she told him.

'Chat in two minutes, Mark,' a large, older bloke who looked like a coach called to him as he jogged past. Joesbury nodded briefly. 'For God's sake, Lacey, don't get yourself involved in anything . . .'

'I need to handle it myself first. It's about trust. And not scaring people. If you tell her I told you, I'll deny it.'

Joesbury looked exasperated. 'What is this? A test? You're trying to find out where my loyalties lie?'

'How devious. I never thought of that. But I guess we will, won't we?'

He shook his head. 'I didn't have you down as manipulative.'

'Liar, I bet there isn't a negative adjective in the English language you haven't applied to me at some point.'

'Dad, do you want a bite of mine? Lacey, we got you one of your own.'

Lacey looked at the ketchup-smeared, soft bread-roll, crammed with bacon, and realized she was genuinely hungry. Another first in a long time. Huck was holding it up to her, expectantly, as though he couldn't imagine anyone turning down a bacon sandwich. His own was more than half eaten. He had ketchup smears around his mouth and a dollop like clown's make-up on his nose. Lacey reached out and wiped the ketchup from his nose with her index finger.

'Huck,' she said, 'if your dad were even half as cute as you, I would definitely be his girlfriend.'

Without thinking, she raised her ketchup-smeared finger to her lips. She was about to open her mouth when she remembered. The sight, the taste, the smell of fresh blood. Nausea washed over her.

She had no right to be here, with these people, who were normal.

'Excuse me,' said Joesbury. 'I need to go and break a few bones.'

'Hi, Barney, enjoying the game?'

Barney turned and looked at Lacey. He saw immediately that she was different. Her face was harder, her eyes colder. She knew. They both did. *So this is what it's like*, he thought, *to have an enemy*. 'Yes, thanks,' he replied. 'Are you?'

Her lips stretched sideways. If a snake could smile, that's what it would look like. 'Oh, I've always been a big rugby fan,' she said. 'Where I come from it's impossible not to be.'

The wind was messing up her hair. It stretched out in his direction, he could almost imagine it wrapping itself around him, pulling him closer, holding on tight.

'Where do you come from?' he asked her, noticing that the others were sidling further away down the touchline. Only Jorge was close enough to be in earshot.

She seemed to think about that for a second, then, 'I was brought up in Shropshire,' she said. 'Very close to the Welsh border. We knew a lot of Welsh people. The Welsh live and breathe rugby.'

'My dad likes it,' he said, fixing his attention on the game. 'A few of my mates' dads play. And one of our teachers from school.'

Seemingly tired of hair in her face, Lacey pushed it back behind her head, then twisted it round at the back of her neck into a knot. She stuffed the loose end into the collar of her coat. He'd never seen a woman do that before. 'I got your text,' she said. 'The one you sent me last night.'

Careful now. Barney saw Jorge stiffening. He'd heard her, too. He just had to hope Jorge had the sense to keep quiet.

'I was at a mate's house last night,' said Barney. 'I sent a couple of texts to my dad. Did I send one to you by mistake? Sorry.'

'No, I mean the one about Deptford Creek. About what you saw down there.'

Barney looked Lacey full in the face. He was a good liar, he took after his dad, this would be easy. The hair she'd imprisoned was starting to break free and fly in the wind again, like ribbons, like weed in a rough sea.

'I didn't send any about Deptford Creek,' he replied. 'Maybe it was someone with a similar number.' He pulled his phone out of his pocket, reeled off his number. 'Anything like that?' he asked her.

'I can't check right now,' she said. 'The police have my phone. It may take them a few days, but they will trace who texted me last night. It will be better to own up now.'

She was bluffing, she had to be. It was a pay-as-you-go phone, it couldn't be traced.

'Barney, I heard you all come home. It was obvious something had happened. Ten minutes later, the text arrived. Whatever you were doing down there, however much you think you might be in trouble, I promise you, the police won't be interested. All they care about is making sure they have as much information as possible about what happened there last night.'

Exactly, thought Barney. *If they find out we were there, they'll find out Dad was. Hatty will describe that sweatshirt and then that will be it.*

'Barney, this is a murder inquiry. A multiple-murder inquiry. I'll come with you, but you have to talk to the police.'

No, he was not going to tell the police that his dad had been at the boat. There would be a perfectly good reason, there had to be.

'I'm sorry, Lacey, I don't know what you're talking about.'

41

Monday 18 February

'SUSAN, IT'S DANA TULLOCH.'

'Hi Dana, anything new?'

'Yes, I think so. I've just had a report back from the lab and it's interesting.'

'Hang on, let me grab a pen.'

Dana waited. She'd never been in Susan Richmond's office, could not picture the room where the psychologist was right now. She looked down at the notepad on her desk. She'd written the name PETER SWEEP in a large circle and was drawing faint pencil lines from one letter to another, in the time-honoured way of solving anagrams. So far she'd come up with Peeper Stew, Peep Wester and Weeper Step.

'OK, fire away,' said Richmond.

'The clothes that Jason and Joshua Barlow were found in were sent away, which is perfectly normal procedure,' Dana told her. 'Their father had confirmed they were the clothes the boys were wearing when they went missing, so potentially what we found on them could be important.'

'I guess you're always hoping for the killer's DNA.'

'Goes without saying. There were quite a lot of hairs and fibres on both boys' clothing, but that's perfectly normal for children of this age who've spent the day at school.'

'Makes sense.'

'There was a lot of blood around the necks of the boys' sweaters, but again that's exactly what we would have expected.'

'I guess.'

'There was also blood, or what appeared to be blood, on Jason's trousers. Left leg, just below the knee. When we had the initial report, we assumed it was just spatter.'

She paused, giving the other woman chance to catch up with her notes. 'And now you know it's not?' Richmond asked after a second.

'It's not even blood,' said Dana. 'Or rather, not real blood.'

'What other kinds of blood are there?'

'It's fake blood,' said Dana, looking at the picture she'd found on the internet. 'The sort you buy in bottles in joke shops. Or theatrical make-up suppliers. You even see it in supermarkets around Hallowe'en. It's actually pretty realistic. Sort of gloopy and shiny and just the right dark-crimson colour.'

'Fake blood?'

'Which the boys didn't have, according to their parents. And which the school tell me would definitely not be allowed on school premises.'

'So you're thinking it came from the killer?'

'Do you remember Sergeant Anderson suggesting our killer might be doing a Ted Bundy? He may have been closer than he knew. Ted Bundy pretended to have a broken arm. What if our guy appears to be badly hurt? What if he's clutching a bleeding wound, maybe asks the child to phone for help for him.'

Silence, whilst Richmond thought about it. 'A lot of children would find that scenario very frightening in itself. A strange man, dripping with blood.'

'Yes, they would,' agreed Dana. But if it were a woman who appeared badly hurt?

'Do you think there could be a woman out there called Pet Sweeper?' she went on.

'Sorry?'

'Oh, nothing. It just occurred to me Peter Sweep might be an anagram of the killer's real name. Not working though, too many Es.'

'Your mystery woman on the beach still a mystery?'

Dana gave up, dropped the pencil and crumpled the paper. 'Completely,' she said. 'No matches even close on the system. Whoever she is, she's not a villain with a police record of any sort. Which is odd, in its way, because I'm not the only one here who thinks she looks familiar.'

'That's interesting,' said Richmond, 'because I showed her picture round the office here, and got no reaction at all. Which would suggest she's not a celebrity or simply someone with one of those common faces. She's someone who just the police are finding familiar. Have you thought about releasing the picture?'

'My boss won't do it without a little more to go on than a sighting under Tower Bridge,' said Dana. 'You have to see his point. She's probably nothing to do with the investigation at all and I'm just wasting time thinking about her.'

'What are you afraid of, Lacey?' asked the counsellor.

Back again, in the torture chamber. It seemed to get smaller and dimmer with every visit. Lacey wondered how the woman coped if she had a claustrophobic patient to deal with.

'Do I strike you as a fearful person?' replied Lacey, who'd learned long ago that if you asked lots of questions in these sessions, there was always less time to give away the important stuff.

'We're all afraid of something,' said the counsellor, who was wearing a darker shade of grey than usual this afternoon. It made her face less pink, her hair more silver. 'Given your recent history, one might expect you to be more fearful than most. You've experienced a very dark side of life. It's bound to have an impact.'

'Yes,' said Lacey. 'You would expect so, wouldn't you?'

'Have you hurt your wrist?'

'What?' Lacey tugged the sleeves of her sweatshirt, bringing the edge of the cuff close to her knuckles.

'You've been rubbing it a lot,' said the counsellor. 'I just wondered if you'd sprained it, with all the weights you lift.'

'I did,' said Lacey, trying not to show relief. 'But it was boxing, not weights. I hit the bag badly. Nothing serious.' Of course, thought Lacey, were she to admit to deliberately cutting herself, taking a knife to her own vein, then running her tongue along the thin, red line, letting the sharp-tasting liquid wash around her mouth, it would be game over. She'd never be signed fit for work again. Especially when she confessed that the need to do it a second time was building.

'I've been wondering how much of this need to get your body to maximum fitness is actually about fear,' said the counsellor. 'Subconsciously, your mind is telling you that the stronger and fitter you are, the more able you'll be to fend off the next attack. Because I think, deep inside, you're afraid of the next attack.'

Sometimes this woman was verging on smart. And sometimes she was completely clueless. Lacey pulled her arms around her body to make herself look vulnerable, and to keep her fingers from worrying at the sore on her wrist.

'Are you still planning to leave the police?' asked the counsellor, after a moment.

Lacey nodded. 'After the Cambridge trial,' she said. 'How much of what we discuss here do you pass back to my superiors?'

The counsellor looked shocked. 'None of it,' she said. 'These sessions aren't about your fitness to do your job, I thought I'd made that clear when we started. They're to help you deal with what you went through in Cambridge. And last year.'

'Yes, you did say that. Sorry, I wasn't thinking.'

'Are you afraid of what people think of you?'

Bless her, she had no idea.

'I'm not scared,' she said, in a small voice.

'I'm sorry, I didn't catch that.'

'I'm not scared,' Lacey went on, speaking louder now. 'I can't feel fear any more. I sometimes wish I could.' She leaned forward, closer to the counsellor. 'I test myself, I go out walking after dark, around some of the roughest parts of London. I walk through deserted open spaces, even along the riverbank at low tide. All the places where women alone are supposed to be at their most vulnerable. Where sensible women wouldn't dream of going.'

'You think you've lived through the worst, what else can there possibly be?' asked the counsellor.

'In a way, but I think it's worse than that.'

'What can be worse than that?'

Lacey thought about Tulloch's eyes upon her in the interview room, about the way Sergeant Anderson, DC Stenning and all her other former colleagues couldn't quite look at her. She thought about Barney and his mates at the rugby yesterday, terrified and fascinated in equal measure.

'I've become what other people are scared of,' she said. 'I'm the thing they fear.'

'I won't keep you long, Sir. I just want to ask you a few questions about the boat you keep at Deptford Creek.'

The detective was tall with dark, curly hair and a friendly, open face. On the doorstep, he'd introduced himself as Detective Constable Stenning and Barney's dad, looking wary, had invited him inside.

'You mean my late father-in-law's yacht, I suppose,' said his dad. 'The *Laird of Lorntie*, moored at the Theatre Arm.'

'Yes, that's the one. You do still own it then?'

'I do, yes. I keep meaning to do it up a bit, put it on the market, but somehow never seem to get round to it.'

'Can I ask when you were last there?'

Barney's dad let his head fall to one side, as though he were thinking about it. 'My son has a better memory than I,' he said, after a moment. 'Barney, can you remember when we were last at the boat?'

Barney had been curled up on the sofa in the kitchen, pretending to be absorbed in his DS.

'October,' he sighed, in his best impersonation of a bored teenager. 'Maybe November. We had to clear leaves off the deck.'

'Sounds about right to me,' agreed his dad. 'I can probably get you an exact date if I look through last year's diary. I had a locksmith go earlier this year when the keys went missing, but he made his own way there.'

'What about when you went to dry it out?' added Barney.

Barney's dad tapped his fingers against his temple, the classic *Lord, I'm so forgetful* gesture. 'That's right,' he said. 'The locksmith called to tell me the boat was looking quite damp. Soggy bedsheets and upholstery, that kind of thing. I had to spend a day there drying everything out. I took time off work. Do you want me to check my diary?'

'Shouldn't be necessary,' replied DC Stenning. 'You weren't there on Saturday evening then?'

'I'm afraid not,' replied Barney's dad. 'This will be about the young boy, I suppose? The one we saw on the news.'

'Tyler King,' said DC Stenning. 'We confirmed his identity earlier today. What about your son?'

'I doubt Barney could find his way to Deptford Creek without me,' said his dad. 'He was at a sleepover on Saturday night.'

'And you were . . . ?'

'I was here. For an hour or two I enjoyed the unusual peace and quiet, then I got a bit lonely. I went to bed early.'

God, his dad was good. A singing sound told Barney he'd received a text message. He pulled out his phone. It was from Harvey.

Check out Facebook now!!!

Tricky one. He didn't want to leave his dad while the detective was still in the house. On the other hand, Harvey sounded pretty desperate.

'Dad, can I go upstairs?'

His dad nodded. 'Yes,' he said, looking at the detective. 'That's unless . . .'

'Oh, I'm done,' said DC Stenning. 'Thank you for your time.'

Barney got up, gave DC Stenning a shy smile and left the room. As he climbed the stairs, he heard the two men talking as his dad showed the detective out.

'We'll let you have the keys back as soon as we've completed the search of the marina. Shouldn't be more than a few days?'

'That's fine,' said his dad. 'I've got a spare set. And I really should get there myself before too much longer.'

The door closed, his dad returned to the kitchen and Barney reached his own floor of the house. His computer was on, he was already logged on to Facebook. It took a couple of seconds to open up the Missing Boys page.

Peter Sweep had posted twenty minutes earlier.

Tomorrow, tomorrow, the killer will come out tomorrow. Take care, my pretty pale boys, watch out for Peter.

The comments stream was building rapidly.

Sick bastard.

Pervert. You don't fool anyone.

Sick twat.

Barney had a vision of Peter, sitting at his keyboard, watching the fury unfold and smiling to himself at how easily people could be wound up. They were like fireworks – light the blue touch paper and retire.

His mobile was ringing. It was Harvey. 'Have you seen it?' he said, as soon as Barney answered. 'Sam's just been on the phone,' he went on, when Barney had confirmed that he was looking at the Facebook page that moment. 'He thinks we should get some kids together and patrol the streets tomorrow. You know, safety in numbers.'

'I think they'll all be safer at home,' said Barney.

'That's what Jorge said when I rang him at the theatre. He said the best thing we can do is encourage everyone to go straight home from school and stay indoors till Wednesday morning.'

'I agree with him,' said Barney.

'Yeah, but they're not safe at home, are they? Home is where they're disappearing from. Somehow he's getting into homes. How is he doing that?'

'He knows them,' said Barney, wondering why he hadn't thought of it before. 'When kids go missing, it's nearly aways someone they know. Someone they don't think will hurt them. Like the school caretaker, or the man at the chip shop.' Or the parent of a— No, he wasn't going there!

'So we can't trust anyone?' said Harvey.

'Dad, if you knew who the killer was, would you tell the police?' asked Barney from the doorway of his father's study.

His dad didn't even look up. 'Of course.' He did though, Barney noticed, close down the screen he'd been working on. Barney stepped a little further into the room.

'What if it was someone you cared about?'

Now his dad looked up. 'What do you mean?'

'What if it was me?'

His dad half smiled, then looked nervous. 'Barney, what are you talking about?'

'What if you found out the killer was me? Would you tell the police?'

'Oh you funny kid, come here.'

Barney didn't move, so his dad did, standing up, pushing back his chair and wrapping his arms around his son. Pressed against his dad's chest, smelling the warm, male scent that was possibly his real earliest memory, Barney felt himself relaxing. He was being stupid. There was an explanation, there was always an explanation.

'The answer to your ridiculous question is that I would not give you up to the police, no matter what you'd done, because you are the one thing in my life I absolutely could not live without. Do you believe me?'

'Yes,' said Barney, amazed. Had he really not realized until now that his dad loved him? Really, deeply loved him. The one thing in life he could not live without? You couldn't feel like that about one child and . . . God, he was an idiot. Downstairs, in the kitchen, something pinged.

'And that's dinner,' said his dad. 'Downstairs in five, young man.'

His dad left the room. Barney turned to follow him and had a sudden thought. His dad had left his computer switched on, which he hardly ever did. Twenty minutes ago, maybe a bit longer, Peter Sweep had posted on Facebook. Twenty minutes ago, his dad had been at his computer. Barney could settle it, once and for all. He moved the mouse to the menu bar at the top of the screen and clicked on History. The menu box dropped down and Barney could see the internet sites his dad had visited since he'd got home from work. He stared, read through the list, counted the sites and then closed the box again.

There was an explanation. There was always an explanation.

Barney left the room and made his way slowly downstairs. In the kitchen he could hear cutlery being placed on the table, water being run into glasses. He sat down at the table, thinking that the hardest thing he might ever be asked to do was to put food in his mouth right now. Because if there was an explanation why his dad had spent the entire evening researching Dracula, vampires and blood lust, he really couldn't think what it might be.

42

Tuesday 19 February

AFTER THE FRONT DOOR HAD CLOSED AND HIS DAD'S footsteps faded away down the street, Barney made his way upstairs to put into practice what he'd just learned how to do on the internet. He was planning to conduct a systematic search of his father's bedroom, study and bathroom.

The study would be the hardest, what with all those books and cupboards, so he was starting with the bedroom. Besides, if his dad was hiding anything, it was more likely to be in here. He and his dad respected each other's privacy. They rarely went into each other's bedrooms. He paused on the threshold, pushed open the door and looked in.

He wasn't going to find anything, there was nothing to find, but sometimes you just had to be able to close a door and bolt it. And leave the bolt to rust. He was going to settle it, then he was going to take down all the stuff in his room about the murdered boys and throw it away. He'd become too involved, his imagination was starting to play tricks on him.

He was going to use the grid method. Start in the corner, make his way down the wall, then turn back. He'd search a strip of the room twelve inches wide with each pacing of the room. He was the boy who found four-leaf clovers in meadows that had millions of leaves all the exact same shape and colour. This was going to be easy.

He started walking, letting his eyes lose their focus and the patterns form. Near the head of the bed, he spotted a toe-nail clipping. At its foot he knelt on the carpet and peered beneath. Dust balls. A feather or two. A safety pin and a dry-cleaning label. Something else he didn't immediately recognize. Barney pulled it out and held it up to the light. It looked like something he couldn't remember ever seeing in the house – the pump from a hypodermic syringe.

He sat back on his heels, thinking. There was no reason to have a hypodermic syringe in the house, and plenty of reasons not to. Injections were one of the few things that put the wind up Barney. He couldn't explain it, he understood perfectly that the pain was small and short-lived, it was just the suspense of waiting, of knowing something sharp and insistent was going to puncture his skin.

Forgetting about his carefully planned grid, Barney stood and walked into his father's bathroom. It was a small room, with no natural daylight. Washbasin, shower cubicle, toilet and wall-mounted cabinet. The towels and the shower mat were cobalt blue. The tiles were white with a blue trim. It smelled of antiseptic and spicey old wood and was surprisingly clean and tidy for a room his dad had sole charge of. The cabinet was above the basin, fixed quite high on the wall. It was locked.

Why would anyone lock their bathroom cabinet?

Barney sat on the loo seat to think. Locking your bathroom cabinet was one thing, but keeping the key any distance away was another. Who wanted to hunt down a key every time they cleaned their teeth? It would be in here somewhere. He jumped up on to the loo seat so that he could see on top of the cabinet. Nope. He turned to look at the rim of the door-frame. There it was. Jeez, what sort of moron did his dad think he was?

A second later, the cabinet door was open and Barney stretched up to see inside. Toothpaste, shaving soap, razors, dental floss, ear drops, Clinique for Men aftershave, Night Nurse, headache pills. Syringes. Lots of them in little sterile packs. And six small, plastic, colourless vials of liquid. Barney had never seen them

212

before. He turned the first to read the label properly. Octocog Alfa.

Upstairs at his own computer, Barney typed Octocog Alfa into Google and, a few seconds later, had his answer. Locked in his bathroom cabinet, his dad kept a drug, and the means to administer it, that had a primary purpose of making blood clot.

Barney felt like there was a wild animal in his head. One that was scratching and clawing and tearing, desperate to be out. He couldn't sit still. He couldn't watch television. Reading was impossible. Every few minutes he checked Facebook and the twenty-four-hour news websites. The rest of the time he spent walking the house.

His dad was obsessed with Dracula and all things to do with vampires. How else to explain the endless websites he'd been trawling through on his computer. He kept supplies of a drug that made blood clot. He was out of the house on Tuesdays and Thursdays when the killer struck. He had a boat at Deptford Creek where two bodies had been found, a boat he visited but lied about. Lied to the police as well as to his son. He'd brought sheets home to wash, the same night the Barlow boys had been found beneath Tower Bridge. One of their gloves was, even now, in his coat pocket. Jeez, how much more proof did he want?

The phone was ringing. Barney looked at his watch. His dad had promised to phone every half-hour but he hadn't been gone that long. He didn't want to talk to his dad right now, but if he didn't answer, he'd probably come rushing home.

'Hello?'

'Barney, it's me.' Harvey. 'Nothing's happened yet.'

'It might not happen at all,' said Barney. When his dad phoned, he'd say he was ill. That he had serious stomach cramps. His dad would come straight home then, surely? He'd put Barney first, wouldn't he, before anything else he might have planned for that night? 'You're not out patrolling then?' he asked.

'Jorge told Mum and she said not in a million years was I leaving the house tonight.'

'No. Don't.'

'Yeah, but Jorge gets to go out. He's gone with a couple of his mates to football training. I don't see why he gets to go and I don't.'

'He's older. Whoever's doing this doesn't seem interested in teenagers.'

'That's what he said. I don't see why I couldn't have gone with him.'

'What about Lloyd and Sam?'

'They're both at home too. Makes no bloody sense to me. Every kid that's gone missing has been taken from home. It's like, let's put our children where they're going to be in most danger. Hang on, someone's at the door.'

Christ no, Harvey!

The line went dead. On the Missing Boys page, people were actually taunting Peter now.

Come on then, put your money where your mouth is.

We knew you were all talk, weirdo!

Harvey was back, thank God. 'Sorry, had to let Jorge in. Daft sod twisted his ankle, Mr Green had to bring him home. He's well pissed off. I'd better go. Call me if anything happens.'

Barney put the phone down.

His dad loved him. Barney believed that completely. Could you love one boy and want to kill others? Could you stalk, capture and kill boys who were so similar, in so many ways, to the one you did your best to protect?

Right, he couldn't stand this. He was getting his dad home. He'd phone an ambulance if necessary, fake a burst appendix. By the time they found out he was fine, the danger would be over. It would be too late.

Someone was at the door.

Four loud knocks, the sound of someone determined to get a response. Delivery men always knocked that way. Friends and neighbours gave polite, rhythmic knocks, rat, tat-a-tat, tat. People wanting to sell you something were polite too, but more formal, usually giving four crisp, business-like taps. Delivery men, though, didn't bother with niceties. They had something to deliver, they had a right to attention and they were determined to get it.

Four even louder knocks. Whoever was at the door wasn't messing about. Delivery men didn't come at eight in the evening. Ignore it.

On the other hand, wasn't he safest boy in London right now? What did he have to fear from a stranger on the doorstep?

He wanted to be wrong about that, though. More than anything, he wanted to be wrong.

Enough to want the real killer to be on the doorstep?

Just go and look. There were strong locks on the door. Barney ran down the stairs and to the window of the living room. A tall, thin man was on the doorstep, in a motorcycle helmet with the visor still down. He was staring straight at Barney.

Useless to pull back now, he'd been seen. Barney stared back at the man. His dad's height, but thinner. His face was almost impossible to see but Barney had the impression he was young. He was holding up a thin, square, white box, pushing it towards the window, then pointing at the door. At the kerb was a motorcycle with a large storage box on the back. The box had a familiar name and logo on it.

He was a pizza delivery-man.

Barney went to the hallway and unlocked the door. He opened it the full four inches the chain would allow.

'Pizza for Roberts,' came the muffled voice from behind the visor.

'Sorry, didn't order one,' said Barney. The face behind the visor looked white, surrounded by very dark hair.

A heavy sigh of impatience. 'Your name Roberts?'

'I didn't order a pizza.'

'Well, maybe someone else did, kid. Look, it's been paid for so you might as well have it.'

'My dad's in the shower.'

'Do I look like I care? You having this, or not?'

Take it, it could be a clue. The man had taken off his heavy motorcycling gloves, there would be fingerprints on the box. Barney tentatively stuck his fingers out through the gap, ready to pull back at any time if the man looked as though he were going to grab him.

The man gave another exaggerated sigh. Was this how he did it then? Made the children feel guilty that they were being difficult? 'You have to sign for it,' he said. 'I can't get my machine through that gap.'

There were voices in the street. A mother and two teenagers were walking along the opposite pavement. Witnesses. Nothing could happen while people were so close. Barney slipped the chain off the door and opened it. He took the pizza box, warm under his fingers, and tucked it beneath one arm. The man was holding out a small, rectangular box with a display screen on it. Barney had seen his dad sign them several times. He picked up the pen and scratched his name on the screen.

'Thanks, mate,' said the man, bending down to pick up his gloves. 'Enjoy.'

Barney watched him walk the few yards across the pavement to his bike, check that the box on the back was locked, and then kick it into life. A second later, he was gone.

Pizza? His dad had made supper like he always did. He never ordered food to be delivered unless the two of them were at home together. What if the pizza delivery-man had been the killer, and that was how he got to the boys? Maybe he delivered the pizza and went away again to get their trust, then came back later saying something like he'd delivered the wrong one. OK, first things first, he had to phone his dad and make sure he hadn't ordered it. He found his phone, but a text message came in before he could dial. From Harvey.

Facebook. Now!

'I am knackered, starving and if I drink any more coffee I'll be tap-dancing naked on the ceiling,' complained Tom Barratt from the middle of the incident room. What time can we go home, Sarge?'

'When I say so,' answered Anderson, who'd been trawling his way through the door-to-door statements collected after the Barlow brothers had been found on the South Bank.

Dana looked up from the corner desk where she and Susan Richmond had been re-reading witness statements. 'If nothing's happened by ten o'clock we can assume it's a hoax and call it a night,' she said.

Barratt spun on the spot. 'Sorry, Ma'am, didn't see you there.'

'Don't mention it. I'd still like everyone to be ready for a call-out though. Staying off the booze might not be a bad idea.'

'I can't find anything, Boss,' said Stenning, leaning back in his chair and rubbing his eyes. 'Not a single official news website running with the story.'

'Don't tell me the media have actually had an attack of conscience,' said Dana. 'That will make me start thinking about Twilight Zones.'

'What do you think about this Sweep character, Susan?' asked Anderson. 'Is he our man?'

Richmond shook her head, but in a *who knows?* kind of way. 'There's a lot that doesn't ring true,' she said. 'If you look back at his early posts, there's nothing about vampires until that bright spark Hunt starts talking about Renfield's Syndrome. Now it looks like this Peter's trying to quote the entire novel at us.'

'Jumping on the bandwagon,' said Anderson.

'Exactly. The real killer, to my mind, would be livid we'd misunderstood him. He'd be more likely to be trying to put us right.'

'Or it's a blind alley he's very happy for us to go down,' said Dana. 'Don't killers enjoy feeling the police are stupid?'

'I think it's safe to say he's in a pretty good mood right now,' said Anderson. 'How you getting on, Gayle? Can you give us a status update?'

'Yeah, very funny, Sarge.' Mizon was as pale-faced and sore-eyed as anyone. She'd spent the day monitoring the social media sites but, as she complained, given how quickly they were updated at times it was quite easy to miss something. 'Nothing yet. Except the usual load of nonsense. Uh-oh!'

'What?'

'Peter Sweep has just posted.'

Everyone in the room made their way over to Mizon's terminal. Dana arrived last, determined not to be seen panicking.

Oliver Kennedy will not be going home tonight. Oliver Kennedy is going on an awfully big adventure.

For a moment, no one spoke.

'Could be a wind-up,' said Anderson.

Silence, all eyes fixed on the screen.

'He's never given us a heads up before,' said Stenning.

They waited for the comment thread to build. It was slow. The rest of the world seemed as stunned as they did.

'OK, we need a list of Kennedy families in South London,' said Anderson. 'Pete, you up to that?'

Stenning nodded and sat back down at his desk.

'When you have the list, we're looking for sons aged eight to eleven,' Anderson went on.

'If he really has taken someone, they'll be in touch with us before we can track them down,' said Mizon. 'People won't delay reporting a missing ten-year-old at the moment.'

'Not necessarily,' said Anderson. 'Kids can be missing for some time before they're missed, if you get my drift. Quick as you can, Pete. Tom, give him a hand.'

'Sarge, do you want me to get on to Facebook?' asked Mizon. 'See if we pin him down this time?'

Anderson nodded. 'Has to be worth a try. Tell 'em it's urgent this time.'

'How difficult is it to keep an eye on your kids?' said Dana. 'What is this Oliver Kennedy doing out on his own? Do his parents not love him?'

The door opened. 'Is it true?' Weaver was in the doorway.

'It's true our Peter Sweep friend is claiming he has another victim,' said Richmond. 'Could still be a sick hoax. To be honest, I've been half expecting something like this.'

'No reports of missing children?' asked Weaver.

'None yet,' Anderson told him. 'We've started looking for kids called Oliver Kennedy, but there's going to be a few.'

A phone rang. Barrett answered it. After a few seconds, he hung up and crossed to the TV in the corner.

218

'There's about to be a news bulletin,' he said. 'They're going to interrupt the programming.'

A collective groan murmured around the room. Weaver walked over to the TV screen. Dana stayed where she was.

'Keep going, Pete,' said Anderson. 'We need to find that kid.'

'We interrupt this programme with a news bulletin,' said the presenter, a dark-haired, blandly handsome man in his forties. 'A contributor to the social-media site Facebook, who has, in recent days, claimed to be the Twilight Killer, is believed to have abducted his sixth victim. Scotland Yard press office tell us they have received no reports of missing children yet, so we are appealing to the parents of Oliver Kennedy, believed to be between eight and eleven years old, to get in touch with us by contacting the number below.'

'Good God above,' said Weaver, running a hand over his face.

'They're interfering directly with the investigation,' said Richmond. 'Can they do this?'

'No law to stop them,' said Dana.

'Joining me in the studio is forensic psychologist Dr Bartholomew Hunt,' the presenter continued, as the camera angle widened to show the man sitting further along the desk. 'Dr Hunt, you believe this latest abduction was predictable?'

'Entirely so,' said Hunt. 'Twenty-four hours ago, the killer him-self warned that he would take another victim. In my opinion, the Metropolitan Police have to explain why the families of London weren't warned.'

'Switch that crap off,' said Dana.

'Boss, we need to keep a handle on what's being said,' said Anderson.

'I am not having this investigation hijacked by a bunch of moral delinquents who would probably prefer Oliver Kennedy to be found dead by morning because it will increase their viewing figures. *We* are running this investigation and that's the way it's going to stay. Unless you have a problem with that, Sir?'

Weaver looked troubled but he shook his head. Reluctantly, Mizon switched off the TV and returned to her desk.

'Any luck yet, Pete?' asked Dana.

Stenning was still hunched over his computer. 'Working our way through the list of Kennedys,' he said. 'Found one possibility. Family in Blackheath.'

'Ring them,' said Dana. 'Make sure they know where Oliver is. If they can't see and touch him right this minute, we get local uniform out to them.'

'I'll do it,' said Weaver, crossing the room and perching on Stenning's desk. 'You just keep finding me numbers.'

'I guess by the end of the evening we'll know whether this Peter is our killer or not,' said Anderson. 'If all Oliver Kennedys are accounted for, we know he's been pulling our collective plonker.'

The phone rang. Everyone stopped what they were doing and looked at it. Somehow they all knew. Anderson stood up.

'I'll get it,' said Dana.

Wherever she sat in the living room, Lacey could see the knife drawer. Plain white melamine, it hovered at the edge of her vision like her nemesis. If she left the room she could still see it. It had been tormenting her all day, like the bottle of Scotch in the cupboard of an alcoholic.

She could not do it again. Once was forgivable, understandable even. Once could be considered an experiment. Twice meant she had a problem. Twice meant that, far from making a recovery, she was actually sinking fast.

But she'd felt so much better. All day Sunday, and most of Monday, she'd felt as though she'd taken a miracle drug. That feeling inside her, like a coiled spring, had gone. It had felt like the first warm day after winter. Lacey stood and walked across the room, trying to think about something else.

The MIT still had her mobile phone. Presumably they hadn't yet managed to trace where Saturday evening's text had come from. But if the Met couldn't prove Barney had sent her the text, how on earth could she? And what did he have to hide, anyway? He was eleven years old. How could he be involved?

She was in the kitchen again, dangerously close to the knife drawer. Impossible to stay indoors. She grabbed a jacket and her helmet and went outside. The night was dark and cold, the wind coming directly from the river.

On the embankment, the police presence seemed unusually heavy. Uniformed officers were making their way along the pathway, chatting to groups of teenagers who'd braved the cold. Tuesday evening. They were expecting the killer to strike again.

Maybe they'd even been given her description, told to look out for a thin, pale woman who haunted the riverbank once night had fallen.

Suddenly self-conscious, Lacey left the river and set off east, avoiding the main roads, peddling as fast as she dared in London traffic. Only when she got as far as Bermondsey did she risk heading back to the water. When she reached a stretch of the embankment that seemed quiet, she got off and pushed her bike towards the embankment wall.

The river was lively tonight, the tide coming in fast and the wind blowing hard in the opposite direction. Choppy little waves were dancing across its entire surface and the long, smooth blackness was continually broken by tiny fountains of white spray.

A police launch was heading downstream, in the exact centre of the river. It was too far away for Lacey to be sure, but it looked exactly the same as the one Joesbury had forced her on to the previous autumn, after a ducking had given her a temporary fear of fast-moving water. He'd introduced her to his Uncle Fred, a sergeant in the Marine Unit, and the launch they'd been travelling on had been called out to intercept a dinghy of illegal immigrants. The dinghy had overturned, Lacey had jumped into the water to rescue a young girl, and bloody hell, had she got herself in trouble, from both Uncle Fred and Joesbury. But her fear of rivers had gone as quickly as it had come.

There was just something mesmerizing about large, powerful watercourses: about the never-ending motion, the way they were continually moving and changing but always constant, always there. As the song said, they just kept on rolling, and somehow, this river in particular always managed to calm her. If she could live close to it, if by some miracle she could afford one of these riverside properties, if she could fall asleep to the sound of its journey, she wouldn't need to—

'Oh, Jesus!'

Sudden pain winded her. There was a clatter of metal against concrete and someone hit her hard.

Barney stared at the screen. Peter Sweep had posted four minutes earlier. Short and very much to the point. Oliver Kennedy? Who was Oliver Kennedy? People on Facebook were asking the same question. Comments popped up one after another like pop tarts from a toaster. Someone thought he might go to the same school as his younger sister. Another said there was someone called Kennedy in his cub pack, but he thought his first name was Jacob. Nothing else from Peter, but that was his way. He didn't join in the conversations. Then a comment that looked genuine.

I played tennis with Oliver tonight. He left with Joe Walsh. Has someone phoned his house?

Barney flicked screens to the news channels, but there was nothing there. Not that he would have expected it this soon. Back to Facebook. The comment thread was growing but most of it looked speculative and alarmist. People were enjoying the drama. Barney felt sick. He hadn't realized just how much he'd been hoping the pizza man had been the killer.

Barney sat up and leaned towards the screen, as though physical proximity might make him understand more. Peter had posted again.

Take care, he said, take care how you cut yourself. It is more dangerous than you think in this country. First cut is the deepest. Hold still, little Olly.

'Why didn't you warn us?' Tom Kennedy demanded. 'That's what I want to know. You knew someone called Oliver Kennedy was going to be taken. Why wasn't it on the news when we could have done something?'

Oliver Kennedy's father hadn't stopped moving since Dana, Susan Richmond, Tom Barrett and a uniformed constable had arrived at the Kennedys' home in Lambeth.

'We didn't know that,' said Dana, in the gentlest voice she could manage. 'Oliver wasn't mentioned by name until this Peter Sweep claimed he already had him.'

'But you knew he was going to take a kid tonight. If we'd been told that, we'd never have let him out.'

For the love of God, thought Dana. *Five boys have been killed in the past six weeks in this part of London and that wasn't enough for you?*

'I understand how you feel, Sir, but I promise you, we are doing everything we can to find—'

'Do you? Do you have any idea what it's like to hear on the friggin' television that a maniac has hold of your son? Do you have kids?'

'This isn't helping!' came a wail from across the room.

Oliver's mother had barely moved from the sofa since Dana and the others had arrived. She clutched the neck of her oversized pink sweatshirt, her face a waxy shade of green. At her side sat a teenage boy, similar enough to his father for Dana to be sure he was Oliver's older brother.

'Thank you.' Dana addressed the mother directly. 'Now it will really help if you can tell us exactly what Oliver's movements were this evening.'

'We've already told that first lot you sent round,' said Kennedy Senior. 'Get your information from them. We need to go and look for Oliver. Come on, Caz.'

As the father made for the door, the mother looked uncertain.

'I'm afraid I need to speak to you both before you go anywhere,' said Dana. 'It's in Oliver's best interests, I promise you.'

'The TV are organizing a search party. That doctor bloke is coming down himself. At least they're doing something.'

'Sir, I cannot let you go just—'

'If it was a ruddy Paki kid, you'd be out looking for him, wouldn't you, you heartless bitch!'

An audible gasp from Susan, then silence in the room.

Dana took a step closer to the man. 'Mr Kennedy, if we don't find Oliver safe and sound, my failure to bring him home to you will haunt me for the rest of my life. I swear to you that's the truth.'

He glared back. For a second, she could have sworn he was about to spit at her. She was almost flinching. Then his eyes closed. 'I'm sorry,' he said.

'I know,' Dana said. 'Now, I have thirty uniformed officers conducting a house-to-house search both in Lambeth and in Deptford Creek, another place we're interested in. They will make sure the volunteers who arrive to take part in the search are properly directed. In a little while, if you still want to, you can go out and join them, although one of you will need to stay here in case Oliver gets in touch. Now, please can we all sit down?'

He nodded. Dana made herself sit on the nearest sofa. One by one, the others followed her lead. She looked at the teenager. 'You're Oliver's older brother, is that right?'

He nodded.

'I'd like you to go upstairs with the constable here and look through Oliver's room. Touch as little as you can, and the constable will help you, but you're looking for anything out of the ordinary. Any notes, bus tickets, anything that strikes you as a bit unusual. Can you do that?'

The boy nodded. 'I know the passwords for his computer,' he said. 'Do you want me to check that, too?'

'Yes, please. Look through his recent emails, any posts he's made on Facebook or Twitter or anything. The constable will be watching everything you do, not because we don't trust you, but because if you find anything, it needs to be properly recorded.'

When the two of them had left the room, Dana turned back to Oliver's parents. They were sitting side by side, holding on to each other.

'I need you to tell me where Oliver was this evening. Starting from when he got home from school.'

Mrs Kennedy spoke, her husband holding on to her hands, giving her little pats and squeezes whenever she threatened to break down. Oliver had arrived home from school on time. He came home by bus, travelling with several other kids from his class. There were always several parents on the bus, too, so his mother never worried about his safety. She left work at 3.30pm and walked to the bus stop to meet him before they walked home together.

He'd had a snack, a glass of squash and a packet of crisps,

changed out of his school uniform, then gone out to play tennis at some local courts. He walked there and back with a mate, Joe Walsh.

At six-forty, by which time Oliver would normally have arrived home, she'd gone out with her older son to look for him. Seeing nothing of either Oliver or Joe, they'd gone to Joe's house to find him already home.

'Joe told us he'd left something at the clubhouse,' she said. 'They'd just got into the recreation ground when he remembered. He jogged back, leaving Oliver waiting for him at the entrance to the park. He wasn't out of sight for more than a couple of minutes, he said, but when he got back Oliver was gone. He shouted for him a couple of times, then got freaked out and ran home. His mum was just about to phone me when we got there.'

Dana nodded. There had been practically no time at all for Oliver to disappear.

'Why did Joe go back, did he tell you?'

'He realized his phone wasn't in his pocket,' Mrs Kennedy replied. 'The kids always hang their coats up in the clubhouse while they're playing. Joe got to the park and realized his phone was missing.'

'Did he find it?' asked Dana.

The woman nodded. 'It was in the clubhouse, he said. Must have fallen out of his pocket.' She turned to her husband. 'Except it couldn't have fallen out, could it?' she went on. 'Remember, Joe said he found it on the worktop by the sink.'

'Someone could have picked it up off the floor,' said Barrett, who was pulling his own phone out of his pocket.

'Or someone could have taken it out, in the hope of separating the two boys,' said Dana. 'If you can let us know who's in charge of the club, we can talk to everyone who was there this evening. We'll also talk to Joe again. If Oliver's abductor went to the tennis club this evening, someone will have seen him.'

'Talk to you in the hall, Ma'am?' said Barrett.

'What is it?' asked Oliver's mother, like a hound with a scent.

'Our guv just needs a quick word with DI Tulloch,' said Barrett. 'You too, Susan.'

225

'I'll be right back,' Dana told Oliver's parents, before following Barrett and Richmond into the hallway.

'That was Gayle on the phone,' said Barrett, when the door had closed behind them. 'Another Facebook post, give me a sec.'

The two women waited, while Barrett found the right app on his phone and opened the page.

'Can we rule the parents out of having anything to do with it?' asked Dana.

The profiler nodded. 'I think so,' she said. 'They're falling apart. They've no idea where he is.'

'Here we go,' said Barrett. Richmond, standing closer, saw it first.

'Oh my God,' she said. 'We can't show them this.'

Dana took the phone being offered to her. A photograph had been posted on the Missing Boys page by Peter Sweep. It showed a small boy tied up and blindfolded. From the position of his mouth, he looked to be whimpering.

'We have to,' said Dana. 'They need to identify him.'

'Well, we know Peter Sweep's for real,' said Barrett.

A thudding noise upstairs. 'Mum! Dad!' Oliver's brother appeared at the top of the stairs and came hurtling down. Dana stepped forward to stop him at the bottom.

'Have you been on Facebook?' she asked the scared boy.

'It's Oliver, there's a picture!'

'I know,' she said. 'Come on, we'll tell them together.'

Lacey took a second to get her breath back. What had happened to her police instincts? She'd had no idea anyone had been close. Had it been a real attack, and not just a careless jogger falling over her bike, she'd have been helpless.

The jogger in question was bent over in the road, rubbing his ankle and scraping the sole of his shoe against the kerb at the same time. Quelling an instinct to apologize, she reminded herself that the pavement was nearly two yards wide and there was absolutely no way that either she or her bike had been blocking it. So if this guy was going to get lippy, good, she was in the mood. He looked up. Early forties, sallow skin, rather good-looking. His face was damp with sweat. He was wearing jogging bottoms and a black

226

fleece sweater, a woollen hat pulled down over his ears and a fleece scarf around his neck. She'd seen him before.

'Christ, dog shit.' More scraping and rubbing of lower limbs.

Lacey leaned back against the embankment wall and folded her arms. He was going to pick up her bike, and he was going to express the hope that he hadn't damaged it. He looked up again.

'I'm not seriously hurt, if you were wondering,' he snapped.

'I wasn't,' said Lacey. 'I was thinking about my bike.'

'I bloody well fell over it.'

'There was bloody well no need to. The path here's wide enough for half a dozen bikes. And it's perfectly well lit. I can hardly be held responsible for your clumsiness. Unless you're planning on blaming me for the dog shit as well.'

He glared for a second longer, then his face relaxed.

'Sor-ry,' he drawled at her. 'Although actually, it was trying to avoid getting too close to you that was the problem. Most women get the jitters when they see a man running towards them at night. I went too close to the kerb and slipped in dog shit.'

He bent down, picked up her bike and leaned it back against the railing. 'Looks alright,' he said, giving it the once over.

'How's your leg?'

He looked down. 'Looks alright,' he said again. 'You were at the rugby on Sunday, weren't you?'

She knew she'd seen him before.

'I saw you talking to Barney Roberts,' he said, before she could answer him. 'I'm his games teacher, Dan Green.' He held out a gloved hand for her to shake.

'Lacey Flint,' she said, taking it. 'Barney's next-door neighbour.'

Politeness in his eyes became genuine interest. 'Not the detective? He's mentioned you.'

'Really?'

'Yeah, you might have a new recruit there in a few years' time. Got a very investigative mind.'

'And this is often apparent in games lessons, is it?'

He gave the easy, relaxed laugh of someone who laughs often. 'No, my wife is his form teacher. He's a bit of a pet of hers. I can see why, he's a nice lad. Bit odd, but a good kid.'

A nice lad who just might be concealing evidence in a murder inquiry.

Green put his hands behind his head, stretched his arms back and did a little jog on the spot.

'How's the injury?' asked Lacey.

'Not nearly serious enough to stop me running home, un-fortunately,' he replied. 'Why is it always harder to start again once you've stopped?'

Knowing exactly what he meant, Lacey couldn't help smiling.

'I tell you what, there's some heavy police presence out tonight,' said Green. 'All along the embankment. Anything to do with you?'

'I imagine it's something to do with the murdered boys,' said Lacey, 'but I'm not working at the moment, so I'm only guessing.'

Green nodded. 'Well, I'm only putting off the inevitable. Nice meeting you, Lacey.'

He gave her one last nod and set off. In spite of his fall, he ran fast and well, a natural athlete. As the river turned a bend, he looked back, saw her watching and waved. Then he was gone.

The Theatre Arm at Deptford Creek was still and silent when Barney arrived. Police tape cordoned off the area where they'd found the body, but otherwise, there was no trace of what had happened on Saturday evening.

What *had* happened on Saturday evening? It was all very well to be blasé when the others were around, talking about freak waves and animals; it was a different thing entirely now that he was here again, alone, with an extremely vivid memory in his head of a dead child leaping out of the water. Of blind eyes that, for a second, had looked directly at him.

No wave could have done that. And it hadn't been an animal they'd heard in the water. It had been something much bigger. Harvey had sworn he'd seen an arm, large protruding eyes in a pale face. He hadn't been lying. Mistaken, possibly, but not lying, he'd been too scared. So had his older brother. Barney had never seen Jorge lose his cool before.

A flock of birds was flying towards him, low in the sky, following the course of the Creek as though it marked some ancient, avian pathway. As they passed overhead, Barney looked up and, for a second, their sleek graceful shapes changed before his eyes, becoming shorter and squatter. Their flight was no longer straight and smooth through the air but undulating and sensuous. Beaks shrank and eyes grew bigger and brighter. For a second the birds became bats. Then the moment passed and they flew on.

Telling himself to get a grip, Barney took a step closer to the water. What he was dealing with was bad enough without any supernatural rubbish thrown in. Christ, if the police managed to prove a blood-sucking creature of fiction was responsible for the murders, he, for one, would be hugely relieved. He was the last person in London to be scared of vampires. Keeping his eyes away from the patch of concrete where the remains of Tyler King had lain, he stepped from the yard on to the first of the boats.

If the theory he still didn't want to give words to, even in his head, were true, someone would be on the boat. His dad was supposed to be working late, giving lectures and meeting students at the university. If he wasn't, if he was here – well, he'd think about that when he had to.

He was much closer to the water now. The river was full and fast and the tide probably at its highest. Could there be a better way of getting rid of blood than in a fast-flowing river when the tide was on its way out? Especially one that fed into one of the largest rivers in the world? Blood, even the blood from a whole body, would disappear without trace in this river. As always when he thought about blood, Barney started to feel a bit light-headed.

He could think about that later. First he had to know if anyone was on board. Remembering how Hatty had climbed on to the boat on Saturday and knowing he had to create no noise or movement, he swung first one leg over and then the other. Then paused for a moment. What would his dad do, if he caught him here? If he had to choose between his son and his freedom, which would he pick?

He hadn't come all this way to go home with no answers. Dropping low, Barney crawled along the deck to the nearest window, the one that looked out from the main saloon on the starboard side. The curtains were drawn but there might be a gap.

The first two boys to be killed had been found at Deptford

Creek. That probably meant they'd been killed here. When a third body needed to be disposed of, the killer had found a new dumping ground. He hadn't wanted to draw too much attention to the Creek. He hadn't wanted the police to find the place where he kept and killed them.

The curtain on the first window was fully drawn and Barney could see no light behind it.

His dad had had new keys cut for the boat over Christmas and, ever since, had been unusually secretive about where he kept them. He could have invented the missing keys, to make sure that no one but he could access the boat. And the damp the locksmith had reported? Could that have been the result of someone trying to wash the boat down?

Barney carried on crawling.

His dad had been on the boat on Saturday night, when Tyler King's body had appeared from the water. Barney had seen him, so had Hatty, she just hadn't recognized the sweater. Yet he'd lied, claiming to be home all night. He'd even lied to the detective. No one lied to the police unless they had something big to hide.

Impossible to see through any of the windows. Barney crawled along the cabin roof and slid his fingers under the hatch. This time it didn't move. It was going to be impossible to see inside, but if he lay still and listened, he'd hear anything that happened below. He let his head fall silently against the wood of the hatch.

He'd been in position for only two minutes when he heard movement below. A bump. A low moan. Then a laugh. His dad's laugh.

'Good evening, Barney,' said a voice above him.

43

L ACEY STAYED WHERE SHE WAS ON THE BANK. THE LAST thing she needed right now was to get into a scuffle with a kid around deep water. It was the right call. Barney, after a last glance at the hatch of the boat, began making his way towards her. Once off the yellow boat he moved quickly, as though eager to reach her. She almost told him to take it easy.

'I'm not trespassing,' he announced, when he'd joined her on the wall. 'That's my granddad's boat.'

'And is Granddad at home?' Lacey asked him, looking back at the yellow painted yacht with the green trim and wooden deck. It looked old, but cared for. A well-loved classic.

'He's dead,' said Barney. 'The boat's empty. No one goes there now.'

The child stood next to her, looking awkward and uncomfortable. Lacey took a step back, further from the river, hoping he'd follow her. He did.

'So you're back again,' said Lacey. 'What keeps bringing you to Deptford Creek at this time of night?'

'I don't know what you mean.'

She nodded towards the boat she'd found him on. 'Is your dad with you?'

'No!'

Extraordinary reaction. She mentioned his father, he looked terrified. Why would the kid be scared of his dad?

'Does he know you're here?'

Shake of the head. 'He's working. Miles from here. Are you going to tell him?'

Definitely afraid of something. 'Not necessarily,' she said. 'But I need you to come back with me now. It's not safe for you to be here on your own this late.'

Barney didn't argue. If anything he seemed eager to get out of the yard. They collected their bikes and wheeled them back towards the main road.

'What were you doing there?' Lacey tried again, after a few seconds.

Nothing for a while. Then, 'I got curious,' said Barney. 'I saw on the news about how they'd found a body here and I just wanted to see the place for myself.'

She watched him, waiting for him to make eye contact. When he did, he looked at her steadily, without flinching. Young as he was, he was pretty unflappable.

'I saw on Facebook that another boy had gone missing,' said Barney, after they'd walked in silence for some minutes. 'Is it true?'

Everywhere she went, people were determined to drag her into that case. 'I'm not sure,' she said. 'If it is, it'll be on the news when we get back.'

They walked on, the only sound being that of the bike wheels on the wet road.

'Why does he do it?' said Barney, in a small voice. 'Why does he kill kids?'

The question the whole country was asking. Barney, still a child, would expect a grown-up, a detective, to know the answer. 'There are lots of reasons why people kill,' she said. 'And usually those reasons make no sense to people like us.'

'What do you mean?'

Lacey sighed. She was wet, cold, some way from home and this kid wanted a psychological profile. 'There may be something wrong with his brain,' she said. 'Maybe it was injured in some way that stops him feeling compassion and pity. Or maybe he went through a terrible experience when he was a child, bad enough to damage him, even if not in a physical way.'

Barney had been watching her face rather than where he was going. He pushed his bike a little too close and almost knocked her off balance.

'Steady!'

'Sorry.'

They walked on, until, in a quiet voice, Barney asked, 'Can he get better?'

'Better, as in . . . ?'

'Can he stop doing it? Is there a way of making him good again?'

They had to cross the main road at this point. Lacey waited for a gap in the traffic. 'I don't think so,' she said, when they'd reached the other side. 'I think when people are as damaged as he is, the only thing you can really do is stop them hurting anyone in the future.'

'You mean send him to prison?'

'Well, it might be to a secure hospital, but it would still seem very much like a prison.'

'What if he's got . . .'

Lacey slowed down. Barney was no longer making eye contact. When she was looking straight ahead, his eyes never left her face, but the second she turned to him, he looked away. What was he hiding? 'Got what?' she asked him.

'Nothing. Why does he kill kids, though? Why not grown-ups?'

Wow, he wasn't holding back with the tricky questions.

'Well, that's probably a question only he could answer, but usually when killers go for one particular type of victim, it's because those victims remind them of a person in real life. Maybe someone who's hurt them. They can't kill the one they really want to, so they choose – do you know the word surrogate?'

'I think so. You mean he's killing ten- and eleven-year-old boys because there's one particular ten- or eleven-year-old he really wants to kill but can't?'

'Well, it probably won't be quite as simple as that, but basically— Barney, what's wrong?'

He was crying. The tough, defiant kid had tears gleaming in his eyes. Knowing she'd seen them, he brought his fists up to his face like a much younger child, to hide the tears and wipe them away at the same time.

Lacey looked up the street and spotted a café still open. With one hand on Barney's shoulder, the other steering her bike, she led the child across the road towards it. When he asked for Coke, she ordered two to save hassle and led him to a table next to the wall.

'Going to tell me?' she asked, when nothing but gulping sounds and sniffs had come from Barney for quite some time.

'I've been trying to find my mum,' he said, as though he'd only been waiting for her to ask.

'I didn't know you had a mum,' she replied.

He looked up at her with eyes that were suddenly so much brighter than the grey they usually seemed. 'Everyone's got a mum.'

'I know, sorry, I just assumed . . .' She stopped. She hadn't assumed anything, she hadn't really given it any thought. 'What happened to her?' she asked.

'She left,' said Barney. 'When I was little. I don't remember her at all. I've got a picture, though, I know what she looks like.'

'Does your dad know where she is?'

'I don't know. He never talks about her. All I can remember is him telling me she had to go away for a while. But that means she's going to come back, doesn't it? For a while means not for ever. Why would he tell me she's gone for a while if he knew she wasn't coming back?'

To soften the blow, of course, thought Lacey. *Hoping you'd forget, just get used to her not being around. Oh Barney!*

'Have you never talked about this with your dad?' she asked him.

'Not for a long time. I think when I was little, I used to ask where she was and he always said the same thing. Mummy's gone away for a while. After a bit, I just stopped asking. I've been looking for her myself though.'

Lacey listened, as the cappuccino machine hissed and spat, and while Barney told her about how he'd divided the whole city into zones, and researched the various newspapers and free-sheets in each area. That he was advertising in the classified columns, doing an area at a time, ticking them off when they were done and he'd got no response. He told her how he funded the cost of the advertisements from money he earned working at the newsagent's, and about the secret email account that he checked every morning.

God love him, it would never work. Even if his mother was still in London – in itself quite unlikely – what were the chances of her combing the local newspapers on a regular basis?

'It won't work, will it?' said Barney, as though he'd read her mind. 'You think I'm mad.'

'I think you're brave and intelligent and resourceful,' said Lacey. 'But you're right, I'm afraid. It won't work.'

His face crumpled. They were facing each other across the table and all she could do was reach forward and pat his hand. She wondered how long it had been since a woman had hugged him. She sat there, feeling helpless and awkward, until he gave a massive sniff and looked up.

'The police could find her, couldn't they?' he asked, and now his face had taken on a sly look. 'They know how to find missing persons.'

'The police have procedures for tracing missing persons,' said Lacey cautiously, 'but even they don't always work. If people want to stay missing, they usually do.'

'How do they do it?' said Barney, leaning forward. 'What do I have to do to find her?'

'You know what a database is?'

He nodded.

'Well, the first thing the police would do is search through the various databases,' she said. 'We'd probably start with the police national computer. I'm sure this wouldn't be the case, but if your mum has ever been arrested or given a police caution, there'll be a record of it. Assuming that didn't trace her, we'd check the electoral roll – you know, the list of people who are eligible to vote; then the DVLA, the people who issue car licences; the department of work and pensions, Her Majesty's revenue and customs, the various utility companies – phone companies, especially. Unless your mum has disappeared from sight completely, she'll be on one, probably more, of those databases. They would give us a last known address and we'd take it from there.'

'How long would it take?'

'If you were in a real hurry, you could probably have it done in a few days.'

'If I told them my mum was missing, would they look for her for me?'

Oh, the poor kid. 'Your dad would have to report her missing,' Lacey said. 'But as she went such a long time ago, I doubt they'd consider it a good enough reason to look now.'

'But she is missing, and if anything happens to my dad, I'll have no one to look after me.'

He wanted Lacey to look for his mother. The unspoken question was shining out from his eyes. And she could, no doubt about it. How ethical it would be was another matter entirely.

'Barney, if I could talk to your dad about it, I might be able to—'

He looked at his wristwatch. 'I should get back now,' he said. 'My dad will be wondering where I am. Don't say anything to him, please. I don't want to worry him.'

Lacey stood and carried both coke cans to the bin. 'What's your mum's name?' she asked.

'Karen Roberts. Why?' asked Barney, hope lighting up his face.

'Do you know her maiden name? What she was called before she was married.'

'My granddad was called Prince,' said Barney. 'Is that what you mean?'

'Karen Roberts, née Prince. Barney, I'm making no promises, but I'll have a think about it. Now, come on, let's get you home.'

44

A T THE FRONT OF THE INCIDENT ROOM, A LARGE WHITE screen had been hooked up to the internet. Four detectives sat watching the Missing Boys page update itself every few seconds. They'd already tried, and failed, to track Peter Sweep via the usual route – email address and internet service provider. This evening, Facebook had told them, Peter was posting using a smart phone. They'd been happy to supply the number, but all BT had been able to tell them was that it was being used within half a mile of a base station not far from Lambeth. The effort and thought Sweep had put into concealing his identity and where-abouts had done more than anything to convince most members of the team that he and the killer were one and the same. Most, not all.

'Dana, I just don't think it's him,' said Richmond.

Dana watched Anderson stop pacing the room and turn on the spot to face the profiler. 'What the hell do you mean?' he demanded. 'He's got a picture of the kid. Scroll it back, Gayle. Let's all have another look at the poor little bastard, shall we?'

Richmond sighed and ran her hands through her hair. 'I know that and I know what I'm saying will sound like it's making no sense, but everything is telling me that this is not your man.'

The room was empty but for the four of them: Dana, Anderson, Richmond and Mizon. The rest of the team were out looking for

Oliver Kennedy. Anderson had made no secret of his desire to join them out in the field.

'Go on,' said Dana.

'Boss, with respect, I think I can be more use out on the streets. At least I can knock on doors, ask questions. Sitting here is doing my head in.' Anderson had walked to the door now, practically had hold of the handle.

'I know that, but I need you here, Neil. Somebody has to do the thinking.'

'Not my forte, Boss. If it's all the same to you, I'll leave that to the women.'

'Sit down, please, Sergeant Anderson, Susan has something she wants to tell us.'

Anderson, red-faced and hard-eyed, sank clumsily into the nearest seat and glared at Richmond.

'I won't say our killer is the most controlled I've ever come across because that would mean relatively little,' said Susan. 'The chance to work with serial killers doesn't come along very often.'

'Well, excuse us for not providing job satisfaction,' began Anderson.

'Stop it!' snapped Dana. 'I'm sorry, Neil, but we're all on edge here. Just try and hold it together, will you?'

Anderson gave a heavy sigh and shook his head.

'But those of us who do this line of work keep 100 per cent up to date with what's going on elsewhere,' Richmond continued. 'Every time a new serial killer raises his head, whether it's here or overseas, most commonly the US, we hoover up every bit of information we can find. Every big case has reams written about it and we read everything.'

'OK, we get you're well informed, what's the point?'

'The point, Sergeant, is that this is one of the most controlled killers *anyone* has come across. Highly intelligent, exceptionally organized, no hint of anger of any sort. He made one mistake, right at the start, when he didn't leave Tyler's body where you'd be bound to find it, but since then, nothing. He plans what's he's going to do, he stalks his victims for days, maybe for weeks, gets his snatch absolutely right. There is nothing sexual or angry about what he does to them. He keeps his cool throughout, then he leaves them for us to find. He is an ice man, or woman.'

Dana found herself, once again, thinking about Lacey Flint. Ten minutes ago, from the privacy of her office, she'd asked local uniform to check whether Lacey was in her flat.

'But suddenly, tonight, that's all changed. Suddenly he's like a kid who's had too many blue Smarties. He boasts in advance about what he's going to do, he names his victim within minutes of having got him, now he's giving us a blow-by-blow account of what he's supposedly doing to the poor kid. There's a malicious, impish glee about it all and it's completely out of pattern.'

'Another one,' said Mizon from her desk. 'This is starting to turn my stomach.'

'What is it this time?' asked Anderson. 'More blood-lust bollocks?'

Mizon nodded. 'You know what? I think it is him,' she said, 'but something has made him go a bit mental. Maybe it's all this talk about vampires.'

'No,' said Richmond. 'He's enjoying the vampire angle. We've had – what – three references to blood-drinking in the past hour? But all pretty samey and unimaginative. He keeps talking about the warm, nourishing taste of blood, it's stuff straight out of a cheap vampire thriller.'

'I get that,' said Dana. 'I really do, but isn't this just the sort of escalation we see with serial offenders? Isn't it possible that his need for greater public attention this time is just part of the escalation?'

'If he were showing any sign of reckless behaviour, I might agree with you,' said Susan. 'But he isn't.'

'You don't think telling the world what he's doing is reckless in itself?' suggested Mizon. 'Suddenly he's the most hated man on the planet. If ever there were a candidate for public lynching, he's it.'

'Another reason why I don't think it's him. I don't think our killer wants to be hated. I think he wants to be understood.'

Anderson gave a short, guttural cough, beneath which the word 'bollocks' could be plainly heard.

Richmond stared Anderson straight in the face. He looked away first. 'We have to concentrate on what he's doing to these boys,' she went on. 'He's draining the blood out of them. Now, we have no idea why he's doing that, and I certainly don't believe he's drinking it, but he will have a reason. It's part of some ritual that is very important to him and I know he does it calmly and in a controlled fashion. He will want to be alone, to give it his full attention. He won't want interruptions and he won't want to break off every few minutes to give an update on Facebook. Killing is an intensely personal, private experience and he will not want to share it.'

Dana's desk phone rang. She listened for a few moments, then replaced the receiver. Lacey Flint's whereabouts were unknown.

'Deep down, I don't think he wants to hurt these boys. I think he can't help himself. He may even be deeply ashamed of what he's doing. This freak-show going on right now feels completely wrong.'

Up on the large screen, another post appeared.

Oops! I think that last one was a bit deep. Oliver isn't moving any more.

'Oh, God help us,' muttered Anderson, dropping his head into his hands.

'*Oops?*' snapped Richmond. 'Now seriously, did you ever hear of a vicious killer using the word "oops" before? This pillock is playing with us! He's getting off on making us sick to our stomachs, but he isn't killing Oliver at the same time.'

Anderson glared at her. 'You have no idea how much I hope you're right.'

'I think she could be,' said Dana. 'He's never killed a child the same night he abducted him before.'

'Ladies, I would be with you a hundred per cent, were it not for the small matter of Oliver Kennedy being missing and a picture of him tied up and screaming being on the ruddy internet.'

'Is it possible the photo isn't Oliver?' asked Susan. 'Just some other kid who looks like him? I know his parents identified him, but they were under a lot of stress.'

'He's still bloody missing.'

'This is getting us nowhere,' said Dana. 'OK, I'm going back to talk to his parents. Neil, can you check on how the searches are going? Gayle, you OK to—'

'Keep watching Facebook? Yes, Ma'am.'

45

'LACEY, CAN I TELL YOU SOMETHING ELSE?'

They were home. Once they'd left the café, Barney had been anxious to get back so they'd ridden fast. Lacey had insisted Barney stay in front and wait for her at each junction. More than once, passers-by had glared at her, no doubt thinking her highly irresponsible to have a child out on his bike so late. Now they were both out of breath, warm despite the cold wind and drizzling rain. Lacey leaned her bike against the railings above her flat.

'Of course,' she said, wondering what on earth was coming now.

'I think there's something wrong with my brain.'

She honestly never knew what this child was going to say next. 'Barney, you're the most intelligent child I know.' No need to tell him he was practically the only child she knew. 'I really doubt there's anything wrong with your brain.'

He looked pleased, then doubtful, finally uncertain.

'Why do you think there's something wrong?' she asked, removing her helmet. Her hair, damp with rain and sweat, clung to her head.

'I have episodes,' he said, after a moment.

'Episodes?'

'It's the right word. I looked it up.'

'What sort of episodes?'

His eyes fell to the rain-streaked pavement. 'I lose time,' he said.

'I just don't remember anything. Hours can go by and I haven't a clue what I've done.'

'And when do these episodes happen?'

'Usually when I'm alone,' he said. 'At home, or out skating. But it happened in class once. The bell rang and I realized I hadn't a clue what I'd been doing for about half the class, since Mrs Green told us to work through our maths books. I'd done the work, I just couldn't remember doing it.'

'Sounds like a daydream to me. I had them a lot when I was your age.'

She had, too. It had been her way of dealing with a pretty awful life. 'You say hours can go by?' she asked him. That had been an exaggeration, surely. Daydreams lasted minutes at most.

'This one time, I was sitting at my computer and I realized I'd no idea what I'd done all evening. I couldn't even remember getting home from school. I think I'd been out, because my coat was wet, but I just didn't know.'

He was getting upset again. The skin around his eyes was turning pink, the contours of his mouth stiffening. He was shivering too, his smaller body had chilled down quickly. He needed to be indoors with a hot bath and hot chocolate, to be looked after properly. Oh, she was so out of her depth with this. 'Have you told your dad?'

He shook his head. 'They seem to happen when he's out. I don't want him feeling guilty.'

Well, it was about bloody time he felt guilty. An eleven-year-old kid suffering black-outs and his dad was leaving him on his own? 'Is your dad out at the moment?' she asked him.

He nodded, but couldn't look at her again. 'I think so.'

'When does he get back?'

'I'm not sure. I'm usually asleep.'

'Do you want me to come in and wait with you?'

'No. Don't tell him I told you. Please. Or about Mum. Or about me being at the boat tonight. Please.'

What was he so afraid of?

'OK, listen to me, Barney. A few years ago, when I was a bit older than you are now, but still quite young, I had episodes too. Periods

243

of time that I had no memory of. It was like someone had taken a whiteboard rubber and just wiped away my memory.'

'Yes,' he said. 'That's what it's like.'

She made herself smile at him, even though she felt like crying.

'It was a very difficult time for me,' she said. 'And I think the periods of memory loss were caused by sadness and worry. I think there were times when I was just so unhappy my mind couldn't cope, so it sort of went to sleep. Does that make sense?'

He nodded.

'I think something similar could be happening to you. I think your anxiety over your mum could be the main cause of it. The important thing to remember is that for me it didn't last, and I don't think it will for you either.'

'Really?'

'Really. Now, it's late and you need to be in bed. I'm going to think hard about everything you've told me and we'll talk again. Are you sure you don't want me to come in with you?'

He shook his head, but he looked a bit happier. At that age, having a grown-up take charge was always going to be a relief.

'You've got my number?' she said. 'I'm just next door.'

He smiled at her again. She watched him unlock the door and disappear. When she heard the sound of the deadlock being turned on the inside, she went down to her own flat.

Lacey found Barney's mother in a little over an hour. She double-checked her facts and then got up and walked out into the garden. Somehow, it was always easier to think out here. Sometimes, if she closed her eyes and zoned out the roar of the traffic, she could almost imagine she could hear the river.

From the shed door she could see directly into the window that she'd always assumed must be Barney's because she often saw him just behind it, working at the computer. The room was in darkness and the curtains drawn.

She really needed to talk to someone. Someone who was a parent. Someone whose judgement she trusted. Shit, was there really no one else?

The handset of the landline phone was in her pocket, because she'd already decided she was going to call him. Maybe she'd even been glad of the excuse. *You're number one in Favourites*, that funny cute kid had told her. She, on the other hand, had no need to save his number as anything: she'd known it off by heart for months.

'Hi,' said the familiar voice a second later.

'It's me,' she said, unnecessarily. He'd have caller ID, he'd have known exactly who it was.

'If this is a booty call, you're about to make me a very happy man.'

'Are you in the middle of something? And it isn't, by the way.'

'I'm on the embankment, heading home. Something up?'

'Sort of. I need advice.'

'Blimey, I'd have been less surprised if you'd wanted sex.'

No, she couldn't do it, she couldn't be in the same room as him, especially not this late, not feeling like this. 'It's quite late,' she said, backtracking. 'It can wait till the morning.'

'I'll be with you in ten, Flint. Put the kettle on.'

Barney closed the front door and saw the pizza box where he'd left it before fleeing the house earlier. Not really wanting to touch it, he knew he couldn't leave it there. He'd never sleep. Still with his gloves on, he carried it through to the kitchen. About to put it in the bin, he had a sudden thought and opened the box.

The pizza was American Hot: chilli beef, spicy pepperoni and jalapeno peppers. His favourite. The sort he always ordered. It hadn't been a mistake, it had been meant for him.

For a second, he toyed with the idea that he might have ordered it himself, during one of his 'episodes'. But how could he have paid for it? He didn't have a credit card.

Some time later, Barney realized he was sitting on the hard tiles of the kitchen floor. He had no idea how long he'd been out of it. His dad had been on the boat. Oliver Kennedy – or more likely, by now, Oliver Kennedy's body – was on the boat and his dad was the killer. Even if he said nothing – and how could he send his own dad to prison? – even if he kept quiet, the police would find him. They always did and then he'd be completely on his own. But maybe

Lacey would find his mum. Maybe she'd find her in time. He dragged himself upright and climbed the stairs.

On his own floor, Barney wanted nothing more than to go straight to bed. Somehow, though, he just couldn't resist opening up Facebook one last time. Just to see if there was any news on Oliver. Unable to stop himself, he read through the various postings Peter and others had left throughout the evening.

Jeez, that wasn't his dad. He just knew it. No way would his dad be that sick.

Without even bothering to log out, he was about to turn away when he spotted a message waiting for him. Messages on Facebook were private. Only the sender and the recipient could see them. He clicked open Messages. It was from Peter Sweep.

My new obsession is you. How was the pizza?

'Let me get this straight. You offered to use Metropolitan Police resources to help a disturbed eleven-year-old boy conduct a missing-persons search?'

Lacey glared over the top of her mug. It was the first time she'd ever willingly invited Joesbury into her flat and she'd expected to be jumpy as hell. Instead, she was finding his presence strangely soothing. The knots that had been clenched up inside her for most of the day were loosening. But Christ, why was her flat so unwelcoming? Why did she insist upon plain white, picture-free walls, Spartan furniture, a complete absence of ornaments or personal possessions? She didn't like clutter, but would a few cushions hurt? And those light fittings had probably been trendy in 1965.

'Give me some credit,' she said. 'I promised him nothing. He told me his mother's name and I said I'd give it some thought.'

'OK.' He nodded at her to go on.

'I did then remote-access the system, so if you want to report me to Tulloch, I'm sure she'll be delighted.'

One eyebrow flickered. 'Save your breath, Flint, I'm not getting involved in your cat fight.'

'She started it.'

The eyebrow went up. Five wrinkles appeared between it and his hair-line.

'First thing I did was to run her through the box. Nothing.'

Joesbury nodded. The box was slang for the Police National Computer. 'So we know she's not banged up somewhere,' he said.

'Then I thought I'd better make sure she's still alive,' Lacey said. 'Because I'd feel a proper pratt if I spent hours trying to track her down, only to find out she'd gone under a bus five years ago.'

'And did she?'

'Go under a bus? I wish.' Lacey got up, pressed the space bar on her computer to activate the screen and looked back at Joesbury. He crossed to join her. He hadn't been home all day. There was no trace in the air of the lightly spiced cologne he wore after a shower. He smelled of London, of fast food and traffic and smoke and beer.

Knowing exactly what she was doing, and how it would be interpreted, she stepped closer to him. Their shoulders brushed and stayed together.

'Oh lord,' said Joesbury, as he took in the information on the screen.

It was a coroner's report, dated seven years earlier. The report itself ran to some ten pages and contained police statements, medical details, post-mortem reports. The summary was just two paragraphs long and told them that Karen Roberts, aged thirty-six, of Lambeth Road in Kennington, had taken her own life after several years of mental illness, including severe post-natal depression. She'd taken a whole load of diazepam, lain down in a warm bath and drawn a knife across her femoral artery. Her body had been discovered by her four-year-old son, Barnaby.

'He doesn't remember anything?' said Joesbury.

'Apparently not, although . . .'

'What?'

'What age do kids start remembering things?'

Joesbury made a *who knows?* gesture. 'Round about three, I would have thought. Huck says his first memory is going to feed the ducks one Sunday morning and falling in because I was talking to one of the mums, who was blonde and pretty. He was two and a half at the time. On the other hand, his mum's told the story so often he probably just thinks he remembers it.'

'I wonder if at some level he does remember it,' said Lacey. 'Barney, I'm talking about now. Remembers it, but just doesn't want it to be true.'

'Why do you say that?'

'He's a very switched-on kid. Very computer savvy, for one thing.' She explained about his systematic search for his mother. 'There was press coverage of Karen Roberts's suicide. Not much, but reporters invariably attend coroners' inquests and a kid finding his mother's body would be a story they'd be bound to cover. I found the coverage with a quick Google search. I can't believe he's never done the same thing.'

'You think he knows but he's in denial?'

'I think it's quite possible. He also told me he has what he called episodes. Memory black-outs. I think he found out about his mum, wiped it from his head and now his brain is playing odd tricks with him. That would make him a pretty screwed-up kid, wouldn't it? Acting out this elaborate charade of looking for his mum when all the time he knows she's dead.'

Joesbury said nothing. He didn't need to.

'What on earth do I do?' she asked him.

He shook his head. 'This is a bloody minefield. You have to talk to his dad.'

She'd known he was going to say that. She could have worked that one out for herself. 'I think he's scared of his dad.'

'Seriously scared, or just a bit wary of an emotionally distant parent?'

'I don't know. I don't know either of them well enough to judge.'

'Lacey, you can't give a vulnerable, disturbed kid potentially harmful information without speaking to his father first. Setting aside for a moment the damage you'd do to him, think about the implications for you if the father makes an official complaint.'

'I know.'

'If you think the kid's being abused at home, then you have to make it official. Otherwise, I tend to think families are best placed to sort their own problems out. Talk to his dad, take it from there.'

He hadn't told her anything she couldn't have worked out for herself. So why, exactly, had she asked him round?

'I will, thanks.'

Joesbury looked at his watch. 'Christ,' he said. 'Well, if I'm not staying, I'm going.'

Ignore the stab of disappointment. 'As obvious statements go, that had an elegant simplicity about it,' she said.

'Goodnight kiss out of the question?'

Don't smile at him. Don't even let your eyes soften. 'I appreciate your coming round, Sir.'

Wrong, too flirtatious! He'd taken hold of her wrist, was pulling her . . . ouch!

'What's up?' He'd seen the flicker of pain, was lifting her left wrist and loosening his fingers to reveal the plaster peeking out from beneath her sweater. A plaster that was blood-stained. She pulled away; he tightened his fingers, around her hand this time, so as not to hurt her.

'What's going on?' he asked her.

Shit, shit, shit. This is what he did. He wormed his way in and dug out her secrets, one by one. He'd keep on going, if she let him, until there was nothing left for him to find, and that would be—

'Lacey?'

'It got infected,' she said, looking him directly in the eye. 'It's a bit sore.'

'That scar's nearly five months old,' he said. 'No way did it get infected. Lacey, what did you do?'

It was none of his business. How dare he ferret his way into her head like this? Her mobile was ringing. No, her phone was still in the custody of the forensics service contracted to the Metropolitan Police. It was his phone. She watched him pull it out of his jacket pocket, check the screen, then put it to his ear.

'Want me to come?' he said after a moment.

He ended the call without saying anything more and slipped the phone back into his pocket.

'You know another kid went missing tonight?' he asked her.

Acutely conscious of the throbbing pain in her wrist and the sharp, twisting guilt in her chest, she nodded.

'Apparently he's now hanging by his ankles from Southwark Bridge.'

Both hands covered her mouth, pain forgotten. 'Dead?' she managed.

He shrugged. 'Not clear yet, but probably.'

'It doesn't fit. He doesn't kill them this quickly. And he doesn't hang their bodies from bridges.'

'If I ever meet him I'll be sure to pass on your disappointment. In the meantime, the line-access team have been called out to bring him down.'

She nodded. One of the specialisms of the Marine Unit was searching at heights and the line-access team was a group of trained climbers. They regularly checked the bridges of London and other high-profile buildings for explosive devices. Joesbury was by the door now. 'Are you coming?' he asked her.

She shook her head.

A sigh, quick and impatient. 'I'm a simple soul, but it strikes me it wouldn't hurt you or Dana to remind yourselves you both work on the same team.'

'She doesn't need me.'

'Have you considered that maybe I do?'

No, she could not be needed. Not by anyone and especially not by him. There was nothing in her to give. 'I can't.'

He dropped his eyes to her wrist again. The pain had become sharp and intense, like tears she couldn't let herself cry.

'Lacey, please sort yourself out,' he told her. She braced herself for the slam of the door, but it closed softly and sadly and he was gone.

46

'CHRIST, IT'S LIKE A FUCKING ROYAL VISIT. DON'T THESE people sleep? Or are they all the ruddy undead?'

Dana and Mark, in oilskins and lifejackets, were on the flybridge of the police launch as, a little over the speed limit, it emerged from the shadow of Tower Bridge and motored upstream towards Southwark. Directly in front of them, the turquoise and gold bridge had been cleared of traffic and pedestrians, but every square foot of pavement on the southern embankment seemed to have someone standing on it. Windows of the buildings that lined the river were awash with faces.

In the forty-five minutes since Peter Sweep had posted on Facebook that Oliver Kennedy was dangling from Southwark Bridge, the news had spread round London like a contagious and particularly unpleasant rash.

'It's sodding mental,' the chief press officer at New Scotland Yard had told Dana ten minutes earlier when she'd spoken to him on the phone. 'I've counted three broadcast crews already and more will be on their way. Just do what you have to do and let us know when you have something to give us. We'll try and keep the feeding frenzy off your back.'

Mark had a baseball cap pulled low over his face and a scarf tied high around his neck. He'd spent his career infiltrating criminal gangs. If his face became known, even appeared once on television, that would come to a sharp end. He was risking a great deal, just by being here. In the cabin below, his uncle, Sergeant Fred Wilson, was at the helm and Neil Anderson and Susan Richmond were standing in frosty silence. As they neared the bridge, a tall man in uniform joined Dana and Mark on the flybridge. Chief Inspector David Cook was the officer in charge of the Metropolitan Police's Marine Unit. He'd known Mark since he was a child.

'The lad's on a ledge about twenty feet above river level,' he told them. 'He's in some sort of black bag, possibly a heavy-duty binliner. It's difficult to see in the dark, but my lads have been under there already with binoculars and lights, so we know it's there.'

'What happened to dangling by the ankles?' asked Mark.

'Poetic licence on our friend's part, thank God,' said Dana.

'There,' said Cook as the boat reached the shadowed water beneath the bridge and slowed. 'Count along four of those vertical iron struts, starting at the pillar. About twenty feet above the water.'

'OK,' said Mark.

'Go directly up for about three feet, and you should just be able to make out a dark shadow. That's it.'

The boat passed under the bridge and the three of them looked up. A dark, shapeless mass was all Dana could make out.

'How the hell did he get it up there?' asked Mark.

Once on the other side, Fred turned the launch towards the south bank. From overhead came the sound of a helicopter.

'I hope to God that's one of ours,' said Cook, glancing up.

'I didn't call one,' said Dana. 'I think we can assume it's not.'

'Friggin' circus,' said Cook.

'I think the question is, how did it get down there?' Dana said to Mark. 'David thinks it was swung on a rope and dropped from above. There might be something attached to the bag to help it snag, but basically it was touch and go whether it would catch on something or just go tumbling down into the water.'

'So what's the plan?'

'The plan is to send a climber up to release it and lower it down to us,' said Dana. 'We're just going to pick up and brief Spiderman, apparently.'

Mark did his one-eyebrow trick. 'Who else?' he said.

'Spiderman's the nickname of our best climber,' said Cook. 'Young officer, not been with us long. Bit of a loose cannon, just between us, but he got his name for a reason.'

'He didn't meet us at Wapping because no one ever knows what bed he's going to be sleeping in,' said Dana. 'There's a list of young women police officers and the team have to go through them systematically. It takes a while.'

'He answered his mobile on the first call and he's on his way,' said Cook. 'He's a complete teetotaller so we never have to worry about calling him out. He's the right man for the job, Dana. That's a tricky climb, it's dark and it's wet. If the kid were definitely dead, we'd be taking much more time to prepare. Possibly even waiting till morning. If I send a less experienced climber up there's every chance he'll slip.'

'And you don't want footage of one of your officers dangling in mid air from Southwark Bridge while the world waits for us to bring down a child's body,' said Mark. 'The man's got a point, Tully.'

'He's arrived, Sir,' Fred called from below. 'He's just kitting up.'

'I'm rather curious to meet this bloke,' said Mark. 'Must get his autograph for Huck when it's all over.'

When this was all over, they'd be transporting the body of a child exactly Huck's age to the mortuary and she'd be on her way to tell his parents. Dana told herself to take it easy. Black humour was stock in trade for police officers. It was how they detached.

The launch reached the embankment, where another, smaller, police launch was tied up. Waiting for them at the foot of the steps was a very tall, very thin man in his late twenties.

Mark had already left the flybridge. Dana watched him throw a line to a constable on the other launch and slide a fender along the hull a few inches so that the two boats could moor up together without one damaging the other. The tall constable, followed by a squatter, older man similarly dressed, stepped on to the first launch and strode across to board theirs.

In the dim cabin light, Spiderman's hair looked black as soot and his face would have been stunningly handsome had it not been just a fraction too thin. His hands were thin too and looked twice as long as Dana's. He blinked hard as though to drive away the last vestiges of sleep. He towered above everyone else on the boat. He had to be six foot five.

'Have you had a look, Finn?' asked Cook.

The young officer hitched his harness a little higher around his waist and was prevented from replying by an enormous yawn. The older man had followed him into the cabin.

'We've got a line down from the ledge above,' the older man explained to Cook, while everyone in the cabin tried not to copy the yawn. 'We'll fasten that to Finn before he sets off and I'll guide it up. That's our last resort. He'll run a safety line up himself so that if he slips he won't go far and should be able to sort himself out.'

'Why would I slip, Sarge?' asked Spiderman. 'Did you grease it to make it extra interesting?'

Dana waited for Cook to give the young pratt the dressing-down he deserved. Instead, like an indulgent uncle, Cook gave him a pat on the shoulder. 'This is DI Tulloch,' he said. 'She's in charge of the South Bank Murders investigation. Dana, Constable Finn Turner.'

'Ma'am,' said Turner respectfully. His eyes were a warm chestnut brown and the look he gave her was anything but respectful.

'We need to do this as discreetly as possible,' she said. 'While you're climbing, can you keep radio transmissions to an absolute minimum? Assume that everybody out there, including all the news crews, can hear you. Obviously, if you need help, or you're stuck, then of course you have to talk to us.'

He nodded quickly in agreement. The look in his eyes said, *You are kidding me, Ma'am.*

'But try not to comment at all on what you find up there. If it is Oliver Kennedy, I want his parents to know first and I want them to know from me.'

'Of course,' he said and she couldn't help feeling she amused him.

'I think we're all set,' said the line-access sergeant from the doorway. 'Jim will take you across on the other boat, Finn. Give me a minute to get up top.'

Turner yawned again, raising his arms above his head. The roof wasn't nearly high enough for him to stretch out fully. 'Showtime,' he said, and followed his sergeant from the cabin.

Dana, Mark, Cook, Anderson and Richmond went on deck too and watched the two members of the line-access team cross back to the neighbouring launch. If anything, the crowd on the embankment had grown. A line of constables was trying to keep the press at bay, but they started calling out questions as the line-access sergeant climbed ashore and the two launches released their lines. As Uncle Fred steered them away from the embankment, all five passengers stayed on deck.

Southwark Bridge carries the A300 across the Thames and links the city of London on the north bank with Southwark on the south. Nearly eight hundred feet long, it is constructed of stone and iron, with four wide arches spanning the river. Constable Finn Turner would have to step off the bow of the other boat on to the third stone pier from the south bank, somehow scale the ten feet or so of pillar and then climb up and across the iron work that formed the arch. It would be damp. The stone would be slippery, the iron very cold.

Lights shone from the base of the piers, Victorian-style lanterns ran along the edge of the bridge and the apex of each arch had amber coloured navigation lights, but Dana felt a twist of nerves all the same. The lights weren't nearly bright enough for any of them to be confident about the climb.

When Fred judged he'd reached the middle of the river, he put the engine to idle to hold them in place. Behind them, two more police launches kept other river traffic at bay. On the downstream side of the bridge, Dana could see a couple of RIBs, Rigid Inflatable Boats, doing the same thing. She looked up. They were almost directly beneath the bag that held the body of Oliver Kennedy. The second launch, with Spiderman on board, moved slowly towards the third pier.

'Tide's high,' said Mark conversationally as they waited, each holding on to the rail to balance against the rocking and pitching of the boat. 'Moon must be full.'

'Couple of days yet,' said Cook. 'But you're right. It was nearly a metre higher than forecast at Tower Bridge an hour ago.'

'Why didn't he leave him on a beach this time?' said Anderson, to no one in particular, as they watched Spiderman walk to the bow of the launch, take hold of the line his sergeant had already lowered from above and fasten it to a cleat at his waist.

'Exactly,' said Richmond.

The sergeant on the bridge took up the slack on the safety line and Spiderman did an elaborate stretch then a fast little jog on the deck of the boat. On the shore, cameras flashed.

'Half of me would love to see that twat dangling in the air with his arse uppermost,' said Mark.

'He is a pillock,' said Cook. 'But he's something else when he's climbing. He won't slip.'

'This is all wrong,' muttered Richmond to herself. 'This is not what he does.'

'Am I good to go?' asked Turner over the radio.

'Dana?' said Cook.

Dana raised her radio. 'Go ahead,' she said.

Several yards away, Turner made a long-legged stride on to the stone kerb of the pier. He shuffled his feet awkwardly, slid backwards, gave a little sidestep right, then the same to the left. He moved closer to the pillar and then gazed up at what seemed to be a sheer face. He looked as if he had no idea how to start. Dana felt sick. He couldn't do it, they were going to look like idiots in front of the whole world.

'What the fuck?' said Mark, who rarely let a thought enter his head without articulating it.

'He does this,' said Cook. 'He's getting the measure of the climb. Give him a sec.'

'Bloody theatricals, if you ask me,' muttered Uncle Fred from the helm. 'Here we go.'

Once he started, Spiderman didn't climb the bridge, he danced up it. He scaled the stone pillar as though he really did have sticky feet, and once on the ironwork, his feet hardly seemed to touch one bar before leaping up to find the next. He didn't stop for a second. If he met a tricky section, he played with it, jumping to one side, then the other, sliding down a foot or two before springing back up again. At one point his feet lost contact altogether, he released one hand and swung like a monkey, grabbing another bar and swinging his legs back up until he was suspended upside-down. Then he wriggled up through the ironwork, until he was perched, frog-like, twenty feet above them. He looked directly down into the launch and Dana could have sworn he winked at her.

From there, it was a short crawl to where the body of Oliver Kennedy lay in a black bag. Turner reached it and sat back on his haunches, as though thinking.

'Net and a line,' he said into his radio, a second later.

His colleagues above were ready. Immediately, a line attached to a strong net was lowered down to where the climber was waiting.

'How will they get him down?' asked Richmond.

'If he can, I imagine he'll wrap that net round him and fasten it tight,' Anderson told her. 'Then lower it down to us.'

'It's coming on here?'

'We'll take it back to Wapping nick to do the initial examination,' said Anderson. 'The boss won't make any announcements till we've been able to confirm that it's Oliver.'

Richmond ran a hand over her face. 'I can't believe I got it so wrong,' she said.

'We can't second-guess these bastards,' Anderson told her.

'DI Tulloch.' It was Turner's voice, coming from directly above them, transmitted by the radio.

'This is Tulloch,' said Dana, who hadn't taken her eyes off Turner since he'd begun his climb. He'd pulled the net around the bag and secured it.

'Coming now,' he said, looking directly at her. 'Heads up, Ma'am.'

As the small, black bag with its pitiful contents was lowered from the bridge, Dana counted a dozen flashlights going off and closed her eyes. She felt Mark move her to one side and knew it was about to arrive. She heard Anderson telling Richmond to go and wait below if she wanted to and Richmond refusing to move. She heard the clink of metal that told her someone – Cook or Mark – had unfastened the line. Then the engine firing up. She opened her eyes and saw Finn Turner still watching her. He was trying to tell her something and knew he couldn't use the radio.

'Wait,' she said. 'Fred, hold up. Get him inside.'

'Dana, we have to get him back to Wapping,' said Mark.

'Get him in the cabin,' she repeated. Mark and Cook shared a look, but Mark crouched down and lifted the child. Before he'd even straightened up, he'd looked at her in surprise.

'Inside,' she repeated, her heart thundering, a voice in her head telling her something she didn't dare listen to.

This time no one questioned her. They watched Mark leave the deck and carry the black bag into the cabin. One by one they followed.

'David, do you have a knife?' asked Dana.

Silently, Cook handed one over and she dropped to her knees. The bag wasn't the glossy black she'd expected. It was dull, dirty, spattered with bird droppings. 'We have another bag on board, don't we?' she asked. Now that it came to it, she was almost afraid.

'Of course,' said Cook.

Dana reached out and pressed the knife tip into the plastic. It was heavy duty, thicker than a normal bin-liner, but the blade sliced through it easily. She made a ten-inch cut and pulled the plastic apart. That was enough.

Inside the bag were two pillows, wrapped tightly together with tape, and a dead fox.

'Ten-year-old boys weigh a lot more than that,' said Mark. 'Turner knew before he lowered it down to us. And that bag's filthy. It's even got some sort of weed growing on it. It wasn't left up there tonight.'

'I knew it, I bloody knew it,' gasped Richmond. Out of the corner of her eye, Dana thought she saw the profiler strike Anderson on the shoulder. He, in turn, seemed to shrink as the tension left him. 'You have no idea how glad I am to be wrong,' he replied.

Later, Dana was to think that the sight of Susan Richmond sobbing on Neil Anderson's shoulder was not the least surprising event of the evening.

47

'I WOULDN'T HAVE BELIEVED TELLING PARENTS THEIR CHILD might still be alive would be harder than telling them he's dead,' said Dana, an hour later. She and Susan Richmond had just arrived at an all-night café in Lewisham, a regular haunt of the team when they'd been working late. Mark, Anderson and Mizon were all waiting for them.

Without being asked, the young owner, a Greek Cypriot called Kristos, whom Dana sometimes thought could make a fortune selling information on police investigations to the national press, put mugs of instant coffee and warm bacon sandwiches in front of them.

'How are they holding up?' Mizon asked.

'Barely,' said Dana. 'They understand why we want to hold back the information of what we really found on the bridge tonight. And they've agreed to say nothing publicly until we make our statement tomorrow. Not that I'm taking any chances. The family liaison officer will stay with them overnight, with a uniformed presence outside their house to keep reporters at bay.'

'We won't be able to hold them off for long,' said Anderson.

'I know. The guv's agreed to a media black-out until at least noon tomorrow. Some time in the morning, Scotland Yard press office will send over a draft statement for our approval. I've also spoken to Mike Kaytes. He's the pathologist at St Thomas's we use most of the time,' she explained to Susan. 'He's happy to go along with us. You know Mike, I think he's secretly enjoying the intrigue.'

'You realize the parents will be starting to hope again?' said Richmond.

Dana nodded. 'They almost seemed disappointed when we told them we hadn't found Oliver on the bridge,' she said. 'But I suppose it's easy to judge when you have no idea what people are going through.'

'It's a very common reaction,' said Richmond. 'They want the worst to be over so they can begin to deal with it. People in their situation always say not knowing is the worst. That's until they do know, of course, and then they'd give anything to have that tiny bit of hope back.'

'Is there hope?' said Mizon. 'Is there any chance we might find Oliver alive?'

'I'd say all bets are off with this one,' said Mark, who, as usual, was the first to finish his sandwich and who, as usual, was eyeing up Dana's. 'Fred says the moss we saw on the bag is typical of what you'd expect to see growing on objects left in and around the river for a few weeks. He and Dave are pretty certain it was left there some time ago. Dave's going to get his guys searching the other prominent bridges over the next few days, to see if there isn't another one lying around.'

'That's all we need,' said Dana.

'The fox is puzzling me, though,' Mark went on. 'Presumably it's just a piece of roadkill he scraped up somewhere, in case we brought dogs in. He wanted them to smell blood and the whole farce to become that bit more convincing.'

'Except dogs would have ignored it,' said Dana.

'Exactly, which tells you something in itself.'

Richmond was looking from one face to the next. 'What am I missing?' she asked.

'Cadaver dogs are trained to react to decomposing human flesh,' explained Anderson. 'They ignore animal remains.'

'So Sweep knows a bit about how the police work, but not that much,' said Richmond. 'Which means he's probably not a police officer. Or even someone on the periphery of the investigation.'

'Exactly,' said Mark.

'Something to be grateful for,' said Dana.

'But if he's not one of the good guys, albeit a renegade, then he has to be one of the bad,' said Mark. 'From what I can gather, this Sweep character has known stuff that only people on the inside would know. If he's not one of us, he has to be either the killer, or someone in league with him.'

'I can go through all his comments tomorrow,' offered Mizon, talking directly to Mark. 'Try and come to a view about which really do show inside knowledge and which are just lucky guesses.'

Dana had suspected Gayle Mizon of having a crush on Mark before now. Unfortunately, because Gayle was a nice girl and as straight as they come, he couldn't see past Lacey-Bloody-Flint.

'That would be a tiresome job but useful, thank you,' said Dana. 'We really need to know whether we can rule him out or not.'

'What do you think, Susan?' asked Anderson, and in spite of everything, Dana had to hide a smile. The profiler had been Anderson's public enemy number one since she'd been introduced to the investigation. Now her opinion was important and she was Susan.

Richmond shook her head. 'I daren't send you off on the wrong track while Oliver could still be alive,' she said.

'Go out on a limb,' said Anderson. 'We will neither act upon it nor hold you to it.'

'Promise?'

Were those two flirting?

'Peter Sweep isn't your killer,' she said. 'He's a mischief-maker. I think when Gayle does her analysis tomorrow, she'll find that every bit of his so-called insider knowledge is either a result of closely watching what's actually going on, or lucky guessing. Creating the sort of public mayhem we saw tonight is what he gets off on. He will have been there, watching everything unfold, rubbing his hands with glee.'

'Creaming his jeans,' said Anderson, nodding in agreement.

'Not the phrase I would have used, but I can't argue.'

Good God, Anderson was blushing.

'Oliver is still missing,' said Mark. 'Could a mischief-maker have engineered that?'

'And Sweep knew about it before his parents did,' said Dana.

'This is doing my head in,' said Anderson.

'Could it be a prank?' suggested Mark. 'Could Oliver be hiding up with some mates somewhere? Maybe a bit scared now at the furore they've unleashed? There is something pretty childish about the whole bloody circus we had tonight.'

'Oliver and Sweep fellow pranksters?' said Dana. 'It would take a pretty disturbed kid to put his parents through what the Kennedys have been suffering tonight.'

An electronic singing sound made them all jump. It was Mark's phone. He looked at the display, then instantly up at Dana. He held eye contact for a fraction of a second before glancing down again. Not a look she'd seen on his face before. An expression that looked a lot like guilt. He began tapping out a response, leaning back in his chair so that no one would see the screen.

She was being stupid. Anyone could be texting him, even at this time of night. It could be someone from Scotland Yard, a mate, even his ex-wife. So why did she know for an absolute fact it was Lacey Flint?

48

'I*'VE REMEMBERED SOMETHING ELSE. DO YOU WANT ME TO TELL you about it?'*

'If you'd like to.'

'Do you want me to tell you?'

The patient was getting agitated again. 'Yes, I do,' said the psychiatrist.

'Shit.'

The psychiatrist said nothing. She sat, still and unmoved, maintaining eye contact with the patient.

'I said shit.'

'Yes, I heard. What about it?'

'That's what I remember. The smell of shit. They all shat themselves, just before they died. It was running down their legs, staining their pants, all over the floor.'

'Well, that's not so surprising. When people are terrified, which those boys must have been, they often lose control of their bodily functions. It's normal.'

'It's disgusting. I didn't mind the blood, the blood didn't make me feel funny at all, but the shit. Just turns my stomach. Why'd they have to do that? Why'd they have to shit?'

49

Wednesday 20 February

'MORNING, MA'AM,' IT WAS STENNING. 'I'VE GOT GOOD news and bad news.'

'Give me the bad.' Dana was only half awake. Christ, they'd found him. Oliver Kennedy had been found on a grubby, oil-streaked beach somewhere.

'Bartholomew Hunt has already been on TV this morning, announcing to the world that he seriously doubts we found the body of Oliver Kennedy last night. He says in his view it was a massive hoax, that the killer does not dispatch his victims so quickly, that Oliver is still alive somewhere and being fed upon and that the shambles that is this city's law-enforcement agency (that's us, by the way) has endangered his life by wasting time and resources on a wild-goose chase.'

'Somebody's tipped him off.' Christ, she could count on the fingers of one hand how many people knew it wasn't Oliver on the bridge last night. 'OK, Pete, I appreciate the heads up. I'll see you at the station.'

'Hold your horses, DI Tulloch. I said good news and bad. I've only given you the bad.'

Suddenly, something was pulling the sides of Dana's throat together.

'What?'

'We've found him.'

'Say that again?' Wide awake now, bolt upright, the only thing keeping her from jumping out of bed was the fear of missing Stenning's next words.

'We've got Oliver Kennedy. Safe and sound. Cold as an icicle and seriously frightened, but basically fine. I'm behind the ambulance now, following him to St Thomas's. Even his parents don't know yet.'

'Christ, I can't believe it.' Dana was up, looking round the room for clothes. Anything would do.

'Neither could we, to be honest, Ma'am. We got the call about half an hour ago. I was on my way in and just went straight there.'

'OK, Pete, don't tell me any more now. Do your absolute best to keep this quiet and don't let reporters anywhere near Oliver or the medical staff treating him. I'll get his parents and bring them to the hospital. If we can keep this under wraps, we might be able to use it.'

'Will do, Ma'am. See you there.'

The living child was as pale as the dead ones had been and, frankly, not much more animated. There was a red bruise on his left cheek, and the skin on his right cheekbone had been scraped. Huge shadows under his eyes. But this one was sitting up, clutching his mother's hand tightly, blinking his tears away.

'Hi, Oliver,' said Dana, letting the door of the private hospital room close softly behind her. 'I'm Dana. I'm a detective. I need to ask you some questions, if that's OK.'

Oliver's mother, leaning out of her chair to be closer to her son, glared at Dana as though she might bite her if she got too close. 'He needs to sleep,' she said.

A few hours ago, she'd have promised Dana anything to have her son back again.

'This won't take long,' said Dana, pulling up a chair and sitting down. 'Well, Oliver, you've given us all a bit of a fright. Can you tell me what happened?'

It took longer than it should have. In spite of everything she could say to reassure him, Oliver was frightened of her. She suspected he'd be frightened of anything and everything unfamiliar for a long time to come. He was another victim, even if he was still alive and relatively unhurt.

Eventually, though, she'd heard everything he had to say. He told her that when Joe had gone running back to the tennis club, he'd hung around at the gate of the park, keeping Joe in sight and making sure he stayed beneath a streetlight. Oliver had just seen his friend reappear from the clubhouse when someone jumped him from behind. A large sack had been pulled over his head and then he'd been picked up and carried.

'Were you put in a car or a van?' Dana had asked.

Oliver had shaken his head. 'He just carried me,' he said. 'I don't think we went far.'

They hadn't gone far. Oliver had been found in the choir stalls of a nearby church, less than five hundred yards from where he'd gone missing. Once inside the building, his abductor had flung Oliver down hard on his face, kneeling on his back to prevent him getting up. He'd tied his wrists and ankles and then put a gag around his mouth and a blindfold around his eyes.

'I couldn't really breathe,' said the child. 'It got worse if I struggled, so I had to stop. I thought I was going to suffocate.'

'You've been very brave,' said Dana. 'Can you tell me anything about this person's voice?'

Oliver shook his head. 'He never spoke to me,' he said.

He never spoke? So how could they be sure it was a he?

'Not at all?' asked Dana. 'Not even to tell you what to do?'

'No, he just pushed me and pulled me.'

'Oliver, this is quite a difficult question, but can you tell me anything about how big this person was?'

Oliver looked puzzled, so she tried again. 'I know you didn't see him,' she said, 'but he carried you and got quite close to you. For example, did he seem as big as your dad?'

Alan Kennedy was around five foot eleven and strongly built. Oliver looked at his dad, standing silently in the corner of the room, and shook his head. 'More like Martin,' he said.

Martin, Oliver's teenage brother, looked at his dad in alarm. 'I was at home all night, wasn't I, Dad?'

Dana smiled at the older boy. 'I think Oliver just means whoever attacked him was about your size,' she said. 'Which is very useful to know.'

Martin Kennedy was about Dana's own height, somewhere around five feet four inches tall. The height of an average-sized woman.

'So if he didn't speak to you, he didn't threaten you at all?' said Dana.

Oliver shook his head.

'Can you tell me what happened next?' asked Dana.

'It all went quiet,' replied Oliver. 'I heard the door being closed and the key turned, so I figured he'd gone. I didn't dare move for ages, but then my arms and legs started to hurt so much I had to.'

Oliver's mother inched herself closer to her son. Her right arm was stretched over his pillow, her left hand clutched both of his together.

'I realized I could move my wrists a bit,' said Oliver. 'I had quite a thick coat on and he'd taped my wrists together round the sleeves. When I twisted them around and rubbed them together, it got looser.'

'He's got tiny wrists,' said his mother, reaching out one finger and gently stroking the back of her son's wrist. They looked pink, a bit sore.

'Go on, Oliver,' said Dana.

'I managed to get my hand free,' said Oliver. 'It took ages and it hurt, but I kept on going because I knew once he came back he would . . .'

'Your son is an extremely brave young man,' said Dana, turning to the boy's father, giving Oliver chance to take a breath and his mother time to wipe away the tears. When she could hear his breathing had calmed, she turned back. 'Once you had a hand free, were you able to get the rest of the tape off?'

He nodded. 'Off my eyes and mouth first. Then my legs. I was in some sort of room. It was really dark. I couldn't see much but I could hear buzzing, like machines. It was like the boiler room at school.

But I couldn't get out. He'd locked the door. I banged on it for ages but nobody came.'

Jesus, the search must have passed within yards of the church.

'So what happened?'

'In the end I gave up. There was another door and when I opened it I was in the church. I knew where I was then, but I still couldn't get out. I couldn't even find a phone. I thought there might be one in the vestry but it was locked.'

'So you just had to wait?'

Oliver nodded. 'There was a bolt on the boiler-room door. On the church side, I mean, so I locked it. So if he came back, he wouldn't be able to get to me. Then I went and hid in the choir stalls. I don't know if he came back. If he did, I didn't hear him.'

'You brave, clever boy,' said Dana, as, across the room, the door opened fractionally. Neil Anderson looked in.

'This is Sergeant Anderson, he's a detective too,' said Dana, noticing how alarmed the child became suddenly. 'Will you excuse me for a second?'

She got up and followed Neil outside. 'SOCOs are still in the church, but they've finished with the boiler room, where Oliver was left,' he said.

'Anything?' asked Dana.

'They say they're pretty certain the boiler room isn't where the other boys were killed. They say you can't spill that much blood and not leave a trace. Especially as neither the floor nor the walls lend themselves to thorough cleaning. And there's no drain of any description.'

'Did they find anything we can rely on?'

'Some footprints that are too big to be Oliver's but not as big as most men's. They've taken photographs, obviously. Also there were some fibres on Oliver's jacket. Black, look like some sort of wool mix. They could be important, especially if they match nothing at the Kennedy house.'

Dana stopped, turned and leaned against the corridor wall. Anderson did the same.

'How's the kid?' he asked, after a second.

'Good as you could expect,' said Dana. She looked at her

watch. 'I have to be at the Yard in less than an hour,' she said.

'Have you decided what our official line is on Sweep yet?'

'We're going to announce that we no longer believe him to be the killer, simply a malicious prankster. He will be found and brought to justice, but he's no longer a major focus of our inquiries. We've asked Facebook to block the Missing Boys site. From now on, we're going to ignore him.'

Anderson pursed his lips in a silent whistle.

'You think we're being rash?'

'Boss, what if he did take Oliver last night, but something prevented him from going back to finish him off? All the shenanigans on Facebook could just have been the real killer venting his frustration.'

'Possible.'

'In which case, taking away his soapbox and announcing to the world we're not taking him seriously any more could just make him do something stupid.'

Dana straightened up. 'I hope so,' she said. 'Because until she does, we won't catch her.'

Barney's dad was in the kitchen, eating breakfast, when Barney came down. He looked up and his face creased with concern. 'What time did you get to sleep?' he asked. 'Or did it not actually happen at all?'

'I think I heard you come in,' replied Barney, who didn't think he'd ever felt this tired or ill in his life before. It had been impossible to sleep after Peter's Facebook message. Peter was someone he knew. How else would he be able to order Barney's favourite pizza? He knew who he was, where he lived and what his favourite pizza toppings were. Jeez, fewer than half a dozen people probably knew all three of those things about him.

He sat down and stared at his dad. *Did you order me a pizza last night, Dad? Did you?*

'What?' said his dad, cereal spoon hovering.

If he said nothing, if he didn't mention it, then his dad might. His dad might give himself away. Last night, someone calling himself Peter Sweep had abducted and murdered a ten-year-old boy. He'd tied him up, put his photograph on Facebook, and then kept the world informed when he'd cut open his throat and fed off his blood. Last night, once again, his dad had been on the boat.

'*... usually when killers go for one particular type of victim, it's because those victims remind them of a person in real life ... They can't kill the one they really want to, so they choose – do you know the word surrogate?*'

Barney looked at his father's hands, at the skin around his mouth, as if there might be some traces of Oliver Kennedy's blood. *Is it my throat you want to cut, Dad? My blood you want to drink? Do I have to die to stop you?*

His dad was looking at the TV screen behind Barney's head. The volume was still low. Now he was looking round for the remote.

Shall we just end this now? I'll get the sharpest knife I can from the drawer, I'll lie down on the table and you won't even have to tie me down because if Mum's gone for good and you're a murderer, then I really don't want to live any more.

'They've found him,' said his dad, cranking up the volume. 'Thank God for that.'

'Found who?' Barney managed, before turning to look at the screen. A reporter in a green coat was standing outside St Thomas's hospital.

'That kid who went missing. I nearly had bloody heart failure when I heard about it last night. That's why I was home early.'

Oliver was alive? Barney could hardly believe what he was seeing and hearing. Alive and unhurt. He'd spent the night locked in a church? A church miles away from the boat at Deptford Creek that he'd heard his dad laughing on?

'I tell you what, mate, until this guy's caught, I'm going to have to give up working late. I know you're sensible but I just can't deal with the stress. What's the matter? Barney? Buddy, why on earth are you crying?'

50

'ELLO, I'M LOOKING FOR STEWART ROBERTS. CAN YOU tell me where I might find him, please?'

For the first time in what felt like months, but was probably only just a few weeks, Lacey was wearing formal clothes. An off-the-peg suit that felt looser than when she'd worn it last, a plain white blouse and low-heeled court shoes. Her hair was twisted up at the nape of her neck. It was nothing special, just the clothes she wore when she had to look serious, like a proper detective. It was an outfit in which she never felt herself. Which was perhaps as well, because had she felt like herself, she might never have made it inside the main door.

Stewart Roberts was a lecturer in English literature at King's College, London, the fourth oldest university in England and one of the most highly regarded in the world. He worked from the daunting, pale-stone buildings on the Strand.

Academia – just the thought of it made her shudder. At the start of the year, for only a few days, she'd been a student in the most prestigious university in the land. The experience had almost killed her.

The woman in the office looked Lacey up and down and decided she was a sales rep. 'Do you have an appointment?' she asked.

Lacey pulled her warrant card out of her inner pocket and held it up. 'CID,' she said. 'If Mr Roberts isn't here, please tell me where I can find him.'

'I'll just check.'

A few moments later, Lacey knocked at a blue painted door on the right-hand side of a long corridor. The office behind was large. She counted three untidy desks, two of them occupied. Stewart Roberts stood as she entered the room and she could see that he recognized her. He was an attractive man, she realized, if you went for bookish types. Mid forties, with thick grey hair and neat, regular features. Spectacles that looked trendy rather than otherwise. His clothes were better than you saw on most academics. His jeans looked designer, his sweater expensive. He was frowning at her now.

'My secretary said the police wanted to see me. Did she mean you?'

'*Our* secretary,' mumbled the large, middle-aged woman at the other desk, without looking up.

'Is there somewhere we can talk privately?' Lacey asked.

The woman visibly stiffened. There was no way she was moving.

Stewart looked at his watch. 'I have a lecture at three. What's it about?'

Lacey glanced at his colleague and raised her eyebrows. He got the message. 'We'll go to the chapel,' he said. 'No one's ever in there.'

'This is beautiful,' said Lacey a few minutes later as they stepped inside a Victorian chapel filled with gold light and jewelled colours. To either side of the nave, crimson pillars supported elaborately panelled archways; beyond them were stained-glass windows. Above were more pillars, more arched windows and then cross-beams and an intricately decorated ceiling. Directly ahead were five more stained-glass windows above the altar, the central one a strikingly realistic depiction of the crucificion.

'Yes, it is quite something,' said Stewart. 'Restored in 2001.'

'And no one uses it?'

'Slight exaggeration on my part. There are services here most days. So what can I do for you, Lacey, isn't it? I really do have a lecture at three.'

'It's about Barney.'

Instant alarm on his face. 'Has something happened to him?'

'No, he's fine. That is, I'm sure he's safe and well, but I am worried about him.'

She waited for the reaction. Upon being told their kids were in trouble, parents invariably went on the attack. It was usually difficult to predict in advance whether the object of their aggression would be the child, or the officers who'd come to report, but it was invariably one of the two.

Stewart, though, surprised her. He walked slowly and deliberately to the front pew and removed the coat he'd thrown over his shoulders as they'd left his office. He sat down, leaving room for her to sit beside him without feeling crowded. Then he waited for her to tell him more.

'I thought you should know that Barney has been looking for his mother,' she began. 'For the better part of a year now. He's been placing ads in the classified sections of local papers. He has a plan to hit all the papers in greater London and then gradually spread out over the south-east. Every penny he earns at the newsagent's he spends on advertising. He wants me to help him now. He wants me to get her put on the missing-persons list, to launch a proper police inquiry.'

When she glanced over, the man beside her had visibly paled. He'd wrapped his jacket around his lower arms like a muff, or a comforter. 'Barney's mother is dead,' he told her.

'I know that. I did an online search for her after I spoke to him.'

Stewart shook his head slowly. 'I had no idea he still thought about her,' he said. 'He hasn't mentioned her in years.'

'I'm afraid she's on his mind a great deal. Do you never talk about her at all?'

He was fiddling with something on the coat, twisting it, worrying it. 'Never,' he said. 'I've been waiting for him to ask. I should have known the fact that he didn't was a problem in itself.'

Both afraid of being the first to raise the forbidden subject, each waiting for the other to bring it up.

'He found her, did you know that?'

'Yes, I did,' said Lacey.

'He and I had been out for the day. He wasn't an easy baby. Completely adorable in many ways, but demanding. Needed constant attention and entertainment. Even I found him exhausting and I wasn't with him most of the day. Karen just couldn't deal with it and I was trying to give her a break. I thought a bit of peace and quiet for a few hours might help. When we got back, he went running round the house looking for her. He'd climbed up the stairs before I even knew where he was and pushed open the bathroom door. By the time I got up there, he'd climbed in himself. I think he was trying to get her out . . . God, the two of them, the water had splashed everywhere. It looked like the whole room was covered in blood.'

'I'm so sorry,' said Lacey. 'How terrible for him. For you both.'

'For the first few weeks, he asked for her a lot. Just Mummy, Mummy, over and over again. And he had very bad nightmares – it wasn't difficult to imagine what they were about. After a while, he just stopped asking and I suppose I was relieved. It seemed so much easier just to pretend he'd never had a mother. Jeez, I really screwed up, didn't I?'

Yes, thought Lacey. *It's what we do. We screw up, and those we're supposed to protect are the ones who get damaged.*

Stewart was looking at his watch. 'I really have to go,' he said. 'Thank you. I'll take care of it.'

Lacey watched him pull his coat back on and walk down the central aisle. Only when the heavy oak door had closed behind him did she realize he'd left something on the pew, something that must have fallen from the pocket of his coat while he'd been fidgeting with it. A small, black glove.

PART THREE

51

Saturday 8 March

OFTEN, IN THE OTHER WORLD, LACEY TRIED TO PICTURE the hall where those who were imprisoned physically met with those who served time in other ways, and could never do it. Yet once inside, it became as familiar as her own bedroom. Creamy yellow, scuff-marked walls, dust collecting in corners, high barred windows that never seemed to show anything but grey cloud. Often, when she was in here, Lacey felt as though she'd been in this large, dusty, echoing space for ever and that the world outside was nothing more than vague memories and mostly-forgotten dreams.

'So how long since anything's happened?' the prisoner asked.

'Nearly three weeks,' said Lacey. 'Two weeks, four days, to be precise, since Oliver Kennedy was found alive and well. The clocks will go forward soon, the evenings will be light again. People are actually starting to wonder if it's over.'

Pretty eyes blinked and narrowed. 'Has there been a deathbed confession?'

'Not that I'm aware of.'

'Then it's not over. If he's still alive, he's planning that someone else won't be.'

'You sound very sure of yourself.'

Shoulders rose, fell, the prisoner rolled her eyes and pulled a face.

277

'You're right,' she agreed. 'What could I possibly know about serial killers?'

'And there was I, thinking the police and the medical profession had black humour all sewn up.'

'You want to spend some time in a high-security prison.'

'If DI Tulloch has her way, I probably will.'

Across the room something fell and shattered. There was a scurry of movement, a muttering of recrimination. Sound always seemed much louder in here, shrill and grating, and when someone yelled, Lacey could almost feel the vibrations spinning round in her ear-drums.

'I take it diplomatic relations have not been resumed?'

'She's had me into the station three times,' Lacey said. 'She clearly doesn't believe I know nothing more about the discovery of Tyler King's body than I've already told them.'

'She's a cow. But in fairness to her, you do.'

'Hardly. Without any evidence of where that text came from, all I have is a hunch I can't prove. And yet she has someone watching my flat every Tuesday and Thursday. I'm sure she'd have it searched if she could get a warrant.'

'She's jealous.'

'Of what, exactly? My meteoric career? Dazzling social life?'

'She's jealous because he loves you.'

Lacey told herself not to grin like a half-wit, that it really made no difference whether he did or he didn't. Except, wasn't the belief that he did, in spite of everything, the reason she was able to go on?

'She's gay,' Lacey said.

Hazel-blue eyes twinkled. 'Maybe she's jealous because you love him.'

'I'm not going to dignify that—'

'Yeah, yeah, so are you still seeing the shrink?'

'Don't have a choice on that one if I want to keep my job.'

Eyebrows twitched. Eyelids narrowed. 'You haven't resigned then?'

Lacey braced herself for an argument. Or an I-told-you-so moment. 'I haven't changed my mind. I'm just not prepared to leave under a cloud.'

'That's my girl. Does seem a bit of a waste, though, when you can get all the therapy you need here for free.'

'And believe me, you do me much more good.'

The prisoner leaned forward an inch or so and tipped her head first one way and then the other. Then she sat back and stared for several long seconds without speaking. 'Hmmn,' she said eventually. 'You sure?'

Half-amused, Lacey waited the silence out. As if she was going to fall for the steely-eyed stare. Hadn't she taught it to this girl in the first place? Sure enough, fewer than ten seconds had gone by before boredom set in.

'So, what's the latest on Peter Sweep?'

'What do you know about Peter Sweep? You can't be allowed to use Facebook?'

'Not officially. But we can access the internet under supervision. And nobody pays too much notice. Why would they? All the porn channels are blocked. So, go on, Peter Sweep?'

'The official line is that he was a time-waster,' said Lacey. 'Some nut milking the case for his own twisted ends. He wanted attention, to be the centre of a massive media storm, and got rather more than he'd bargained for. The reaction to his kidnapping of Oliver put the wind up him and he's lying low.'

'As, coincidentally, is the killer.'

'Peter Sweep isn't the killer, the MIT have been very clear about that.'

'And of course they're never wrong. Now, when are you going to tell me what's up with you?'

Somehow they never stayed on safe ground for very long. Lacey shook her head. 'I'm OK. I'm struggling with that business in Cambridge, but I'm coping.'

Silence. She was getting the steely-eyed treatment again. Well, that was OK, she just had to sit it out.

Seconds ticked by. At least six, maybe she even made it to seven.

'I've done something really stupid,' she said, and could feel the tears smarting behind her eyes.

The other woman was marble still. 'I doubt that, but I'm listening.'

Lacey tried to smile, didn't quite make it. Then she tugged the sleeve of her sweater up over her wrist. She untied the knot and starting to unravel the bandage. The girl reached out and stopped her.

'It's OK,' she said. 'I know what you did.'

'It's like scratching an itch,' said Lacey, as though pleading to be understood. 'Once you think about it, you can't not do it.'

'Does it help?'

'Yes. It really does. It's like a drug. Like valium. The scream that's been building up inside me just melts away.'

'Until the next time?'

Really no need to answer that. Overcome with shame, Lacey dropped her eyes to the Formica table-top. When she finally looked up, the face opposite hers was that of a crestfallen child.

'I really screwed you up, didn't I?' said the prisoner.

A damp film was swimming across Lacey's vision. Tears were very close. 'I think I managed that one by myself,' she answered.

'Ten minutes, ladies!' called the officer on duty. There was a general flurry around the room as people began the process of getting ready to leave.

'How's Mark?' asked the prisoner.

Lacey sighed. 'Avoiding me. I haven't seen him since – well, since he found out I'm not as tough as he likes to believe. I don't know, maybe he thinks I had something to do with the murders as well. He started out believing me guilty of everything, maybe he's just reverting to form.'

'Ever thought of telling him the truth?'

A long silence. Visitors were starting to leave the room. Prisoners were filing out of a door at the back.

'No, you're right. You can't. And you can't be with someone and keep a tiny piece of yourself back.'

'This is not a tiny piece we're talking about,' said Lacey, keeping her voice low, as people passed close by. 'It's who I am. And not with him, no. For some reason, he's the one person I can't hide anything from. Apart from you, of course.'

'You really do love him, don't you?'

Lacey leaned back in her chair. Love him? Did that really, honestly, come anywhere close?

'If I wasn't around, you could be with him.'

All the light had left the other woman's face. Lacey knew instinctively she was deadly serious. She sat upright again.

'I'm not sure where you're going with this, but I think you need to stop,' she said.

Simultaneously, both women stood. 'Maybe we need to face facts,' said the other. 'If I disappear, you're safe. Nothing to tie you to what happened before. Nothing for anyone to find out.'

'I'm not listening.' Lacey bent to pick up her bag, blood pounding in her ears.

'I'll do it. For you. I'll do it gladly.'

'Stop it. Now.'

Around them, faces were turning their way. Violence erupted so swiftly and suddenly in these situations, everyone was constantly on their guard.

'You are the one person I can be myself with,' said Lacey, not caring who heard, as long as the girl in front of her got the message. 'If I didn't have this time with you, I'd be lost.'

'If you lost me, you could have him.'

A heartbeat. A decision, made years ago, never articulated before.

'Then I choose you. Do you hear me? I choose you.'

52

'ABBIE, DO YOU REMEMBER MY MUM?'

Abbie Soar, Harvey and Jorge's mum, put down the chopping knife and gave the smallest, saddest shake of her head.

'I don't, I'm afraid,' she said. 'It was just you and your dad when you first arrived at pre-school.'

The kitchen door opened, Jorge's strong, clear voice rang throughout the house and Harvey appeared, tugging at the waistband of his school trousers.

'Mum, can you get me Tommy Hilfiger's boxer shorts?' he asked, heading for the counter, nose in the air, like a hound sniffing out truffles.

'Possibly. But what would Tommy Hilfiger wear?'

Harvey pushed his body against that of his mother. 'You know what I mean,' he said, looking up into her eyes and digging his chin into her breastbone in a way that looked pretty uncomfortable but which Abbie didn't seem to mind. She wrapped her hands around his middle and worked her fingers inside his waistband. Then she bent her head and nuzzled her face against Harvey's neck. It was the sort of physical intimacy of which Barney had no personal experience.

He turned away, fixing his attention instead on the photographs on the wall. They were in black and white, all taken by Abbie in foreign countries: black kids dressed as soldiers, who might have been playing a game except for the hollow look in their eyes; women with dark headscarves and startlingly pale eyes, watching out over arid landscapes for men who would never return; people limping from a burning hospital.

It was pretty depressing stuff. Not a single picture on the wall made you feel good about life. But the picture he could see reflected in the glass of most of the photographs was disturbing him even more. A mother, treating her child's body like an extension of her own; her son nestling against her as though they were two adjoining pieces of a jigsaw. For a second, Barney felt rage threatening to overwhelm him.

Not fair, not fair!

OK, Harvey didn't have a dad, but dads weren't the same. Dads earned money and kept you fed and clothed and drove you around the place, but mums wrapped their bodies around yours and made you feel safe. Mums were the ones who cried when you cried, but loved your tears all the same because they had the power to make them go away. Mums were there in the night, when dark, twisting fears were wrapping themselves around you. Mums were the ones who lay down close and whispered stories about riding through tropical forests on blue elephants. Mums were the ones who could put their hands on your bare bum and bite your neck and nobody would think it at all unusual.

Not fair!

He'd heard nothing from Lacey. He'd known it had been bad luck to mention his mum to her. Now he'd done it with Abbie, too. In the picture glass he could see her now, watching him over Harvey's head.

'Tell you what, Hon,' she said to her son. 'Will you go and get my phone for me? I left it in Jorge's room.'

With a heavy sigh, as though there were no end to the effort expected of him, Harvey left the room.

'Did you take all these?' asked Barney, embarrassed now, feeling as though he'd give anything to take back what he'd just revealed about his mum.

'Years ago,' Abbie said. 'Before Harvey was born.'

Upstairs, Jorge had stopped singing. Barney could hear him and Harvey talking.

'I asked your dad once about your mum,' said Abbie. 'Not being nosy, just friendly. He told me it was just you and him. And he said it in such a way that made me feel he didn't want me to ask any more questions. So I didn't. As far as I know, no one else ever did either.'

Barney looked at a picture of a boy of about his own age, gazing up at the camera. A boy with a blood-soaked bandage around his head. 'You've seen some pretty nasty stuff,' he said.

Abbie came closer, until she could put a hand gently on Barney's shoulder. The little finger of her hand brushed softly against his neck.

'Yes,' she said. 'I have.'

53

Monday 10 March

'YOU SAVED ME THE BEST VIEW,' SAID DANA, AS SHE settled into the chair by the window and stiffened against a shiver. It would be cold here, floor-to-ceiling windows made it inevitable in March, but the view from the first-floor Blue Print Café on Butler's Wharf was just about worth it.

'Actually, I didn't,' replied Detective Superintendent Weaver, nodding downstream. Judging by the level of wine in his glass, he'd arrived early. 'That's the one I prefer.'

Dana had been looking past the thousand-year-old Tower of London towards the metallic gleam of the city. Every brick, every steel plate, every pane of reinforced bomb-proof glass sang out power. She turned a 90-degree angle. Warehouses, dock buildings, rotting wooden piers.

'Whistler did a series of sketches of the Thames warehouses,' said Weaver. 'I've got copies at home. I'd have them on the wall, but Mary thinks unsigned prints are naff so I keep them in a folder in my study. Incredibly atmospheric – I'll bring them in some time. Torn sails flapping in the gales, masts brushing against the rooftops, buildings that seem to be growing out of the river and tumbling into it at the same time. Working boats like beached whales, you can't see how they'll ever get out of the mud.

And then the tide comes in and they're off again, to distant shores.'

'Very poetic, Sir.'

'And so many people, scurrying around like ants, with their individual jobs and their collective purpose. In over a hundred years it hasn't changed.'

'I hadn't appreciated luxury riverside apartments and embankment restaurants were popular in Whistler's day,' said Dana, as the waiter approached them.

'Yes, very funny. The detail might have evolved, but the picture remains the same to me. East of here is what London's really all about. The city, on the other hand, could be anywhere. What'll you have?'

With the skill borne of frequent practice, Dana opened the menu and spotted the choices that would be the easiest to force down. 'Salad and the risotto, please,' she said. 'Do you want me to kick off?'

Weaver pulled out a notebook and put it, unopened, on the table. Dana had brought her laptop.

'The exercise we did monitoring traffic in and around the dump sites threw up several dozen vehicles that travelled along more than one of the routes being watched on the evenings the bodies were left,' she began. 'We're following them up to see if any of the registered keepers have a record of any kind. If they do, we want to know what they were doing on the nights the boys went missing.'

'Anything yet?'

'Nothing, but we're not quite through the list. After that, we'll go back to those who don't have form.'

'This doesn't feel like first-offence territory to me,' said Weaver.

'No. But it could just be someone who didn't get caught. Dave Cook's team have finished their search of the main Thames bridges. Apart from the one they found on Tower Bridge, there was nothing.'

The day Oliver Kennedy had been found safe and well in a London church, the line-access team had searched Tower Bridge and found a parcel similar to the one retrieved from Southwark Bridge by Constable Finn Turner. A heavy-duty black bin-liner, stuffed with two taped-together pillows and the decomposed carcass of a pigeon. Peter Sweep, it seemed, had been planning his own particular take on the practical joke for some time.

'Any idea how he got them up there?' asked Weaver.

'The line-access team think "down there",' said Dana. They tried swinging a similar package from above on a line and letting it go. They think Sweep must have dropped his over the side and possibly lost quite a few in the process.'

Weaver nodded. 'As you know, the search of the area around Deptford Creek Marina found nothing,' said Dana.

That hadn't been strictly true. The search of the Deptford Creek marina had unearthed a couple of thousand pounds' worth of stolen goods, stashed away in old vans and Portakabins. All small-scale stuff that Dana had been happy to hand over to local CID.

'And I understand it is quite possible for Tyler's and indeed Ryan's bodies to have been washed up the creek from the Thames?' Weaver asked.

Dana nodded. 'Since DI Joesbury spent his childhood on the river, there's been a big development at the mouth of Deptford Creek,' she said. 'It's altered the way the river flows. Now it's quite common for debris to get carried up the creek when the tide's coming in, and then get trapped there. Once we heard that, we scaled down our search of the marina.'

Weaver glanced down at the screen on his mobile phone.

'The fibres we found on Oliver Kennedy's clothes have been identified as coming from a fleece jacket made by a company called J. Crew,' said Dana. 'They're a popular supplier of casual, outdoor-style clothing. We've traced it to a particular batch and should be able to match it to the garment itself, if we ever find it.'

For a second she thought she'd lost her boss's attention. He was staring across the river towards Wapping.

'One of those Whistler sketches features the police station,' he said. 'The distinctive shape of the roof, the bay windows on the front. Over a hundred years ago, a senior police officer sat in Dave Cook's office and looked across to where we are now. I mention it because I've just had a bill for the search of the storm drains he had his dive team do. Is it too much to hope it gave us anything?'

A joint operation of the Marine Unit, Lewisham MIT and the Environment Agency had conducted a search of the two-mile stretch of the south bank between Tower Bridge and Bermondsey. They'd been looking for traces of blood around the storm drain and sewerage outlets. In summer – even in dry autumns, the team from the Environment Agency had told them – there would be no question of it being a search for a needle in a haystack. All polluting substances entering the Thames would leave a trace of some sort. But in March, given the above-average rainfall they'd had in the past few weeks, it had been a long shot. One that hadn't paid off.

'We still haven't found out who sent Lacey Flint that text,' said Dana, mentally making her way down her checklist. 'Nor are we likely to, unless Flint herself comes clean with us.'

'Sent from a pay-as-you-go phone, is that right?' said Weaver.

Dana nodded. 'Bought with cash, topped up with cash. If we find the phone itself, we've a chance, but other than that, forget it. The phone company tell us it's a model that parents typically buy for their kids, and that fits with the sightings we had of kids at Deptford Creek that night, but that's as far as we've got. Equally, we've had no luck unearthing our mole.'

'Bit of a worry, that one.'

'I don't think it's anyone on the immediate team, Sir,' said Dana. 'There's any amount of information they could have passed on if they'd been inclined. We're still looking, of course, but it's a question of priorities.'

Weaver nodded. He knew all about priorities. 'Still think we could be looking for a female?' he asked.

Dana told herself to stop obsessing over Lacey Flint. The fact that the woman was perfectly capable of murder didn't, in itself, make her actually guilty of it. 'Some slightly encouraging news on the footprints,' she said. 'They believe the depth of the prints isn't consistent with what you'd expect from even an average-sized bloke. There's also some evidence of the edge of the print being indistinct, as though the boot was sliding around. They believe it's perfectly possible that the boots were worn by someone much lighter and smaller than the size-ten prints would have us believe.'

'A woman trying to give the impression of being a bloke?' said Weaver.

'Exactly. And Oliver Kennedy believed he was abducted by someone of a similar size to his fourteen-year-old brother. We also have the possible use of fake blood in the abductions, as a way of throwing the kids off their guard, and the use of pressure-point compression to subdue them. It all points to our perpetrator not having the brute strength of a man.'

'Well, I can't say I'm exactly excited by that news, Dana,' said Weaver. 'Unless you have some actual female suspects for me.'

Almost of their own accord, Dana's eyes moved back towards Tower Bridge. A woman on a beach on a wet winter's night. A woman who'd run.

'Found your mystery female yet?'

'No sir, I'm afraid not.'

'Anything else?'

'Do you remember that Facebook page we were monitoring and had blocked?' she went on. 'Facebook wanted to remove the block and we agreed. So far the visitors seem to be behaving themselves. There's no sign of Peter Sweep anywhere.'

'What's the latest thinking?'

'Split between those who thought he was a complete time-waster who got scared by the furore he created, and those who believe he is the killer, whom resourceful Oliver Kennedy managed to foil.'

'What do you think?'

'Susan Richmond believes he wasn't the killer, and she makes a very convincing case. She thinks Peter Sweep is a teenage prankster with good enough IT skills to be able to stay one step ahead of the publicly available information.'

Weaver was nodding. 'Clocks change soon,' he said. 'Evenings will be light again. He's going to find it a lot harder to dump bodies along the Thames without being seen.'

'Well, that's something to look forward to.'

'You don't think he's stopped, do you?'

'Guv, nobody thinks he's stopped.'

54

Tuesday 11 March

'BARNEY!'

Barney stopped at the door of the changing room and turned to face his PE teacher. 'Well played today,' said Mr Green as he caught up with the line of boys. One by one they disappeared inside the changing room, leaving Barney and Mr Green alone in the corridor.

'Thank you, Sir.'

'Some good passing. You're a generous player, you don't hog the ball.'

Barney smiled. He'd tried, once, to explain that it was watching the patterns the ball made on the field that gave him the buzz, far more than the ability to put the ball in the back of the net, and the recipient of his rather long-winded explanation had glazed eyes before he'd finished his third sentence. He hadn't tried since. Let people think he was a generous player.

'I was wondering if you wanted to join the élite training squad on Tuesday and Thursday evenings,' Mr Green said.

Mr Green's élite squad was made up of the best players in their school, the adjacent secondary school and several other local schools. Jorge, Lloyd and Harvey were all part of it, Sam was desperate to be asked.

'Thank you, Sir, I'll ask my dad.'

From beyond the changing-room door came the scuffling, banter and high-pitched giggling of several young boys in a confined space, free of clothes and supervision. Mr Green hammered on the door. 'Quieten it down, you lot,' he yelled.

The noise abated fractionally, then picked up again.

'It finishes at eight, which is quite late,' said Mr Green, who was leaning against the door, one arm outstretched. 'But I can drop you off afterwards. I usually go on to the gym after football and I drive very close to your house. It won't be a problem.'

'Thanks. But my dad might be able to pick me up,' said Barney. 'He doesn't work in the evenings any more.'

'Really? I thought you told me he always worked late on Tuesdays and Thursdays?'

Barney shook his head. For the last couple of weeks, since Oliver Kennedy had briefly disappeared, his dad had been coming back at his usual time and spending the evening at home. He'd rearranged his tutorial responsibilities, he'd explained, when Barney had questioned him. 'Not for a few weeks now,' he said.

'Mr Green, it might not concern you that the boys in your care have ripped the hooks off the walls in there, but my English class and I are finding it rather difficult to concentrate.'

Mrs Green had appeared from the nearest classroom and had the look on her face that usually meant she'd been watching you talking for several minutes when you should have been finishing off your maths. Only this time, Mr Green was getting the brunt of it.

'I'm very sorry, Mrs Green,' he replied. 'I know how you hate your normal routine to be disturbed.'

Uh-oh, something wasn't right between those two. Normally when teachers addressed each other as 'Mr' and 'Mrs' they did it in a half-jokey way, as if they were really saying, *Yes, we both know we don't normally talk like this, but we're pretending as we're in front of the kids and actually it's a bit of a laugh, isn't it?* These two weren't joking at all; Barney could almost see the words coming out of their mouths like little silver darts. Stab, stab, stab. Barney hadn't much experience of married behaviour, but even he could spot the under-currents of a row.

291

'I'd better get changed, Sir,' he said, stepping forward, ready to go past Mr Green and into the changing rooms. In fairness, it was pretty loud in there.

'And I'd better nail the hooks back on to the wall,' said the PE teacher, following him in without another word to his wife.

Barney was the last in the changing rooms, some five minutes after the second-last boy to leave. It was always a mistake, being one of the stragglers. If he were first to finish, which he usually tried to be, it was relatively easy to walk out of the door, but if the room was almost empty then no matter how hard he tried, he absolutely could not leave it without tidying up. Never a pleasant experience, picking up sweaty, muddy socks, even underpants sometimes, and putting them in the right places, but better by far than spending the rest of the day with the mess preying on his mind.

By the time he finished, it was at least two minutes after the bell had gone: he was going to be late for his last class of the day. Barney hated being late almost as much as he hated mess. One last look round the room, a last sock to be folded, hands washed and he was out.

The door to his classroom was half open; he got to it and stopped. Mrs Green was in there, alone, talking on her mobile phone. Barney caught her last words, just as she heard him at the door.

'I'm not sure I can wait much longer,' she said, and then, 'Promise me?' She turned on the spot, phone clamped to her ear. 'Gotta go,' she told the caller and cut off the call. 'Hi!' she said to Barney.

Barney opened his mouth to say sorry, wondering why, of the two of them, Mrs Green was the one who looked guilty. Actually, not so much guilty as sad.

'Were you tidying the changing rooms again?' she asked him.

No one was supposed to know he did that. He couldn't remember telling anyone at school he did that. He always waited till everyone was gone. He shrugged.

'I need my science folder,' he said, glancing across the room to his desk.

'Better hurry up then,' she said.

Barney crossed the room, grabbed his folder and made for the door again. Mrs Green watched him every step of the way. She often watched him. Sometimes in class, if he glanced up suddenly, he saw Mrs Green watching him, just staring at him, not in an angry way, in fact a bit like the way his dad looked at him sometimes. He never saw her looking at any of the other children in the same way. Just him.

'Barney,' she said, as he was about to disappear. He turned back.

'If Mrs Lafferty tells you off for being late, tell her I asked you to stay behind.'

'Thanks, Miss,' said Barney, because it would be impossible to explain that it was the being late, not the telling off, that bothered him.

'Although I guess it's the being late that bothers you. Go on, you funny boy. Get a move on.'

55

'YOU KNOW SOMETHING? UNTIL I STARTED SEEING YOU, no one ever talked to me about what happened that day. The day it all started.'

'Never?' asked the psychiatrist.

'Not once.'

'Why do you think that is?'

'They were just hoping I'd forget. Because I was so young, not much more than a baby, they all thought I wouldn't remember anything about it. You're not supposed to start remembering things until you're quite a bit older than I was then. So I expect they thought, even if it's in there somewhere, it's buried so deep it will never find its way out.'

'But you do remember? Some of what happened?'

'I remember everything.'

'Why don't you tell me? Tell me what you remember.'

56

Thursday 13 March

SIX CHILDREN SAT HUDDLED BENEATH THE CORRUGATED-metal roof at the top of the skateboard ramp. Raindrops bounced from rooftop to ramp and caught the gang in the backsplash, but damp clothes and stiff bodies seemed a small price to pay for a few more minutes of freedom from adult control.

'It's five to nine,' said Lloyd. 'I need to go.'

'We'll all go together,' replied Jorge. 'At nine o'clock.'

Barney, at the edge of the group, was watching the reflections of the streetlights on the rain-drenched ramp. One reflection, from the light immediately behind them, shone directly across the playground to the mural on the opposite wall. The large green crocodile with the alarm clock rammed between his teeth looked set to leave the brick wall and waddle along the orange path towards them. There was something rather menacing about that crocodile.

A flickering streetlight caught his eye. It was just outside the old municipal building on the next street along. From the top of the ramp, Barney could see the second and third floors of the abandoned building. It was dark red, like the community centre, with ornate brickwork around the flat roof. Funny – two of the windows on the second floor were boarded up. He was pretty sure three of them had been the last time he'd looked.

'Planet Earth to Barney. Come in, Barney.'

Barney turned back to the others. He'd done it again, gone off into his own little world. He was tempted to ask how long he'd been zoned out, but didn't really want to draw attention to the problem.

'So what do you think, Barney Boy? Has he stopped or will he kill again?'

'It's been three weeks now,' said Barney.

Of the group, only Jorge openly registered that that wasn't anything like an answer to the question. Had he stopped, or would he kill again? It was a question Barney asked himself several times a day. Since Oliver Kennedy had been found alive and well, he'd allowed himself to hope. Twenty-two days had gone by and nothing.

Oliver Kennedy had been nowhere near his granddad's boat. And if the boys weren't being killed on the boat, what difference did it make that his dad had been there on the Saturday night they'd found Tyler's body or on the Tuesday that Oliver had disappeared?

Was it a coincidence, though, that in the last twenty-two days, when there had been no disappearances and no bodies dumped on the banks of London's rivers, his dad had stopped leaving the house on Tuesday and Thursday evenings?

'I can't sleep with the light off any more,' said Hatty. She was the only one who ever talked about the night they'd found the body. None of them ever mentioned it, unless Hatty did first, but equally, no one seemed to mind when she did. They'd nod understandingly, as though grateful to her for articulating what they all felt. 'I keep seeing his face,' she went on.

'It was just decomposing tissue,' said Lloyd. 'If you see a dead fox or cat in the road, chances are it'll be covered in maggots. It's horrible, but it's not scary. So why should a dead human be any scarier?'

None of the others looked convinced.

'I think he's stopped,' said Barney, and his right hand, tucked deep inside his coat pocket, had its fingers crossed. 'We may never know why exactly, but just as there was a trigger that made him start, there was another that made him stop.'

'He hasn't stopped,' said Jorge. 'He's just biding his time. He probably already knows who he's going for next, he's just waiting for the right moment.'

Silence, and then Hatty gave a theatrical little shudder. 'I'm so glad I'm a girl,' she said.

'Yeah, but in dim light, that's not always obvious,' retorted Jorge.

There was a moment of scuffling, of good-natured complaint, as Hatty hit out at Jorge and he dodged out of her way, pushing Lloyd out into the rain.

'So why has he done nothing for nearly three weeks?' Barney asked.

'People got too careful,' Jorge replied. 'No one was letting their kids out any more. Dads were coming home from work early to meet their kids at school. Cops were going to every school in the area, warning people, telling them to stay in groups, not to trust anyone they didn't know very well. It got to the point where kids wouldn't even answer their own front doors.'

'So you think he'll move on?' asked Sam. 'Go to another part of London, maybe another city?'

'Nah! No need. People will have forgotten all about it in a couple more weeks.'

'No, they won't,' said Barney, more quickly than he'd meant to.

'Well, not forgotten exactly, they'll just get more relaxed again. You can't live in a state of red-alert for ever. Know what this guy's biggest weapon is?'

'Fangs,' suggested Harvey.

'Complacency,' said Jorge.

There was a short pause. Several of the group were wondering what, exactly, complacency meant.

'Nobody ever thinks it's going to happen to them,' said Barney.

'Exactly. Even here, in the midst of it all, everyone thinks it's going to happen to someone else. Even us. We found one of the bodies, but I bet all of us, if we're honest, think we're going to make it home safely. Don't we?'

'Stop it,' said Hatty, only half giggling.

Barney stood up. 'My dad is pretty serious about nine o'clock being the latest I'm allowed out and it's gone that already. I'm going to have to skate like crazy.'

297

'No you don't, Barney Boy.' Jorge got to his feet, too. 'Come on, you lot, we all go together.'

Jorge, Harvey and Hatty left Barney at the end of his road, just a hundred yards from his house. On blades, Barney was at his front door in seconds.

As he searched for his key, he realized he hadn't seen the green Audi for a while. Huck Joesbury's dad must have got tired of stalking Lacey Flint. Just as well, really, given that she had a new stalker. Him!

There was light shining behind the curtains of Lacey's basement flat. She was at home and, for a second, Barney thought about running down the steps in his socks and knocking on the door. He hadn't seen her since he'd asked her to look for his mum. She didn't go out running at the usual time anymore. When he'd seen her in the garden she'd kept her head down, as though determined not to look up to his bedroom window, not to make eye contact. He'd even knocked on her door a couple of times, but she never answered. She was avoiding him. Either she hadn't looked for his mum yet, or she had looked and hadn't found her. Either way, she didn't want to let him down.

Barney opened the front door. The hall light was on but the house beyond was in darkness. For the first time in nearly three weeks, his dad was out on a Thursday.

Barney didn't bother with the lights. In his socks, he padded lightly down the hall and into the kitchen. There was a note on the table.

Had to work late, unexpectedly. Call me when you get in.

Barney found his phone and walked to the window. He couldn't see into Lacey's garden, but the amount of light coming from it told him not only that the shed lights were on, but that the door was open. She never left the shed unlocked if she wasn't in it. Barney put down the phone and opened the back door.

57

IT WAS TEN PAST NINE WHEN LACEY LEFT THE SHED. HER shoulders were sore and her head ached. She'd pounded the punchbag till she could barely stand.

The rain hadn't stopped all evening. It was cold, hard rain, the sort that seemed to seep through your skin, chilling your bones. How long would it take, she wondered, for blood to congeal in these temperatures? For the rain to wash away all traces?

As she locked the shed door she saw that the house next door was in darkness and she wondered, not for the first time, if Stewart Roberts had told Barney yet about his mother. When she'd met him that day at the university, he'd been vague and, knowing it was barely her business, she hadn't pushed. Now, though, it was awkward and until she knew for certain, she couldn't talk to Barney. For the past couple of weeks she'd been avoiding him, and she was pretty certain Stewart had been avoiding her.

It was all beyond her anyway. Whatever problems Barney and his dad had, they would have to sort out for themselves. She couldn't think about anything but the knife in the kitchen drawer. Four nights now, she'd managed to hold off. Another one just wasn't in her. She'd take off her clothes – no point creating unnecessary laundry – switch off all the lights in her flat and stand in the garden, letting the rain wash over her body, just as long as it took for the bleeding to stop.

In her bedroom, she pulled off her trainers and socks. She'd left the conservatory door open and could hear rain behind her, bouncing on the tiled floor.

The front of her flat was never properly dark, too much light from the street seeped its way in through the curtains, but at the back, especially close to the house, no-one would see her. What she did at the back of the house was her business alone.

The knife handle was so warm, the only soft, warm thing in the flat; it nestled in her hand like a small creature seeking shelter. Lacey walked back towards the garden, tugging at her shirt with her free hand. Cold air was pumping into the flat now and she could almost imagine the walls billowing out like a balloon.

There was a dark, human shape in her conservatory.

Lacey froze. Someone was standing at her desk, looking down, absorbed in something he'd spotted there. The computer was switched off; the intruder could only be reading the contents of one of the files she'd left on her desk.

Lacey took a step forward, gripping the knife, anger flooding through her at the frustration of a task unfinished. Maybe the blood she needed to see this evening didn't have to be hers. The intruder was small, slim, jumpy. Wearing football kit! He heard her approach and jumped back, the file still clutched in one hand.

'Barney?'

The boy, all eyes and quivering limbs, stared back at her. His mouth opened, a croaking noise came out.

'Barney, what are you doing here?'

'*No!*'

Astonishing, the way a strangled whisper could sound like a howl. What was wrong with the child?

Then she remembered. The file on her desk, which she'd never thought to lock away because no one ever came into her flat, was the file on Barney's mother.

He was stumbling back. The rain was soaking his hair. Moving quickly, Lacey dropped the knife on her desk, pulled him indoors again and closed the conservatory door. She turned the key and slipped it into her pocket.

Barney stared back at her. She put a hand on his shoulder.

He could have been made of stone, for all the reaction she got.

'Barney, come and sit down.' She pushed him gently, feeling resistance that seemed too strong for a child so young. 'I'm so sorry you had to find out like this.'

He turned, looked at the door to the garden.

'Come on, let's sit down,' she repeated, and he allowed her to steer him through the bedroom and into the living room. She switched on a light and turned to face him. God, it could be a different child. Lacey didn't think she'd really appreciated until now the impact grief could have. Damn his father for not telling him.

'Barney, sit down,' she tried one last time and gave up. This boy was not going to sit down. He didn't look as though he was ever going to move again.

'I'm so sorry, Barney,' she said again. 'To be honest, I suspected it might be the case when we spoke last and I found out fairly quickly. I found the coroner's report and some newspaper coverage that same night.'

No response, but the child had started moving. His hands were twisting together furiously, in a continuous motion that seemed to be a pattern repeating itself: clasp one way, then the next, bang knuckles together, stretch out fingers and slap, over and over again, faster and faster till it looked as if he might rip his fingers out.

She put a hand out to stop him, but he slapped her away and carried on. Lacey took a step back. She wasn't afraid – how could you be afraid of an eleven-year-old, but even so . . .

'We need to go and talk to your dad.' She tried a different tack. 'We should go together, now. Come on.' She gestured towards the door. His eyes didn't leave hers.

'I went to see your dad the very next day,' she said, knowing that being less than honest now could be disastrous. 'I told him about our conversation, what you'd asked me to do and what I'd found out. I'm sorry, I know you didn't want me to, but when I found out what had happened to your mum, I had to get your dad involved. He had to be the one to tell you.'

'He killed her!'

For a second, Lacey thought the boy had struck her, the way he'd dived forward, the ugly twist on his face. She expected to feel the pain of the blow, but no, there had been no contact. It was just words.

'Barney, we need to go and talk to him. Come on, I'll come with you.'

'He's out. He's always out on Tuesdays and Thursdays. That's when he does it.'

Does what? What the hell was going on with these two and why, why, did they have to drag her into it? She wanted to stand in the rain, feel cold streams run down her body and watch the skin part, the red bubbles burst on the air . . .

'He killed my mum. Now he's killing *them*. He wants to kill me, but he can't, so he kills them instead.'

'Barney, she was very ill. She didn't really know what she was doing. The coroner's report said she had post-natal depression. Lots of women get ill after they . . .' She stopped. How could she tell him his mother had become sick after she'd given birth to him and never truly got better again? He'd think it was his fault she'd died.

'He killed her. That's why he never told me about her. He's frightened I'll remember.'

The room was so cold. Lacey couldn't stop shivering. It was as though the walls had become permeable and the cold air outside was seeping through. And in front of her, an eleven-year-old boy was trying to remember the day his mother had died. His eyes were darting around, his breathing picking up pace, as he flicked through his store of early memories. She could almost see it herself. A small boy, alone and scared, hearing his parents arguing on the floor above. His mother screaming for help, wanting to get to her, trying to stop his dad. She could see the phantom memories forming, and knew he might never know whether they were real or not.

'Barney, please stop doing that with your hands, you'll hurt yourself. I know your dad should have told you, but he didn't want you to be upset. He was trying to protect you.'

'My dad is the murderer. The one they call the Twilight Killer. I've known for ages. I wasn't going to say anything because if the police take him away I'll have no one to look after me, but now I know he killed Mum I don't care.'

He was hurling accusations around, trying to hit out as he'd been hurt.

302

'Barney, you're upset, you're not thinking properly.'

'He knows all about vampires. He reads about them all the time on the computer. We have three copies of that Dracula book.'

'Barney . . .'

'He takes them to the boat. That one at Deptford Creek. He was there, that Saturday night I sent you the text. That's why I wouldn't admit it was me – I didn't want you to find out he was there. He's never home on Tuesdays and Thursdays but he brings sheets home to wash because they've got blood on them. There's a drug in his bathroom. I can't remember what it's called but it makes blood clot. And I found a glove. A kid's glove that wasn't mine. He took it from one of the boys he killed.'

'Barney, stop this now!'

Lacey reached for the boy, hardly knowing what she was going to do except that she had to stop him pulling his hands apart and she had to try to calm him down somehow. Seeing her move, he struck out and caught her off balance. As she stumbled back, he pushed her again and shot to the front door. The chain was off, the lock turned and Barney was gone.

Still barefoot, Lacey stepped outside. No Barney. She ran up the steps, cold and slippery beneath her feet, to the front door of the next house. Still no sign of Barney anywhere.

Banging on the front door brought no response. She waited a few seconds and knocked again. Then she pushed open the letterbox and listened. No sounds at all from inside the house. Christ, it was nearly half past nine at night, a child of Barney's age could not be running around on his own.

Back in her own flat, she found the number of the university. The number rang and switched to other extensions several times before there was finally a response.

''Lo?'

'I'm trying to find Stewart Roberts. He's one of the lecturers in the English department. It's a family matter.'

'Yeah, I know Mr Roberts. He's not here though.'

'Are you sure? It's really important I find him. I understood he had lectures or tutorials on Thursday evenings.'

'Lectures finish at five o'clock. There are one or two late tutorials, but none on a regular basis. In any case, Mr Roberts left at six, like he always does. Has a young kid, from what I understand, doesn't like to leave him on his own too much.'

'Thank you. I'm sorry to have bothered you.'

Just a few minutes outdoors had soaked Lacey to the skin, and she was freezing. Could she just leave it now? Trust in Barney's common sense, hope he'd calm down and bring himself home. It really wasn't her problem. She barely knew the boy or his father, had certainly never asked to be dragged into their affairs.

The file on Barney's mother was on the conservatory floor in a puddle of rainwater. She bent to retrieve it, to tuck the loose papers back inside. The poor kid, to find out like this. And he'd be freezing, too – as wet and cold as she was. Only he was still outside.

Nothing she could do. She had her own problems. Other people's pain couldn't drown out her own, all it could do was distract her for a short while. Her own soon came flooding back. And the knife was where she'd left it on the desk.

Too cold now to go back outside, Lacey picked up the knife. In the bathroom, white porcelain gleamed at her. *Scarlet drops on white, like blood on snow.* She gripped the knife more tightly and held her arm out over the bath.

Damn it, Barney had to be found. Lacey dropped the knife into the washbasin and went back to her desk. She had no way of contacting Stewart other than at the university. She'd have to talk to her colleagues at Southwark. If she explained, they'd probably keep the search for Barney low-key, but somebody had to be out looking for him.

She picked up the phone.

My dad is the murderer. The one they call the Twilight Killer.

Boy, she really didn't want to be a fly on the wall when those two got together again.

He takes them to the boat. That one at Deptford Creek. He was there, that Saturday night I sent you the text.

He'd admitted it. Not only had Barney been involved in finding Tyler's body, as she'd been pretty certain all along, but he'd lied to protect his father. He, too, had been at Deptford Creek that night.

But the police at the scene would have talked to everyone on the boats. If Stewart had been there, they'd know about it. There would have been no need for Barney to keep it a secret.

I found a glove. A kid's glove that wasn't mine. He took it from one of the boys he killed.

Stewart had dropped a child's glove in the chapel the day she'd been to see him at work. She still had it in the flat somewhere.

He wants to kill me, but he can't, so he kills them instead.

Good God above, it wasn't possible. Was it?

'Lacey, it's not a great time.'

Pete Stenning's voice was unusually low, as though he was whispering into the handset, maybe even had his hand wrapped around it to muffle the sound. It sounded as if he was at work, though.

'Sorry, Pete. I can talk to someone else. I'll try Gayle at home.'

'Gayle's here. We all are. But I don't think anyone . . . Lacey, do you not know?'

'Know what?'

'Jeez, hang on.'

Footsteps. A door opening. Sounds fading. For the whole team to be at Lewisham at this time of night could only mean one thing. Another child had either disappeared or been found dead.

He's never home on Tuesdays and Thursdays.

Mr Roberts left at six like he always does.

He brings sheets home to wash because they've got blood on them.

'Lacey, there's no easy way of telling you this, and I'm probably going to get murdered just for talking to you.'

Fear sliced into Lacey like a blade. And she'd thought nothing could really hurt her again. She was about to find out how wrong she'd been.

'What?'

'Mark Joesbury's son went missing a couple of hours ago. No one has a clue where he is.'

58

'**M**A'AM.'
        Dana stopped at Gayle Mizon's desk, grateful for the delay, even if it would only last a couple of minutes. In a glass-walled meeting room, Mark, his ex-wife Carrie and her new partner Alex were waiting for her. The last thing she wanted to do was go back in amongst them and admit, yet again, that there was no news.

'Peter Sweep's been on Facebook again,' said Gayle. 'Two minutes ago.' Her eyes raised towards Huck's family. 'I haven't said anything,' she went on. 'It's not what they want to see.'

It wasn't going to be what Dana wanted to see either. Nevertheless, she looked over Gayle's shoulder.

Got my hook into a Huck. Slice and dice.

'Same tactics as when Oliver went missing, I'm afraid, Ma'am. He's posting from a smart phone, almost certainly bought second-hand, with a pay-as-you-go SIM card. He's close to the same base station in Lambeth as last time.'

'Have you seen this?' Dana asked Anderson, who was at the next desk. He nodded.

'We've had an absolute black-out on Huck's disappearance,' said Dana. 'Peter Sweep must be the killer.'

'We have, Boss,' answered Anderson. 'But his mum phoned everyone she could think of when he wasn't waiting for her at the football ground. The news is out there and we can't assume anything as far as Sweep is concerned.'

Behind Dana the door opened and Detective Superintendent Weaver came into the room.

'What do we know?' he asked her in a low voice, as though worried anything he might say at normal volume would carry to the meeting room.

'Huck went to football practice as usual at six thirty this evening,' Dana told him. 'His mum dropped him off. She went to pick him up at eight and he wasn't there. Whatever happened to him, he left quickly, because when the register was taken at six thirty-five, Huck didn't answer to his name. Twenty-eight boys were at training tonight and we're contacting them all to see if anyone knows anything. As they all live in roughly the same area and as they all appear to be at home, it isn't taking too long. Trouble is, most of them didn't notice Huck at all tonight. Three did, but only in the first few minutes after he'd arrived.'

'Nobody could have taken him out of a crowded changing room without being seen,' said Anderson. 'So we have to assume he was one of the last to leave the changing rooms and that he was waylaid on his way from the pavilion to the all-weather pitch.'

'We're very keen to talk to the head coach, a Daniel Green,' said Dana. 'He was at training tonight, but had to leave ten minutes before the end and no one knows where he is now, not even his wife. She says he typically goes to the gym after training, but he isn't there.'

'If he left ten minutes before the end, he was still there for eighty minutes when Huck wasn't. He can't be involved.'

'Exactly, Sir. He's Huck's PE teacher, and DI Joesbury plays rugby with him. We're not worried about him, we just want to talk to him.'

They'd reached the meeting room and entered it together. Three pairs of eyes met Dana's. Hope flickered for a second in each.

'We've got the go-ahead for a TV appeal early tomorrow morning,' said Weaver, after introducing himself to Carrie and her partner. 'You'll be OK for that, won't you, Mrs Joesbury?'

Carrie Joesbury, a tall, dark-haired woman in her late thirties who, over a decade ago, had asked Dana to be one of her bridesmaids, so determined had she been to appear relaxed around her fiancé's female best friend, looked anything but OK. She straightened up in her chair and shook her head.

'Now!' she said. 'We have to do it now.'

Two hands reached across the table towards her. At the last second, Mark pulled back, leaving Alex to cover Carrie's hand with his own. Alex was younger than Carrie, prettily handsome and rich, having worked in fund management since he left university. He and Mark couldn't be more different.

'We're too late for the main evening news.' Weaver was using his soothing voice. Dana wondered, for a moment, if it ever worked; it certainly wasn't about to with these three. 'If we do it in the morning, it will go out three times or more on the main news programmes. We'll get far more exposure.'

'It's the sensible thing to do, Carrie,' said Dana. 'I'll do it with you, of course, and perhaps Alex?'

Carrie's head shot round to her ex-husband. 'Mark will do it,' she said. 'Won't you?'

Mark's face seemed to have lost all its colour. 'I can't,' he told the table top.

For a second, Carrie looked as though she hadn't quite heard him. Then, 'you are kidding me!'

Mark flinched, his eyes stayed down.

'Is this about cover? You'll put your precious frigging cover over our son's life?'

Weaver glanced round nervously. Beyond the glass partition, people were trying hard to look as though they weren't listening, but Carrie's voice was too loud.

'This is all your fault,' Carrie spat at the side of Mark's head. He might not even have heard, for all the reaction she got. 'You should have been with us. Looking after him. He's your responsibility, but you could never get that, could you?'

Dana pulled out a chair and leaned across the table towards Carrie, trying to catch her eye.

'Mark can't appear on television,' she told the terrified woman. 'And that's about protecting Huck – not himself or his job. If he's recognized, if word gets out that Huck's father is a senior police officer, especially one who's been involved in the sort of operations Mark has, then whoever has Huck could panic. It will put him in more danger.'

'We've got thirty officers conducting a search of the area,' said Weaver, after a second. 'And we're about to make the news public. Officially. We'll be asking householders to check their garages, garden sheds, anywhere they think a small boy could possibly be hidden away.'

Silence in the room, while everyone tried to think of something to say.

'Carrie, you need to go home now,' said Dana. 'There's nothing else you can do here and you need to be at home in case Huck manages to come back by himself. I'll be sending someone with you.'

Carrie didn't move. After a few seconds Alex got to his feet. 'Come on, babe,' he told her. 'They'll let us know the minute they hear anything.' He looked at Dana for confirmation.

'The second,' she told him.

'What about the boys who were with him at football training?' said Mark, as Carrie and Alex moved towards the door. 'I want to talk to them. Can you let me have a list?'

Dana took a deep breath. 'Mark, you're going home too.'

'What?'

She couldn't back down. 'You know the score. You're not capable of functioning properly, and your being here will jeopardize the work the rest of us have to do.'

How could her best friend look at her like he hated her? Didn't he realize how much she was hurting too?

'You are not sending me home.'

She stood up. 'While you keep me here arguing, I'm not looking for Huck.'

For a second she thought he was going to hit her. Nor was she alone. Weaver took a step towards her. Then Mark stood up, pushing his chair back. He raised his fist and hit out. The glass wall of the meeting room cracked around his hand but the pieces held. He pushed past Alex, pulled the door open and strode out through the incident room. If he saw the young woman standing just inside the door, he made no sign.

He was gone, and the air of the room seemed thick with his pain.

59

MARK HADN'T SEEN HER. LACEY DIDN'T THINK HE'D SEEN anything much, his eyes had been full of tears. The hand that had reached up to push open the door had been blood-stained and twisted. He might even have broken it.

For a second, she almost turned and followed, with no idea of what she'd do or say when she caught up with him, only knowing that no one in his position should be alone.

Then she saw the slim, white-faced woman being led across the room by a tall man in an expensive suit. This was Huck's mother – impossible to mistake the heart-shaped face and the tiny nose. She was trying to make eye contact with people as she left, holding back sobs as she did so. 'Thank you,' she kept repeating. 'Thank you for your help. Please find him.' As they reached the door, she looked up and met Lacey's eyes. Her lips moved, she tried to smile, then they were gone and everyone in the incident room was looking at Lacey.

'What are you doing here?' Dana Tulloch's voice was like an icy shower on a cold day. She was at the far side of the room, Detective Superintendent Weaver standing directly behind her.

Lacey moved further into the room. 'I want to help,' she said.

'I've got no time for theatricals.' Slowly, deliberately, her heels clicking on the tiled floor, Tulloch stepped towards her. 'You're not on full duties and you're certainly not part of this investigation. You need to go home.' As she stopped talking, she stopped moving. She stood and stared.

'I'm another pair of hands,' said Lacey, conscious of every member of the team watching them. There were tears on Gayle Mizon's face but she was holding it together. DS Anderson was red around the eyes. Even Stenning was the same off-white shade as the paint on the walls. She'd never seen them like this before. And she knew that there was no one she could rely on in the room to back her up. However well disposed towards her they might be privately, they'd support Tulloch when it came to it.

'I can watch CCTV footage, I can trawl through witness statements, I can run HOLMES searches. I've got a good eye for detail, you can use me.' Before the words were out, she knew it was no use.

Tulloch glanced at the detective closest to the door. 'Tom, would you please take DC Flint to her car?' she said.

A second's pause, and then Tom Barrett stood up.

Lacey felt her temper rise like water coming to the boil. Tulloch had no right to put private antagonism before the search for a child. Especially that child. As Barrett stepped towards her, she put up a hand to stop him.

'I have information,' she said. 'Directly relevant to the case. If you won't let me help, then I have to make a statement.'

Around the room, detectives were sliding glances at each other, then flicking between her and the DI. Tulloch narrowed her eyes and moved closer. She couldn't have looked more cynical if she'd been practising in front of a mirror. 'What information?'

'I can tell you who sent me the text about the body at Deptford Creek and I have the name of a possible suspect.'

The mood of the room changed then, subtly, but unmistakably. When she'd arrived, they'd been sympathetic, even if they hadn't dared show it. Now, she could sense their allegiance changing as they registered the possibility that she'd been holding out on them.

'Tom, take her downstairs. I'll be down in five minutes.'

No, Tulloch was not going to have it all on her terms. 'I want Sergeant Anderson to take my statement,' said Lacey. 'Gayle or Pete can accompany him.'

Tulloch was close to her now. Close enough to spit, close enough to strike. Either looked decidedly possible. 'You do not get to choose to whom you speak,' she said.

'With all due respect, Detective Inspector Tulloch, I believe you have a personal prejudice against me. If you insist on taking my statement, I want a solicitor with me. If the Sergeant does it, we can start straight away.'

It took a split second for Tulloch to realize that waiting for a duty solicitor could take an hour or more. Wearing heels, she was almost exactly Lacey's height, and Lacey could feel her breath on her face as she spoke.

'If anything happens to that child, I will hang you out to dry. Do I make myself clear?'

Lacey didn't blink. 'Likewise,' she replied, then deliberately turned her head away. 'Shall we start, Sergeant?'

'Why didn't you tell us this the night we found Tyler?' asked Anderson, as she'd known he would.

'I had no proof Barney sent me the text,' Lacey replied. 'It was nothing more than a hunch and the fact that very few people have my mobile number. I couldn't turn a vulnerable child over to a murder investigation without something more than that. I thought I could make him confide in me, that he and I would come in together. I also thought you might be able to trace the text from my phone, but that doesn't seem to have happened.'

'It was sent from a pay-as-you-go phone,' said Stenning. 'Cash transaction, impossible to trace.'

'And the first you've heard of his suspicions about his father was tonight?' asked Anderson.

'Absolutely. I didn't really take in what he was telling me at first. I felt too bad and too angry that he'd had to find out about his mother the way he did. I thought he was just hitting out. But then, after he disappeared, I started thinking. I know Stewart is out of the house on Tuesdays and Thursdays – I've noticed before now that Barney is on his own then. But the security bloke I spoke to at the university said he always leaves at six because he has a young kid. So, he's telling work he's leaving early to be with his son, and he's telling his son he's working late.'

313

'So where is he going?' said Stenning.

'Exactly. And Barney insisted he was at Deptford Creek that Saturday night we found Tyler's body.'

'That boat was empty when we checked it,' said Anderson. 'At least, we assumed it was. Locked up, in darkness, people nearby said it had been empty for months.'

'I went to their house a few days later,' said Stenning. 'I remember it because it's right next to where you live, Lacey. Mr Roberts told me they hadn't been near the boat for months. Mind you, the kid said the same thing.'

'He was protecting his father,' said Lacey. 'He also talked about blood-stained sheets from the boat. Blood-clotting drugs in the bathroom. And the glove.'

She nodded at the small black glove that was now in an evidence bag in the middle of the desk. 'Assuming it's the same one – Barney said it wasn't his,' she reminded them. 'Why would Stewart have a child's glove that isn't his son's?'

'Ah shit, I remember now, Sarge,' said Stenning. 'The kid mentioned that the boat was reported wet. By the locksmith, I think he said. The boat was damp inside and the boy's dad had to take the day off to go and dry it out. Roberts himself neglected to mention that. Claimed he'd forgotten until his son reminded him.'

'We need to bring him in,' said Anderson. 'And get a warrant to search his house and the boat. OK, thanks, Lacey.'

'Sarge, you need to find Barney, too. I dread to think what's going through his head right now. He's in no state to be out on his own.'

'We'll get right on to it. Christ, the last thing we need right now is another missing kid.' Anderson stood up, switched off the recording equipment and stretched to ease the muscles in his back.

'What happens now?' asked Lacey. 'Can I leave?'

Anderson nodded down at her. 'Course you can. But stay close to a phone and answer it immediately if we call. I'm sure I don't need to tell you to stay in the area.'

'Are you sure there's nothing I can do to help?'

Anderson opened the door and allowed Lacey to precede him out. Stenning brought up the rear.

'If I were you, love,' he said, as the door slammed shut behind the three of them, 'I'd go and find DI Joesbury. I'd say that's where you can be most use right now.'

60

THE FLAT ON THE TOP FLOOR OF THE WHITE STUCCO HOUSE in Pimlico was empty. Lacey was sure of it. She'd sat in her car looking up, waiting for lights to come on. After a while, she'd walked round to the rear of the properties. Nothing. Joesbury wasn't home.

There were police cars outside the Roberts's house when she got back. The front door was open and a uniformed constable was standing guard. DS Anderson had wasted no time. There was no sign of Tulloch's Mercedes, which was something to be thankful for. Lacey crossed the street, pulling her warrant card from her pocket. She was about to show it to the constable on duty when a familiar figure appeared in the hallway.

'Pete, it's me,' she called.

Stenning saw her and came outside. 'Stewart Roberts is at Lewisham,' he said in a low voice, once they reached the foot of the steps. 'The DI's talking to him, but he's freaking out about his kid. Refusing to talk until we find him.' Stenning kept glancing over her head, as though he was uncomfortable talking to her.

'You haven't found Barney then?'

Stenning shook his head. 'We've put a bulletin out, but we're stretched pretty thin. Everyone we've got available is looking for Huck.'

'Please let me help,' said Lacey. 'I can phone round his friends' houses. He has to have gone somewhere.' As she waited for Stenning to think about it, she realized the last thing she wanted was to get dragged into the search for Barney.

Talk about being torn in two. All she wanted to do was find Joesbury and help him look for his son. Yet Barney, with no mother and a father in police custody, had no one to look out for him. And it was her fault he'd run off.

'We've got it covered,' Stenning replied after a moment. 'Better you keep out of it all.'

'Have you found anything in the house?'

Stenning glanced behind, then lowered his voice even further. 'You didn't hear this from me,' he said, 'but we've got an expert taking his computer apart. Roberts had a Facebook account, but he was mainly keeping an eye on what his son was doing. Of more interest are numerous internet searches about vampires and blood-drinking. And some very dodgy-looking drugs in his bathroom cabinet. I imagine they're the ones the kid told you about.'

'So if the post-mortems of the murder victims show traces of the same drug, then . . .'

Behind Stenning another detective appeared. Stenning practically jumped away from Lacey. 'I'll see you,' he told her, before pushing past her, crossing the road and jumping into his car. He hadn't promised to keep her informed or to get in touch with her again. Nor would he. She had no role in the investigation and Stenning, of all people, would toe the line.

OK, did she go in or stay out? Instinctively, out felt right. She'd be on the move, able to look in parks and on scrubland, around garages, even clamber into gardens and peer into outbuildings. It would be pointless, of course, nothing more than keeping her body on the move to stop her head exploding. Trying to find two young boys in the whole of South London.

As she let herself into her flat, the phone was ringing. *Joesbury.* She grabbed it.

'Lacey, it's me.'

The most familiar voice in the world, one that she'd never get used to calling her Lacey.

'Are you OK? What's happened?' Behind the woman's voice she could hear others arguing, heavy doors slamming shut. The everyday noise of a women's prison. And what she didn't need right now was a crisis in the north-east. She could not leave London.

'I won't have long, but I had to talk to you,' the prisoner said. 'What I saw on the news tonight, about the latest child that's gone missing. Is it his? Joesbury's son?'

Conscious that precious seconds were ticking away – phone calls from prisons never lasted long – Lacey found it impossible to answer. If she didn't say anything now, it might not all be true. She wouldn't have seen the glass of the interview-room wall shattering, the man she loved in pieces, the pale-faced mother thanking the people whose inability to do their jobs would cost her her son before the night was out. The woman on the phone took the answer as read.

'Is it significant, do you think? That he's a senior police officer's kid? Or just chance?'

'Probably just chance,' Lacey managed. 'Huck is the latest of seven. None of the others had any connection to the police. He just got very unlucky.'

'Lacey, you have to find him. If he loses his son, he'll never get over it. You don't recover from something like that. He might look the same, but inside he'll rot away.'

Like you did, Lacey thought. *Is that going to happen to everyone I love?* 'I'm not part of the investigation,' she said. 'Besides, they have a suspect in custody.'

'Who is he?'

Forcing herself to keep talking, Lacey explained that the odd boy from next door had accused his own father of the killings; that he'd been suspicious for a while and that finding out about his mother's death, and jumping to the conclusion that his father had been responsible, had been the last straw.

'And what do you think?' the woman asked, when Lacey had finished. 'You know this guy. Does he strike you as being a killer?'

'They never do,' said Lacey. 'But there's a case to answer. Even the Dracula stuff fits. Stewart's a lecturer at King's College. His speciality is Gothic literature. You remember the stuff I used to read? Ann Radcliffe, *The Monk*, *Frankenstein*? Well, Dracula's probably the best-known example of Gothic literature in two hundred years. He would have known it backwards. Barney told me they have several copies in the house.'

'No.'

'What do mean, no?'

'He's not your man. Oh shit, Lacey, this is awful. All the police energy will be focused on him now, persuading him to give up information he doesn't have. And it's your fault.'

Was everyone going to blame her for what was going on?

'Lacey, are you still there? OK, I listened to everything you said and frankly, out of the father and the son, I'd be more worried about the son, but just put that to one side for a second. The vampire stuff is the clincher for me. I had some time in the IT room today and I managed to look back through all the quotes from the novel that appeared on Facebook – the ones from the bloke who claims to be the killer. In fact, I've got them all with me, and I promise you, whoever this Peter Sweep is, he's never read *Dracula* in his life.'

'What?'

'OK, on the sixteenth of February, the same day that Hunt character started sounding off on TV, he posted this: *Do you not know that tonight when the clock strikes midnight, all the evil things in the world will have full sway?* Later that day, we had: *There are mysteries which men can only guess at, which age by age they may solve only in part.*'

'Yes, but—'

'No, keep listening. Next day, this appeared: *No man knows till he has suffered from the night how sweet and dear to his heart and eye the morning can be.* A few hours later: *Listen to them, the children of the night, what music they make!* Two days after that: *Take care how you cut yourself. It is more dangerous than you think in this country.*'

'What are you saying, they're not from the book?'

'Of course they're from the book, but Peter Sweep didn't get them from the book, he got them from an internet search. He did exactly what I did. Typed "Bram Stoker Quotes" into Google and got a list of the most famous ones. They're the ones he's been using. He even used the same order. The vampire stuff has always been just smoke and mirrors. Sort of like what I did, but not nearly as well thought through. Whereas someone who knows the book well – someone like your Stewart Roberts, who sounds like a pretty bright bloke – would be a bit more subtle, don't you think? He'd find the more obscure references, the less obvious ones.'

Shit, she was right. 'Then I really hope we're back to Peter Sweep not being directly involved at all,' said Lacey. 'Because if Stewart is clean, then we have nothing.'

'Yes, you do. Well, I do. And Peter Sweep is definitely your man. He just jumped on the vampire bandwagon to muddy the waters. Fair play, I'd probably have done the same thing given the chance.'

'Ca—' Lacey stopped just in time. She could not call the other woman that. Ever again. 'Toc,' she said, reverting to an old nickname. 'We're running out of time.'

'Ok, I've been going through all the references on social media to the killings, mainly those on Facebook, but I've kept an eye on the others as well and two things about the Missing Boys page stand out from the beginning. The first is that Peter Sweep had knowledge of what was happening in the case before it was officially made public, and the second is that there was a literary reference running through right from the very beginning. Not Bram Stoker, a different book altogether, and the references were very subtle and very cleverly woven in. No one would have had a chance of spotting them until there'd been at least three or four. And I doubt even I would have done if I hadn't been reading and re-reading every book in the prison library over the past few months. Right, have you got a pen handy?'

Lacey was at her desk, her computer switched on. She sat down, tucked the phone behind her ear and pulled her keyboard closer. 'I can type,' she said.

'*Ryan Jackson's body found at Deptford Creek earlier this evening. I imagine he was slightly damp when they pulled him out.*'

Lacey typed it out, thought about it. Nothing.

'Go on.'

'*Noah Moore washed up at Cherry Garden Pier. Sorry end for His Nibs.* Anything striking you yet?'

'Some old-fashioned language being used. Other than that . . .'

'Oh, that's my girl, you're nearly there. Now, when you and your young friends found Tyler King at Deptford, there was a reference to whether his lovely curly hair had been eaten away by the fishes. But if you look at a picture of Tyler, his hair was straight as an arrow. Not a ringlet in sight. Then, when the Barlow boys were found by Tower Bridge, there were no fewer than six references to the fact that they were twins. So what have we got: Slightly. Curly. Nibs. Twins. Come on, you were always the reader.'

'Oh my God!'

A heavy sigh of satisfaction down the line. 'And that, my friends, is the sound of the penny dropping.'

'The Facebook page. The Missing Boys. Missing – lost. It was obvious from the start. Slightly, Curly, Nibs. The dead boys are the lost boys.'

'And if you had time – which you don't, so I'll fill you in – you could look in a thesaurus and you'd find out that another word for the verb to sweep is to pan. Peter Sweep is Peter Pan.'

Silence. A second of near overwhelming excitement and then the sharp realization. The other woman was almost certainly right, but how much further did it really take them?

'Does it help?' she asked now, as though thinking exactly the same thing.

'In time it has to,' said Lacey. 'But we may not have time. And it doesn't tell us who he is. No thoughts on that, I suppose?'

'Hey, I've done my bit. It's up to you now. I've really got to go this time. Love you. Trust you. Go find him.'

The line went dead. The call would have cost the other woman a small fortune in prison currency. With everything screaming at her to get up and get moving, Lacey took a few moments to look back through the Facebook postings. The prisoner had quoted them absolutely correctly. Was there really any doubt? None that she could see. OK, this was no time to play the Lone Ranger.

'Gayle, it's Lacey,' she said, when her call was answered. 'I need to run something past you.'

61

'HAVE YOU FOUND MY SON YET?'
Each time Dana had seen Stewart Roberts this evening, he'd changed, and not for the better. The crisp, steel-grey of his hair seemed to have seeped down and stained his skin. His forehead and cheeks were more lined than before. His hands were shaking and, in spite of the heating in the room, he shivered continually. He might be a guilty man about to crack. Equally, he could be a normal parent terrified for the safety of his son.

Wreck or not, they hadn't been able to break him yet. They'd talked to him twice. Both times he'd denied being at the boat at any time since the one-off day in January when he'd gone to deal with water damage.

'We're looking,' she told him. 'Sergeant, can I have a word?'

'I don't believe you,' Stewart called after her as Anderson rose to follow Dana from the room. 'You're looking for that other kid. You're not interested in mine.'

As Dana and Anderson left the room, Stewart's solicitor put a hand on his client's arm and spoke to him in a low voice. The door clanged shut.

'How's it going, Ma'am?' asked Anderson, rubbing his eyes.

'We've had the coroner's report into the death of Karen Roberts, Stewart's wife,' she told him. 'He's off the hook for that, at any rate.

322

She spoke to a relative on the phone after Stewart and Barney left the house, and she'd been dead at least an hour by the time they got back. He couldn't have killed her.'

Anderson nodded, then shrugged. 'We're getting nowhere in there,' he said, indicating the interview room. 'He claims the internet research he's been doing is background work for a lecture he's got coming up. All the renewed interest in vampires gave him the idea, apparently. And gothic literature is his specialist subject, so naturally he's going to have all sorts of spooky books. He's hiding something, but until he starts talking, we've got nothing other than the word of an hysterical – and missing – kid.'

'Oh, we've got a bit more than that,' said Dana, letting a small smile creep on to her face. 'We've got a cabinet full of blood-clotting drugs and hypodermics, which don't strike me as everyday toiletries, and we've got traces of blood on the houseboat.'

Anderson looked instantly awake again. 'You're kidding me?'

'Too soon to say whose, of course. We've also got a magazine dated first week in February. A woman's magazine, interestingly, but it still puts the nail on his story about not being there recently. What do you say we have another word?'

'After you, Ma'am.'

Dana picked up her case. This time, when they opened the door, the eyes of the solicitor met them. 'Mr Roberts is ready to make a statement,' he told them. 'In return, he wants an assurance that you are doing everything possible to find his son.'

'Of course,' said Dana. She picked up the phone and requested that someone bring a progress report down to the interview room. If Stewart was about to tell them something valuable, she didn't want it compromised down the line when he claimed undue stress as a result of worrying about his son. She took her seat and Anderson dropped heavily into the chair beside her.

'What would you like to tell us, Mr Roberts?' she said.

Stewart looked her straight in the eye. It was the first time he'd done so except when he'd been asking about his son. 'I was at Deptford Creek on Saturday the sixteenth of February,' he told her. 'On my father-in-law's old boat. I arrived at around seven in the evening. I left just after one in the morning, when I judged the police had finally left the site.'

Dana told herself to stay calm, not to react with anything more than polite interest.

'I've also been going to the boat most Tuesday and Thursday evenings,' he went on, 'since the middle of November. There was a period over Christmas and the New Year when the keys went missing and I had to get the locks changed. I couldn't use it then. And I haven't been the last couple of weeks. With everything that's going on, I haven't liked to leave my son alone and he hates babysitters.'

'Why do you go to the boat?' asked Dana, with an odd urge to reach out and squeeze Anderson's hand. If more had ever depended upon an answer to a question, she honestly couldn't remember it.

Roberts looked down at the table, then at his solicitor, then back at her. 'I go to meet my girlfriend,' he told her. 'I didn't tell you earlier because I was trying to protect her. It's become obvious that that isn't going to be possible.'

Dana told herself not to panic. 'Why the secrecy?' she asked.

'Because she's married. But I imagine you already guessed that.'

It might not be true. It might be a delaying tactic. If he didn't admit the girlfriend's name straight away, that would be a sign that he was just playing with them.

'We're going to need her name,' said Anderson.

Stewart nodded his head. 'I know,' he said. 'Her name is Gillian Green. She's my son's form teacher. Her husband is his games teacher. You can see now why I can't entertain her at home.'

No. They could not have wasted the past three hours on a man who was guilty of nothing more than an affair with a married woman. She was going to kill Lacey Flint.

'Was she with you at the boat on the sixteenth of February?'

'She was. When we heard the fuss going on around us, and the talk of the police being called, I told her to slip away quietly. I was going to follow when I'd locked the boat up. I didn't get chance, so had to wait till it was all over. I sat on the dark boat and waited. Your people knocked at exactly 11.42. I ignored them.'

Dana could feel the tension building again in the back of her neck. He didn't look as though he was lying.

'Why do you meet on Tuesdays and Thursdays?' she asked him.

'Her husband coaches a football club till eight, then does his own circuit training at a local leisure centre. After that, he goes to the pub. He's rarely home before midnight.'

Dana felt Anderson's eyes on her. She turned. His eyebrows were raised. *Daniel Green*, he'd written on the pad in front of him. She nodded.

'And the black glove you've been getting so excited about is hers, by the way,' Stewart went on. 'It's not a child's glove, it's a one-size stretch glove. She uses them for playing tennis.'

He had an answer for everything. Did he? She reached into her case and pulled out an evidence bag. 'Can you tell me what this is?' she asked, putting the bag on the table in front of Stewart. He bent forward to look at the clear plastic vials inside.

'It's my medication,' he said.

'For what?'

He looked directly at her. 'I'm a haemophiliac. I inject myself a couple of times a week as a preventative measure. Otherwise, if the knife slips when I'm chopping the carrots, I could bleed to death. Actually, I don't use knives if I can avoid it. Hardly worth the risk.'

No, this was not all slipping away from her. 'Your GP will confirm this?'

'Of course. Would you like her name and number? I also made a point of telling your custody sergeant when he booked me in. Did he not mention it?'

An answer for everything.

'So why was your son surprised to find it?' asked Anderson, who seemed a lot more on the ball than she was. 'Why did he mention it to one of our officers?'

'Barney doesn't know about my condition. Wisely or not, it's one of several things I decided to keep from him.'

'Why?' asked Anderson. 'Surely it would be a precaution for him to know. In case anything happens.'

'Barney is terrified of blood. Probably because he found his dead mother in a bath of it when he was four. I've always taken the view that knowing I'm in danger of bleeding to death as well would be a bit too much for him to deal with.'

'We're going to have to talk to Mrs Green,' said Dana.

'I know. Is it worth my asking you to be discreet?'

Dana stood. 'My godson could be in the hands of a killer,' she said. 'And you've already wasted enough of my time. Frankly, saving your girlfriend's marriage isn't high on my list of priorities.'

'One second, Ma'am.' Anderson's hand was on her arm. 'There's another matter we need to ask Mr Roberts about.'

Was there? Christ, she really wasn't up to this. Thank God for Neil.

'Our crime-scene investigators found traces of blood on your boat,' said Anderson, as Dana sat back down. 'We can't identify whose yet, but we will. Anything you want to say?'

Stewart glanced at his solicitor. 'Where was the blood?' he asked.

'Why don't you tell me?' said Anderson.

Stewart sighed. 'Gilly cut herself a few weeks ago,' he said. 'She bled quite a lot. On the bed and the cabin floor. I thought I'd cleaned it up.'

Anderson glanced at Dana. She nodded. The report had referred to traces of blood on the wooden floor of the boat and to a half-washed-out stain on bed-sheets that was almost certainly blood.

'How did she cut herself?' asked Dana.

Stewart looked down at the table-top. 'She was trying to take the foil off a bottle of wine with a knife,' he said. 'It slipped. Can I go now? I want to look for my son.'

Dana got to her feet again. 'You're going to have to leave that to us for a while,' she said. As she left the room, Stewart dropped his head into his hands. It could have been a gesture of guilt, but it looked an awful lot like grief and fear to her.

'I'll get someone to bring down information release forms,' she said to Anderson, once the door had closed. 'We might as well check the haemophilia business with his GP.'

'So Stewart Robert's girlfriend is married to Huck Joesbury's football coach, whom we still haven't managed to track down,' said Anderson, as they made their way back up the steps to brief the team. 'Is this starting to feel a bit incestuous to you, Ma'am?'

'It's starting to feel a bit beyond coincidence.'

'Are you going to phone Mark?' Anderson asked, bringing a

picture into her head of Mark, alone at home, sitting in the dark, staring at the phone. Dana shook her head. She couldn't do it. She simply couldn't tell him they'd spent hours chasing a lead that was now slipping away.

Gilly Green had the sort of looks that other women rarely notice but that men find quietly intriguing. Dana, being a woman who habitually noticed other women, spotted her appeal immediately. She was slim, with clear, fair skin and a small, neat face that was pleasantly pretty rather than striking. Close to midnight, she was still dressed.

'My husband isn't back yet,' she was saying as she led them to a small, snug sitting room to one side of the hallway. 'He's not been answering his phone. Is there any news of Huck?' She looked at the clock above the hearth and frowned.

A coal fire was burning in the grate and scent sticks in a jar gave off a smell of apples and cinnamon. The walls were a soft shade of mushroom and there was a lot of natural wood. It was the sort of room in which Dana felt instantly at home. There was a pile of exercise books by one armchair, one of them still open on the padded seat. Mrs Green had been marking class work, probably to take her mind off where her husband might be. 'Has something happened to Daniel?' she asked.

'Not to my knowledge, Mrs Green,' Dana replied. 'And Huck Joesbury is still missing. Can I ask where you were on the evening of Saturday the sixteenth of February?'

Mrs Green stared at her for a second, glanced at Mizon, then seemed to shrink a little. She sat down, pushing the exercise book out of the way. To her credit, she made no attempt to look as though she were thinking about the question. She didn't look puzzled, didn't ask to see her diary, she just looked resigned. And rather sad.

'I was on a boat at Deptford Creek,' she said. 'It belongs to a friend of mine. I left around eleven o'clock.'

Dana asked permission to sit down and then both she and Mizon perched on the edge of the sofa. 'Were you aware the body of a young boy was found there that evening?'

Blue-grey eyes looked directly back at Dana. 'Yes, of course. I saw it on the news the next day.'

'And you didn't think to let us know you'd been there? That you were a material witness in a murder inquiry?'

The woman's head jerked back a fraction, registering the criticism. 'If I'd seen or heard anything I would have been in touch with you immediately,' she replied. 'I teach children of that age. I teach Huck Joesbury. But I couldn't have told you anything. I was below deck the whole time.'

'Alone?'

Gilly shook her head. 'I was with Stewart Roberts. He owns the boat.'

'How long have you been having an affair with Stewart Roberts?'

Her chin lifted a little higher. 'I don't refer to it in those terms, but we've been seeing each other since last November. We meet at the boat, on Tuesday and Thursday evenings. Not so much recently.'

'The sixteenth was a Saturday,' said Dana.

'My husband was out, Barney was at a sleepover. It was an opportunity.'

'Mr Roberts told us there was a period when you couldn't use the boat. Is that the case?'

Gilly nodded her head slowly. 'We couldn't get into it over Christmas,' she said. 'The keys went missing. We still met up, though, we just had dinner or a couple of drinks.'

So far, their stories matched perfectly.

Dana reached into her bag and pulled out an evidence bag containing the black glove Lacey had given them earlier. 'Do you recognize this, Mrs Green?' she asked her.

Gilly peered at it. 'It looks like mine,' she said. 'I've been missing one for a couple of weeks now. How did you—'

'This fits you?' Dana asked. Gilly's hands weren't big, but the glove looked to be half their size.

'It stretches. It's a one-size-fits-all. I'll show you, if you want.'

Dana looked at the glove again. She didn't want it removed from the bag. She could Google the make when she got back, but she doubted Mrs Green was lying about that, at least. One more thing

328

to try. Dana moved across the room to stand close to Gilly's chair. 'Can I see your hands?' she asked her.

A puzzled frown. 'My hands?' Gilly Green was looking down at them herself now. They were slim, well-shaped, the nails painted a pale pink.

Dana held out her own hands, expectantly. Gilly stood up and, rather nervously, held her hands out for Dana's inspection. Dana looked at the palms, then turned them over to see the backs. 'Where was the scar?' she asked her. 'I'd have thought it might still be there.'

'What scar?'

'You cut yourself on the boat on the fourteenth of February,' Dana said, keeping up the pretence of looking at the other woman's hands. 'A bad cut, from what I've been told. You lost a lot of blood. I'd have thought there'd be some trace of it still. But there's nothing I can see.'

'I don't remember cutting myself,' Gilly said, hesitantly.

Dana felt a surge of excitement. This was a part of their story they hadn't thought to agree on and it wasn't matching up. She'd argued all along that a woman had to be involved. A woman and a man, working together. 'Really? Not on the boat?' she said. 'Because we've been told that the blood we found is yours. If it's not, we'll know very quickly and then it really won't look good for either of you.'

Gilly closed her eyes and sighed. She didn't look nearly as frightened as Dana would have liked. 'Stewart told you I cut myself?' she said.

'Did you not?'

'He was being delicate, Detective Inspector. The blood you found is almost certainly mine. But I didn't cut myself.'

'So what happened?'

Gilly's small mouth twisted. 'It wasn't the most convenient time of the month for intimacy to take place,' she said, looking slightly defiant. 'But when your time together is limited, you tend not to be too particular. And it was Valentine's Day. The sheets were a mess, Stewart had to take them home to wash them. I thought I'd cleaned the floor. Apparently not.'

Damn. All too feasible. And all too easily provable. If the blood turned out to be Gilly Green's, they had nothing.

'Do you have children, Mrs Green?'

A startled look. Then a shake of the head.

'Then why the subterfuge? If you've met someone else, why can't you just move on? Stewart Roberts isn't married.'

Blue eyes glinted. 'I do want to move on. And I want to be with Stewart. But leaving Daniel at the moment feels impossibly callous. We did have a son, you see. We lost him to meningitis just over two years ago. He was ten.'

'What do you think, Ma'am? Misguided woman in love or cold-blooded killer?'

Dana ran her hands across her face. 'Can't call it either way,' she said.

The two officers were outside the Green's home. Before leaving for Lewisham police station to be interviewed formally, Mrs Green had given Dana permission to conduct a search of the house. Not having to wait for a warrant would save them valuable time. On the other hand, her cooperation almost certainly meant she didn't believe there was anything to be found.

'She looked guilty when we told her Barney was missing.'

'You think so? I thought she looked scared. I think she could be fond of him.'

'So neither Mr nor Mrs Green are where they should be on Tuesday and Thursday evenings,' said Mizon.

'They can't be working together,' said Dana. 'Mrs Green can be alibied by Mr Roberts.'

'She and Roberts could be, though.'

Dana nodded. 'We need to find something on that boat. A hair, a fingerprint, something. Anything.'

It was approaching midnight by the time Dana got to the lock-up yard that led to the houseboat community. She showed her ID to the constable at the gate and made her way gingerly across rubbish-strewn concrete and then down the steel ladder to the boats.

'Oh, feel free,' muttered a voice from the cockpit of the first boat she stepped down on to.

'Sorry to disturb you, Sir,' she replied, making her way around the bow of the boat, the way she'd seen Mark do several times in the past. 'It's more polite,' he'd explained once. 'Sort of like walking around the edge of someone's garden rather than directly through their living room.'

'Evening, DI Tulloch,' the chief SOCO greeted her when she'd climbed down into the cabin of the yellow yacht.

She made herself smile. 'Please tell me you have something.'

He shook his head. 'It's a bit of a love nest,' he replied. 'Certainly some evidence of sexual activity. Including a half-full packet of condoms in a cupboard in the heads. We've also got wine, candles, some nice glasses, olives.'

Dana looked round the cabin, surprised. She'd imagined it narrow, low and cramped, fitted out with plastic seats and hard edges. Instead, the main saloon was high enough even for the men to stand upright, and panelled in a warm-coloured wood – cherry or walnut. The wall-lamps were mock Edwardian, sumptuous and gleaming in the harsh lights the forensic team had brought on board. The chart table looked like a gentleman's desk and the book-shelf above it held copies of Dickens, Trollope and Austen, instead of the maps and pilot books it had been built for. The upholstery was dark-red leather, and ornate brass handles shone everywhere. The cabin felt like the private study of an old London club.

To one side of the saloon was a fold-out dining table, which looked easily big enough to strap a young boy to, but . . .

'If five boys had their throats cut in here, the place would be swimming with blood, wouldn't it?' she asked. 'Even a good clean-up would leave traces.'

'It would,' the SOCO agreed. 'Mind you, we're finding traces of detergent and disinfectant, which would suggest recent cleaning. Another thing of interest is several small patches on the ceiling where the varnish on the wood has peeled away.'

Dana looked up to where police marking tape indicated the sites the SOCO was referring to. She could see nothing.

'The sort of mark Sellotape leaves behind when it's pulled off,' the SOCO explained. 'Could be nothing. Or it could be where he stuck up clear plastic sheeting to stop the blood staining the walls and ceiling.'

'Which?' said Dana. 'I need to know which.'

The SOCO pulled an *I understand, but there's a limit to my powers* look. 'Tomorrow we can have the boat lifted and moved to where we can look at it properly,' he said. 'If a lot of blood has been washed away, there'll be traces in the bilges, even if the cabin itself is clean.'

Tomorrow was no good to her. Tomorrow Huck could be lying dead on a beach somewhere. Dana's phone started ringing again and she stepped back on deck to take the call. It was Anderson, calling from Lewisham.

'Good news, Boss. You might want to get back here pronto.'

Funny, how you could be so keyed up that the expectation of good news felt as difficult to deal with as bad. 'What's happened?' Dana demanded, hardly daring to hope that Huck had been found.

'We picked up Dan Green in the pub. The one several of the circuit trainers told us he might be in. Guess what we found tucked into the inner pocket of his gym bag?'

'What?'

'Huck's mobile phone. Cheeky sod was carrying Huck's phone with him.'

Dana looked up and closed her eyes; the fine drops of rain felt like starlight on her face. Oh God, they were close, they were going to find him. Just as long as he was still . . .

'Are you sure? Are you sure it's Huck's?'

'Definitely. It has his mum's number programmed in, his dad's, his best mate's. Even yours.'

'I'm on my way. Has anyone talked to him yet?'

'Not yet. And Gayle found a fleece sweater in the Greens' house. In one of the drawers in the bedroom. Black, J.Crew. Just like those fibres we found on Oliver Kennedy.'

Dana took a massive breath to clear her head and gave Anderson orders to get the preliminaries in order: the background checks that would establish whether Green had any history with the police; details of property he owned; of relatives in and around the capital. As she climbed from one damp deck to the next she told herself that Green was a well-known sports coach. All the dead boys had played football or rugby and Green was involved with both. The boys might all have known him from football fixtures they'd taken part in. They wouldn't know him well, but he would have been a familiar enough figure for them not to feel threatened if he approached them. And he'd lost a son of exactly the same age as the dead boys.

Dana got back to her car, put the blue light on top and set off towards Lewisham. And when the tiny voice at the back of her head tried to remind her that she'd never believed the killer to be a man, she ignored it.

62

'I HAVE NO IDEA HOW IT GOT THERE,' SAID DAN GREEN. 'It doesn't really matter how many times you ask me, I can't give you a different answer.'

'Your fingerprints are on it,' Dana reminded him, which, strictly, was a moot point. A partial print had been found on the phone that appeared to be a match for Green's right index finger. It would never hold up in court, but, so far, they hadn't revealed how flimsy a piece of evidence it was.

'I keep my keys in that pocket. It's quite likely I touched the phone when I put them in or pulled them out. Look, my bag was on the touchline for over an hour while we were training. I didn't have my eyes on it the whole time. Anyone could have slipped something in it.'

Green was a good-looking man, but not, Dana had noticed with interest, at all similar to Stewart Roberts. Taller, younger, more muscular, with thick, dark hair, bright enough but hardly Brain of Britain. This man was an athlete, not an academic. When she'd first entered the interview room, she'd glanced down at his feet. Even in trainers they looked larger than average. Size eleven or twelve, at a guess. Bigger than the wellington boots that had left the prints on the beaches. And that was panic rearing its head again, wasn't it? Because something about this just didn't feel—

'Who took the register tonight?' asked Dana.

334

'James did,' said Green, referring to his assistant coach. 'I was there when he did it.'

'So you knew Huck hadn't turned up?'

'I knew he hadn't answered the register.'

'You didn't see him?'

'No, I don't remember seeing him at all tonight.'

'You didn't think to phone his mother when he didn't show up.'

Green sighed. 'In hindsight, I really wish I had. But up to five kids don't show most weeks. Usually because something unexpected has cropped up at home, or they just don't feel up to it. I can't chase 'em all up.'

'Some of the children there tonight say they saw Huck at the beginning of the session.'

'So I understand. I didn't.'

'How can a child be there one minute and not the next?'

'I have no idea.'

'Did you talk to him at the beginning of training?'

'No, I didn't see him.'

'Did you ask him to wait for you in your car for a few minutes?'

'No, I didn't see him.'

'If Huck has been in your car recently, we'll find evidence.'

'Huck has never been in my car.'

'Your wife believes you go to circuit training on Tuesday and Thursday evenings after football training. That isn't strictly true, is it?'

'I used to believe my wife stayed home and did her marking on Tuesday and Thursday evenings. Turns out that's not strictly true.'

'What do you mean?'

Green shrugged. He wasn't going to be shaken easily. Time to turn up the heat a bit.

'Are you referring to the fact that your wife is having an affair with Stewart Roberts?' said Dana.

Green exhaled loudly through his nose. 'Is that who it is?' He gave a short, bitter laugh. 'I wondered why she always took such an interest in Barney.'

'You didn't know?'

'I knew it was happening with someone. I guess the details aren't that important.'

Green's sallow skin had paled and his eyes had narrowed. He might be feigning nonchalance but she was getting to him. She reached down into her case and pulled out the silver-framed photograph Gayle had found in his house. His reaction was immediate.

'How dare you touch that?' Green asked her.

Dana pretended to study the ten-year-old boy in the photograph. It had been taken at school and showed him wearing a maroon sweater and a maroon and black striped tie. Benjamin Green had looked a lot like his father.

'I'd say the dead boys look very like your son, Mr Green,' she said, knowing she was on dodgy ground. Benjamin had been darker haired and more sallow of skin that the victims. 'Is that how you choose them?'

Green gave her a look of pure contempt and closed his eyes. She watched him breathe in and out three times.

'For the benefit of the tape, the suspect is refusing to answer the question,' said Anderson, after twenty seconds had gone by. Green's eyes shot open.

'For the benefit of the tape,' he said, 'the suspect thinks you are a bunch of incompentent half-wits.'

'We can make your life very difficult if you don't cooperate, Mr Green,' said Dana.

'Detective Inspector, my son is dead and my wife – who I still love, by the way – is about to leave me. Trust me when I say that you and your friends don't even come on to my radar screen.'

'We could always leave him in a cell with Mark for half an hour,' said Anderson, when they left the interview room ten minutes later. 'He'd be singing after five minutes.'

'I don't doubt it, but he still couldn't tell us anything. It isn't him, Neil.'

Anderson gave a heavy sigh. 'Boss, Huck's phone was in his bag. Fingerprints. Black fleece.'

'Did you see his feet? Bloody enormous. There's no way he could squeeze into size-ten wellingtons. Or leave a shallow, slightly wobbly print in the mud. And would a killer as careful as we've continually told ourselves this one is leave his latest victim's phone in his bag for anyone to find? If Green were guilty, he'd have been expecting us to talk to him. He would have got rid of the phone.'

'So how did it get in his bag?'

'My best guess? Huck dropped it in the changing room – he's always leaving it lying around – and one of the other boys picked it up and dropped it in the coach's bag for safe-keeping.'

'So what – are we back to Mrs Green and her shag bunny? Because I can't believe none of the three are involved.'

'Mrs Green and her shag bunny, as you so charmingly call him, alibi each other. We need actual evidence on the boat or in one of their houses to pin it on them. And while we're looking for it, Huck is out there.'

Suddenly, Dana could no longer summon up the energy to put one foot in front of the other. She stopped and leaned back against the wall, almost setting off the panic alarm. She couldn't look at Anderson. He waited, gave her time. Huck didn't have time. No choice – she had to hold it together. She stood upright again.

'Hold the fort upstairs for a bit?' she asked him.

'Going somewhere, Ma'am?'

'I need to talk to Huck's mum.'

'What will you tell her?'

'God knows. But I promised.'

Lacey saw the boy by the gates of the community centre and called to him. He turned and watched nervously as she ran towards him. She pulled her warrant card from her jacket as she struggled to get her breath back. It was only midnight but she felt like she'd been up all night. Or been drinking heavily. Something was slowing her down and it was starting to feel a lot like despair.

'You're a friend of Barney's, aren't you?' she said.

The boy was about her height, very slim, with fair skin and hair. A beautiful child, on the verge of turning into a man. Around fourteen years old, wearing a mud-spattered tracksuit and trainers. 'Someone from the police phoned our house about him. Have you found him?' he asked.

She shook her head. 'I wanted to ask if you could think of anywhere he might have gone,' she said. 'The police will have checked the houses of all his friends. I was thinking maybe of a den or a place you like to hang out. I'm Lacey, by the way. I live next door to Barney, but I'm also a detective.'

'I know,' the boy said. 'He's mentioned you. I'm Jorge Soar.'

'Can you think of anything, Jorge?'

'We mainly meet here,' said Jorge, nodding his head back towards the community centre. 'I've just been in there now, checking it out.'

Lacey turned to look at the old factory building with its high perimeter wall. Through the iron bars of the gate she could see the murals glowing in the lamplight. A forest gleaming green and silver. Shadowy figures that might have been Red Indians hiding behind trees.

'It looks closed up to me,' said Lacey.

'It gets locked at nine,' Jorge told her. 'That's when the caretaker leaves. But there's a way in at the back. Can you believe Barney and Huck are both missing?'

Barney and Huck. Lost boys.

'Do you think they're together?' asked the boy, surprising her. She shook her head.

'I hope they are,' he said. 'Barney's sensible. He'll look after Huck.'

'You should go home,' said Lacey. 'I know you want to help, but it's not a good idea for you to be out this late.'

'I sneaked out,' confessed Jorge. 'Mum'll kill me if she finds out. But Barney's my brother's best friend. He wanted to come too, I just didn't think it would be safe for him.'

'It isn't. Not for you either. Do you want me to walk with you?'

He shook his head. 'We're only five minutes away. You're right, though, Gran'll freak if she looks in my room and sees I'm not there. I hope you find him, Lacey. Huck, too.'

At the corner of the street, when Jorge would have faded out of sight had it not been for his hair shining silver in the streetlights, he turned and waved. Then he was gone.

63

'O F ALL THE BRIDGES, OVER ALL THE RIVERS, IN ALL THE world, she had to walk on to . . .'

Joesbury's voice caught, like a jagged fingernail being dragged over silk, and he gave up the attempt at humour. He looked back down at the speeding water. Lacey approached slowly. His hair and jacket were soaking wet.

'I've been looking for you all evening,' she said. 'The minute I stop, there you are.'

Finally accepting that she was never going to find either Huck or Barney by running around London like a headless chicken, Lacey still hadn't been able to go indoors. There would be something so final, somehow, about closing the door of her flat for the night, knowing the boys were still out there. Telling herself she'd think more clearly in the open air, that cold stimulated the brain, that the river always soothed her, she'd ridden her bike to the closest bridge over the Thames. Vauxhall.

Traffic had quietened down for the night and the bridge was empty of pedestrians. Except one. At the apex, a tall male figure was leaning against the railings, looking downstream.

When she was close enough to touch, Joesbury raised his right arm. Lacey moved into its circle and felt it close around her. The hand dangling over her shoulder showed the marks of a fresh wound. The skin was broken and puckered, the blood already congealed. They looked towards the dancing, shining lights of the city.

'Have they sent you to break the bad news?' said Joesbury.

'No,' she said quickly. 'I don't know anything.'

Hardly true, but how could she tell him the MIT were following leads that would take them nowhere? And that it was her fault? As for the latest idea, she would just sound crazed. Peter Pan? Lost Boys? How did that help – really?

Mark was looking at the display screen of his phone. 'Dana's phoned a couple of times. So has Anderson,' he went on. 'I can't talk to them. If it's happened, I don't want to hear it. I want to stay here. Not knowing.'

She reached her hand up, brushed her fingers gently over his, feeling him flinch when she touched the wound. 'It's not over yet,' she said.

'I did try to phone you,' he said. 'For some reason, you were some-one I felt I could talk to. I got Number Unobtainable.'

'My phone is wrapped in an evidence bag and filed away in a locker somewhere,' Lacey told him. 'I haven't got round to replacing it yet.'

His hand dropped from her shoulder and he reached inside his jacket. When he brought it out again it was holding a phone that she knew wasn't his. A different make, very new model.

'I bought this for Huck a couple of weeks ago,' he said, balancing it in the palm of his hand and holding it out so the nearest street-light shone on it. 'I've been having an ongoing argument with his mother about whether I can give it to him or not. She says it'll get nicked and doesn't want him having unrestricted access to the internet. I say that when he loses it, as he does several times a week, we'll be able to trace it without turning two houses upside-down.'

'He'll love it,' said Lacey firmly. 'But for the record, I agree with his mum.'

For a second, Joesbury's hand tipped, as though he were about to let the phone slip into the water below. Lacey reached out and brought it back within the confines of the bridge. She took the phone from him and slipped it into the side pocket of his jacket. If he noticed what she was doing, he didn't comment.

'I watched you go in here, remember?' he said.

Remember? As if she could set foot on this bridge without having flashbacks to a night in October, nearly six months earlier. To a hand grasping her shoe, horrified turquoise eyes looking down at her, the sensation of slipping, then a sickening plummet to the river below.

'Not the sort of occasion you forget easily,' she admitted.

'I've been thinking I might just slip over the edge myself some time between now and morning.'

He didn't mean it. He was far too tough to take that way out. *Deal with it, but keep it light.* 'Well, then I'd have to come with you,' she said. 'Can't break with tradition.'

He turned to look at her. 'Can't live—' he began.

Lacey didn't skip a beat. 'If you don't,' she finished.

For a split second, she knew she'd pulled him back. She, not Huck, was at the front of his mind. He was close enough to kiss, all she had to do was stretch up on tiptoe and lean forward. She'd never wanted to more. It had never been less appropriate. Then the moment was gone.

'I wish you could have known him,' he said, turning back to watch the river again.

No, don't talk about him in the past tense. 'I do know him,' she said. 'He's you in miniature. Or rather, he's you before you got all tough and grumpy and cynical.'

The muscle in his cheek jumped. In different circumstances, that would have made him laugh. 'No, he's me as I should have been. He's the good bits of me – what few there are – with his mother's sweet nature and common sense.'

'He's certainly very cute.'

A shudder, and then something between a sigh and a sob. 'Lacey, he was the cutest little kid you can imagine,' he said. 'When he was a toddler, I couldn't take my eyes off him, and when I wasn't watching him I was videoing him. Carrie used to think I was morbid because I'd sit and watch the footage with tears in my eyes, because with every month that went by it felt like we'd lost something. I used to think the hardest thing in the world was to watch your child getting older.' He stopped, ran a hand over his face. 'Course, that was until I had to face the possibility that I might never watch him grow up.'

Finally, the effort was too much. He bent forward and laid his head on his arms. She could see his shoulders tensing with the effort not to give way to sobbing, and it felt as though the pain was all inside her. Just taking another breath was going to hurt too much. And then – oh!

Her eyes still fixed on the man at her side, her thoughts a thousand miles away, Lacey took a step back. Was it possible?

Mark sensed her retreat and looked up. His face was wet with tears. At any other time the sight would have melted her.

'I have to go,' said Lacey, as gently as she could.

His face twisted as though he didn't believe what she was telling him. Then his eyes narrowed. He pulled himself upright.

'What?' he said. 'What have you thought of?'

The one man in the world she could never hide anything from.

'Maybe nothing.' She took another step back. Her bike was just yards away. Another step, watching him nervously as though he might spring at her any second. 'I need to go.'

A step forward; he was following her. 'Not without me, you don't.'

She shook her head, continued to back away.

'Jesus, Lacey, this is my son we're talking about.'

She held out both hands. 'I know,' she said. 'I need to think now. I need to think really, really hard and I can't do that when you're around.'

'Of course you can. We can work it out together. I'll help.'

'Stay safe, please. As soon as I know anything I'll call you, I promise.'

He was following her along the bridge. 'Lacey, don't you dare leave me like this.'

'Please. I need to be on my own. Just for a while, just to think.'

He was close. He grabbed her, held her tightly by the shoulders. He opened his mouth, but the yell came out of hers.

'OK, this is it, Joesbury. Do you trust me or not? Because if you do, then you have to let me go.'

He stared at her for a second. His hands fell away.

'I'll call you,' she said, reaching for her bike. 'Don't go far and answer your phone.'

He threw up his hands in exasperation. Or despair. 'How?' he demanded. 'You haven't got a frigging phone any more!'

Shit, he was right. While she was thinking what to do, he pulled Huck's new phone out of his pocket once more and held it out. 'I'm saved in Favourites,' he said. 'You've got an hour. Then I'm coming after you.'

Lacey turned her bike, pulled it on to the road and set off. She'd be home in under ten minutes. A couple of phone calls to make and one last piece of the jigsaw to put in place.

. . . until I had to face the possibility that I might never watch him grow up.

The boys who wouldn't grow up. The Lost Boys. Spirited away to Neverland by Peter Sweep, aka Peter Pan. Peter Pan wouldn't let his friends grow up. He wanted to keep them young for ever, like him. Peter Pan was a child.

The killer they were looking for was a child.

64

'HELLO.'
The voice was sleepy, with just a hint of concern, the classic response to an unexpected late-night phone call.
'Evi? This is Lacey Flint, from the Metropolitan Police.'
Silence on the line. Just beyond the conservatory windows, rain was falling steadily. Already it was the wettest March on record and still it came: relentless, unforgiving rain – that might run scarlet with a small child's blood before the night was out.
'You called me Laura. Laura Farrow, remember? In Cambridge.'
'Good lord, of course.' A second's pause, while Lacey imagined Evi looking at the clock, giving herself a little shake, telling herself to wake up. She'd met Dr Evi Oliver, a psychiatrist specializing in problems affecting young people and families, just weeks earlier in Cambridge, when Evi's concern over an unprecedented number of student deaths had led to an undercover police operation. In only a few days, Lacey had come to trust Evi in a way she rarely trusted anyone. When they'd said goodbye, neither woman had expected to be in contact with the other again. Undercover police officers did the job and then disappeared. It had to be that way.
'How are you?' asked Evi, sounding wary but not unfriendly.
'Not good at all. And I've no time to chat. Evi, I'm really sorry to do this to you, but I need advice. Can you help me?'
No hesitation this time. 'What do you need?'

'So we're no longer looking for Dracula, we're looking for Peter Frigging Pan!' Dana stopped pacing when the wall got in her way and turned to face the group, who were almost cowering before her. Mizon, Stenning, Richmond, Anderson and Barrett, the only members of the team she hadn't been able to bully into going home. 'Can I have a volunteer to explain that to the world's media tomorrow morning, after my godson's body has been washed up by the tide, because I really don't think I'm—'

'Dana!'

Anderson was on his feet. 'I am very close to going to the Super and requesting that you be removed from this case too,' he said.

As they stared at each other, Dana could almost hear the sharp gasps going on around them. She wasn't the only one who didn't believe what she was hearing.

'Like DI Joesbury, you are just too close,' Anderson went on. 'The only reason I'm not doing so is that when you're on form you're the brightest police officer I've ever worked with. I happen to think the young lad needs you.'

This wasn't happening. Neil gave her unquestioning back-up. Always.

'But he needs you at your best, not falling apart, so you'd better decide which you're going to be and you'd better decide quick.'

It was a disciplinary offence, talking to a senior officer this way. She had to nip this in the bud, right now.

'Now, Gayle has been working on something all evening.' Anderson turned briefly to Mizon and gave her a quick, encouraging smile. 'Don't think I haven't noticed. And we are going to pay her the courtesy of listening to her.' Attention back on Dana now. 'Are you staying or not?'

'Of course I'm staying,' Dana said. 'I'm sorry, everyone. Go on, Gayle.'

Mizon's throat clenched as she swallowed. 'Well, the first thing I want to show you is this,' she said, indicating her screen. The others gathered round, Dana just a second behind everyone else, to see a photograph of red roses filling the screen.

'I went to the website of David Austen Roses,' Mizon went on.

'They're probably the biggest supplier of roses in Europe, my mum uses them all the time. Anyway, not really expecting anything, I typed "Peter Pan" into the search facility and look – this is the same photograph that Peter Sweep's been using on his profile page.'

'So all these weeks we've been looking at a patio rose with double blooms and bright-red flowers called Peter Pan,' said Anderson.

'Yes,' said Mizon. 'I guess he thought a boy in green tights would have been too obvious.'

For a moment, Lacey felt like a beleaguered general spotting reinforcements on the horizon. She hadn't realized how much she'd missed Evi. 'Is there such a thing, such a condition, as a fear of growing up?' she asked. 'Have you ever come across children who are terrified of the whole business of puberty, of entering the adult world?'

It was way past midnight, and Evi Oliver had almost certainly been dragged out of bed. On the other hand, she was the woman who, despite severe physical disabilities, had twice been instrumental in stopping exceptionally serious crimes. 'Many times,' she said. 'I'd say most pre-teens will experience anxieties about the onset of adolescence.'

The rain was shrill on the flat, glass roof of the conservatory and Evi's voice was pitched low. Lacey had to listen hard.

'And how do these anxieties manifest themselves?'

'The usual ways. Bad behaviour, sulking, truancy, minor problems with the police. Let's see, shoplifting, category-C drug use. It's called being a teenager, Laura. I mean, Lacey.'

'OK, that all sounds completely normal. But have you ever come across kids whose reactions have been more extreme? Violent, even?'

A couple of seconds went by as Evi gave herself time to think. Lacey watched the rain and tried not to think about the water level rising steadily higher. About the tide on the turn. She told herself to hold it together, to think about the man who might still be on the bridge in the rain, counting on her.

'Sometimes,' said Evi, after a moment. 'I've treated some pretty disturbed teenagers. They'll start lashing out at parents, siblings. They might get involved in gangs, playground fights.'

Unable to bear the indoors any longer, Lacey pushed open the conservatory door. The sound of the rain intensified, like the drumbeats of an approaching army. 'What about extreme violence?' she asked. 'Could a child be so disturbed by the fear of growing up that it drives him to kill?'

A heavy sigh on the other end of the line. 'Oh Lacey,' said Evi. 'I did so hope they hadn't got you involved in the South Bank murders.'

'So what does everybody think?' Dana asked a short while later. 'Susan?'

On the whiteboard in front of them were the quotations pulled from the Missing Boys Facebook page that referred to the fictional lost boys of the J. M. Barrie's story. Gayle Mizon had just outlined her theory that the killer could be a child – a child with a Peter Pan complex.

Dana stared at them. It was almost too ridiculous, except hadn't she had a feeling from the outset that these boys weren't being killed by the classic male paedophile? She'd assumed the killer had to be a woman. What if she'd been right on the first count, but had jumped too quickly to the next neat solution?

'It's an interesting idea,' said Richmond, which Dana had learned in their short acquaintance meant she hadn't yet formed an opinion. Trouble was, they didn't have time for her to consult the literature, organize group discussions and mull it over for days.

Without speaking, Stenning stood up and walked back to his own desk. He moved the mouse around, opened up a search engine.

'The problem I have with it all,' said Anderson, 'notwithstanding the rigour of the work that Gayle's done, is that children want to grow up. They crave independence, the ability to do cooler stuff. I can't imagine what could make a child terrified of growing up.'

Richmond got up too and paced a long, slow circle, rubbing her temples all the while.

'How about if, whoever this kid is, his mother has a lot of boyfriends, is even on the game,' said Mizon. 'He's going to view the sexual act in a very negative way. Maybe he's been sexually abused.

It could all add up to a child who views sex as inextricably linked with the adult condition and as something to be avoided.'

'Susan?' prompted Dana.

The profiler turned to face the group.

'Sadly, that scenario is all too common,' she said. 'Most sexual offenders will have an early history of sexual abuse or disturbing sexual experiences. Our killer isn't a sexual offender, though.'

'Well, what if he's afraid of the responsibility of adulthood,' said Mizon. 'What if he's made to feel guilty for not being a breadwinner yet. You can see it, can't you? "When are you going to do something useful with your life instead of taking from us all the time?"'

'You've given this a lot of thought,' said Richmond.

Mizon's eyes dropped to her lap.

'But I doubt either of those factors would be enough,' said the profiler.

'What if there's more than one?' said Anderson. 'This is South London. We have some pretty dysfunctional family units.'

Richmond was silent.

'Is it possible?' asked Dana.

'Everything's possible,' said Richmond. 'Whether it's likely is another matter. I can think of no documented cases where a fear of entering the adult world has led to a child taking extreme measures to prevent others from doing so.'

'You think Gayle's wrong, don't you?' said Dana.

'She isn't wrong,' said Stenning, turning to face them again. 'Come and look at this.'

'What turns children into killers?' asked Lacey.

'Nothing,' Evi replied. 'They're born that way.'

Lacey took a moment to process the answer she really hadn't been expecting. 'That's a bit radical.'

'You've not had much to do with kids, have you?' said Evi. 'The average two- or three-year-old will get into a murderous rage on a regular basis – screaming, kicking, hitting.'

'That's just a tantrum,' said Lacey.

'And what's a tantrum but an expression of completely

uncontrollable rage?' said Evi. 'You put the means to do serious harm into the hands of a toddler in the middle of a full-blown tantrum and the chances are he'll use it. Children are passionate little creatures, capable of the same strength of feeling as adults, and they have the same dark impulses that we have. The question you should be asking me is what stops children killing.'

'OK, what stops children killing?'

'Social conditioning, mainly done by two loving parents, within a calm and stable home environment,' said Evi. 'The child learns that the world doesn't revolve around him alone, that others have feelings and rights, too. Most importantly, he has to learn that if he acts on a violent impulse, there will be consequences. But no one should underestimate how much effort goes into this. Conditioning a small human being takes a huge amount of work.'

Lacey stood in the shelter of the conservatory roof, looking out at foliage that seemed to slump under the weight of the rainwater. Each drop that fell into the garden bounced off leaves and branches, sometimes more than once, multiplying the sound of the rainfall. Her tiny patch of lawn had turned to mud already.

'That all makes perfect sense,' she said. 'And I can see how lots of children don't get the chance to learn those lessons. But wouldn't that mean we have a whole load of juvenile delinquents?'

'Well, I think some people would argue that's exactly what we do have,' replied Evi. 'There are people who will tell you that a major part of our society is facing meltdown because parents are opting out of the social responsibility of bringing up their kids to know right from wrong.'

'It's that simple?'

Evi gave a small laugh. 'Nothing ever is.'

'Evi, if I'm right, that the killer is a child, he can't be a young one. Anyone under the age of ten or eleven just wouldn't have the strength or the independence of action. Is that fair?'

'Sounds sensible. Killers under the age of ten are almost unheard of. Do you have a particular child in mind?'

Frankly, out of the father and the son, I'd be more worried about the son.

Do you think they're together? Barney and Huck.

'Yes,' Lacey said. 'His name is Barney.'

'I think I've got him,' Stenning called over, hurrying them along. Awkwardly, as though they'd grown stiff from sitting in one position too long, the group gathered around his desk.

'I've done a search of the CCTV footage we collected from the access roads,' he said. 'Just two of them, Horseleydown Lane and Jamaica Road, I didn't have time to do any more. A kid wouldn't be able to drive a car, right, which could explain why the previous searches threw up zippo, so I did a search for bikes.'

'You think he transported a body on the back of a pushbike?' said Dana. 'Two bodies, in the Barlow boys' case?'

'I think that might be exactly what he did, Boss. Take a look at this.' Stenning dragged the mouse across the desk and clicked. The team saw a still picture of Horseleydown Lane, off which led the Horseleydown Steps. The steps weren't in shot. A second still picture came into view, and this one showed a slim figure on a bicycle. The bike was dragging an enclosed baby trailer. The third shot showed a closer view of both bike and trailer.

'There's something in that trailer,' said Gayle. 'Could you fit two nine-year-old boys in there?'

'Yes,' said Anderson. 'We've had one since Marcus was three. He and Abigail both still get in it from time to time. They're over the weight limit, but in the park it's safe enough.'

In the fourth shot, the bike and trailer had disappeared from view.

'Eighteen minutes later, he comes back,' said Stenning, who was jiggling the mouse again. 'Remember those large bins just by the steps? I reckon it would be easy enough to park the bike behind them and carry the boys one at a time down on to the beach. Here we go.'

Dana stepped closer to the monitor as the bike and trailer came back into view. It could be just wishful thinking, but the rider seemed to be pedalling faster now, as though pulling a lighter load.

'How would he get them in there?' she asked. 'When they're alive, I mean. Once they're dead it would be reasonably straightforward.'

'If this is a young teenager, he's not going to seem particularly threatening,' said Richmond. 'Quite the opposite, in fact. Younger kids love hanging out with older ones. Maybe he just offered to take them for a ride.'

'And if that didn't work, he had the Vulcan pressure points to fall back on,' suggested Anderson.

'Fake blood to throw them off guard,' said Dana. 'Looks like he had a whole bag of tricks.'

'Do we get a better look at the rider at all?' asked Anderson.

'Slightly,' said Stenning, 'at the next scene. Give me a second.'

They waited.

'Here we go,' said Stenning. 'Camera on the corner of Jamaica Road and Bevington Street.' He flicked through still shots and the team watched the bike and trailer getting closer. As he reached the corner, the rider braked and, for the first time, looked up.

'Definitely not a man,' said Anderson.

'Slim woman or teenager,' said Richmond.

'I don't think that's a woman,' said Mizon. 'Women and teenage boys just don't move in the same way. Look at him. He's holding his shoulders like a man. And there's no way he's dressed for the weather. That's a thin jacket he's wearing. A woman would dress properly. It's not a woman.'

'No, it's not,' said Dana. 'Well done, Gayle. You too, Pete.'

'Bloody good job,' said Anderson. 'Now we just need a friggin' name.'

'Barnaby Roberts,' said Mizon. 'His father's in custody downstairs. I think we might just have been focusing on the wrong member of the family. And, much as I'm enjoying your praise, this isn't my theory. It's Lacey's.'

'Tell me about Barney,' said Evi.

Lacey took a deep breath, told herself to concentrate. This wasn't the time for running around, this was thinking time. 'He lives with a largely absent father whom he seems to fear,' she said. 'His mother committed suicide when he was four and he found the body. But then he wiped the memory from his mind and convinced himself not only that she was still alive but that he could find her by advertising in local papers.'

'Poor kid,' said Evi.

A poor kid who might, at this moment, be slitting the throat of another child. Lacey looked up. In the light of the solar lamps, the trees and shrubs in her garden were glowing vivid shades of green, as though the downpour had washed away all traces of city grime. Her garden looked strangely beautiful, but beyond it was a big, alien city, and it was no place for anyone to be out alone, especially not a child.

'He's exceptionally bright,' said Lacey. 'Has incredible powers of observation. But with issues. Almost certainly has OCD. I see him doing things with his hands, muttering to himself when he thinks I don't see. He's very knowledgeable about tides and the river, he knows stuff the killer would need to know. And he's been taking a very keen interest in the murders. Wanting to discuss them with me.'

'Where is he now?'

'We don't know,' she said. 'But another child has gone missing tonight. Wherever Barney is, he could be with his latest victim.'

'Hence the sense of urgency.'

Urgency? Jesus, she wasn't sure how much longer she could stay in one place. She wondered how Gayle Mizon was getting on, sounding out the Peter Pan theory with the MIT.

'Evi, a few minutes ago, you said you'd hoped I wasn't involved in the South Bank murders. I was just asking you about seriously disturbed kids. How did you know what case I was calling about?'

Evi gave a heavy, sad sigh. 'I've been keeping a watching brief on the South Bank case,' she said. 'Quite a few of us have, actually, because it's been so completely atypical. No violence, no sexual motive. It's all been about showing off, misdirections, fooling around. One of my colleagues spotted the Peter Pan quotations, and that got us thinking. Some of the references have come from the book, rather than the stage play, which isn't so readily available. Others have come from the official sequel, *Peter Pan in Scarlet*. Quite a lot have even come from the 2003 film. Typically, who's most familiar with the Peter Pan story? Kids.'

'You didn't say anything?' Lacey knew she sounded judgemental, just couldn't help it.

'Lacey, what did we really have other than an idea? Possibly a completely daft one? Child killers are extremely rare. The few we have almost invariably come from a background of serious neglect and abuse. They've been brutalized from a very young age and they deal with it by passing the violence on. Are you with me?'

'Of course.'

'But the South Bank murders show no violence, which argues against them being the work of an abused kid. It was a feeling, a hunch. Nothing more. Only now it seems you have the same one.'

'Except I was thinking of a child who identified with a character from literature. Someone who wanted to stay a child for ever and keep his buddies with him.'

Silence again, while Evi was thinking. *Come on, come on . . .*

'The victims didn't know each other, though,' she said. 'They weren't buddies. And the killer can't have known them all even slightly well or there'd have been a connection you'd have spotted.'

Suddenly, it was hard to breathe. Lacey strode outside, almost panting with the effort of just moving forwards. 'Shit, you're right. I've just sent the investigation team off on another wild-goose chase and his little boy is going to be dead before the night's out.'

'Lacey, get a hold of yourself. You're almost there. I do think your killer could be a child, and from what you've told me about this Barney, he seems a very likely candidate. I just don't buy your afraid-of-growing-up theory. No, stay with me. As I understand it, murder is driven by compulsion. Sex, avarice, rage. Strong but very simple emotions. Fear of growing up? No, that's too complex. I think the Peter Pan business is just an idea he's been having fun with. He's been playing with you. He has no intention of flying off to Neverland, he's enjoying himself too much. His real motivation will be much simpler, much deeper. But for heaven's sake, you can worry about what's driving him when he's caught.'

The rain had finally stopped. The garden looked like a tiny patch of rainforest after a tropical storm, like a dense, storybook jungle – like a painting she'd seen on a wall.

'Flying off to Neverland,' said Lacey.

'Sometimes, Lacey, there is no reason. People kill and there is no neat, understandable motive. What did you say?'

'Evi, thank you.'

'What? Are you OK?'

'I have to go now,' said Lacey. 'I know where he is.'

65

'MY SON WOULDN'T HURT ANYONE.'

'Yes, thank you, Mr Roberts,' said Anderson, taking the seat opposite Stewart. 'We've taken note of everything you've told us about Barney's inherent gentleness and his habit of nursing injured birds back to health when he was small. The fact remains, though, that both he and a younger boy are missing, and it is extremely important that we find them.'

'Barney is terrified of blood. He goes ape-shit if he cuts himself. I practically have to sedate him to get him to have a vaccination. There is no way on earth he could cut someone's throat.'

Dana took the seat beside Anderson and flicked open the notes facility on her laptop.

'Do you actually know what your son gets up to when you leave him alone two evenings a week?' she asked.

Stewart's eyes narrowed. 'What do you mean? He does his homework, watches TV, plays on his computer and goes to bed. He's a sensible kid.'

'He goes out, hangs around with a gang of older children and spends an inordinate amount of time looking for his dead mother. I'd say he's a child with problems,' replied Dana.

'You know nothing about my son.'

'He also experiences episodes when his memory deserts him completely. Large chunks of time when he claims he has no recollection of where he's been and what he's been doing. I'm starting to wonder how much you know about your son.'

Lacey found a torch, latex gloves and a dry jacket. She was out of the house in less than a minute. At her destination in fewer than five.

Fly off and join them in Neverland.

How many times over the last few weeks had she lurked in the shadows and watched Barney and his mates speeding down the skateboard ramp at the community centre? *You look like you're flying,* she'd told him. They hurled themselves down impossibly steep slopes at terrifying speeds with only balance and the force of gravity to keep them upright. The wind caught their hair and pulled at their clothes. When they spread their arms for balance they genuinely looked as though they were soaring through the sky.

And the illusion was made perfect by the mural painted on the brick wall behind them. A picture of a night sky, stars and the moon, plump, billowing clouds, and three children, the Darling children, flying for the very first time in their lives with the aid of happy thoughts and fairy dust. The community centre, the place where Barney and his mates hung out, was Neverland.

The grim Victorian exterior of the community centre had been softened and made child-friendly by extensive mural paintings. The pictures ran around the main building and inside the perimeter wall. One of the outbuildings, she was sure, showed a bay with mermaids on rocks. There was the enormous green crocodile with the alarm clock grasped between its teeth. A pirate ship in full sail. Wigwams to represent the Indian village.

At the gates, Lacey took Huck's phone out of her pocket. Was she certain enough to call for back-up? Whilst the paintings could have given Barney the idea in the first place, was it feasible that children were being held and killed in a community facility that, every day, was swarming with people? She could not call the MIT here to find an empty building.

If they were taking her theory seriously – and if they still believed it to be Gayle Mizon's they probably would be – they'd concentrate on finding the places that Barney had access to. The houseboat and the boatyard were obvious ones. Maybe the Roberts family owned a garage or lock-up somewhere. They'd be talking to his friends, trying to find out if there were any dens or meeting places in old, abandoned buildings. God knows there were enough of them around South London at the moment. That was the sort of ordered, logical search that would find Huck. Pulling them away from it to pursue yet another harebrained idea could be dangerously irresponsible.

Thirty-five minutes before Joesbury was expecting to meet up with her again. She couldn't phone him either. If there was even the remotest possibility that his son was being held in the community centre, he'd tear down every door in the place trying to find him. She couldn't put him through that until she was sure.

Dana pushed open the door of the incident room, knowing she was going through the motions. She'd just about lost the ability to think. All she could do now was follow procedure and hope others on the team were functioning better than she was.

'OK, we've spoken to the families of all Barney Roberts's close friends,' she told the team. 'He was at the local community centre until nine o'clock, and then three of his friends – Jorge and Harvey Soar and Hatty Bennet – walked home with him. Harvey seems to be his best friend so we may have to talk to him again. None of them can think of anywhere he might be other than his own house or possibly the boat at Deptford Creek.'

'I've just had a call from the uniformed team we sent down there,' said Anderson. 'There's no sign of him, and it's not that big an area. They really don't think he's gone there.'

'We haven't spoken to DC Flint again,' said Dana, 'but for now it looks as though hers was the last sighting we have of him.'

'Neither DC Flint nor DI Joesbury are at their respective flats, Ma'am,' called Stenning from across the room. 'DI Joesbury's still not answering his phone.'

Dana acknowledged Stenning with a nod. 'I think we have to assume DC Flint and DI Joesbury are pursuing their own independent investigations,' she said. 'Let's hope they're together and at least stand a chance of keeping each other out of trouble. In the meantime, if Barney is the one we're looking for, it seems safe to assume he's gone to wherever he's been keeping and killing the boys. If we find Barney, we find Huck.'

The entire complex was in darkness. But Lacey knew she'd often seen Barney and his mates in the yard after the centre had closed. In fact, hadn't Jorge, less than an hour earlier, told her he'd just been inside?

The heavy gates were padlocked. The brick perimeter wall was around five feet high, but iron railings on top of it took it up well above her head.

If Barney and his mates could get inside, she could.

At the corner of the street, the railings gave way to the outside wall of the outbuildings. Round the corner, the street was both narrower and quieter. It was still difficult to see a way in. The outbuildings were single-storey, with steeply sloping tiled roofs and no obvious way over them. Lacey followed the wall to the end and turned the next corner.

This time she was in an alleyway between two streets. No one around. Plenty of shadows. Lacey found her breathing escalating. She'd spent weeks telling herself nothing could scare her any more. Was she about to find out that she was wrong?

On this side there was another door. Unlike the wide, iron gates at the front of the yard, designed to allow vehicles to drive right inside, this one was a pedestrian access only. Lacey stretched out a gloved hand to try the handle. Locked, of course, but to the right of the door one of the railings had broken away, leaving a narrow gap.

Lacey jumped down into one of the darkest corners of the yard. All seemed still. No sound came from beyond the outer walls except the ordinary night-time percussion of London. OK, Barney could not be in the main building. It was used for twelve hours or so every day. People were constantly coming and going in every part of it. There was no way abducted children could be hidden in there.

What about the outbuildings?

Four doors faced on to the yard. Each shed had a small window, set high in the wall. Switching off her torch, relying only upon the light from the streets, Lacey made her way towards the first shed.

And with every step, the fear she thought she'd left behind for ever was growing.

There were too many hiding places. Too many shadows. Beneath the skateboard ramps, around corners, even inside a collection of plastic Wendy houses by the main doors. Children could hide anywhere. They could squeeze their bodies into the smallest spaces.

The outbuildings were definitely the most likely place. In the young children's play area Lacey found a plastic cube that would bear her weight. Balanced on it, she could see through the window that the first shed was packed to the roof with piles of chairs, stacked trestle tables, cardboard boxes. She'd struggle to open the door, never mind move around inside. Nevertheless, she tried. Locked.

The next was full of sports and games equipment, outdoor stuff that wouldn't be needed until the spring. Locked like the first. The third shed looked like the overspill of a busy office. Two desks were piled high with books and files. Filing cabinets lined one wall. Paper littered the floor. Black bin-liners, close to bursting apart, were piled in one corner. The door was locked.

The fourth and last shed in the line had been used as a workshop. Against the far wall was a long Formica counter, interrupted only by an old-fashioned Belfast sink. An immersion heater was fixed to the wall. Empty paint tins lay along the counter. There were woodworking tools, saws, hammers fixed to the walls. Locked like the rest. And, like the rest, quite plainly no one was inside.

Lacey felt panic rising up again. Panic that would creep into her thoughts and throw them off kilter, stealing away her ability to think straight. She couldn't give into it. Not yet. Victorian buildings nearly always had cellars.

She started to move again, looking down for the tell-tale ventilation grates or the reinforced opaque glass squares that allowed daylight to reach underground. Nothing around the outbuildings. Nor around the main factory building either. There was no way of getting inside to check. Time to face facts: there was nothing more she could do on her own.

Lacey pulled her borrowed mobile from her pocket. Unsure who to call first, Mizon or Joesbury, she hesitated as a flickering of light caught her eye. She looked up. There it was again. A light inside the building, in an upstairs window? Gone. Shit, had she seen it or not?

Lacey ran straight at the skateboard ramp and let the momentum take her up. At the top, from where Barney and his friends regularly launched themselves into the night, she could almost see through the upper windows. All seemed dark. Then the flickering began again – which was nothing, after all, just the reflection of a malfunctioning lamppost in the next street along, and time was running out.

The lamppost started flashing again, drawing her attention to the building immediately behind it. A derelict Victorian house, large and square, with ornate red brickwork, very similar in architectural style to the community centre. She'd walked past it many times, could even remember when it had housed local council offices. Once officialdom had moved out, it had become a hang-out for drug addicts and homeless people, until complaints from local residents had resulted in tighter security and regular police inspections. She'd even visited it herself once, back when she'd been in uniform.

It was taller than the houses in the adjacent streets, taller by a whole storey than the community centre, and the upper windows looked directly into the yard. Into Neverland.

Movement at Dana's side made her glance up from the computer screen. Susan Richmond was approaching with two mugs.

'May I?' she asked, indicating the vacant seat.

'Of course,' replied Dana. 'You know, I'm still not sure.'

'About what? About the killer being a child?'

Dana shook her head. 'Lacey's a bright officer,' she said, 'but she's impulsive. Gets an idea and has to act right away. She doesn't necessarily think things through. If we're looking for a child who doesn't want to grow up, how do the multiple cuts fit in?'

Richmond thought for a second. 'You mean if he wanted the kids dead, he'd just want to get it over as soon as possible?'

'Exactly. the multiple cuts suggest to me it's about the cutting. The cutting is what he gets off on.'

'The important thing is, he didn't kill any of the other boys the first night. We still have time.'

'Ma'am.' Anderson had approached. 'For what it's worth, we know who our mole was.'

Dana had forgotten all about the mole, that someone had been feeding information to Bartholomew Hunt.

'That was the pathologist, Mike Kaytes, on the phone,' said Anderson. 'He's working late on another case and found a half-finished email his nerdy young assistant Troy was writing before he got called away. Guess who it was to?'

'Hunt?' tried Dana.

'Bang on. Turns out Hunt is young Troy's mother's cousin. He admitted everything when Mike pressed him. He'll be instigating disciplinary proceedings in the morning, he just wanted us to know.'

'Thanks, Neil.'

'Doesn't really seem that important right now, does it?'

The windows on the ground floor of the house were boarded up with plywood. Lacey inspected each in turn, looking for loose nails, but there was no way in at the front that she could see. The huge double-door, beneath the carved sign reading MERCIER HOUSE, BOROUGH OF LAMBETH, PARKS AND AMENITIES DIVISION, didn't budge an inch when she tried the handle.

Same at the side. Four large, rectangular windows, all boarded up. The rear of the property was enclosed by a tall brick wall with a wide gate. The gate swung open when she pushed it and Lacey walked through into the ghost of a garden.

A rose had rambled the entire length of one wall, its branches clambering into the trees overhead, twisting and fighting with a bramble for tendril-holds. Berries from the previous autumn, shrivelled and rotting, clung to thorn-strewn branches and littered the ground. Further in, old fruit trees, their limbs dried and splitting, seemed to rely on the brick walls and the memory of former days to stay upright. One of them still bore fruit. Lacey blinked – apples in February – but they were real enough. The tree had lost its leaves but kept its fruit. In the street-light the apples shone rosy-red, gleaming on the bare branches like baubles on a

Christmas tree. More apples lay at its foot, rotting, the red skins smeared across the ground like bloodstains. She really had to get a move on.

An echo of a path took her towards the house. Brown stalks lying prone across the gravel were all that was left of the summer's weed growth. Lacey passed a stone bird-bath that lay crumbling on its side. Closer to the building was a skip, a quarter-filled with refuse. Running along half of the rear wall were the remains of an elaborate Victorian conservatory.

The glasshouse stretched up to a high, vaulted roof, much of which looked intact, but as Lacey drew closer she could see splinters of glass scattered around like diamonds on the ground. The door she pushed at, more out of habit than any real expectation, opened.

The exotic hot-house plants had long since shrivelled and died, but the raised beds of the original conservatory remained, as did the slim, rectangular pool that ran lengthwise down its centre. The interior still retained the smell of damp, warm vegetation that greenhouses never seem to lose, but the smell was deceptive. Even sheltered from the wind, the conservatory was freezing cold; the glass panes were starting to mist over at the touch of her breath. The wall between the conservatory and the interior of the house had two windows, both boarded up. The half-glass door that led into the building had been similarly secured. Lacey was on her way to check the door when she saw the bike.

Tucked against the house wall, it looked modern, designed for a woman, with a low crossbar and with a plastic-covered baby-trailer attached to the back. Before she was close enough to touch it, Lacey could see that the coloured plastic of the trailer's roof was wet. Raindrops. And yet the bike was completely sheltered beneath the glass roof. Some time in the last hour, this bike had been out in the rain.

Crouching, Lacey peered inside the trailer, looking for any trace, even a scent, of Huck, but there was nothing. She tried the back door to the house. Locked and boarded. There was no easy way into this house and panic was rising up again, muddying her thinking and telling her it was hopeless.

Back in the garden, she pulled out Huck's phone. Joesbury would come like a shot if she called, but apart from some vague thoughts about Neverland and a baby trailer, what did she really have? She needed to get inside.

The windows on the next floor up were open to the elements, but reaching them would mean scaling the iron framework of the conservatory. Almost as an experiment, Lacey reached up, and the stabbing of a tiny shard of glass was a reminder of her own stupidity. No child, even a strong and agile one, could scale the conservatory with another child on his back.

She had to go, find Joesbury, tell him her hunch had come to nothing. He could probably organize a search of the house, just to be sure, but it would be little more than ticking the box. Lacey had almost turned away from the house when something caught her eye. At the corner of the building, strung from an upper window, was a collapsible rubble chute.

Conscious of her heart beating faster again, Lacey stepped over to it. It was black, or she might have noticed it sooner, a long, wide pipe stretching from the upper floor of the building, designed to allow sharp rubble to be thrown safely to the ground. It was constructed in sections: when not in use or in transport each piece could slip inside the next so it became a manageable size. At one point, it had probably been directed into the skip.

Suddenly, the hunch was alive again. This was the perfect way to get the body of a young boy in and out of the building. The lost boys had all been small, skinny, ten-year-olds. Some sort of rope and pulley system could have lifted them to the top floor via the chute. Once they were dead, the chute would have got them back down again.

In the bike, she had the means of getting them around London; in the rubble chute, a way of getting them in and out of the house. The house gave the killer somewhere to work, but was too close to other people for him to risk keeping the boys alive for long. Was it enough? She looked at the phone. Still twenty minutes before Joesbury came looking for her. If she called him now, he'd tell her to wait for him. He'd alert Tulloch and the team, who would insist she wait outside. It was the only sensible thing to do. But how would she ever get Huck's face out of her head, if she stood here doing nothing, while he . . .

Lacey tucked the phone back in her pocket, returned to the conservatory and started to climb.

The vertical ascent wasn't difficult. Clambering across the arched roof, though, she had to avoid putting any weight on the glass. Her limbs were shaking by the time she reached the window, but one last effort and she was inside.

Just in time to hear a low-pitched whimper.

People around her were exhausted. Dana knew she had to send them home. She'd tried already and they'd ignored her. They were staying as long as she stayed, and she was staying until the end.

Across the room, the phone started ringing. It was a measure of how tired everyone was that no one rushed to answer it. After a couple of seconds, Anderson got up and crossed the room.

'OK, listen up, guys, this is important.'

Heads lifted. Several people were blinking hard.

'That was SOCOs down at the Creek,' Anderson said. 'They've found more blood on the houseboat. Tiny amounts. Someone's done a pretty good job of cleaning up, but there's no doubt. There are at least two distinct types, both definitely human. And before you ask, neither are Gilly Green's.'

'I'm not keeping up,' said Mizon. 'I thought we'd ruled out Stewart Roberts.'

'We ruled him out,' said Dana. 'We didn't rule out the boat.'

Lacey made herself keep still, ignore the urge to run from room to room, shouting out Huck's name. There were procedures to be followed, the first of which was to understand the size and nature of the building to be searched.

The room she was standing in was large and high, with a carved ceiling-rose and picture rail. There was a cheap filing cabinet that no one had thought worth removing, a metal chair lying upturned on the linoleum floor and stacks of loose files to one side of the door. A door she had to open, slowly and silently.

The door opened on to a landing above a wide, ornate staircase. On either side of where Lacey was standing, two further flights of stairs gave her a choice of passage up to the next floor. In the hallway below her was the wide front door and – she counted quickly – at least five more rooms.

Oh, this wasn't an empty house, somehow she just knew it. This house was alive and breathing, watching her. She could almost see the gentle, respiratory movement of the walls. The wind, which was somehow finding its way in from outside, ruffled loose papers, stirred old cobwebs, chased dried leaves across the floors. The woodwork shifted and tensed, bracing itself, waiting for her next move. Reluctant to leave the relative safety of the room she'd entered by, Lacey knew she was committed. Having entered the house, she had to complete the search.

Police training told her to check and secure the ground floor first. Instinct screamed at her not to go down. Down meant no way out. Down was the equivalent of being trapped in a cellar.

Besides, the chute had led from the top floor of the house. Logically, anything happening in this house would be happening above her. Which meant there was no point checking this floor either. She had to go up.

Leaving the doorway to take to the stairs was like finding herself in the middle of a maze, in which danger could come from any direction. This was a huge house, with any number of rooms, corners and cupboards. Barney was small and agile. He could be anywhere. He could be watching her right now. If it came to it, could she fight an eleven-year-old boy? One who was desperate, and possibly armed?

Before she was halfway up the stairs, Lacey had the over-whelming feeling that she'd taken the wrong flight. The urge to turn, head down and then back up the left-hand stairs was so strong it was all she could do to force herself to carry on. Then a muffled but distinct yelling stopped her in her tracks. The sound a terrified child makes when his mouth is covered.

Stewart Roberts looked Dana straight in the eyes, but there was something rather defiant about his face now. He'd grown paler, the muscles in his jaw were twitching and his eyes were beginning to look damp.

'I want to talk about the time you went to the boat to dry it out,' she told him. 'The second week in January, I understand.'

Wary, he inclined his head. 'The locksmith I sent there said it looked damp,' he replied. 'Thought perhaps a hatch was leaking. I went a couple of days later and found he was right. There were small pools of water on the floor. And most of the soft furnishings were damp.'

'Did you find a leak?'

He shook his head.

'For the benefit—'

'For the benefit of the tape,' he interrupted, 'I didn't find a leak. None of the hatches had been left open, to my knowledge. The boat seemed completely sound. I had no idea, and still don't, how the boat could have been wet.'

Dana pressed a key to take her to a different page.

'Our crime-scene investigators have found traces of blood on your boat,' she said. 'At least two distinct types, neither originating from Mrs Green this time. Could either be yours?'

Slowly, reluctantly, he shook his head. 'I keep a record if I cut myself,' he said. 'It happens very rarely. I'm extremely careful.'

'What about Barney?'

His breathing was quickening. 'Barney hasn't been on the boat since last October. And when he cuts himself, the world knows about it.'

'You do realize that if the blood we've found matches any of the victims, then they could only have been killed by someone with access to your boat?' Dana said.

Stewart didn't reply. For a few seconds she watched his chest rise and fall.

'More than once now,' she said, 'you've referred to the keys to the houseboat going missing late last year. Mrs Green said the same thing. What can you tell us about that?'

'The keys were missing over Christmas,' Stewart told her. 'I had the locks changed.'

'Can you give us some dates?'

He sighed and pulled out his phone. He looked at the screen for several seconds, tapping various apps. 'The last time I was at the boat before Christmas was the thirteenth of December,' he said after a moment. 'That was a Thursday. The following Tuesday, the eighteenth, Gilly and I met for a drink. I imagine the keys went missing some time over the weekend in between.'

Dana looked at her laptop calendar. Anderson leaned closer so he could see it too. Tyler King had disappeared on the twentieth of December, Ryan Jackson on the third of January. Both bodies had been found in or by the Creek.

'When did you get the locks changed?' asked Anderson.

Stewart had been anticipating the question. 'The eleventh of January,' he said. 'Friday morning.'

On the tenth of January, Ryan's body had been found on the beach at Deptford. From the following day, the killer would have been unable to access the boat. He'd found somewhere new. Somewhere he didn't dare risk keeping the boys for too long. So he'd started killing them faster. It was all starting to come together, except . . .

'Any idea how the keys went missing?' Anderson asked.

Stewart shook his head. 'I kept them on a hook by the front door with all the house keys,' he said.

'I think you told us before you don't have many visitors,' said Anderson. 'Barney doesn't like people in his house. I think you said that's the reason why you never used babysitters.'

Stewart seemed to shrink a little. He shook his head, but the conviction had gone.

'Who, apart from you and Barney, could have taken those keys?' asked Dana gently.

'No one,' said Stewart. 'No one comes into our house. Just me and Barney and occasionally his mates. He can tolerate kids, you see, because he stays in charge. Other than a few kids, though, no one.'

Silence. The man across the desk remained perfectly still. Outwardly, he was unchanged. Inside, Dana knew, he was crumbling.

Knowing that if you're going to attack, you do it fast and hard, Lacey ran up the last few steps. She burst through the one door on the upper landing and in the tangerine light of the street lamps had a moment to take in the huge, high-ceilinged room, the bloodstains festooning the walls and rafters like forgotten party-streamers, and the sickly, slaughterhouse stench of the place. Then she spotted the small, slim boy tied to the trestle table in the middle of the room. Eyes open. Body wriggling. *Huck.* Still alive, thank God. Duct tape had been tied across his mouth but he was making a hell of a noise from behind it. His hands were taped together and so were his feet, and tape had been wound round and round his body to secure him to the table. His head was jerking from left to right but his eyes never left hers.

Then they did. At the exact moment that Lacey heard the swish of air behind her, Huck's eyes darted to the left. Without that second of warning, the blow might have been fatal. As it was, her right arm deflected the flying sledge-hammer and it caught the side of her head. The next blow, coming only a split second later, was that of a body hurtling through space and flying directly into her. She fell to the ground, sickened and disorientated. As she went down, she spun to the left and caught sight of the second trestle table. Lying on it, trussed and gagged exactly like Huck, was Barney.

'Ma'am.' Tom Barrett was at the far side of the room. He had to raise his voice to be heard.

'What is it, Tom?'

'I've been running checks on all those kids Stewart Roberts told us were friends of Barney's. I think you're going to want to see this.'

Dana crossed the room to Barrett's desk. He stood to let her sit down, but she shook her head, leaning on the desk instead. His screen showed the webpage of a CNN newsite.

'Barney Roberts's best mate is a kid called Harvey Soar,' Barret told her, as first Mizon, then Anderson, Richmond and Stenning gathered around the desk behind her. 'Harvey has – or rather had – some famous parents.'

'Abbie and Rob Soar,' said Anderson. 'The British journalists who got caught up in the Ivory Coast atrocities. Remind me when this was?'

'Twelve years ago,' replied Barret. 'Abbie must have been pregnant with Harvey at the time. There was a massacre in a school

– over a dozen boys were killed, supposedly so they couldn't grow up and join the government-controlled army. The Soars were there, caught up in it, and they had their two-year-old son with them.'

'They came across the school just as the rebels left,' said Dana, who'd been reading ahead. 'I remember this happening. Abbie took photographs – they went all round the world afterwards. They got away, but the rebels caught up with them. Rob Soar was killed in front of his wife and son.'

'Rob Soar had his throat cut. He fell with his kid on his back and bled to death in the river,' said Barrett. 'And the boys in the school were killed in the same way. Over a dozen young lads, all with their throats cut.'

Dana scrolled up the page, back to the photograph at the top. It was of Abbie and Rob Soar at an awards dinner. She needed only a second to look at the slim, elfin woman with short fair hair.

'That's her,' she said. 'That's the woman on the beach.'

Lacey never actually lost consciousness. She was aware of shock rather than pain, then a crippling weakness in her limbs. She thought perhaps the hammer hit her again, this time between her shoulder blades. Then she wondered if someone was kneeling on her back. Her face was pressed against the rough wooden floorboards – boards that smelled of a terrified child's blood. She knew that any second now she was going to vomit.

Breathe in, breathe out, stay alive.

Her hands were behind her back. Too late she realized they were being taped together. Whoever was kneeling on her bounced, pressing her chest against the floor and squeezing the air out of her body. *Don't fight, take a breath.* When the weight lifted, she could kick, struggle to her feet. This was only a kid.

But the kid was on the other table. Two trestle tables. Huck on one, Barney on the other. There was someone else here. Someone who was reaching for her legs, trying to tape her ankles together. She kicked, bucked, but whoever was sitting on her was too heavy. *Do something, he's almost won.*

He had won, she couldn't move. The darkness was changing, taking on deep shades of blue and purple, becoming more solid, wrapping itself around her. She had to rest, just for a minute. *No, don't pass out. Stay conscious. Get upright.*

Rocking on to one side, she drew her knees up towards her chest and pushed hard against the ground with her right shoulder. The pain across her collarbone almost made her give in to the darkness but she told herself to hold on, keep breathing, think about Huck, think about Barney.

She was in a large, rectangular room at the back of the upper floor. A room that could have been the studio of an insane painter with access to only one bright colour. A room with so much blood it was making her head spin. The high, peaked ceiling had several areas where the arterial spray was concentrated. The boys who had died in here hadn't been killed in the same spot. They'd been moved around, as though the killer wanted an individual and permanent momento of each on the walls. Nor had the boys' killer bothered getting rid of the blood. The blood was all still here, she could smell it. The boards beneath her were slick with it. Lacey felt her ears start to buzz, her head to grow thick. She couldn't faint.

Only one door, the one she'd come in by. Three windows high in the rear wall looked out on to the night. Too high for jumping to be a safe escape option.

As the dizziness faded, Lacey became aware that three pairs of eyes were watching her. Two belonged to the forms prone on the trestle tables, the third to the elf-like figure squatting on the ledge of the far window, clinging to a rope. The rope was attached to a pulley in the ceiling and secured to a cleat beneath the window, and the elfien creature had knocked her to the ground by swinging at her. It was poised to swing again if she moved.

The killer was slim and strong, dressed in green. With spiked fair hair and eyes of an odd intensity. A malevolent sprite. Peter Pan.

'My daughter-in-law's out. She's working.'

'We'd like to talk to the boys please. Jorge and Harvey.'

'They're both asleep.'

Dana, Gayle Mizon and Susan Richmond stood at the door of the tall terraced house and faced the faded, elderly woman on the threshold. She smelled of gin, exotic cigarettes and cheap perfume.

'I'm so sorry,' said Dana. 'We wouldn't dream of disturbing you at this hour if it wasn't urgent.'

'I don't want them upsetting any more. Jorge's already been out this evening, looking for Barney. Harvey cried himself to sleep.'

'Mrs Soar, two children are missing and your grandsons know one of them very well. They may be able to give us some clue as to where they might be.'

'You'd better come in. I'll see if I can wake them up,' the woman said.

Dana and her two companions stepped into the hallway and closed the front door behind them. The elderly woman turned to walk away from them. The hallway was tall and narrow, in the manner of old houses. The cream walls were lined with photographs. Just ahead, Gayle Mizon stopped and nodded at one particular shot. Dana stepped closer. It was the original of the photograph they'd seen minutes earlier on the CNN website: Abbie and Rob Soar, receiving an award for news coverage in the Congo.

The sound of a key turning in the lock made all three women start. They turned, to see the front door open and the woman they'd just been discussing walk through.

Slim, fair-haired, around thirteen or fourteen years old, Lacey figured, looking at the figure in green poised to swing down at her again. Just a kid. She'd been right about the kid. Just chosen the wrong one. And thanks to her, the MIT was following the wrong lead again. Thanks to her, Dana Tulloch and her team would be looking for Barney, tracking down places he might be hiding. They wouldn't be looking for the older brother of his best friend. And yet, in spite of her growing despair, there was some element of relief in finally being able to give the killer a name.

'Hello, Jorge,' she said.

'What's going on? Are the boys alright?' The woman with short blonde hair looked from one police officer to the next, then to the top of the stairs. 'Sylvia, what's happening?'

The elderly woman seemed to sway. Both Richmond and Mizon took a step towards her. Dana fixed her attention on the new arrival.

'These people want to talk to the boys,' she heard the grandmother say. 'One of their friends is missing. I was just going to wake them up.'

'I don't want them disturbed.' The younger woman's eyes were darting around the hallway, doing anything other than meet Dana's.

'You recognized me the other night, didn't you?' Dana said.

'You're a reporter. I've seen you at press conferences.'

The boy's mother made a move to get past Dana. 'I'm a photographer,' she muttered to the tiled floor.

Dana stepped forward, blocking her route to the stairs. 'I called out to you, but you ran away. Why did you do that?'

'I don't know what you're talking about. I'd like to check on my sons.'

The stairs were empty. The grandmother had gone.

'You were on the beach beneath Tower Bridge,' said Dana. 'Why would you go there on such a bad night?'

'It was a crime scene. I was taking photographs.'

'You weren't carrying a camera.'

Another step forward. The two women were almost nose to nose. 'It was in my bag.'

'You weren't carrying a bag.'

'Abbie!' The grandmother was calling from the top of the stairs. 'Jorge isn't in his room. He's not with Harvey either. I think he's gone out again.'

Abbie seemed to droop.

'Abbie,' said Dana. 'How long have you known about Jorge?'

When Lacey fell, the reality for Barney finally hit home. Until that moment, he'd been half waiting for Jorge to burst out laughing, to cut him and Huck loose, to say, 'Got you!' and admit it had all been the biggest possible wind-up.

He'd bumped into Jorge after he'd fled Lacey's flat and, in his misery, had confided his fears about his dad yet again. Jorge had been completely understanding, seeing exactly where he was coming from, but assuring him he was wrong. In urgent whispers that had been so convincing, he'd told Barney he had a feeling he knew who the killer was, that he didn't want to say more now, but that it was someone they both knew and that it would be a massive shock for everyone. If Barney would come to the old house with him, he'd said, they could break in and get proof.

Half drunk on the knowledge that his father might be innocent after all, Barney had followed Jorge to the house, up the framework of the conservatory and then to the top floor of the house. He'd been scared, of course, close to petrified, but Jorge had given him courage somehow and when they'd heard Huck whimpering, Jorge had gone straight in. Barney had actually been having fantasies about the two of them being heroes when Jorge had jumped him. Even then, he hadn't quite taken it in.

Not until he'd seen the look on Jorge's face as he'd flown through the air and swung the huge hammer at Lacey's head had he even begun to believe that his best mate's older brother, the coolest guy he knew, was a killer.

Even when Lacey sat up, blinking, her eyes unable to focus on anything, Barney had a second of hope that it was the 'Surprise!' moment at a party, when suddenly all the mystery was laid open.

'Who knows you're here?' Jorge was asking Lacey.

Tell him you're the first, willed Barney. *Tell him half the Metropolitan Police will be bursting their way through the door any second. Scare him. Panic him. Make him run.*

'No one,' gasped Lacey, giving first Barney and then Huck a strange, intense stare. 'I came on my own. I love what you did on Facebook, by the way. Peter Sweep, the Missing Boys. Really clever.'

What was she doing? Even Jorge wasn't sure. His eyes narrowed, searching for sarcasm in the detective's face. A movement to the left caught Barney's eye and he glanced at Huck. The kid was no wimp, you had to give him that. He'd been bucking and pulling and wriggling since Barney had been thrown into the room. Now he was rubbing his face against the wood of the trestle table, trying to get the tape off his mouth.

'You're in a show, aren't you?' said Lacey. 'I saw your photograph in the local paper. You're actually playing Peter Pan in the West End. God, you even look like him.'

Peter Pan? Peter Sweep? What was she talking about? If Jorge was Peter Sweep that made sense, it explained how Peter knew so much about Barney. And yes, everyone knew he was playing Peter Pan in the show, but what had that—?

'Come away with me to Neverland,' sang Jorge, still crouched on the window ledge. 'Lacey, gonna teach you to fly.'

'The police haven't a clue,' said Lacey. 'They're still chasing round looking for a vampire.'

Jorge actually sniggered at that.

'Did you really do it by yourself?' Lacey was saying now, like she was some kid meeting a pop star for the first time. 'Five boys, and now these two. It's incredible. They'll be writing books about you.'

A look of scorn washed over Jorge's face. He didn't mean it, though. Barney had seen the flash of hunger on his face.

Lacey stopped and coughed. She looked as though she was about to be sick. Then she seemed to make a massive effort. 'I know what I'm talking about,' she said. 'I've studied real-life serial killers for years. The ones who really catch the public imagination are the women and the young ones.'

And the ones who never get caught, thought Barney. *Don't tell him that.*

Lacey's face seemed to darken, and for a second her eyes lost focus. Then she took a deep breath. 'You know what you should do now,' she said, still speaking directly to Jorge. 'Go to the nearest police station and tell them to organize a press conference. They'll do it, if you say it's about the case. And they'll have heard of you. I mean, you're practically a celebrity. Then you can announce to the whole world it was you. You could say you knew the police were never going to catch you and you just got bored with it.'

Barney watched Jorge's face for a reaction. If Lacey could just persuade him to leave the building, she could get herself free and call for help. Even if Jorge took her phone, she could untie him and Huck. She wouldn't let Jorge catch her off guard again. Huck's duct-tape gag was almost off. He'd be able to yell soon.

'What will they do to me?' asked Jorge, surprising Barney. It was the question of a child. Lacey obviously thought so too. She was giving him a reassuring smile.

'You're too young to go to prison,' she said. 'They'll probably send you to a special facility, just for a few years, just till you're eighteen.

Then they'll give you a new identity, maybe send you somewhere really cool like Australia and you can sell your story. I wouldn't be surprised if they make a film about you.'

Jorge was nodding and Barney felt a rush of hope. It was going to work. There were plenty of sharp edges in the room – once they were left alone, Lacey could free herself in minutes. But then Jorge stood, tensed his whole body and leaped forward. The rope carried him into the centre of the room and he let go, landing lightly beside Lacey.

'Or I could kill these two, and then you, and make it look like you did it before killing yourself out of remorse.' Jorge smiled, and suddenly looked nothing like a child. 'I wouldn't even have the bother of getting rid of the bodies then. I know what I'm talking about, I've studied real-life serial killers for years.'

Barney closed his eyes, and gave up.

'I don't know anything,' said Abbie. 'Sylvia, have you any idea what time he went out?'

'We always wonder, when there's a killer amongst us,' said Dana. 'We ask ourselves, have I seen him, spoken to him, do I know him? I've been on the news saying "Someone knows him" over and over again. I wanted everyone in London to ask themselves that question.'

Abbie Soar hadn't moved from her spot at the foot of the stairs.

'But you had more reason than most, didn't you?' said Dana, trying to recall the conversation she and Susan Richmond had had on the way over. 'After what you and Jorge went through when he was young. What happens to us in the first three years of life has a massive impact upon who we are as people.'

Huge pale-blue eyes couldn't quite meet Dana's. 'I thought Jorge was dead too, that day,' Abbie said. 'When I pulled him out of the backpack, he was covered in his father's blood.'

'He doesn't remember it,' said his grandmother. 'He was only a baby. We've never talked about it.'

'What happened to you and your family was on the news all over the world,' said Dana, ignoring the older woman. 'There's a huge amount of coverage on the internet even now. We found it in seconds. Have you never wondered if Jorge has done the same thing? He might even have convinced himself that he remembers it all.'

'She wasn't even allowed to wash him,' said Sylvia. 'The two of them were put straight in the truck and taken to the capital. Four hours in that hot, stinking truck, and all the time that poor baby covered in blood.'

'It was the blood that made you suspicious, wasn't it?' said Dana, still talking to Abbie. 'Blood on his clothes?'

'Jorge washes his own clothes,' said the grandmother, still at the top of the stairs. 'He insists on that. I did spot some blood one time, but it was fake blood, from that show he's in. I know he was telling the truth. He has a bottle of it in his room.'

Abbie's blue eyes were still fixed just a few inches over Dana's shoulder.

'And he was always out when a boy disappeared or when a body turned up,' Dana went on. 'Always at football or at the youth club or whatever it is that he does in the evenings. He's always out, isn't he? On Tuesday and Thursday evenings?'

'That's when he rehearses,' said Sylvia. 'He's in a show in the West End. He's playing Peter Pan.'

Behind Dana, Gayle Mizon gave a small whimper.

Abbie came to life then. She made a move to push past Dana and the others. 'I need to find my son,' she told them.

Dana stood her ground. 'No,' she said. 'You need to sit down and tell us where we can find him.'

Huck, Barney, now Jorge. How many more boys would be lost before the night was done?

'You wouldn't have a chance,' Lacey told the silver-haired child with the dead eyes, knowing that the way Tulloch felt about her, he actually stood a very good chance of convincing the police she was the killer. It would be a nice, neat ending for the case. Overly disturbed police officer going on a murderous rampage, mis-directing her colleagues to cover her own tracks, until she couldn't live with the guilt any more. Except—

'Take that gag off Barney and he'll tell you I wasn't in London for the first three weeks of this year,' she said. 'There's no way I could have killed Tyler or Ryan.'

Jorge glanced over at Barney. 'Then it'll have to be Barney who did it,' he said.

Shit, that would work. The MIT would certainly believe Barney was the killer. She had done so herself until a few minutes ago.

Jorge reached into the back pocket of his jeans. 'Which means you're next,' he said to her.

She'd lost track of time. Joesbury had said he'd come looking after an hour. The hour was definitely up, but by how much? Probably not enough.

'Which bit do you enjoy the most?' she asked Jorge, as he took a step closer. He was holding something in his right hand. Within the cup of his fingers, she could see the gleam of a blade. Behind him, Huck was straining to lift his head from the table. His wide blue eyes were watching in horror. Barney, on the other hand, had his eyes fixed to the ceiling. The fingers on both his hands were flexing and pointing, like claws going into spasms. 'Do you enjoy the moment the knife breaks the flesh? Or when you see the light leaving their eyes?'

Jorge stopped moving. His eyes were staring, his mouth twisted. He looked like a child who'd been unjustly told off. He looked as if he was about to moan that it wasn't fair.

'Are you sexually excited by young boys?' asked Lacey.

For a second she thought she'd gone too far, that he'd launch himself at her.

'I'm not a pervert,' he told her. 'I don't do it for pleasure.'

'Why, then? Why do you do it?'

'Honestly?' he asked her.

She nodded. 'Yes,' she said. 'Tell me honestly.'

'Honestly,' he repeated. 'I just don't know.'

Sometimes, there was no reason. Except . . .

'I do,' she said. 'I know why you do it.'

Jorge turned from her then, walked back to the two trestle tables, right up to where he could look down at Huck on one side and Barney on the other. The Barlow twins had died in this room. The bloodstain down the table leg closest to Lacey was unmistakable.

Jason and Joshua had bled to death here. Probably others as well. Terrified young boys had lain in this room and felt their blood seeping out as their bodies got colder and the darkness grew at the edge of their vision. Jorge was looking from Barney to Huck, at the point of their necks just below their chins, as though deciding which one to cut first.

'I know,' she repeated.

She could see the dilemma in his face. Half of him wanted to shut her up, the other half to hear what she had to say.

'It's like a tension inside you,' she said. 'It grows all the time. You feel it in your head, your stomach, even your fingers and toes, and it gets stronger and tighter, and with every hour that goes by it gets a firmer hold on you, until it feels like your entire body is screaming. And then that cut. That moment the knife slides across the skin and it falls apart, there's something almost magical about it. Then the blood comes fizzing up and flows out and it's like all that noise in your head just goes away.'

He was shaking his head slowly, his eyes never leaving hers.

'The blood makes all the noise, all the pain, just slide away,' said Lacey.

His head was saying one thing, his eyes another entirely. How much time had gone by? Enough?

'You're wondering how I know, aren't you? I know because I do it too. Only I cut myself. I've never been quite as brave as you. Don't you believe me? Untie my wrists and I'll show you the scars.'

His mouth twisted – he wasn't going to fall for that one. But at least he wasn't looking at the boys any more.

'You'll have to cut Barney's wrists, you know,' she said. 'If he's the one you're planning to pin the blame on, you can't cut his throat. They'll never believe an eleven-year-old would cut his own throat. You'll have to cut his left wrist first, because that's what right-handed suicides always do. And you'll have to get the angle right, or they'll know. Will you remember all this?'

'Shut up.'

'And another thing you should know is that it takes a lot longer for people to die when you cut their wrists than when you do their throats,' Lacey called out. 'It takes longer to bleed out. And the wounds will start to heal themselves. The blood will coagulate. You may have to make more than one cut. It will take time. Won't be pleasant.'

'Shut up!'

'You've never killed a friend before, have you? You hardly knew the other boys. Are you sure you can do this to someone you like?'

Jorge looked from her to Barney, then to Huck. He stepped closer to Huck.

'One last thing,' Lacey called out. 'It's really important I tell you this.'

'What?'

'I have Huck Joesbury's new mobile phone in my pocket.'

As Jorge's eyes opened wide in surprise, she turned quickly to Huck. 'Your dad bought you a new iPhone,' she said. 'He lent it to me because the police have mine, but it's yours. He hasn't given it to you yet because your mum thinks you're a bit young for it, but he's got it all set up for you. The numbers of all the people you know are in it – your mum, your dad, DI Tulloch, your godmother.'

'If this is about trying to make me think you've made a call, forget it,' said Jorge. He dug his hand into his jacket pocket and held something out towards her. 'It fell out of your pocket when I hit you.'

'Is it damaged?'

Unable to stop himself, Jorge glanced down at the screen and pressed the small round button that would activate the home page. Lacey saw the gleam of light and colour. The phone wasn't damaged.

'The reason it's important,' she said, 'is that there's a very useful app on that particular phone – you might have heard of it, it's called Find My Phone. If two iPhones are connected by the same computer, then one phone always knows where its partner is. It's done by GPS. So all Huck's dad has to do to find us – and can I just say, he is one mean son-of-a-bitch when he's mad, isn't he, Huck? – all he has to do is to open up the app, put in a password and his phone will tell him exactly where this one is.'

'You're lying.'

'No, I'm not. I saw Huck's dad just over an hour ago. That's when he gave me the phone. He's been tracking me ever since. It's what he does. It's his job. He knows exactly where I am.'

'Liar!'

'I'll prove it. Activate the app. Take Huck's gag off – oh, clever boy, he's done it himself – and get him to give you the password. And I'll bet you anything you like that it tells you Detective Inspector Joesbury's Iphone is right outside that door.'

'Dad!' screamed Huck.

Then everything happened at once, in a blizzard of noise and movement. Jorge ran for the door. He'd almost made it when the door fell off its hinges and crashed into the room. As Joesbury stepped inside, Jorge backed up and ran to the window, taking the rope with him. Joesbury ran after him. Jorge leaped. They heard a sharp cry, a loud clatter and then nothing. Joesbury had reached the window. He pulled out his radio. Lacey didn't catch the words as he briefly spoke into it. She must have closed her eyes for a second, because when she opened them again Joesbury was leaning over his son's prone body. He got Huck free and picked him up. With his son in his arms, he staggered across the room before collapsing beside her. She could feel the cold dampness of rain, the warmth of perspiration, the stickiness of tears. She felt as though their three bodies had merged into one clinging, shaking heap.

It seemed a long time before Huck's voice broke the silence. 'Dad,' he said. 'What about Barney?'

66

'*FOUR OF US WENT INTO THE SCHOOL THAT DAY. MY MUM AND dad, a local man who was our guide, and me. His name was Billy, I think, the guide. I remember him being really worried about Mum taking pictures and Dad filming. He kept trying to hurry us out, get us moving. There were lots of people, around, the ones the rebel soldiers hadn't killed. The women and the older people.'*

'*So not everyone was killed?*' asked the psychiatrist, Dr Evi Oliver.

'*It was the boys they wanted. They didn't want the boys growing up and becoming government soldiers, so they killed them all, in the school, where they were probably having a maths lesson or a spelling test or something.*'

'*And your parents took you into the school too?*'

'*I think they forgot I was with them. They did that a lot. They had this rucksack-type thing that they put me in, and I'd be on Dad's back or Mum's back and they just used to get on with everything. I was on dad's back that day. I remember seeing Mum taking pictures of the dead boys.*'

Silence. Jorge's eyes closed. Evi waited, gave him time. Then they snapped open. '*People have been trying to tell me that these memories I have aren't real,*' he said. '*That I'm making it up.*'

'*I don't think anyone believes you're making it up,*' replied Evi. '*What you went through is a matter of record. I think the difficulty they have is that you were very young.*'

'*I'm not making it up.*'

'Of course not. Somewhere, everything you went through that day is still with you. But you describe it all in such detail. For such a small child to take all that in and retain it would be quite remarkable.'

'I was there. I saw it. I was there.'

'Of course you were. I think what people are suggesting is that in addition to your own memories, you've heard other people talking about what happened that day, maybe you've read about it in newspapers or on the internet. It's possible that real memories and newspaper coverage and speculation have become—'

'What? Mixed up?'

He was getting agitated again, rocking backwards and forwards in his chair. Evi glanced to one side to check the handset with the panic button was on the desk.

'No,' she said. 'More like interwoven. But you know, it doesn't really matter how much of what's in your head is from actual memory and how much is acquired. What's important is how real it is to you. Why don't you tell me what happened after you left the school?'

Jorge reached out and drank from the plastic beaker of water on the desk in front of him. 'We knew we had to get out of there,' he said. 'People started talking about how more rebels were coming, how we had to get away. Most of the villagers were leaving. There were some women – mums, I guess – who were crying over the dead boys, but everyone else was just trying to get away. They all went into the forest, but Billy said we had to follow the river to try and meet up with the government forces, so we did.'

'And what happened then?'

'We walked for a long time. It was hot and I was thirsty. I think I cried a lot. Maybe I fell asleep. Then I remember more soldiers. They all looked very young, not much older than the dead boys we'd seen in the school, and their uniforms were torn and dirty. They didn't look like proper soldiers, just like kids pretending, and I think I was waiting for my dad to tell them off, to make them get out of our way, when they cut his throat.'

'That must have been terrible.'

'This boy, this kid, came up to him, like he was just going to have a chat, but he didn't stop walking, he just went really close to Dad, then he lifted his hand up and there was a knife in it. Swish. My dad's blood was flying into the air like a firework.'

'And you were still strapped to his back?'

'I don't think they saw me at first. They were looking at Mum. Dad started to fall down, into the river, and I was going too, obviously, because I was on his back. Then there was shooting. I don't remember much more. Just watching my dad's blood make patterns in the river.'

'The shooting was from the government soldiers, is that right?' asked Evi.

Jorge nodded. 'They shot all the rebel boys. Then put me and my mum in a van. We drove for hours. I was covered in Dad's blood, but there was nothing to wash it off with. Then I think there was a plane. That's all I can remember. Can we stop now? I want to go back to sleep.'

'Of course,' said Evi. 'We'll talk some more tomorrow.'

Jorge got up and limped to the door. The leg he'd broken the night he'd been caught was healing, but wouldn't be sound for a few more weeks yet. In the open doorway he turned back to Evi.

'I never wanted to hurt anyone, you know,' he told her. 'Not really. It was always just about the blood.'

67

'VERY APPROPRIATE,' SAID DANA, SITTING DOWN BESIDE Helen in the Peace Pagoda and looking out over the river.

'How did it go?' asked Helen.

Dana pulled the collar of her jacket up a little higher and moved closer to Helen. Since the rain had stopped, a cold front had hit London. The forecasters were even talking about snow.

'I apologized; she said, Don't mention it,' replied Dana. 'We talked about the weather for five minutes and then she got up to leave.'

Helen reached out and put a hand on her arm. 'It's a start,' she said. 'Lacey's hardly the kiss-and-make-up type. Did you ask her whether she's coming back to work?'

Helen could never bear the idea of someone bright and young leaving the service.

'She's put in a request for redeployment,' Dana told her. 'She's going back into uniform.'

Helen was watching a flock of geese make their way upstream, flying low, almost skimming the water. 'Wow,' she said.

'Says she needs an easy life for a while,' said Dana. 'As if Lacey Flint will be able to stay out of trouble for long.'

A young family were walking along the path towards them. Mum, dad, newborn twins in a double buggy, so wrapped up against the cold that only their noses could be seen. Dana sat up a little taller, her eyes fixed on the buggy. Babies. When had they become so completely fascinating?

Helen had spotted what she was up to. She took hold of Dana's gloved hand. She did it slowly, as though half expecting it to be pulled away. 'I wish you'd told me,' she said.

'I hardly knew myself,' said Dana.

Silence.

'But really, Mark Joesbury as a sperm donor? I can't see it.'

For a second, her own body's shaking scared her. Then Dana realized she was laughing, and it felt like a long time since she'd done that.

'There are things we can do, you know,' said Helen, after a moment.

Dana turned to face her. 'There are?'

Her partner nodded. 'Lots of women in our position have children. Where there's a will.'

A couple of hundred yards away from them, the geese had landed on the riverbank. They were strutting, over-confident, noisy creatures.

'Is there?' said Dana, when she'd plucked up the courage. 'Is there a will?'

Helen rocked her head, shrugged, pulled her face in a couple of different ways. She was thinking about it. Dana held her breath.

'You'd have to do the pregnant thing,' said Helen at last. 'Not sure I'd be up to that.'

Dana's hands shot to her face. She gulped. Tears filled her eyes. 'Oh my God,' she said. 'Pregnant?'

Helen leaned back against the bench, hands laced behind her head. 'It's the usual prerequisite, from what I understand.'

'Pregnant? Me?' Dana was staring down at her stomach, as though just talking about it might have made it happen.

Helen shook her head. 'And already it's addling her brain. Come on. Let's go and look at some websites.'

The two women got up. Arm in arm, they followed the newborn twins and their parents out of the park.

*

'OK.' The older of the two Joesburys looked at his watch as they crossed the narrow canal that ran through Regent's Park zoo. 'We've got an hour. So I suggest penguins, otters, meerkats, and I suppose you could talk me into the insect house. But not the butterflies. Butterflies scare me.'

Huck was looking at the map in the zoo guide they'd bought on their way in. 'African hunting dogs, Komodo dragons, lions and tigers,' he announced before looking up at his dad. 'And finish with the gorillas. Did you know they ripped a woman's head off last year?'

Joesbury shook his head. 'Where do you hear such rubbish?'

'Alex Welsh told me. She broke in at night and went into the gorilla cage and they ripped her head off and the keepers found them next morning using it as a football.'

'What was the score?'

Huck gave him that *you can take the piss if you want to, but I know what I know* look and the two of them walked on. Joesbury had his hand on his son's shoulder. He found it difficult these days not to be close enough to touch. And when he was close enough, next to impossible not to maintain some sort of physical contact, as though the reassurance of his eyes that his son was still there, still safe, just wasn't enough.

They stopped in front of some monkeys. On a branch above their heads, a mother sat grooming her baby, running her hands over its fur, searching for lice, smoothing, scratching, petting. She bent and nibbled the baby's ear, then ran one hand along the length of its tail. She, too, didn't seem able to keep from touching her child. The young monkey, on the other hand, looked bored. It was watching the other monkeys, half wanting to run off and join in, half needing to stay close to its parent for just a bit longer.

'I'd really like to see something cuddly,' said Joesbury. 'Isn't there somewhere you can stroke goats and rabbits?'

There was a heavy sigh at his side. 'Dad, I'm not traumatized. And will you please tell Mum I don't want to see that counsellor any more? She smells of disinfectant.'

'I'll certainly pass on your thoughts.'

The baby monkey crawled away. The mother watched it go, not taking her eyes off it for a second. It had reached the end of the branch when two larger monkeys, like over-exuberant teenagers, came racing towards it. The baby scuttled back to its mother, climbing up her body as though it were an extension of the branch, clinging tight to her fur. She nipped his ear in an *I told you so* way.

'Bats!' said Huck. 'I want to see the bats!'

Joesbury sighed. The kid was winding him up. 'There is no friggin' way I'm going anywhere near bats.'

'I'll tell Mum you swore.'

He looked down. 'I'll tell her you fancy Kaycia Lowrie.'

Stalemate.

'Come on then, let's go and find the tigers. But if it's feeding time, you're on your own. Which reminds me, where do you want to eat tonight? TGI's? Giraffe?'

'We're going to Trev's,' said Huck, as they set off along the path once more.

'Oh, are we?'

'I booked a table.'

The kid just got better. 'And when did you do that, seeing as how you haven't been out of my sight since I picked you up?'

'I did it when you were in the toilet. You spend a long time in there, you know.'

Directly ahead of them, two teenage girls turned and stared at Joesbury.

'Yeah, thanks for that,' he told his son. 'Am I allowed to know what time?'

'Seven-thirty. Lacey couldn't make it any earlier.'

Now that was just mean. When had his son turned mean? 'I know you're winding me up,' he said. 'You haven't got Lacey's number.'

The look on Huck's face said there was no end to the pain he was expected to endure. 'Dad! For someone who claims he works in IT, you know zilch about technology,' he complained. 'My new phone is linked to yours by your computer. All the information on yours is on mine.'

Joesbury stopped walking and narrowly avoided being run into by a double buggy. 'You've got all my contact details on your phone?'

'Yeah. Who's Nobby McT—'

'Give me that phone!'

Huck darted ahead, turned and did his nah-nah-nah-nah-nah dance in the middle of the path. He pulled his phone from his pocket and waved it around his head.

'Oy, get back here! Now.' Joesbury set off running. 'OK, I'm serious. Huck!' Great, his nine-year-old son could out-run him.

'Someone stop that kid, he nicked my phone!'

Lacey watched Barney lock the cabin and slip the key into his pocket. 'It's a nice boat,' she said. 'A lot bigger than I expected. Thank you for showing it to me.'

A nice boat on which two young boys had died. Tyler King and Ryan Jackson had been taped to the fold-out table in the main cabin below and left alone and terrified for days, while a badly damaged child battled with his demons. Did that bother her? Should it?

'Dad's going to sell it this spring,' said Barney. 'I don't think he'll be able to come here again.'

'Yes, he told me.'

Sensing Barney wasn't ready to leave just yet, Lacey sat down in the cockpit facing the Creek. Barney mirrored her, keeping his back to the water. The tide was high and the boat rocked gently, soothingly, against its moorings. When it was out, the whole of the Theatre Arm would smell of mud. The boat would be grounded, skewed at an angle. No mains water, relying on a generator for electricity, calor gas to cook. And that rubbish-stewn yard to negotiate several times a day. It would be the most impractical place in London to live.

'Was there something you wanted to ask me?' she said, after a moment. Earlier in the day, Barney had been almost too keen to show her around the boat. She'd suspected he wanted to talk to her away from the dad who never seemed to let him out of his sight these days.

'Harvey and his mum and gran have moved away.' His voice was trembling, the way voices did when they were trying to hold back tears. 'No one knows where they've gone.'

'That's normal, I'm afraid,' said Lacey. 'It's called protective custody. A lot of people will be very angry at Jorge. They might be tempted to take it out on his family and that wouldn't be right.'

'It wasn't Harvey's fault.'

'No.'

Silence. There was more to come. Lacey pulled her jacket closer around her. In the time that they'd been here, the best of the afternoon had passed. The air coming off the water was very cold and shadows were lengthening.

'Did you mean it?' said Barney. 'What you said in the house? About how you – you know?'

Lacey pulled up the sleeve of her jacket and showed Barney the bandage on her left wrist. The wound beneath it hadn't been disturbed for nearly two weeks now. It was healing. In a little while, if she wasn't tempted to slide backwards, she might start to wonder if maybe she was too.

'I've been seeing a counsellor,' she said. 'Like you, like Huck. Only I've been seeing mine for a while now and I haven't been honest with her. I didn't tell her about things she could have helped me with. I've decided I'm going to tell her about this. Next time I see her.'

'It's weird,' said Barney, staring at the bandage. 'I thought I was weird, but—'

'You're not weird,' said Lacey, tugging her sleeve back in place. 'You're different and interesting and quirky, but you're not weird. And you've had a lot to deal with lately.'

Barney looked at the slatted wooden floor of the cockpit. 'You mean thinking my dad was a serial killer?' he said.

'Well, don't feel bad about that. I thought *you* were.'

He looked up again. His lips twitched. So did hers. Neither one of them was quite ready to smile about it yet. 'What I meant was, you've lost your best friend and your mum,' she went on. 'At least, the hope of having your mum back one day. That's a lot, by anybody's standards.'

Silence.

'I think I knew about Mum,' he said. 'Deep down. I just didn't want it to be true.'

Silence again. She nodded, wanted to reach out and take his hand, didn't quite feel able to. But he needed someone who would. Before he grew up thinking there was no love, no warmth in the world. His father, with the best will in the world, was never going to be the demonstrative type.

'Your dad said he'd told you about Mrs Green,' said Lacey. 'Does that feel a bit strange?'

'He wants her to move in with us,' said Barney. 'Not yet. Not until I go to secondary school, but soon after that.'

'Well, it will take some getting used to, but she seems quite nice to me.'

'If they get married, she'll be my stepmother.'

'Are stepmothers always bad?'

He thought about it for a moment. 'Guess not,' he said. 'She makes nice biscuits. And I expect she'll help with homework.'

Lacey smiled, and for a second, the small, fair-skinned face in front of her had turquoise eyes and dark, spiky hair. 'Biscuits and homework,' she said. 'I'll remember that.'

Splash, splash.

'What was that?' Barney was on his feet, had turned to look out over the water, and taken a step closer to her.

'Just the water banging against the hull,' said Lacey, puzzled.

'We should go.' Already he was on the side deck, swinging his leg over the guard-rail.

'Of course.'

She let Barney lead the way around the boats and on to the bank. Twice she had to ask him to slow down and be careful. The river was high enough for them to step off the nearest boat on to the yard. Barney walked several paces away from the edge before he turned.

Earlier in the day, when she'd met Dana Tulloch for coffee and peace talks, the DI had told her that none of the children at the Creek that night had wavered in their story that Tyler's body had leaped out of the water at them.

'What do you think happened?' asked Barney, and she knew he was thinking about the same thing.

'I think Jorge threw the body overboard, expecting it to be washed out to sea, and that somehow it got caught between two of the boats,' said Lacey. 'I think it stayed there for several weeks, and then one night, when there'd been a lot of rainwater and a high tide, it worked its way loose.'

'Harvey saw someone swimming.'

The sun was getting low in the sky and had all but disappeared behind a tall building. The yard was taking on an eerie look in the half-light, the Creek beginning to shine black and dense.

'I think Harvey saw Tyler's body being washed around by the tide, and in the dim light it looked like it was moving independently,' replied Lacey.

'It jumped out of the water at us,' said Barney in a small voice.

'I believe many things,' said Lacey, 'but I don't believe dead bodies can move. I think what happened was caused by a freak wave, or maybe even wash from a big boat out on the river.'

He nodded, looking far from convinced. Even she had to admit that, as explanations went, it was weak. Sometimes the easy answers just weren't there.

'I don't think I'm going to come here again,' he said. 'Are you?'

'Not sure,' said Lacey, turning back to look at the yellow yacht, so much bigger and cosier below than she'd expected. She thought about curling up in front of the wood-burning stove, about gentle waves rocking her to sleep each night, gulls waking her in the morning. 'Come on,' she said. 'I promised your dad I'd have you back before sundown.'

'He said I had to ask you to come for supper,' said Barney.

Since when did Lacey Flint have a social life? 'Well, that's very kind,' she said. 'And another time I'd love to, but I already have plans.'

Plans? What was she talking about? Beyond something to do that evening, she had no plans at all. For the following week. For the rest of her life. And yet, as she and Barney set off across the yard to where she'd parked her car, Lacey had a sense that something tightly coiled inside her had begun to unravel. And the feeling that had been growing for some time now was assuming a recognizable shape. It was starting to feel a lot like peace. She opened her car and the two of them climbed inside.

Splash, splash.

Acknowledgements

My sincere thanks to the Marine Policing Unit, particularly Chief Inspector Derek Caterer (who probably wouldn't employ 'Spiderman'), and the Tactical Team, (who wouldn't need to). Also to Adrian Summons, for continuing to open the right doors and steer me safely along the thin blue line.

For bringing *Like This, For Ever* to the shelves, I'm grateful to Anne Marie Doulton and Peter Buckman of the Ampersand Agency and to Rosie and Jessica of the Buckman Agency. At Transworld, I'd like to thank Lynsey Dalladay, Rachel Raynor, Kate Samano, Bill Scott-Kerr and Claire Ward; at St Martin's Press, Elizabeth Lacks, Andrew Martin and Kelley Ragland; at Goldmann Verlag, Andrea Best.

Martin Summerhayes, once again, prevented me from making too much of a fool of myself over IT, whilst Eleanor Bailey had some scarily insightful comments and is a publishing star in the making.

Any mistakes are mine.

Sharon Bolton is the author of five critically acclaimed novels: *Sacrifice*, *Awakening*, *Blood Harvest*, *Now You See Me* and *Dead Scared*.

Sacrifice was nominated for the International Thriller Writers Award for Best First Novel, and voted Top Debut Thriller in the first ever Amazon Rising Stars. *Awakening* won the Mary Higgins Clark award for Thriller of the Year.

In 2010 *Blood Harvest* was shortlisted for the CWA Gold Dagger for Crime Novel of the Year, and in both 2011 and 2012 S. J. Bolton was shortlisted for the CWA Dagger in the Library, an award for an entire body of work, nominated by library users.

Sharon Bolton lives near Oxford with her husband and young son.

TURN THE PAGE FOR A SNEAK PEEK
AT THE NEXT LACEY FLINT NOVEL

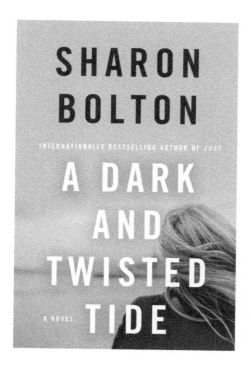

AVAILABLE JUNE 2014

Prologue

'I AM LACEY FLINT,' LACEY TELLS HERSELF, AS DAWN BREAKS and she lifts first one arm then the other, kicking hard with legs that are longer and more powerful than usual, thanks to a stout pair of fins. 'My name is Lacey,' she repeats, because the mantra of identity is as much a part of her daily ritual as swimming at first light, 'which is soft and pretty, and Flint, which is sharp and hard as nails.' Sometimes Lacey is amused by the inherent contrast of her name. Other times, she admits it suits her perfectly.

'I am Police Constable Lacey Flint of the Metropolitan Police's Marine Unit,' Lacey announces to her reflection as she dresses in her pristine uniform and sets off for her new headquarters at Wapping Police Station, taking comfort in the knowledge that for the first time in many months, a police officer feels like who she was meant to be.

'I am Lacey Flint,' she says most nights, as she battens the hatches of her houseboat, turns down the lights and crawls into the small double bed in the forward cabin. 'I am Lacey Flint,' she whispers, as she listens to the water slapping against the hull, the scrabble of creatures setting out for the night. 'I live on the river, work on the river and swim in the river.'

I am Lacey and I am loved, she thinks (but still doesn't quite dare say aloud) as a tall man with turquoise eyes steps once again to the front of her thoughts.

'I am Lacey Flint,' she mutters as she drifts away to the world of what-ifs, could-bes and still-mights that other people call sleep; and she wonders whether there might ever come a day when she forgets that it is all a massive lie.

Saturday 28 June

*T*HE PUMPING STATION SITS NEAR THE EMBANKMENT WALL OF *the river Thames in London, close to the border of Rotherhithe and Deptford, like a woman at a dance who has long since given up hoping for a partner. The small, square building has mostly been forgotten by the people who walk, cycle or drive past it each day, if indeed they ever noticed it in the first place. It has always been there, like the roads, the high river wall, the riverside path. Not a striking building, in any sense, and nothing ever happens in connection with it. No deliveries come to the wide wooden doors on one side and certainly nothing comes out. The windows are all sealed with wooden planks and heavy steel nails. Occasionally, someone lingering on the riverside path might notice that the brickwork is a perfect example of Flemish diagonal bond and that the pattern surrounding the flat roof is beautiful, in an understated way.*

Few do. The roof is above normal sight lines and the nearest road isn't on a bus route. River traffic, of course, is far below. So no one ever appreciates that the pale grey of the building is relieved by bricks of white in a repeating crisscross pattern, and by uniform pieces of stone set at a diagonal angle. The Victorians decorated everything, and they didn't neglect this small, insignificant building, even if few of them would have mentioned its original purpose in polite company. The pumping station was built to pump human sewerage from the lower lying lands of Rotherhithe and discharge it into the Thames. It once played an important role in keeping the streets of the surrounding area fresh, but bigger, more efficient stations and sewerage treatment plants came into play, and there came a day when it was no longer needed.

If passers-by and local residents were curious enough to find their way inside, they'd see that, Tardis-like, the interior appears so much bigger than its external framework suggests, because at least half of the pumping station is underground. All the engineering equipment has long since been taken away, but the decorative beauty remains. Stone columns rise to the roof, their once crimson paint faded to a dull red. The Tudor roses still entwine the tops of the pillars, even though they no longer gleam snow-white. Mold creeps up the sides of the smooth, uniform brickwork, but can't hide that the bricks were originally of the very finest quality. Anyone privileged to see inside the pumping station would consider it a minor architectural gem, something to be preserved and celebrated. It can't happen. For years now, the pumping station has been in private hands and those hands have no interest in developing or changing. Those hands are unconcerned that a piece of riverside real estate this close to the city is probably worth millions. All the hands care about is that the old pumping station belongs to them, and that it serves a purpose particular to them.

It also happens to be the ideal place to shroud a dead body.

In the centre of the space are three iron plinths, each roughly the size of a modest dining table. The dead woman lies on the one closest to the outlet pipe and the killer is panting with the exertion of getting her there. Water streams off them both. The dead woman's hair is black and very long. It clings to her face like the weed on upturned boat hulls at low tide.

Above, the moon is little more than a curled blonde eyelash in the sky, but there are streetlamps along the embankment and some light reaches inside. Together with the glow from several oil lanterns set in the arched recesses of the walls, it is enough.

When the hair is gently lifted away, the pale, perfect face beneath is revealed. The killer sighs. It is always so much easier when their faces haven't been damaged. The wound around the neck is ugly but the face untouched. The eyes are closed and that is good too. Eyes so quickly lose their lustre.

Here it comes again, that heavy sadness. Regret, there is no other word for it really. They are so lovely, the girls, with their flowing hair and long *limbs. Why lure them away with promises of rescue and safety? Why live for the moment when the hope in their eyes turns to terror?*

Enough. The body has to be undressed, washed and shrouded. It can be left here for the rest of the night and taken out to the river tomorrow. Close to hand are the hemmed sheets, the nylon twine and the weights.

The woman's clothes are soon removed; the cotton tunic and trousers are cut away easily, the cheap underwear is the work of seconds.

Oh, but she's so beautiful. Slender. Long, slim legs, small high breasts. Pale perfect skin. The killer's strong fingers run the length of the firm, plump thigh, trace the outline of the small round kneecap and go on down the perfectly formed shin, loving the spreading curve of the calf. Perfect feet. The high, graceful arch of the instep, the tiny pink toes, huddled together like feeding piglets, the perfect oval of the toenails. In death, she is the absolute picture of unattainable femininity.

A rasping sound where silence should have reigned unconquerable. Then something cold and strong clutching the killer's arm.

The woman is moving. Not dead. Her eyes are open. Not dead. She's coughing, wheezing, her hands scrabbling around on the iron block, trying to get up. How did this happen? The killer almost faints away in shock. Eyes that have turned black with horror are staring. More river water comes coughing out of those pale, bitten lips.

Lips that should not have anything more to say for themselves!

The killer reaches out but isn't quick enough. The woman has scrambled back and fallen off the plinth. 'Ay, ay,' she cries, the sound of a terrified animal. The killer too is terrified. Is it all over then?

The woman is on her feet. Bewildered, disorientated, but not so much that she forgets what happened to her. She starts backing away, staring round, looking for a way out. When her eyes meet those of her killer they open wider in dismay. Words come out of her mouth, which may or may not be the words the killer hears.

'What are you?'

And it's enough to bring back the rage. Not who are you? Not, why are you doing this? Both of which would be perfectly reasonable questions in the circumstances, but what are you?

What is it? Good God, what is this freak?

The woman didn't say that. The woman is running round the small, square room now, looking for a window, which she won't find on this floor, or a door, that won't help her. That last was only in the killer's head.

She's spotted the upper floor, is heading for the staircase. There is no way out up there, the windows are all boarded, the heavy door can't be opened, but there are skylights in the roof that she might be able to reach, attracting the attention of people outside.

The killer surges forward, crashing painfully into the iron frame of the steps, catching hold of the woman's ankle, biting hard on the fleshy part of the calf. A howl of pain. Another hard pull. A squawk, then she comes tumbling down.

The killer has her now, but the woman is naked and wet with water and sweat. She isn't easy to hold and she's fighting like an eel. The biting and scratching and the constant, continual wriggling is exhausting. The grip loosens. The woman is up. Reach out, grab. She's fallen, slapped down hard on the stone, hit her head. Dazed, she's easier to manage. Heave. The sound of flesh scraping along stone. Arms flailing, claw-like hands trying to grab hold of something – anything – but they've reached the smooth, metal pipe that, in the old days, took the water out of here. Lift her in. Climb after her. Push her along. The pipe is short, not much more than a metre in length.

The water is below, feet away and gravity is helping now. Lean, pull and – yes – they both hit the water.

And the world becomes calm again. Silent. Soft and easy.

Easy now. Easiest thing in the world. Let go. Let her sink. Let her panic. Wait for her to rise up, to take her last desperate breath, then make your move. Up and out of the water in one massive surge and down again with your hands around her throat. Then down, down into the depths. Down until she stops struggling.

Disgraceful, we don't want it.

Two of them clasped together. A tight embrace. A good way to die.

Stone it. Stone the freak.

Hands appear on all sides. Tiny hands, but strong and determined. Lots of them. Pushing, throwing, shoving and hitting.

The killer is the only one embracing now. The woman has fallen limp and heavy, is pulling them down. The others have gone too. Those others, whom the killer is never quite sure are memories or ghosts, they've fled too. There'll be peace now. Until the next time.

Thursday 19 June (nine days earlier)

A SINGLE DROP OF RAIN FALLING ON THE VILLAGE OF Kemble in the English Cotswolds is destined to become part of the longest river in England and one of the most famous in the world. On its 216-mile journey to the North Sea that single drop will hook up with the hundreds of millions of others that wash daily past London Bridge.

Sometimes, as she swam amongst them, Lacey Flint thought about those millions of drops and her entire body shivered with excitement. Other times, the notion of the unstoppable force of water all around made her want to scream in terror. She never did, though. Catch a mouthful of the Thames this close to the estuary and there was every chance it could kill you.

So she kept her head up and her mouth largely shut. When she opened it to snatch in air, because muscles swimming at speed through cold water need oxygen, she relied upon a prior rinsing with Dettol to kill the bugs on contact. For nearly two months now, since she'd bought the vintage sailing yacht that was her new home, she'd been wild swimming in the Thames as often as tide and conditions allowed and she was healthier than she'd ever been.

At 05.22 hours on a June morning, as close to the solstice as made little difference, the river was already busy and even staying close to the south bank, she had to take care. River traffic didn't always stick to the middle of the channel and no boat pilot was ever looking out for swimmers.

The tide was as high as it was going to get. There was a moment at high tide, especially in summer, when the river seemed to pause and become still. For just a few minutes, ten, maybe fifteen, the Thames became as easy to glide through as a pool and Lacey forgot that she was human, dependent on wet suits and fins and antiseptic rinses to survive in this strange, aquatic environment and became, instead, part of the river.

A sleek, black arrowhead of a gull skimmed the water ahead before disappearing below the surface. Lacey pictured it beneath her, beak open wide, scooping up whatever fish it had spotted from above.

She carried on, towards the jagged black pilings of one of the derelict offshore landing stages that ran along this stretch of the south bank. Not for the first time, Lacey found herself missing Ray. She missed seeing his skinny arms ahead of her, missed the shower of bright water when he occasionally kicked too high, but he'd picked up a summer cold a few days earlier and his wife, Eileen, had put her foot down. He was staying out of the river until he was well again.

Less than thirty metres to the landing stage. Built when London was one of the busiest commercial ports in the world to allow larger vessels to moor up and offload their cargo, they'd fallen into disrepair decades ago. Her senses on full alert, as they always were in the river, something different caught her eye. There was movement in the water, over by the bank. Not flotsam, it had been holding its position. There were otters on the Thames but she'd not heard of any this far down. Other people swam in the river, according to Ray, but higher up where the water was cleaner and the flow more gentle. As far as he knew, he and now Lacey, were the only wild-swimmers this close to the estuary.

Slightly unnerved, Lacey struck out faster, suddenly wanting to get past the landing stages, turn into Deptford Creek and be on the home stretch.

Almost there. Ray usually swam through the pilings, a little ritual of his own, but Lacey never went amongst them. There was something about the blackened, mollusk-encrusted wood that she didn't like to get too close to.

Another swimmer after all, directly ahead. Lacey felt the moment of elation that comes from shared pleasure. Especially the guilty sort. She got ready to smile as the woman came closer, maybe tread water for a few seconds and chat. The woman ahead of her in the water was young, her arms smooth and slim. Her face unlined and pale.

Except, that wasn't swimming. That was more like bobbing. The arm that, a second ago, had seemed to be waving, now moved randomly. And the arm wasn't just thin; it was skeletal. For a second the woman seemed upright. Then she lay flat before disappearing altogether. Another second later she was back. Maybe not even a woman, the long hair Lacey had seen in the dazzling, reflected light now looked like weed. And the clothes, trailing like veils around the corpse, had added to the feminine effect. The closer she got, the more sexless the thing looked.

Lacey drew closer. She'd yet to see a body pulled from the river. Despite her two months with the Marine Unit, despite the Thames' record of presenting its caretakers with at least a body a week in payment of dues, she'd either been off-duty or otherwise occupied on the occasions bodies had been retrieved.

She knew, though, from a briefing talk in her first week, that the Thames wasn't like still water, where a body usually sank and then floated after several days. The Thames had currents and tides that swept a corpse along until it got caught against an obstruction and was revealed at low water. There were sites along the tidal stretch of the Thames that were notorious body traps, that the Marine Unit always searched first when someone went missing. Bodies that went in the Thames were usually found quite quickly and their condition predictable.

After two or three days the hands and face would swell as internal gases began to accumulate under the skin. After five or six days, skin would begin the process of separation from the body. Fingernails and hair would disappear after a week to ten days. Then there was the impact of marine life. Fish, shellfish, insects, even birds that could reach the corpse, would all leave their mark. Often the eyes and the lips would be the first to go, giving the face a startling, monstrous appearance. Whole chunks of the body could be ripped away by boat propellers or hard obstacles in the water. Floaters were never good news.

Very close now. The figure in the water seemed to bounce in anticipation. *I'm here. Been waiting for you. Come get me.*

Not a recent drowning, that much was clear. There was very little flesh left on the face, a few soggy pink clumps of muscle stretching along the right cheekbone, a little more around the chin and neck. Lots of bite marks. And the river's flora, too, had staked its claim. The few remaining patches of flesh were attracting a greenish growth where some sort of river moss, or weed, had taken root.

Small facial bones, hair still attached to the head, weed that seemed to be growing from the left eye socket. There were even clothes, usually the first to go in the river. Except, not clothes, exactly, but something that seemed to have been wrapped round the body and that was now coming loose, trailing towards her, like the long hair. The corpse seemed to be reaching out towards Lacey. Even the arms were outstretched, fingers clutching.

Telling herself to get a grip, that she had a job to do, Lacey began treading water. She had to check that the corpse was secure, if not make it so, then get out of the water and call it in. In a pocket of her wetsuit she carried a slim torch. She found it, took a deep breath, told herself that sometimes you just had to bloody well get on with it, and went under.

Nothing. Utter blackness that even the torch couldn't penetrate. Then a swirling mass of greens and browns, light and shadow. Complete confusion. Shapes that appeared to loom towards her were just optical illusions created by moving water.

And the sounds of the water were so much more intense. Up above, the river splashed, gurgled and swished but beneath, the sounds suggested pouring, draining, sloshing. Beneath the surface, the river sounded alive.

Weird, alien shapes. The black, shell-encrusted wood of the pillar. Something brushing her face. Mouth clamped tight, she was not going to scream. Where was the body? There. Arms flailing, the clothes stretching out. Lacey focused the torch, ran it up and down the suspended figure. The river surged and the corpse was completely submerged. Now its eyeless sockets almost seemed to be staring directly at her. Christ almighty, as if her nightmares weren't busy enough already.

Don't think, just do it, point that torch. Find out what's holding it still.

There! One of the strips of fabric was wrapped tight around the pile. It was anchoring the body in place. It looked secure.

Lacey broke the surface with air still in her lungs and looked past the corpse to the bank. No beach, the tide was too high, but she'd grown cold over the last couple of minutes and had to get out of the water now. The landing stage above her was largely intact but too high to reach. Her only chance would be to clamber up onto one of the cross beams until help arrived. A few yards away there was one that looked solid enough.

She struck out towards it, checking back every couple of seconds to make sure the corpse hadn't moved. It held its position in the water, but seemed to have twisted round to watch her swim away.

The cross beam would hold for a while. Out of the water, Lacey shrugged off the harness she wore round her shoulders. In a small, waterproof pouch that lay in the small of her back was her mobile phone; something Ray insisted she carry with her.

He answered quickly. 'You alright love?'

Lacey's eyes hadn't left the trail of fabric streaming out from the pier. As the waves rose and fell, she caught glimpses of the woman's round, moon-like skull.

'Lacey, what's up?'

No one close, she still felt the need to speak quietly. 'I found a body, Ray. By the old King's Wharf. Fastened round the landing stage.'

'You out of the water? You safe?'

'Yeah, I'm out. And the tide's turned. I'm fine.'

'Body secure?'

'Looks that way.'

'Ten minutes.'

He was gone. Ray had worked for the Marine Unit years ago and knew the significance of a body in the water. Like Lacey, he and his wife lived on a boat moored in Deptford Creek, a nearby tributary.

Ten minutes was an under-estimate, he couldn't possibly reach her in fewer than twenty, but he wouldn't hang around. In the meantime, she had to stay warm.

Easier said than done, wedged between two beams of wood and with the water splashing over her ankles every few seconds. The UK was two weeks into one of the longest heat waves on record but it was still early and the sun hadn't reached the south bank yet.

Below, the water sloshed around the piles, creating mini whirl-pools. The dead woman looked to be dancing, the waves bouncing her playfully, the fabric flying out around her like swirling skirts.

'Hey!'

Lacey almost collapsed in relief. She'd had no idea how tense she'd been. Ray must have flown to get here so – Steady! She felt the beam beneath her give a fraction.

And Ray was nowhere in sight. No small busy engine chugging its way towards her, no wrinkled old boatman frowning into the sun. Yet, for a split second, the sense of another's presence had been over-whelming. She'd practically heard him breathing, felt his sigh on her neck. She'd heard him shout to her.

Lacey stretched up. The embankment was empty. She could hear cars but at a distance. No sounds of bike wheels or jogging footsteps. There was traffic on the river but nothing even remotely close.

There he was, at last, coming towards her as fast as his twenty-horsepower engine would take him. She took the painter he held out and secured the boat, before climbing down.

'Put those clothes on.' He threw a bag her way. 'There's a patrol boat up by Limehouse. They'll be here right away. Now, we will not be talking about swimming. You and I were out on the river in my boat when you spotted the body.'

Lacey nodded as she hid her wet gear in the bag. Swimming in the tidal section of the river was a bylaw offence. Even if you weren't a member of the Marine Unit.

'Are you OK?' Ray asked, as the police launch approached.

'I'm fine,' she said.

The master of the vessel was a young sergeant called Scott Buckle. He looked over at Lacey and waved.

'Part of the job,' Ray told her, in an undertone. 'Won't be the last you pull out.'

'I know.'

'It's a greedy river. People get distracted, a bit careless, it won't give them a second chance.'

Almost a year ago, the river had given her a second chance. It had let her go, possibly one of the reasons she didn't fear it now. 'This wasn't the river.' She watched her colleagues prod the corpse with boathooks. 'And they'll not get it with those. It's fastened tight around the pile.'

'You don't know that,' Ray told her. 'No way would you know that unless you'd stuck your head under. Please tell me you didn't do that.'

'She didn't go in accidentally,' Lacey said. 'She's wrapped up tight like a mummy.'

Ray sighed. 'Jeez, Lacey. How do you do it?'

CPSIA information can be obtained
at www.ICGtesting.com
Printed in the USA
LVHW112313281019
635652LV00001B/120/P